SLASHBACK

Also by Paul Levine

TO SPEAK FOR THE DEAD

NIGHT VISION

FALSE DAWN

MORTAL SIN

SLASHBACK

A JAKE LASSITER NOVEL

PAUL LEVINE

WILLIAM MORROW AND COMPANY, INC. · New York

It is the policy of William Morrow and Company, Inc., and its imprints and affiliates, recognizing the importance of preserving what has been written, to print the books we publish on acid-free paper, and we exert our best efforts to that end.

Library of Congress Cataloging-in-Publication Data

Levine, Paul (Paul J.)
Slashback / by Paul Levine.
p. cm.
ISBN 0-688-11817-8
1. Lassiter, Jake (Fictitious character)—Fiction. 2. Lawyers—Florida—Miami—Fiction. 3. Miami (Fla.)—Fiction. 4. Hawaii—Fiction. I. Title.
PS3562.E8995S57 1995
813'.54—dc20 94-13051
CIP

Printed in the United States of America

First Edition

1 2 3 4 5 6 7 8 9 10

BOOK DESIGN BY CAROLINE CUNNINGHAM

For my agent, Kris Dahl,

who guides me through treacherous waters

Life is the process of finding out, too late, everything that should have been obvious to you at the time.

JOHN D. MACDONALD
The Only Girl in the Game

CHAPTER 1

Dragon's Teeth

Standing barefoot and bare-chested in a moonlit tidal pool, the muscular Hawaiian watched the fat man approach, carrying a canvas backpack, slipping on the wet rocks as the roiling surf crashed offshore. The fat man yelled something but was drowned out by the thunderclap of a wave against the volcanic shelf.

Closer now, the man lost his balance and slid into a depression of muck and seawater. He caught himself on a smooth boulder the shape of a tombstone, polished grayish-white by a million years of salt spray. Gingerly, the man navigated between two sharp rocks embedded in the sand.

"Do you know how much I paid for these boots?" the man asked, mournfully lifting a leg from the slime. "Ostrich skin, hand-stitched in Australia."

As motionless as one of the rocks, the Hawaiian silently watched the fat man, whose voice rose over the howl of wind and waves. "Eleven hundred bucks! I oughta take it right off the top."

A gust lifted the tail of the fat man's aloha shirt—white orchids and red heliconia—that still bore creases from the hotel gift shop. "You and your damn rituals." The man lowered his voice into a formal cadence. " 'Go past the village called Honokahua just behind Makaluapuna Point. Meet me at the rocks they call Dragon's Teeth.' " A roller crashed and foaming water cascaded into the tidal pool. "What horseshit! Christ, I thought the *cachacos* in Colombia were weird, but you Maui Wowies are really two cans short of a six-pack."

"Do you have the money?"

"You got some nerve, punk, you know that?" The fat man's eyes darted toward the Hawaiian's crotch. "Jeez, what're you wearing, a goddamn loincloth?"

"The *malo* is made from the skin of a wild goat."

"You look like some fruit from Fire Island."

"My ancestors wore these when they paddled canoes from Tonga to Hawaii, seven hundred years before Columbus."

The fat man's boots made a squishing sound as he stepped closer to the darker-skinned, younger man. "Spare me another history lesson, okay?" He swung the backpack off his shoulder. "It's all here, which is more than I can say for your deliveries. You shortchanged us by twenty percent last time, and my superiors have changed my orders."

The fat man reached into the backpack and came out with a long-barreled .41-caliber revolver, its satin finish catching the glint of the moon. "I'm sorry about this. You know how I hate violence. If there was any way to work it out, I'd—"

"You should not aim at my head," the Hawaiian told him, placidly. "A simple movement, and you would miss." He tucked his head left, then right, a young Muhammed Ali slipping a punch. "Then I would kill you."

The fat man licked his lips and lowered the gun toward the younger man's heart.

"That cannon is too heavy for you," the Hawaiian continued. "You need two hands to steady it. Or are you just nervous? Are you tasting fear along with your hotel dinner of roast beef and mashed potatoes?"

"Hey, you're the one who should be afraid, beach boy." He struggled to toughen his voice, but the pitch rose just enough to betray him. "You dicked around with the wrong guys."

"Do I look as if I am afraid?"

"No, you and your Polynesian warrior bullshit wouldn't allow it."

The Hawaiian turned toward the crashing waves. Across the Pailolo Channel, the cliffs of Molokai rose from the black sea, silhouetted by the moonlight. "My people had no metal. Their sailing canoes were made of wood lashed together with coconut fibers and caulked with breadfruit gum. The sails were woven from *hala* leaves."

"Who gives a shit?"

"They had no navigational instruments. Just the stars and the moon and their knowledge of ocean currents and the flight of seabirds."

"Seabirds," the fat man repeated, shaking his head. "You been smoking too much of your own shit."

"They followed the clouds on the horizon to find mountainous islands in the sea. All this my people knew."

"What's your point?"

The Hawaiian turned back to face the man with the gun. "What is it that you know, *haole*? Could you survive even one week in the jungle on Molokai barely ten miles from your luxury hotel?"

The fat man shifted his weight uncomfortably. "I was too busy stealing hubcaps to get my Eagle Scout badge, okay?"

"If you and I were alone in the jungle, who would survive and who would die?"

"That ain't the way it is," the fat man said, wagging the gun. "I got Mr. Smith and Mr. Wesson on my side." A wave crashed on the rocks and the spray shot over them.

"On a rocky shore very much like this, the English sailors aimed their guns at my ancestors. Your Captain Cook believed the natives would surely surrender."

"Hey, he wasn't *my* captain."

"Except for wooden fence posts and rocks, we were unarmed." He smirked at the fat man. "And dressed like fruits from Fire Island."

"You sound like you were there."

"Oh, but I was."

Another wave hit, a torrent rushing over them, the backwash tugging at their legs. The fat man's boots filled with seawater and sunk deeper into the muck. He tried to lift a leg. "All right, enough. I gotta get this over with. Finish your damn story. It's the last one you'll ever tell."

The Hawaiian's smile shone in the moonlight. "We were on our own land. There was never any chance we would surrender. We swarmed over the English, while singing praises to our gods. We crushed Cook's skull against the rocks, then stripped the flesh from his bones."

"Great story. I'll watch for it on HBO." The fat man seemed to shiver as the sea breeze picked up and whipped a frothy spray over him. He looked profoundly sad as he drew back the hammer on the large-framed revolver. "Look, I hate this part of the job, but I got no choice." A giant roller tumbled past the rocks and surged over them, filling the tidal pool up to their knees. The fat man coughed and spit. "Shit! I'll take a dark alley in Jersey City over this anytime."

"High tide," the Hawaiian said, looking toward the moon. "You must always know your surroundings. Listen to the earth and the sea, and they will speak to you." He turned toward the fat man and braced himself against a boulder.

"What the hell are you—"

A giant wave crashed past the rocks that resembled dragon's teeth and cascaded over them. The surge twisted the fat man around in his sunken boots and toppled him into the water, the gun flying from his hand. Before the backwash could drain from the tidal pool, the younger man was on him, grabbing him by the neck, bashing his head against a boulder, time and again, the fat man's skull shattering like a coconut under the ax, his cries drowned out by the roar of the ceaseless waves.

CHAPTER 2

The Old Man, the Blonde, and the Bonds

T*he old man loved gadgets, money, and large-breasted women,* and at the moment, he had all three. His thick hands caressed the newest gadget, a sixty-second camera, turned it over and admired its smoothness, a tidy little box cool to the touch. The money came from the sale of Corrugated Container Corp., the company he had founded in the 1920s. The breasts belonged to Violet Belfrey, and she relied on them as an aging fastball pitcher might his slider. Few men remembered a word Violet said, but the image of her full breasts endured for years. A lot of men and a lot of years. With her solid cheekbones and strong jaw, Violet's age was impossible to determine. Somewhere between forty and hell, the old man guessed.

She showed him how to open the camera, her hands touching his and lingering. "Birthday present for you," Violet Belfrey said. "Now, let's take some pictures."

Samuel Kazdoy shrugged his rounded shoulders. "What's to take here?"

They were in his office on the mezzanine of the South Side Theater in Miami Beach. The ventilation was bad, and the theater smelled of age, a tired building in a dying part of town that somehow missed the renaissance going on all around it. Samuel Kazdoy puttered around every afternoon in the dimly lit office and checked in evenings at his twenty-four-hour delicatessen on Collins Avenue. If you've worked for seventy years, you can't turn it off just because the sand is running out of the glass.

"Ah'll show you two things to take," Violet said, peeling off her orlon sweater and slipping out of a sheer red brassiere. She loosened her platinum hair, shaking it in streams over her shoulders, her breasts tumbling free. "How's this for a Kodak moment?"

He squinted through the viewfinder. "Ay, you got some moxie, *bubeleh.*"

"Jes' aim and push the button," Violet said. He did, the flash bleaching the office in white light and casting tiny shadows in the furrows of her forehead. She squeezed out of her tight jeans and high-stepped out of her panties that matched the brassiere right down to the red frilly trim. She turned sideways and arched her back so that her buns jutted skyward like the ramp of a ski jump, and at the same time, squashed her breasts together with her arms. There was no seduction on her lips, no excitement in her eyes. She could have been composing grocery lists for all that her face revealed.

Kazdoy clicked another picture. Eyes smarting from the flash, Violet Belfrey saw a strip joint in Jacksonville a dozen years earlier. She had danced on a table there and even now could smell the stale beer on the wooden bar and feel the salesmen's clammy hands tucking dollar bills into her garter, copping a quick feel as she stepped down. She hated it when the music stopped and she heard the scumbags laughing and the glasses tinkling, no longer able to pretend she was alone.

Violet Belfrey saw more than her share of motel ceilings in Jax, which she figured was the world's largest jerkwater town, a place where the stench of the paper mills clung to your clothes like flypaper on a summer night. She had been stuck halfway between the Carolina mountains and the Florida Gold Coast, and the money was decent even if the men were not. She remembered a blur of flushed faces, of men who leaned close with sour breath and winked that maybe a double sawbuck was the key to her apartment door. Never again, she had vowed, would she sell herself. At least not so cheaply, she later amended.

"Gottenyu!" Kazdoy wore a child's look of astonishment as the instant film developed before his eyes. The legs appeared, the bare round bottom, the breasts filling in, all creamy smoothness, the nipples flat, oblivious to his attention.

Kazdoy loosened his clip-on tie and removed the plaid sports coat. An old sensation tugged within him but he knew it was his memory stirring, not his loins.

He shuffled across the cluttered office filled with photos of company picnics, sketches of new factories, and industry awards. A short man with fringes of white hair, he wore a blue plaid polyester sports coat and a baggy pair of pants that fit better when Ike was president. Placing a hand on Violet's shoulder, Kazdoy said, "Here, *bubeleh*, I got something for you."

She stiffened a moment, an old reflex no matter how many times she'd been down that road. The feeling passed as it always did and she was ready for him, but Samuel Kazdoy walked past her, threw back a soiled blanket that covered a file cabinet, and twirled a combination lock with steady hands. Violet squinted, but the seventy-five-watt bulb tossed shadows, and her eyes still saw blue lightning from the flash.

"How do you remember the combination?" she asked, hoping he would say it aloud. "My little ole head would never keep all the numbers straight."

Kazdoy laughed, touching a finger to his forehead. "My *kop* still works, even if my *schmeckel* don't." He opened the cabinet and Violet saw bundles of papers, legal-looking with fancy script writing and colorful borders. "Coupons," he continued, reaching in with both hands, a kid in a candy bowl. "Put 'em in a safe place. And the first of every month, take 'em to the bank."

The only coupons Violet knew got you twenty-five cents off the kitchen cleanser, so she had no idea what he was giving her, but she figured if you take them to the bank, they can't be half bad. Violet stuffed the documents into the bag from the camera store and quickly put on her clothes. She gave the old man a peck on the cheek.

"Thanks, Mr. K. You're the only thing in pants what's ever been nice to me without askin' somethin' in return."

"You're some *tsatske*," he said with the smile of a young man. His dark eyes were bright and still sparkled with the gift of laughter. "Now run along before I start something I can't finish. I got coupons to clip for the first of December, and so do you."

"You're a sweetie," Violet said, wondering what the hell he had given her and what was left behind in the locked cabinet.

"Sweetie?" Samuel Kazdoy shook his head and smiled

again. "Twenty years ago . . . no make it ten, I'd have given you something sweet. I'd have *shtupped* you from here to Shamokin."

The sign bolted to the stucco wall said SEAVIEW TERRACE, though the drab, three-story building had neither. Violet had moved in shortly after answering the classified ad in the *Miami Beach Sun*: "*Shayna maidel* or *shiksa* wanted as Gal Friday for owner of theater and delicatessen." She figured the job couldn't be worse than the midnight shift at the Sunny Isles Peep Show.

It was only a five-minute walk to the apartment building from Kazdoy's office, and tonight there would be no detours. A few aging widows still lived there, having relocated from Brooklyn or Jersey, but now the tenants were mostly Hispanic. To Violet, they were mostly Cuban, for she made no distinction between the Salvadorans, Nicaraguans, Costa Ricans, Colombians, and a melting pot of others from the Caribbean and Central and South America. All she knew, they jabbered in Spanish so loud you couldn't hear the old Jews hacking up phlegm across the hall.

Violet *could* tell the difference between her Hispanic neighbors and the Haitians who moved in a block away at the Ocean Manor. The Haitians were blacker than midnight, poorer than Georgia crackers, and they scared the bejesus out of her when she walked by their building. No matter that the men looked down as she walked by, Violet feared them for their bare-chested blackness. This night, one of them painted bright pictures on a piece of driftwood, another carved a woman's torso in a piece of dark mahogany. Violet eyeballed the knife as she passed. She clenched the camera store bag until her knuckles were white. Thirty paces from the front steps of her building, a blur flashed from behind.

"*Cuidate mujer!*" Manuel, a skinny twelve-year-old from the second floor, flew by on his skateboard and Violet stumbled off the curb.

"Stay off the sidewalk, you little greaseball!" Violet shrieked after him.

Tingling with anticipation, Violet climbed the stairs. The hallway smelled of fried bananas. Behind the thin walls, a child wailed. Once inside her apartment, Violet's bony hands were a blur of motion. She made a small pot of black coffee. She tied her hair back into a ponytail and sat cross-legged in the tiny living room. She spread the papers onto the living room floor, the cheap shag carpeting matted under the glorious display of colors, blue and orange and purple borders. On top of each one, a finely etched eagle, a magnificent predator with wings unfolding and poised for flight. Violet Belfrey felt like singing the national anthem.

Sipping the strong coffee, she arranged the papers alphabetically, which seemed the businesslike thing to do. First came "Allegheny County Industrial Development Authority Environmental Improvement Bond, United States Steel Corporation Project 6¾ percent."

Bonds, she thought, smiling, for she had heard of stocks and bonds. She had posted bond once on a crummy soliciting charge, but that was different. Posting bond, you paid them; stocks and bonds, they paid you. She folded the bond along its creased lines into a little package. On the front, it said, "Five Thousand Dollars," a wonderful round number. She unfolded the pretty package and inside, attached to the bond, were three dozen little slips with tiny print like an eye exam. Must be the coupons the old man mentioned, she thought. They each said $168.75 payable every September 1 and March 1. Then, what the hell, in the year of our Lord 2012, she would get the five grand.

Too damn long.

Her tits would hang to her hips by then. Tomorrow she would take the bonds to her bank where the vice president with the rat's tail mustache and wandering hands would tell her how the hell to get some money now. Not about to wait six months to cash little tickets like a shitty bolita prize, much less nearly twenty years for the jackpot.

Violet stacked the rest of the bonds in a neat pile. Next came "Brookhaven, Mississippi, Industrial Revenue Development Bond, General Motors Corporation Project 5⅝ percent." The damn coupons here were only $140.62, and the bond said, "Principal due May 1, 2007."

Fucking General Motors. Violet had a Chevy Impala die on her once, and Brookhaven, Mississippi, sounded like shitkicker city. Next, "Dalton, Georgia Revenue Bond, Salem Carpet Mills Project 7.25 percent." Due date September 1, 1998, not so long to wait. But Jesus, why do all the bonds come from stump-jumper towns? These coupons said $181.00 each, and Violet could not figure out why bonds that each said "Five Thousand Dollars" on front could have different amounts on the coupons inside.

Then, "Evanston, Wyoming Industrial Development Revenue Bond, Dow Chemical Company 13 percent," with coupons of $325.00 each. Now we're talking, but the five large ones were not due until September 1, 2014. Jesus, why would the old jerk buy these things? By then, there wouldn't be enough left of Sam Kazdoy for the cockroaches.

Violet's eyes were blurry from the small print, so she stopped reading and counted her neat stack of colorful papers, eleven of them, each with dozens of the tiny coupons, some payable in three weeks on December 1. Eleven times five thousand equals fifty-five thousand dollars. Not bad for a night's work, especially when you don't have to gargle afterward with Listerine.

Then Violet's mind drifted. Her little bundle barely made a

dent in that file cabinet. How many more eagles were caged there, wings stretching even now? Hundreds at least. And the other drawers, thousands maybe, millions of dollars doing no good to an old fool.

That night, Samuel Kazdoy dreamed of Rachel, his wife, buried long ago, and how her pale body trembled under his touch on their wedding night.

Violet Belfrey slept restlessly, the traffic in the street below clicking like the tumblers of a combination lock. When sleep came, she dreamed of an eagle gliding high, wings proudly swept back, talons of steel clutching papers splashed with colors. She called for the eagle to bring her its catch, but the bird soared toward the sea. Again the eagle flew and now there was another and soon the sky was streaked with their inky smears until the birds disappeared and it rained blues and purples and oranges and Violet saw her prize a last time. Glowing in the moonlight, the papers fluttered to earth, tumbled along a beach, and, one by one, disappeared into the cold tomb of a black sea.

CHAPTER 3

Trial Lawyer

Jake Lassiter waited patiently for an answer from number three, a portly thirty-year-old accountant in a gray suit. The man's eyes darted from side to side, and he tightened his arms across his chest. Lassiter stole a glance at Marvin the Maven in the front row of the gallery.

Marvin tugged his right ear, ran a hand over his bald head, and nodded. Either he wanted Lassiter to steal second base or he was telling him to keep this guy on the panel. Some lawyers hire psychiatrists at three-hundred bucks an hour to help pick juries. The shrinks are full of advice: The man who sits with his elbows in his lap is submissive, while the one who encroaches on the next juror's armrests is dominant; the guy who crosses his legs is tense; the woman in a miniskirt with exotic earrings is plaintiff oriented. In Chicago, a cab driver sometimes helps a famous personal injury lawyer by pinpointing jurors' neighborhoods and determining their economic standing. That wouldn't work in Miami where most cab drivers don't speak the language and wouldn't know I-95 from the Tegucigalpa Turnpike.

Lassiter preferred to rely on his own instincts with help from Marvin the Maven and Saul the Tailor, two retirees who spend every weekday, nine to five, in the courtrooms and corridors of the Dade County Courthouse.

"Why . . . yes," the accountant finally answered. "I would agree that just because someone has been injured doesn't mean someone else is at fault."

Lassiter nodded, letting all the jurors appreciate number three's wisdom. He wouldn't have a drink with this guy, but he might let him sit on the jury.

"And you understand that the defense is as entitled to a fair trial as the plaintiff?"

"Of course," the accountant piped up, without hesitation. "Insurance companies have rights, too."

Lassiter nodded at this pearl of tight-assed wisdom. "And you will not be swayed by sympathy for the injured person?"

"Absolutely not."

Lassiter smiled. Bingo!

Marvin the Maven leaned toward Saul the Tailor and whispered, "Fatso saves his sympathy for clients with long-term capital losses."

Lassiter had watched the accountant when he had landed in the third chair in the jury box. Unhappy to be there, he had examined the orange vinyl seat as if a wad of Juicy Fruit might have formed a stalagmite there. Too busy to waste his time, he would likely take out his displeasure on the plaintiff. Which was fine with Jake Lassiter because at the moment he was stuck on the skid row of trial work, the slip-and-fall case.

Only thing worse than defending a slippin' Sylvia suit, Lassiter thought, was a dog bite case.

It would be all Lassiter could do to keep awake while witnesses debated why Mrs. Ana Fraga-Freitas slipped on a slice of papaya at San Pedro's Supermercado and skidded headfirst into a pyramid of Pony Malta bottles. *Bebida de campeónes*, drink of champions. The *Fraga-Freitas* case was not nearly as interesting as one involving the soft drink a few years earlier when Colombian drug dealers laced a shipment with pure cocaine, then overlooked one case after it had cleared customs. A man who bought a spiked bottle at a convenience store ingested enough of the drug to make a buffalo think it was a butterfly. The man didn't last the night.

Lassiter looked across the courtroom at Mrs. Fraga-Freitas. She wore a neck brace, but that was for show. The soft tissue injury was a product of her chiropractor's vivid imagination. The broken collarbone had long since healed, and at a solid five feet three, 230 pounds, she could unload refrigerators at the dock. With one hand.

God, how he hated slip-and-falls. The cases were nearly always identical. The plaintiffs were middle-aged to elderly, and if they didn't slide across the floor at a supermarket, they tripped over invisible cracks in the sidewalk. Every two-bit plaintiff's lawyer with an office in a shopping center and commercials on late-night TV had a fistful of slipping, falling, tripping clients and a stable of orthopedic surgeons better at testifying than operating. The cases took little legal ingenuity but a substantial ability to schmooze with doctors and push them to the limits of their oath, something that became easier when the hefty expert witness fee was paid in advance.

Lassiter had begun voir dire the same as always. *We ask*

these questions only for the purpose of seating a fair and unbiased jury. A little white lie, he told himself. After all, he could hardly reveal the truth: *We seek a jury predisposed by background and experience to favor our clients and to despise the opposition.*

It's an imperfect system, lawyers like to say, but the best one ever devised. Excluding trial by combat, of course.

While trying to decide about the accountant, Lassiter was still concerned about his neighbor, juror number two. A self-employed carpenter, he responded to questions quickly and loudly, then looked around, waiting for the applause. Might want to show off in the jury room, Lassiter worried, get macho and run roughshod over the others. A one-man jury, no lawyer wants that.

There were two other men seated so far, a college student wearing jeans and a cable TV installer in a khaki jumpsuit with his name above the pocket. Three women had survived the cut, a social worker, a flight attendant, and a homemaker. It was a typical jury, but hardly a fair cross-section of Miami. To truly represent the community, you'd have to include drug dealers, boiler-room bullion salesmen, small arms runners, porno filmmakers, swampland hucksters, and goat-sacrificing *santeros.*

Choosing jurors is like going out on a blind date. No matter how much you've been told in advance, there are always surprises. "Look at their shoes," Marvin the Maven always advised. "Leather oxfords, shined up good, that's your foreman." Marvin had owned a shoe store in Pittsburgh, and he could analyze your temperament with a downward glance.

"What about the woman?" Lassiter once asked him.

"Stay away from the ones who show their toes. Especially if they've painted their nails."

Jake Lassiter looked at his notes. The carpenter wore paint-stained, hard-toed shoes, the student sneakers, the computer technician loafers. Only the accountant had shoes with laces. Tied tight, Lassiter figured. Two of the women wore conservative pumps, the flight attendant ankle-high work boots that make SoBe club hoppers look like lumberjacks.

Lassiter squeezed his six-foot-two frame out of the heavy oak chair and walked toward the jury box. Every juror watched him. He gave the impression of filling his space and the next guy's too, had what they can't teach in law school . . . presence. A dozen years since he'd torn down the field to make a tackle—or get his clock cleaned—on a kickoff, but you could still play racquetball against his abdominals. He watched the jury panel through clear blue eyes and tried not to betray his boredom, then pretended to study the juror chart on his yellow pad. Struggling to appear earnest, he stroked his chin and ran a hand through his thick, sandy hair. He looked toward Marvin the Maven who tugged his left ear this time and nodded.

"The defense accepts the jury panel," Lassiter said to the judge.

Lester Jeffries, the plaintiff's lawyer, walked to the podium and bowed formally to the jury before speaking to the judge. The obsequious bastard was trying to score points already, Lassiter thought.

Jeffries was short and squat with a high forehead and sparse, dark hair. He was partial to suspenders and bow ties and cowboy boots, a combination that made no sense to Lassiter. "Your Honor, I believe we tendered the jury panel to Mr. Lassiter without accepting it," Jeffries said. "Therefore, at this juncture, without undue delay and without further inconvenience to the venire, and noting that the lunch recess is nearly upon us, the plaintiff now excuses juror number three."

A lawyer will always use a bushel of words when just a peck will do. Lassiter slumped in his chair and rolled his eyes upward. A heavy teak beam split the middle of the ceiling and connected with rows of smaller beams that spiraled downward toward the walls. A giant spinal column with ribs attached. I'm in the belly of a whale, Lassiter thought, and in a moment, I'll be whale shit. He glumly watched the accountant leave the jury box, then rose from the defense table and strode to the podium, where Lester Jeffries peered into the gallery, smile cemented into place.

"Jeffries, we're gonna be here all week with this lousy case," Lassiter whispered hoarsely.

"C'mon, Jake, that guy was an anal retentive numbers cruncher. It'd be malpractice for a plaintiff's lawyer to seat him."

"Yeah, but I left on the lady social worker with the heart of gold. We could have called it even."

"Maybe next time," Jeffries said.

"Next slip-and-fall, let's make a deal. No peremptories, no challenges. We'll seat the first six people, no matter what. Put your perjurious osteopaths and chiropractic quacks on the stand by ten A.M., case goes to the jury by noon."

Jeffries thought about it and fiddled with his yellow bow tie. "What if a juror doesn't speak English?"

"Doesn't matter," Lassiter said.

"What if they're all illiterates or cousins of the plaintiff?"

"Hell, I don't care if they're illegal aliens or convicted felons."

"Actually, I'd like that," Jeffries said. "Resentment of authority is always good for the plaintiff, but I don't think they're eligible."

Lassiter shrugged. "I'm not kidding. Let's grab the first six people on Flagler Street."

"I'll think about it," Jeffries said, hooking a thumb into his suspenders, trying to look like Gregory Peck in *To Kill a Mockingbird*, but actually resembling Joe Pesci in *My Cousin Vinnie.*

"Gentlemen, gentlemen," whined the judge, "if your colloquy is complete, may we resume picking a jury?"

Judge Morgan Lewis stood five feet three and sat three feet seven. When he sank into his cushioned chair, he disappeared from view, but he was still within earshot, and the lawyers could hear the rasp of the irascible jurist from time to time. Under his breath, Judge Lewis cursed them for their youth, his parents for his shortness, and himself for the dumb-ass decision to become a judge at $93,111 a year, while snot-nosed lawyers drove home in Porsches after knocking off seven-figure verdicts in his courtroom, the by-God biggest courtroom in the Eleventh Judicial Circuit in and for Dade County, Florida.

"Or if you prefer," squeaked the voice from behind the bench, "I'll pick the jury, and you two can keep quiet."

The bailiff, a retired bail bondsman whose primary job was to collect campaign contributions for the judge, summoned a replacement for the accountant. Lassiter watched a woman with dyed-red hair and a leather mini rise from the gallery. As she walked toward the jury box, Lassiter noticed the earrings, large as basketball hoops. On her feet were Roman sandals, the toenails painted fuchsia and embedded with little gold stars. From the front row of the gallery, Lassiter thought he heard a sigh.

On Flagler Street a group of chanting Hare Krishnas competed for sidewalk space with Nicaraguan exiles denouncing the Sandinistas, or maybe these were Sandinistas denouncing the new regime, you could never tell. The fronds swayed gently on the palm trees in front of Miami Center, a skyscraper of brown travertine marble wedged between the bay and eight lanes of Biscayne Boulevard. Near the top floor, black turkey buzzards—ugly as death—glided outside the windows of Miami's high-rise lawyers. Vultures and lawyers, Jake Lassiter thought, birds of a feather. One difference, though. The feathery scavengers arrive from the north each autumn and depart each spring. The birds in seersucker stick around all year.

"The souls of lawyers paying endless penance," a Cuban spiritualist once told Lassiter, pointing at the vultures flying their endless circles.

"Not so," he replied. "Lawyers never repent."

On the ground, Haitian immigrants lounged in nearby Bayfront Park hawking bags of oranges. Old Cuban men in push-carts sold doughy *empanadas* and sweet *pastelitos*, jockeying for position with hot dog vendors. Slinging his navy blue suit coat over one shoulder, Jake Lassiter settled into the elevator of Miami Center, bulky trial bag resting on the handrail. As the elevator door closed, a woman's hand snaked in and caught the rubber bumper. When the doors parted, Lassiter saw the smiling face of Cindy Clark, his secretary. Two middle-aged men in white guayaberas followed her in the door.

"Thought I recognized that hand," he said. "So few women wear rings on all five fingers these days."

"What about Cher?" his secretary laughed.

Cindy Clark, a twenty-two-year-old free spirit, was an aberration in a conservative, downtown law firm that represented banks, construction companies, and insurance carriers. Monday through Friday, Cindy was the perfect secretary, running interference through the law firm's bureaucracy like a blocker leading a sweep. On weekends she could be found on the back of a candy-apple Harley-Davidson Electra Glide Classic headed for the Keys. On the front in a sleeveless leather vest was Tubby Tubberville, all 260 pounds of him, much of which was decorated with tattoos.

If Cindy was different from the upscale secretarial staff, her boss was just as much an outsider. Jake Lassiter's partners in the old Miami firm were buttoned-down MBA types, corporate lawyers who poisoned the worlds of business and law with clinically efficient takeovers, and litigators whose frivolous pleadings tied up opponents in strike suits and class actions. Wimps outside the boardrooms and courtrooms, these lawyers got their rocks off by manipulating the rules for money, power, and prestige.

"You're back early," Cindy said.

"Settled for one-fifty, sent everybody home."

The elevator stopped, and the men in guayaberas got off on seventeen, home of a Panamanian *banco* with few customers but enormous cash transactions.

Cindy was thinking it over. "One-fifty, as in a hundred and fifty thousand?"

"Yeah."

"Jeez, I thought you said her injuries were phonier than Dan Quayle's smile."

"Who?"

"C'mon, Jake. Why'd you throw in the towel?"

"Their orthopod was giving her a fifty percent disability of the upper-right extremity, fifteen percent of the body as a whole, and she's got a whole lot of body. Plus she's got an MRI printout that looks like the Milky Way and her expert is talking nerve damage. Then, there's *Mister* Fraga-Freitas, who's got his lost consortium claim. Says their sex life headed south, or as he put it, '*de mal en peor.*' "

"What's a broken collarbone got to do with sex?"

"I was dying to ask and hoping the answer had something to do with a trapeze or a chandelier."

"So you settled, just like that?"

"I also had a short trial judge, a short plaintiff's lawyer, and a short guy on the jury who might have ended up the foreman."

"Not your Napoleonic complex theory again. What about your defenses? Remember, she showed up for her depo wearing glasses, but the day of the accident . . ."

"Yes, my performance could have rivaled Clarence Darrow's in the Leopold and Loeb trial. 'And now, Mrs. Fraga-Freitas, isn't it true that when you did your half gainer into the soda display, you were not wearing your bifocals?' "

The elevator stopped at twenty-one, and a cleaning crew got in and rode to twenty-two, where they got off.

Cindy said, "Well anyway, it was something to try. The MP's not going to be happy if he thinks you gave the store away."

MP being Managing Partner, not Member of Parliament, though maybe it stood for Major Prick, too. "Yeah, Cindy, I know."

"I mean, San Pedro's Supermercado is *his* client."

"Yeah, but who does he turn to when they're in trouble. Who got them off the hook on health code violations?"

"I remember," she said.

"Cockroaches in the *frijoles negros*. Story of my life."

"Don't knock it. Your closing argument was great."

Lassiter lowered his voice and spoke to an invisible jury. " 'So what if there's a little thorax with the beans, a hairy antenna with the rice. Once you mix in the onions and spices, who can tell?' "

"Don't forget the part about insects being considered delicacies in certain parts of the world," Cindy reminded him.

The elevator stopped at thirty-two with a soft *whoosh*, and Lassiter held the door open.

"I still don't know why you settled," Cindy said. "Your experts would contradict hers, plus you had a chance to win on liability."

"No way. All the witnesses except Mr. San Pedro agreed the papaya was the color of licorice, meaning it had been on the floor long enough that some produce worker should have cleaned it up, if they all weren't smoking reefer out on the loading dock."

"So you caved in?"

"I settled. I didn't want to lose."

They walked together in silence along the burgundy-carpeted corridor of Harman & Fox. The walls were tastefully decorated with oil paintings of the British men's club variety: hunting dogs, whaling ships, and leather riding gear. Lassiter always thought a school of feeding sharks would be more appropriate but the partners' art subcommittee, which reported to facilities committee, which in turn reported to the finance committee, never took him seriously.

Few of the lawyers were in their offices. It was usually that way. Fifty bucks a square foot for a view of the ocean, and hardly anyone was ever there. A few would be in court, a few might be interviewing witnesses, some would be goofing off at the racetrack, but others were just not accounted for, except when they padded their time sheets with the catchall entry for "research."

"I didn't think that's the way you played the game," Cindy said finally. "Just trying not to lose."

"Maybe you thought wrong, or maybe that was another game. I decided I was *saving* San Pedro money by settling, and that happens to be my job."

"Some job," Cindy said.

"It is unnecessary to remind me that playing poker with half-assed lawyers and cantankerous judges is insufficient grounds for sainthood. And speaking of jobs, why aren't you doing yours?"

They stopped in front of Lassiter's office. The door was open, files propped on the desk and credenza inside. The windows faced east squarely over Biscayne Bay, Miami Beach, and the Atlantic Ocean beyond.

"I needed to get out of the ant farm, find some inspiration," Cindy answered. "Listen to this."

November sky,
Bums in park,
Miami.

Lassiter winced. "Haiku again, another lily pad and teahouse phase?"

"It's spiritually uplifting, you should try it."

"Sure thing," Lassiter said. "How's this?"

Back to work,
Type, type, type.
Cindy.

"Oh, Jake, there's more to life than work. Besides, there was another reason I went to the park. I wanted to see the body. A Colombian cowboy got snuffed and dumped in the piss pool."

She swung a handful of zebra-striped nails in the general direction of Bayfront Park and the octagonal Claude and Mildred Pepper Fountain. Much to the dismay of the city fathers, the derelicts used the four-million-dollar fountain for an outdoor urinal. This was the first time, however, a drug dealer had practiced the dead man's float there. Usually, when a deal soured, the losing entrepreneur turned up behind the wheel of a Ferrari at the bottom of a West Dade canal, a neat pattern of entry wounds at the base of his skull. No need for lawyers to resolve those disputes. A MAC-10 leaves no grounds for appeal.

"Sounds gruesome," Jake Lassiter said.

"Nah, except he bled all over, and from the top floor, the water looked like a bowl of punch at the junior prom."

Lassiter groaned. "Any messages?"

"Lots of calls. Thad the Cad, some crappy problems at the bank. Then a guy from Hawaii, something about his fee for coming to Miami for the windsurfing race. And Mr. Kazdoy. He wants you to go to the theater tonight."

Thaddeus G. Whitney, general counsel of Great Southern Bank, could wait. The bank's work was fine if you were the kind of guy who liked sneaking tricky acceleration clauses into mortgages and drafting collateral agreements so abstruse most people would sign them just to avoid reading them. Lassiter wasn't that kind of guy. He would call Keaka Kealia, the Hawaiian who was arriving Tuesday for the Miami-to-Bimini sailboard race. And Lassiter would show up at Kazdoy's theater on Miami Beach for a lecture on Russian-American relations, an Eisenstein film, and a cup of borscht with the old man after the show.

First, though, there was work to do, plenty of work for a good lawyer these days. Miami had become a boomtown. The biggest business was importation—an assortment of weeds, powders, and pills—and the town was awash with dirty money. Greedy bankers laundered millions in tens and twenties for one point of the action. Lawyers formed offshore companies to hide drug profits and sometimes wound up offshore themselves, tied to concrete blocks if they were unfortunate enough to be subpoenaed before grand juries. Sleek women sniffed at a tropical high and attached themselves to swarthy men draped with gold.

To Jake Lassiter, all that was another world. He lived in a tiny house built of coral rock on a lot lush with live oak and red mulberry trees between Poinciana and Kumquat streets in Coconut Grove. He was one of the last Miamians without air-conditioning, preferring a half-dozen paddle fans that stirred the soggy air but did not seal him inside. At night he could hear the cries of herons and terns on their way from the Everglades to the beaches, and he could taste the aroma of a dozen mango trees next door.

Lassiter preferred the beach to nightclubs and cutoff jeans to lawyer's blue suits. He loved Miami for the water and the solitude he found on a nine-foot sailboard on a twenty-knot day, shredding the breaking waves of the Atlantic. Sailing east, hopping the chop, he would watch the sky meet the ocean at the horizon. The world was limitless, possibilities infinite. But jibe and head west, back to shore, and there in the distance were the glass-and-marble towers of downtown. Inside, plush jail cells twelve-by-twelve. The sun glared against the tiny windows, sharp as a dagger in the eye, and Lassiter imagined ten thousand lawyers, bankers, and accountants pushing their papers from one desk to another and back again, a cycle as endless as the orbit of the circling vultures.

Jake Lassiter would rather sail east.

Cindy Clark typed the settlement papers in the *San Pedro* case and returned to her haiku, trying to work "bloody corpse" into a poetic triplet. Jake Lassiter called the Hawaiian and promised that an appearance fee would be delivered before the race. An unusual request, but for Keaka Kealia, the world's greatest boardsailor, it was worth it.

From his high-rise perch, phone cradled on shoulder, Jake Lassiter reached for his binoculars. He watched the surf break on the reef at Virginia Beach on nearby Key Biscayne. He envisioned Keaka Kealia, six thousand miles away where Pacific waves slapped the north shore of Maui. Lassiter wished he were there with the sailors and surfers whose lives mocked his own. He envied their endless summer, conjuring images of sails crackling in steady trade winds, warm nights grilling mahimahi on the beach by torchlight, surrounded by women with bronzed bodies and sun-kissed hair.

The call completed, Lassiter dropped the *San Pedro* file on the floor next to a bulging folder of antitrust pleadings. He sidestepped half a dozen mortgage foreclosures and made his way to the marble windowsill three hundred fifty feet above Biscayne Bay.

"Maui," Jake Lassiter said wistfully, kicking off his black leather wing tips and squinting into the brightness of the bay.

CHAPTER 4

Soda Jerk

At first Violet Belfrey vowed she wouldn't spend a dime, wouldn't even cash in the bonds. But why not go to the bank and find out what gives? The bank vice president fiddled with his mustache and whistled when he saw her, whistled twice when he saw the bonds, grabbing them, instead of her, with clammy hands. He told her to unload them now and talked about interest rates and issue par versus nominal par and a bunch of other things that didn't make any sense except that she could turn the birds into cash.

"Just a slight discount below face value," he said, twisting his mustache.

No harm in that, Violet thought, walking out of there with fifty-one thousand seven hundred dollars in cash, the banker following her out the door, extolling the virtues of a tax-exempt municipal bond mutual fund.

"We're not the Rocker-fellers," she told him. "The Belfreys always hold our own money, and mine's going right into the shoe box with Grandma Mabel's zirconium ring." Violet neglected to say that tax-free investments were meaningless in a family where no one had ever signed a 1040, and few could have, even if they'd wanted to.

The money all might have gone into the shoe box, too, just as she planned, had the bus not passed Potamkin Lincoln-Mercury on the way back to her place. The midnight blue Town Car, five eagles on the wing.

Violet Belfrey never cared much about jewelry, never had the bucks to care much about it. But a watch, that's practical, can tell time and show people you're classy all at once. The gold Rolex from Mayor's on Miracle Mile, two more eagles aloft.

Gambling was for suckers but a weekend in Nassau with Harry Marlin, her man, well, that was a vacation and a well-deserved one. The blackjack table, another bird uncaged.

It seemed like a lot of money at first, but if you wanted to get your white ass out of town, buy a place in the Carolina mountains, the score would have to be bigger. Hell, only walking around money left, and wouldn't be any sugar daddy there to sink your teeth into.

Of course Harry was asking questions, wanting to know where she got the money. At first she said her aunt Emma died, and Harry cracked wise about Violet's family, saying it was even money her aunt was her sister.

"That ain't funny," she said.

"Okay, just don't pull my chain. Your aunt had to leave the house to take a pee, so don't tell me she saved the money in a cookie jar, or that your uncle Clem struck oil in the pea patch like the Beverly friggin' Hillbillies."

He kept pestering, pecking away at her, and finally she told him. Harry listened, eyes wide, and asked her to repeat the part about the combination lock and the file cabinet.

"Gray metal drawers," she said, "a hollow wood door to the office."

"Uh-huh," Harry Marlin nodded, smiling his gold-capped grin. "Security guards, burglar alarm?"

"Nope."

"Uh-huh," he repeated.

"Don't be gittin' no ideas," Violet told him. "If those bonds disappear, who'd he suspect? Him and me's the only ones ever in the office, and ah'll bet dollars to doughnuts he never told nobody else about 'em."

"Maybe, maybe not. What makes you think you're the first one ever took off her clothes for him?"

She laughed and brushed a fall of platinum hair from her eyes. "He might've dipped his wick in Loretta Lynn for all I care, but he's tighter than my granddaddy's hatband. He wouldn't pay for it, I can tell you that."

"So how come he gave you fifty-five large just for showing your tits?"

"Whatsa matter?" Violet asked. "Doncha believe me? Or ain't my tits worth that much?"

"They're million-dollar hooters, Vi, but that's not the point. It's just weird, he could get a hooker with a tongue like a lizard for a hundred bucks, but he pays you fifty-five K just to pose."

"Maybe he's in love with me. Ever think of that?"

He hadn't before, but he did now. After a moment, he said, "So why don't you do something about it? Shit, all that money for posing. What would he pay for a blowjob?"

"Why doncha make him an offer and see?" Violet said, her eyes narrowing. Not that she hadn't thought of sucking some life into the old man, but hearing Harry suggest it, like he was running the show, burned in her gut. Sam Kazdoy was her private fishing hole, and she didn't need any advice on how to bait the hook.

Ever since he had given her the bonds, Violet had been even more helpful at the theater, offering to run errands, and the old man seemed happy enough to have her around. *Ey, bubeleh, get me a coffee, black, and a bagel with a shmeer.* And she did, stepping into the dark office and hanging around, but there was no talk of breasts or bonds. Relying on a lifetime of experience with men, Violet would bide her time. Let him make the first move.

"Harry Marlin, you listen and you listen good," she ordered. "If ah'm going to get the rest of those bonds, ah'll do it my way and in my own time."

Violet Belfrey had a daily routine. Her job was to be the first one at the theater, pick up the mail, turn on the lights and air-conditioning, and make sure the old rummy of a projectionist showed up in condition to load the reels in the right order. She also checked the door to the mezzanine office, just as she had every day since the old man had introduced her to winged eagles with dollar signs. The door was always locked, a cheap Schlage with a skinny bolt, and when she leaned against it, she heard the groan of metal against wood.

On the way to the theater, Violet stopped at the Lincoln Road Grill, a place never mistaken for the Poodle Lounge at the Fontainebleau. She swiveled in and hugged the pudgy counterman from behind, grinding her pubic bone into his butt as he squashed hamburger patties on the grill.

"Seeyuh right after the show," she said.

"I'll be here," Harry Marlin replied, winking at a customer and wiping his hands on a dirty white apron. He was proud that this savvy blonde had fallen for him. Besides being the best lay he ever had, she was a great listener. Harry needed that because he was a great talker. His monologues could last for hours. Schemes and scams, deals with guys whose offices were the trunks of cars, always a big plan for easy money. In fact, Harry Marlin was a loser. When he gambled, he lost. When he sold drugs at his lunch counter, he was paid with counterfeit currency. When he fell for one of his waitresses, she cleaned out the cash register and beat it to Jamaica with a local wise guy who made porno films.

Harry had bounced through a series of restaurant jobs in Detroit and when he moved to Miami Beach fifteen years ago, he took over the lease on the Lincoln Road Grill, a run-down luncheonette. The food was greasy, but he had fresh copies of the *Daily Racing Form* on the counter for his best customers, the bleary-eyed bettors from the dog and horse tracks and the jai alai frontons. And a motley congregation it was—gamblers, aging dancers from the Beach Burlesque, lobster-pot poachers plus assorted retirees, none of whom seemed to mind the stale doughnuts and metallic coffee.

Harry Marlin made it through each day because he had a dream. He would get out of Miami Beach, would say *adiós* to making chili burgers for the menacing teenagers who skulked through the neighborhood. He would read *The Wall Street Journal* each morning and call his broker each afternoon. He would leave behind the wacko bag ladies who had buried their husbands in Cleveland and Newark, and the bearded rabbinical students who ordered seltzer and made faces at anyone eating the chili. Someday . . . when he scored.

Harry wore an unbuttoned white guayabera, the loose linen shirt with four pockets, which he thought made him look professional, a pharmacist maybe. He was forty-three and camouflaged a growing bald spot with back-to-front and side-to-middle brushstrokes. He was short, olive-skinned, and paunchy, with shoulders like a wire coat hanger, but he had a smile born of innocence and the heart of a wide-eyed grifter who could not help but believe that his next scheme was laced with gold.

One look at Violet that first day and Harry knew she wasn't in the running for Orange Bowl Queen. She was the kind of woman who looks better from across the street than across the counter. Still, he admired her style, the way she perched on a barstool, her legs wrapped around the metal post like snakes on a tree trunk. She was fresh talent in a part of town where the favorite nightcap was prune juice. Round, full breasts, low-cut blouse, chiseled features, and hair bleached too often and too harshly. Maybe a cocktail waitress at a Ramada Inn, Harry Marlin thought at first. Probably heard every line from every costume jewelry salesman on the East Coast, but play your cards right, a pushover and no hassle in the morning.

Harry remembered the first words he spoke to Violet. He had patted his thinning hair, smiled, and asked, "How 'bout some chili, honey?"

"How hot is it?"

"How hot you like it?" he replied, flashing the wide grin.

She examined him as if he were a roach on the bathroom tile. "Just coffee, José, and save the bullshit for your *señoritas*."

"My name's Harry and I'm not a Latino," he said, anxious to distance himself from the guys who smack their lips at every *chica* on the block. "My family's from Beirut."

"Mine's from Macon," she said, "a shithole full of clover kickers. Where's Baberuth?"

"Lebanon. And it's not doing so good neither. Haven't seen your classy chassis around here before. This is my place, you know. But just temporary. I'm working on a couple of big deals. You know anything about the stock market?"

"Sure, a little."

Violet Belfrey knew as much about the stock market as she

did about nuclear fission, but for a reason she could not explain, she wanted the soda jerk with the sappy smile to like her.

"Great, let me tell you about my investments, all imaginary of course, for the time being." So Harry talked about his mythical stock portfolio, his puts and calls and selling short. He invested the way some guys play the ponies, with a make-believe grubstake on paper. "Today I'd be a rich man if I'd had the dough to put in."

Violet listened and the romance began. She would have dinner at Harry's after selling tickets at Kazdoy's theater. On Sundays, the Grill was closed and Harry treated Violet at an Italian place with a clean checkered tablecloth, and afterward they walked along the empty boardwalk and listened to the gentle shorebreak.

With a full moon over the Atlantic, they crawled under the walkway, where Violet's skilled fingers stroked him with the light touch of a pool shark on a cue stick. She bent over him and Harry leaned back, legs spread in the sand, watching Violet's platinum hair streaked by moonlight filtered through the slats of the boardwalk. Then he closed his eyes, at peace with the world, and thought, Harry Marlin, you sumbitch, you've let your sorry ass fall in love.

It had been a month since she'd told Harry about the bonds when he finally asked, "How much you figure the old codger has in that cabinet?"

"Never you mind."

But the same question kept haunting her. How many eagles were perched there with only a thin, hollow door and a combination lock in the way?

So close to paradise. Maybe it was time.

She wore her tightest jeans to the theater and wiggled her can like a bitch in heat. Still no rise from the old man.

She asked if he'd like his shoulders rubbed and he said no.

Like me to clean the office?

No again.

Anything you want?

Nothing, thank you, darling.

Shit, getting nowhere fast. She had a buzz in the back of her mind, worked it over, slept on it, finally was sure about it. Next morning, she told Harry.

He shook his head. "You want me to do a B and E?" he asked. "No friggin' way. Never had a felony rap. Don't think I could do hard time at my age."

"Harry Marlin, what kinda man are you? You wanna play the stock market for real but you don't have jackshit. You been a-fussin' about them bonds ever since I let on about 'em. Now let's see if you got the hair on your balls to do somethin' besides talk."

CHAPTER

5

The Cranes Are Flying

Jake Lassiter parked his 1968 Olds 442 convertible in the alley behind the theater. Lincoln Road was empty of pedestrians. Wealthy matrons once shopped there, riding trams from store to store, wrapped in mink at the first breath of November. Then Saks closed, restaurants and art deco hotels were boarded, and the street was taken over by *Marielitos*—the tattooed Cuban prisoners—who urinated in empty door fronts and terrorized the neighborhood's feeble retirees.

Five blocks away, Ocean Drive was rejuvenated with New York money and New York names. South Beach was now SoBe, where young couples of various genders sought out the newest cafés the way computer-guided missiles target tanks in the desert. Leggy models in Lycra shorts wove around traffic on rollerblades. Photographers and artists and Eurotrash dressed in trendy black walked the walk and talked the talk, but here, just half a mile inland, aged survivors of the Depression or the Holocaust shuffled along with canes and walkers, mumbling to themselves or long-lost relatives.

Violet Belfrey greeted Lassiter at the front door. "Show's started," she said. "You missed Mr. K.'s speech. Something about Lenin's experiment and Roosevelt's big deal."

"New Deal."

"Whatever."

"How you been, Violet?"

"Busted, disgusted, and can't be trusted." With that, she grabbed his bottom, gave a firm squeeze, and guided him through the turnstile. "Nice toe-kiss," she said.

"*Tuchis*, Violet. Sam should teach you better Yiddish."

"You'd be surprised how much learnin' I been doin' from old Mister K."

"And I'll bet you could teach him a thing or two," Lassiter said.

In his retirement Sam Kazdoy kept busy clipping bond coupons and showing Russian films at his movie theater. For the last six months, Violet Belfrey sold the tickets and changed the marquee. And hung around, Lassiter noticed. Rich old man and street-smart younger woman, a classic combination. Jake Lassiter saw cunning in Violet's dark eyes and scavenger's claws in her bony hands. Years ago, before age and wealth had dulled his senses, the old man would have seen it, too.

When Violet answered the employment ad, Lassiter wanted to do a background check. "Let's find out if she's ever been arrested, sued, divorced, done drugs," he told Kazdoy.

The old man refused. "Don't worry, *boychik*. Ey, she's got

some *titskes,*" Kazdoy chortled, cupping his hands two feet in front of his chest. Lassiter never brought it up again and Violet became a fixture at the old man's side.

Jake Lassiter followed a trail of ancient stains on the threadbare carpeting to a seat in the third row. The chair sagged until the metal seat scraped the floor with the sound of fingernails across a blackboard. Once a showplace—home to ten thousand matinees—the theater now was a dank tomb, the air heavy with dust and humidity, ceiling fans struggling against the tropical night.

Lassiter was the youngest moviegoer by thirty years. Most were aged widows and widowers, born in czarist Russia. The crowd was an orchestra off-key, playing tunes simultaneously in English, Yiddish, and Russian, the sounds of Babel rising to the empty balcony. Some chattered throughout the show, their whispers rattling like old mufflers, unaware that as their hearing diminished, their voices took up the slack.

Kazdoy showed double features, an old American film followed by a Russian classic. The Hollywood comedies and musicals were from his personal collection, bought on the gray market, so he paid no royalties to the movie studios, which he thought were still run by Louis B. Mayer.

"Tell the whoremongers Samuel Kazdoy don't pay no blackmail," he had said to Lassiter a half dozen years earlier. He had hired Lassiter to defend him when the studios sued for copyright violations. The old man settled, paying no royalties but agreeing to refrain from showing copyrighted films, a promise he regularly violated. There were no more lawsuits but Jake Lassiter and Samuel Kazdoy became friends, often having dinner together after a movie.

On this night, Lassiter dozed through *The Battleship Potem-*

kin, the classic Eisenstein film. After the show, a beaming Kazdoy moved quickly to the stage on steady legs and, using a microphone, began his weekly sociological essay.

"*Oy*, what a mess we've got here in *Goldeneh Medina*, this golden country. They're knocking down *zaydes* and *bubbes* for their Social Security checks. In Moscow, even with no government worth a damn anymore, it's still safer than New York.

"Something else, too many lawyers. Everybody's suing everybody else. I read in the paper, so I believe it even though it's not the *Daily Forward*, that a woman got hurt in a bus accident, she's suing the city saying the injury made her a whatchamacallit . . ."

"A nymphomaniac, Sam," said a man in the front row, a dapper eighty-year-old in a lime-green polyester leisure suit.

"A *nafka*," said a heavy woman next to him, her brown support stockings drooping around thick ankles.

"Feh!" sputtered the man in green. "No, no, no. A *nafka* charges money, a nymphomaniac does it for fun."

"So who would do it for fun?" the woman asked.

"That's right, a nymphomaniac," Samuel Kazdoy said. "Now, maybe if I was on that bus, she'd have a case." Kazdoy paused and the crowd roared. "But to get sued for too much *shtupping*? It's *meshugge*. Yessir, too many lawyers we got."

Kazdoy was squinting into the lights, trying to spot Lassiter. "Now take my lawyer. Please!"

The house erupted. They loved his corny jokes even more than the pickled herring at the old man's delicatessen.

"Here he is, Sam," a man with a silver toupee croaked. The man sat directly behind Lassiter and recognized him from previous evenings at the theater. Head bobbing, toupee sliding, the man jabbed a finger into Lassiter's shoulder blade. "Here's your mouthpiece, Sam." Lassiter slumped in his chair as heads turned and arthritic necks craned.

"Ah," Kazdoy said. "There's Jacob Lassiter. He's a good

lawyer, and he got those *gonifs* in Hollywood off my back. If you need an estate plan, call him up, but he'll charge you an arm and a leg, then you won't have a ruble left for your kids, but so what when they're in Scarsdale and don't come see you anyway?"

"How much you charge?" said the man with the sliding toupee, his finger now rapping the back of Lassiter's seat.

"I don't do wills," Lassiter said, hoping the old man would change the subject. He was in luck.

"In the Old Country," Kazdoy said, his voice dropping to signify the importance of the next observation, "they told me that the streets in New York were paved with gold. When I got off that stinking boat in 1912, the first thing I see is a man following a horse with a broom and pail, but what he was sweeping wasn't gold."

Then an abridged version of the familiar tale of the arrival at Ellis Island, of working for a cousin making corrugated boxes, and of starting his own small factory and finally retiring with six mammoth ones.

That story done, Kazdoy looked ahead. "Tomorrow, first we'll see a short subject, and I don't mean Mickey Rooney. It's about the Moscow subway system and it's beautiful to look at. They scrub those cars every night, you could eat off the floor. Have any of you ridden in a New York subway recently?"

A knowing murmur swept the crowd, heads bobbing in affirmation.

"Then a great war film that shows the horrors, the losses, the sacrifices . . ."

Oh no, Lassiter thought, how many times can they watch *The Cranes Are Flying*?

"*The Cranes Are Flying*," Kazdoy said. "I know all of you love it." And again, an appreciative stirring rustled through the theater, patrons content that they would revisit the familiar.

After the show, as Violet was making her way to Harry's place, Lassiter and the old man locked up the theater. "Let's get a bite to eat, Jacob," the old man said, as always. "Maybe the Chicken in the Pot is better than last time."

Kazdoy's All-Nite Deli was on Collins Avenue along the ocean but thirty blocks south of the high-rent district and ten blocks north of the trendy club scene. From the window booths, you could see the marquee of a triple-X movie theater advertising an all-male film festival. Next door was a noisy bar frequented by dockworkers who would be shipped out on the next freighter if Immigration ever pulled a raid. On the sidewalk, young women in short shorts and halter tops moseyed along in the universal stroll of the working gal with nowhere to go and lots of time to get there.

The Chicken in the Pot was no better. A layer of grease coated the soup, heavy noodles sinking to the bottom, while rubbery chicken parts floated near the surface.

"Eat a little something," the old man commanded. "Enjoy!"

Lassiter had a whitefish platter, the smoked fish surrounded by coleslaw and potato salad, last week's mayonnaise sharp on the tongue. They ate silently, Kazdoy growing tired, the excitement of the crowd wearing off. Lassiter munched a pickled tomato and wound his fork with sauerkraut. Finally, the old man asked, "How about you come to the theater this weekend?"

"I can't. I'm organizing the windsurfing races on the Key."

"Windsurfing." Samuel Kazdoy shook his bald head. "You make any money at that?"

"Not a cent."

"*Meshugge*. Why do it?"

"I like the challenge of riding a rough sea with just the wind for power and a chunk of fiberglass under my feet. It's a thrill to go faster than the lugheads in their half-million-dollar powerboats. It also keeps me sane, makes me forget about my sweaty-palmed partners and my clients who've never lost anything but their scruples."

The old man narrowed his eyes. "You got no clients you like?"

"Only you, Sam, and nobody's sued you lately."

"*Nu*, who should sue me? When those *momzers* in Hollywood tried, you kicked them in the ass."

Lassiter laughed. "As I recall, we entered a consent order. I assume you've stopped buying bootleg films."

Sam Kazdoy worked his crumpled face into a look of childlike innocence. "That's for me to know, and Samuel Goldwyn to find out. But you did a good job then, and I haven't forgotten."

"Neither have I. You were my first paying client after I got out of the PD's office. Plus you always brought me apple strudel. Nowadays, my clients bring postdated checks and perjurious witnesses."

"I'm surprised you have any clients. Half the time you're at the beach, windboarding or sailsurfing or whatever *mishegoss* . . ."

"Sam, didn't you ever play golf or tennis or go skiing?"

"Skiing?"

You might as well have asked him to eat suckling pig. "Didn't you ever have any hobbies?" Lassiter asked.

"Hobbies? I should live so long."

"But you must have done something besides run your businesses."

"I did religious work."

"You?"

"Sure, I made a lot of women Jewish, if only by injection," Kazdoy chuckled.

"Well, you should come to the beach this weekend just to watch," Jake Lassiter said. "Lila Summers from Maui will be there. She's young and beautiful and one of the world's great athletes. What more could a man ask?"

"To be seventy again," Samuel Kazdoy said.

CHAPTER 6

Cat Burglar

"*W**hadaya mean don't take 'em all?" Harry Marlin asked.* He was unnerved, pacing in the tiny apartment, throwing his hands around, sweat beading on his balding head.

Violet Belfrey watched, worried that he couldn't handle it. Look at him, the little soda jerk—let's face it, she thought, that's what he is—coming unglued only hours before he should be grabbing fistfuls of eagles, enough to fill Lincoln Road with three feet of birdshit.

"You take 'em all, the old man's liable to croak," she said. "Besides, if you only take some, like a couple hundred thou, he won't make such a fuss, maybe not even report it to the police."

"Vi, baby, you don't know what you're asking me to do. It's like saying, 'Harry, only stick it halfway in.' I might promise, but I get the door open, you know damn well I'm gonna ram it home."

"Maybe you should just keep it in your pants, you got such little control, and I can do this myself."

Harry smiled a crooked, gold-capped grin. "Then what about your alibi?"

He had her and had her good. Violet would be with the old man when the B and E was coming down. Someone else had to do the job and Harry was the one.

"Awright," Violet said. "Ah'll keep the old man happy as a clam at high tide, but why be greedy?"

She had finagled an invitation to Kazdoy's apartment, agreeing to broil some chicken—dry it out good, *bubeleh*—and once there, high heels kicked off, yawning and slipping out of tight blouse and frilly bra, she'd cook his goose.

Harry would have all night to root around in the metal drawers.

If he didn't fuck it up.

But look at him now, nervous as a dog shitting razor blades. Should be so easy. But the little man, sweet as he is, couldn't break into a pay toilet. Now he wants to take 'em all, cause a big ruckus.

"Vi, you gotta think big. You said yourself there might be millions there. Millions!"

"That's what ah'm worried about. The bigger the haul, who knows, the FBI might be here tomorrow givin' me the third degree."

"The FBI don't give a shit about an old man's bonds. They got stolen cars to worry about."

Harry stopped pacing to look in the bathroom mirror and

adjust his black wool ski cap, pulling it down over his eyes. Nice touch, changes a guy's looks, harder to get a make on a guy. An army surplus store had provided the essentials of the evening's attire, black turtleneck sweater rolled up to his ears, ski cap pulled down, baggy green army jacket, camouflage pants, and black lumberjack boots, plus a backpack that held a flashlight and crowbar. In that getup and with a four-day growth of beard, he didn't look like Cary Grant in *To Catch a Thief*, more like Yasir Arafat after a tough week in the Bekaa Valley. It never occurred to Harry that a burglar on Miami Beach shouldn't look like a guy who would blow up a synagogue.

Harry smiled into the mirror. Nice change from the guayaberas, he thought. He looked tough, weather-beaten, mean. And truth was, he'd wear a daffodil up his ass to keep from adding a blue chambray shirt with a six-digit number to his wardrobe.

Violet was fixing her hair, trying to get the lank, bleached strands to puff up into a beehive or bird's nest, or some other den for small animals, Harry thought. Each time she almost had it, some pins gave way and a side of the nest crumbled like a seawall in a hurricane. Soon she gave up and let gravity carry her hair down over her shoulders. Then she stepped into a black cotton miniskirt that was so old it was back in style. She wriggled her feet into black high-heeled shoes with sequins and spun around in front of the mirror to evaluate herself.

Harry watched her preening until Violet noticed. "Whatcha lookin' at, anywho?" she asked.

"Whadaya mean?"

Violet's face crinkled into a thin-lipped smile. "Ah'm just wondering why you're quiet as a church mouse right now, when most times you're flapping your gums like a preacher on Sunday morning."

"No reason," Harry said, softly.

"Oh, Harry, I believe you're jealous that ah'm gonna see that old man tonight but you're too damn proud to say so."

"No, Vi, if you wanna go out looking like that, it's okay."

"Harry darlin', ah'm gettin' all gussied up so the old man'll ask me to stay the night so you can get the bonds and ah'll have an alibi that's tighter than a lug nut on a sixteen-wheeler."

Harry looked away and shrugged. "It's okay."

"You're so damn-fire cute to be jealous, I just love you to death. But git your mind on business. Now lookee here."

Violet used a paper napkin to draw a map of the South Side Theater, showing the alley leading to the fire door, the stairs to the mezzanine office, and the drawers tucked away in the corner. Harry concentrated hard and memorized the layout before melodramatically torching the napkin with a seventy-nine-cent lighter. A paunchy and chintzy 007. Then she showed him one of the remaining bonds so he'd know what he was looking for and told him she'd tape over the latch on the fire door.

After Violet left, Harry watched television for an hour, tried to take a nap but couldn't sleep and paced until eleven-thirty. His hands were shaking when he turned the key in his ten-year-old Plymouth—four doors, blackwalls—that looked like two tons of scrap metal and sounded like liftoff at Cape Canaveral.

He headed north on Washington Avenue, turned right, and curled back south on Ocean Drive, driving in circles for an hour, watching the models long-leg it past the cafés and grills and clubs that he lacked the confidence to enter. These were places with women who would never return his glance. Men with flat stomachs and full heads of hair who knew how to dress and what to say, laughing all the way to the next party. To Harry Marlin, the invitation to the party was money, and it was within his grasp.

He let the night swallow him, counting the minutes. Traffic was light on South Beach and he liked that. He turned onto Collins and headed north, still killing time. Just past the bridge to Arthur Godfrey Road, lots of cars were jammed up, trying to get out of the Fontainebleau, Miami Beach cops directing traffic. Harry cruised by and caught a glimpse of an older crowd, rich dudes wearing tuxes, their women in long gowns, some carrying floral centerpieces, and the valet parkers going crazy trying to unscramble all the Mercedeses in the lot. Another one of the charity balls finishing up, and Harry imagined himself buying a table for a thousand bucks for the Alzheimer's Gala, giving away the tickets to his friends, wondering which of the gamblers and con men would like to dance to Big Band sounds.

Harry slid the Plymouth through a U-turn, tires squealing in front of Seacoast Towers, then headed south on Collins. At Seventeenth he turned right and headed away from the ocean past the Jackie Gleason Theater where the marquee said *42nd Street*, and the show must have been over because all the old farts were pulling out of the municipal lot in their Fleetwoods and Town Cars. Again, uniformed patrolmen directing traffic, thank Jesus, all the cops tied up tonight and it's going to be fat city. He headed toward Alton Road and shivered when he passed the darkened windows of Zilbert-Rubin Funeral Home, which reminded him what the whole damn city was about, a cemetery. He turned south on Alton, passing Lincoln Road on his left. A siren wailed from behind and Harry saw a flashing red light and the adrenaline pumped, but then he saw it was a Miami Beach taxi, an ambulance. Another heart run out of voltage.

The old Plymouth wheezed and coughed to a stop three blocks from the theater on Española Way, Harry parking in front of a two-story apartment house—rentals weekly, air-conditioned—and walked to Lincoln Road. A warm, steady ocean breeze rattled the fronds on a line of queen palms. The sound sent shivers up Harry's spine. He strolled twice around the block, casing the joint, ski cap pulled down over his ears, nylon backpack hanging loosely from his shoulders. It was nearly one A.M. and the Road was dead. The breeze, a straightaway easterly, pushed discarded newspapers into darkened doorways and against concrete planters.

Harry walked the deserted sidewalk, pretending to look in the windows. The first time he missed them. Jeez, was he blind, or did they just appear in the pet shop doorway next to the theater? Two of them, slouching against the window, teenagers, skinny in jeans, T-shirts, and running shoes. One had a glove and a bat, the other was flipping a hardball, from one hand to the other.

Small but mean-looking. Friggin' *Marielitos.* No, closer now, he could see one's shirt had the drawing of a frog, a *coqui*, and the slogan "I Love Puerto Rico." A PR and proud of it, Harry thought, like boasting about having the clap.

Real close now, they eyed Harry. Both were tattooed, green scorpions winding across stringy arms. "Got the time, man?" one said to Harry.

"Chuck you, Farley," Harry said, sensing a rip-off. Lift an arm and your watch is gone.

Harry kept walking, did another orbit of the block and the kids were gone. He ducked into the alley at the side of the theater and quickly found the fire door in back. He paused long enough to put on the rubber gloves he bought at the drugstore, the kind the doctor wears to check your bunghole for the Big C. Then he yanked the heavy door open without a sound. He slid inside, removed the tape from the latch and let the door close, loving the sound of the lock clicking into place. In a moment his eyes adjusted to the darkness. The only lights were the red EXIT signs, so he took his flashlight out of the backpack and looked for the stairs to the mezzanine.

The theater smelled of ancient carpeting with too many candies and colas stuck in the woof. The air was musty. The wind slapped a loose shingle against the roof, and Harry listened to the groans from the building's plumbing. And another sound, too. His own heartbeat.

His footsteps on the rubber-matted stairs squealed in his ears as he followed the beam of the flashlight, a heavy three-foot Kel-Lite like the cops use to bust your skull. The door to the office was right where the map had shown, and it gave a little to the push, so Harry pried it with the small crowbar, which clawed the cheap veneer but didn't open the door. What the hell—he gave the door a solid smack with a shoulder and the wood shrieked.

Another smack, another shriek.

The flimsy door still stood between Harry and everlasting bliss, so he stepped back, drew his right knee toward his chest and unleashed a kick with his newly purchased lumberjack boots. The bottom hinge tore out of the soft plaster and it was just like in the movies, except Clint Eastwood doesn't fall on his ass.

The door was swinging on its top hinge, mortally wounded, and Harry scrambled to his feet. He used the Kel-Lite to search the office. First he emptied the desk drawers, messing things around, making it look like a dumb-shit burglar didn't know what was there. The flashlight picked up something—what was it—a photo. Violet, her buns shoved up in the air, arms squeezed together, eyes tiny red dots from the flash. He put the picture in a pocket of the army jacket.

Now where's the cabinet? There, in the corner under a ratty blanket, everything according to plan. He didn't have the combination to the cheap lock, but he had a crowbar. It took only a moment to pop the latch on the top drawer . . . sweet Jesus, let it be . . . seven come eleven . . . but *empty*! Oh shit no.

Second drawer, two tries, the crowbar slipping and scraping

off the paint, the flashlight beam skittering off mark as he pried with one hand and held the light with the other. Then the latch gave way and he tugged the drawer . . . c'mon, baby, oh shit, snake eyes . . . *empty* again.

One drawer left and he prayed because this was his last chance to get out from behind the counter, to fly first-class and play the stock market and order the menu items that said market price and walk into clubs and peel off a Ben Franklin for the doorman.

He opened the drawer and looked inside. Then he cursed. It was full, but not with neatly folded bonds printed with fine-colored inks, and Harry Marlin was plumb out of drawers and shit out of luck.

Garbage! Thousands of little slips of paper, all the same size as if shredded by one of those machines the bookies use to get rid of betting records.

Garbage! The old fool moves his bonds and keeps trash in his office, Harry thought angrily.

Alone in the dark office, no eagles in sight, his world crumbling, Harry Marlin did not shine the Kel-Lite onto the little slips of paper or try to read the print smaller than a box score in the paper. If he had, he would have been confused, what with words like "redemption" and "successor trustee" and "legal tender for payment of public and private debts." But he was looking only for eagles and there were none in the cage.

Harry Marlin opened the back door a crack and peered into the alley. No cars, no people, just blackness and the greenish glow of a mercury vapor light two buildings away. He eased silently outside and the door closed and locked behind him.

Two steps, no more.

He saw nothing but felt it. He ducked, tucking his head below his shoulders.

It slammed into the fire door with the crash of metal on metal, the sound so close it stung.

Harry stumbled and it came again, not as hard, not as much time for a backswing, but it caught him across the shoulder and sent him to the asphalt, where he felt the gravel dig into his palms, and he saw the shapes now in the greenish light. Two of them with one baseball bat and it swung again, chopping down at him, and he thought of Juan Marichal whacking away at Johnny Roseboro's head with a Louisville Slugger, but this bat was aluminum, and the kid swinging it was no major leaguer. One of the skinny punks from out front. Harry rolled on his side and the bat pinged when it hit the asphalt near his head.

It doesn't hurt much to get kicked in the stomach by a sneaker on the foot of a 130-pound greaseball. That's what Harry thought as the second kid started stomping him. The one with the bat bent over, scooped up the backpack and tossed it to his buddy, all in one motion. Good field, no hit, but goddamn it, the crowbar was in there and he could use it now. Then, as Harry rolled over, his hand touched the round shape of the Kel-Lite which had fallen from the pack and his fingers closed over it, and like the caveman with a piece of bone, he swung at his enemy, a good swing for a guy on his knees and it caught the leadoff batter square on the kneecap and there was a satisfying crack and a high-pitched scream.

The kid dropped the bat and hopped away on one foot. The other one, the kickless shit, kept the backpack, snatched the bat, and ran after him. Harry dusted himself off and inspected the damage—a tear in his camouflage pants, a searing pain in his left shoulder, and a most beautiful dent in the Kel-Lite.

Violet Belfrey listened to the phone ring a dozen times. No answer. Where the hell was he? Sitting in jail, spilling his guts?

No, the bird brain couldn't get arrested if he tried. Lost maybe? Or did he lock himself in the theater somehow?

Everything should be perfect. Sam Kazdoy was sleeping the sleep of the contented, and she had a twenty-four-carat alibi. At the precise time of the heist—if Harry didn't fuck it up—she was on her knees between the old man's legs. Christ, it took so long, she nearly got lockjaw.

The old man lived in a penthouse apartment in Bal Harbour, a hundred blocks north of South Beach. The windows looked straight over the Atlantic and the view at night was overwhelming blackness. No stars or moon tonight and from the balcony that jutted over the beach, the world was painted with tar. An ocean breeze sent the old man's brass chimes pinging into each other in a discordant cacophony.

Violet sat on the balcony so she could use the cordless phone with no chance of waking the old man. Not that he was about to stir. Probably sleep till, whadatheycallit, Hahnoocha, the Jew Christmas. She had dialed her apartment every ten minutes since two o'clock. Harry was supposed to be there, a flock of eagles in the bag. In another two hours, some pink would show over the Atlantic. Where the hell was he?

"Hullo."

"Harry! What happened?" She lowered her voice. "Didja get 'em?"

"Nothin' to get, Vi. He musta moved them to a safe-deposit box, just little slips of paper in the bottom drawer. All I got to show for the night is a shoulder that hurts like hell, had to beat the shit out of two greasers who—"

"Little what?" Violet asked.

"Huh?"

"In the bottom drawer . . ."

"Garbage!" he said, spitting it out. "A million little slips of paper."

"All the same size?"

"Yeah. So what?"

"With lots of little writin' on 'em?"

"Yeah."

"You brought 'em home, right?" Violet asked, her voice pleading, hoping, praying.

Silence.

She knew it. He would find a way to fuck it up and he did. "Harry!"

"No, Vi baby, I left them there. They looked like garbage," he said defensively.

"Them's the kew-pons, dickbrain!" Violet shouted through the phone, forgetting about the old man sleeping on the other side of the glass door. "Them's what you turn in to git the money. He musta clipped a bunch of them in advance." Violet heard a rush of air into the phone, as if Harry had taken a shot to the gut.

Silence again. Violet waited, thinking, staying calm, trying to use her new knowledge of high finance to assess the situation.

"I didn't know," Harry whined. "You told me to look for eagles, for packages that fold up like a road map."

Harry sounded as if he might cry. he had let the birds slip through his fingers. Now he was out of control.

"Calm down, Harry. Just drag your ass back there and get them kew-pons."

"Can't, Vi. The fire door's locked now. And I lost the crowbar. I can't get back in." Harry was in no mood to try again, to maybe run into the punks or six of their cousins.

"Goddamn it, Harry, you fucked it up, now you fix it. Once

the old man sees there's been a break-in, he'll move 'em quicker than shit through a goose. The key's in my jewelry box in the bedroom. Just walk the fuck in the front door like you owned the place."

It was easier the second time, just as Violet said it would be. No backpack this time; Harry carried a large plastic garbage bag that he stuffed with little slips of paper. Back at the apartment Harry built a mountain on the kitchen table. A dozen coupons floated to the floor. Let 'em go, walking-around money.

In his excitement Harry didn't notice what was missing from his jacket pocket, didn't even remember picking it up in the first place, so much had happened that night. But in the alley behind the theater, on the gravel-covered blacktop, amid flattened popcorn boxes and the unidentifiable flotsam of a city's byways, was the unsmiling, red-eyed, Polaroid face of Violet Belfrey, arms squeezing breasts together, bottom arched skyward.

The sun was on its way up, sizzling in the Atlantic. The clouds were silver turning pink. The wind had died as it clocked around to the south, and the brass chimes on Sam Kazdoy's balcony hung straight and still. Violet, sleepless and puffy-eyed, dialed her own number.

Harry let it ring six times. Let her think about it. Bitch came down too hard on me tonight. Been bustin' my chops. I'm the one had his dick on the chopping block. Twice. Coulda gotten killed by those friggin' greasers. Would have, except one swung a bat like a rusty gate and the other kicked with spaghetti legs.

Awright.

Enough.

Now I'm calling the shots. He picked up the phone but was silent.

"Harry. Harry. Answer me. You got 'em?"

"The eagles have landed," Harry Marlin said firmly, sounding very much like a man who had the world by the balls.

CHAPTER 7

Linebacker Drill

*Doctor Charles W. Riggs used a stubby thumb to push his lop-*sided glasses up the bridge of his nose, cleared his throat, scratched his bushy beard, and said, "Diethylstilbestrol."

The court reporter squeezed her eyes shut and tried to take it down phonetically on her Stenograph. Winston P. Hopkins III, two years off the Andover-Princeton-Yale express, studied the 173 questions he had prepared in longhand on his yellow pad. His first solo deposition.

"*Dethel still . . .*" Hopkins muttered.

Jake Lassiter sat at the end of the polished teak conference table. His job was to watch Winston Hopkins depose the plaintiff's expert witness and fill out a scorecard on his performance. Law firm bureaucracy.

The plaintiff's lawyer, Stuart Zeman, leaned back and dozed. Manicured and immaculately groomed, he wore a fifteen-hundred-dollar suit of beige silk. The wages of representing the widowed and crippled. His client, a beefy Air Force sergeant with a brush cut and tiny ears, tugged at the choking collar on his dress-blue shirt and loosened the regulation knot in his solid black tie. They were gathered in the thirty-second-floor deposition room at Harman & Fox, a hallowed, dark place where many thousands of hours have been billed at enormous rates.

The bearded pathologist paused and chewed on his cold pipe. His testimony, delivered in deliberate, measured cadences, resembled a lecture by a well-prepared professor to a class of nitwits. "Diethylstilbestrol is synthetic estrogen, commonly called DES. Thirty years ago, doctors prescribed the drug to pregnant women to prevent miscarriage. A generation later, the women's daughters began dying from cancer. Instead of protecting the female offspring, technology was killing them. That's what happened to Gladys Ferguson . . . the late Mrs. Gladys Ferguson." Doc Riggs nodded across the conference table in the direction of Sergeant Claude Ferguson, USAF, the widower and father of a baby boy.

"But how can you be sure of that?" Winston Hopkins whined. The young lawyer had removed his suit coat to reveal paisley suspenders against his white-on-white custom-made shirt. The left cuff was emblazoned with a monogram in blue script "WPH." Fighting the boredom, Lassiter scribbled imagined middle names across a legal pad. *Percival . . . Pilkington . . . Plimpton.* "Her cervical cancer could have been caused by a host of things, could it not?" Hopkins asked.

Dr. Riggs gave the young lawyer a kind, forgiving smile. "Given the history of Mrs. Ferguson's mother using DES, given

Mrs. Ferguson's age and the fact that she acquired cervical cancer following childbirth, statistically there can be little doubt. I have concluded to a reasonable degree of medical certainty that the DES was the *causa causans*, the initiating cause of the cancer. But for the DES, she would not have contracted cancer, and hence, she would not have died."

The sergeant's face was puffy. A single tear gathered, then rolled down a cheek. Seeming not to notice, Winston Hopkins stormed ahead. "But for the DES, Mrs. Ferguson might never have existed, correct?"

"How's that?" Doctor Riggs asked.

"Her mother might have had a miscarriage without the drug."

"No sir!" Riggs yanked the pipe from his mouth and gestured toward the young lawyer. "That's the irony here, the damned tragic irony. DES never worked, never prevented miscarriage. If a woman was going to carry to full term, she'd do it with or without the drug. Gladys Ferguson would have been born, fine and dandy, hale and healthy, without that damned DES. As a drug, it was totally useless except to poison one's female issue."

Jake Lassiter looked up from his doodling. If they had been in a courtroom, the spectators would have oohed and aahed, the reporters would have scribbled notes, and Marvin the Maven would have smacked his gums. It was one of those moments when a witness drives a stake through the heart of your case. Give Doc Charlie Riggs a second chance, and he'll give that stake another whack.

"One moment, please," Hopkins said, pretending to review his notes while trying to regroup without peeing on his Italian kid leather loafers. If the kid took on Doc Riggs again, the savvy old coroner would probably spank him and send him to bed without his dinner.

A lifetime of experience on the witness stand, thirty-two

years as medical examiner of Dade County, now retired and living in a fishing cabin on the edge of the Everglades, Doc Riggs was as sharp as ever. He had dueled with the city's best criminal defense lawyers, savvy street fighters who could eviscerate a weak or confused witness. But they never got to Charlie Riggs. He had never botched an autopsy. Never lost a tissue sample, never failed to weigh, measure, or test the right organs, fluids, and gristle. A small man with dark, unkempt hair and a full beard, Charlie Riggs looked at the world through eyes that twinkled with a mixture of boyish delight and lethal wisdom.

Jake Lassiter wondered if Winston Hopkins was smart enough to shut up. Lassiter looked at the deposition scorecard, Form B83–184 in the firm's parlance. The product of endless partners' meetings, the scorecard had three categories: *Preparation, Poise, and Thoroughness.*

"PPT," Managing Partner Marshall Tuttle formally announced at one law firm meeting, as if the term were inspired by genius. Lassiter figured *preparation* meant ripping off a checklist of questions from the computerized form files, *poise* required equal portions of arrogance and callousness, and *thoroughness* could be demonstrated by asking the same question three times or until the opposing lawyer began snoring, whichever came first. Lassiter cast the partnership's only dissenting vote, saying his grading system would use *Balls, Brains, and a touch of Humanity.*

"How do you measure balls?" the managing partner had sniffed.

"If you gotta ask, you ain't got 'em," Lassiter said, a remark he figured cost him ten grand in the pig pool, the year-end division of profits.

Winston P. Hopkins III plucked at his suspenders and flipped through his yellow pad. He had colorless eyes, a weak jaw, and hair that was thinning before its time. He shot a look at Lassiter, who gave him no signals, then back to Doc Riggs, who waited patiently. Across the table, Sergeant Ferguson stretched his thick neck and cracked his knuckles, one at a time, the sound of cartridges ejecting from a Beretta 9 mm.

"You're being paid for this performance today, aren't you, Dr. Riggs?" Hopkins asked, finally.

Stuart Zeman emerged from his postlunch nap, examined his diamond-encrusted Piaget, yawned, and swiveled toward the court reporter. "Objection to the form . . ."

"I'll rephrase the question," Hopkins said, with just the hint of a sneer. "You're being paid for your time, Doctor?"

"As you are," Riggs said, pleasantly.

Lassiter hoped the twit would shut up soon. He knew Hopkins was a weasel but didn't figure him stupid.

"And how much is the plaintiff paying for your testimony?"

"For my time, young man, Mr. Zeman offered to pay me two hundred fifty dollars an hour. Because of my feelings about DES and the gross irresponsibility of your client in marketing it, I agreed to accept only my expenses plus an Orvis graphite fly-casting rod."

"What . . . what . . . are you telling us you're doing this for practically nothing?"

"To a fly-fisherman, an Orvis rod is hardly that."

Hopkins's laugh was an annoying snort. "Dr. Riggs, really now, do you expect us to believe that you're studying medical records, reviewing the written authorities, testifying at deposition today and then at trial, and all for a fishing pole?"

Why not just walk onto I-95 in front of a semi, Lassiter thought.

"*Homo doctus in se semper divitias habet*," Charlie Riggs said, and the court reporter grimaced.

Hopkins swallowed. "Huh?"

"A learned man always has wealth within himself."

Another minute of paper shuffling, then Hopkins shot the French cuffs on his left sleeve, ostentatiously letting his eighteen-carat watchband catch the glow from the recessed lighting, and said, "Inasmuch as we still have another deposition to take, I have nothing further at this time, subject to the right to recall Dr. Riggs prior to trial."

Charlie Riggs bounded out of the conference room on short bowed legs, and Sergeant Ferguson moved into the hot seat.

Lassiter scooped up his scorecard and followed Riggs into the corridor. Once out of earshot of the conference room, he said, "I wish you were on our side of the table, Charlie."

"You're too late and you're on the wrong side, Jake. DES, for God's sake, one of the chemical catastrophes of the century. How can you even defend the manufacturer?"

"It's my job," Lassiter said, wearily.

"Some job."

"Funny, that's what Cindy said the other day."

Riggs grumbled his disapproval. "It isn't you, Jake. Your heart's not in it. A man has to find himself. Now, take me. What if I'd have gone into a private pathology practice, just looking at damn slides all day. Probably would've made more money than poking around in stiffs all these years, but would I have had the satisfaction, would I have nailed the woman who laced her husband's meat pie with paraquat? Or the sulfuric acid murderer? Nothing left but the teeth, but that was enough for a *corpus delicti*. Or the insulin overdose in the hospital with no injection puncture on the body?"

"I remember," Lassiter said. "You were the only one who thought to look at the intravenous tube."

"Hard to miss under the microscope, a hole made by a syringe. Then I checked the spinal fluid. Sugar count way too low. The attending nurse had a locker stashed full of insulin and a psychiatric history as long as your arm."

Jake Lassiter smiled. "You're the best canoe maker . . . sorry, coroner, this town has ever had. No one can speak for the dead like you."

Doc Riggs gave Lassiter an affectionate shoulder squeeze.

"I remember when you saved my ass in Dr. Salisbury's murder trial," Lassiter continued, "figuring out what ruptured Philip Corrigan's aorta."

"Kind of you to mention it."

"My adrenaline was pumping then, Charlie. Just like the old days in the PD's office."

Charlie Riggs took the cold pipe from his mouth and jabbed it toward Lassiter's chest. "You were alive then. Bring it back, Jake, that same fervor. Even when we were on opposite sides, I always respected you. You defended vigorously, hell, you were tough, but you never manufactured evidence or suborned perjury. You were also a great cross-examiner."

"A left-handed compliment, Charlie. Telling me my life's not worth a hot damn anymore."

"Someday you'll thank me for helping you out. Defending DES cases, for crying out loud! What's next, representing asbestos manufacturers?"

Charlie Riggs tamped some fresh tobacco into his pipe and struggled to light it. "I'm sorry to be so tough on you, Jake. It's only because we're friends. Now, better get back in there. That little prick—*doctus cum libro*, nothing but book learning—is liable to say anything."

That was it, Lassiter thought. Winston *Prick* Hopkins.

When Lassiter eased back into the Brazilian leather chair, he found Winston Hopkins trying to chisel away at the widower's damage claim.

"Prior to her death, weren't you and your wife contemplating divorce?" Hopkins asked in the smart-ass tone young lawyers mistake for toughness.

The sergeant's eyes shot to his own lawyer, then to Hopkins. "No, of course not. We have a baby."

"But you sought marriage counseling?"

"We sought counseling from our minister after Gladys became ill."

"For marital problems."

"No. She was depressed. We needed to—"

"To discuss a divorce."

The sergeant's closely shaved cheeks flushed just below his ears, and the muscles of his jaws tensed. "Hell no!"

Stuart Zeman, wide awake now, slapped the table and leaned toward the court reporter, who was bent over her silent machine. "Objection. I think we've heard just about enough on that subject, Mr. Hopkins. Please move on."

"Well, Mr. Zeman, your client here claims a ton of money for mental anguish at his wife's death, and if I can demonstrate that this marriage was washed up, that's a relevant line of inquiry . . ."

Lassiter figured he should tell the jerk there's a difference between being aggressive and being an asshole, but he didn't have time. The sergeant had a lot of quick for a big man. He flew across the conference table and grabbed the Ivy Leaguer by his noodle neck. There was that moment of disbelief when everything stops dead, Lassiter watching Hopkins's eyes bulge, the sergeant's hands—powerful, working-guy hands—squeezing, then the moment when Lassiter could have stepped in and didn't, silently hoping the sergeant would extract Hopkins's Adam's apple with his bare hands. Then, and it all took no more than five seconds, Lassiter moved, coming up behind them. They were wedged into a corner of the room, Hopkins bent backward, his buttocks hanging over a rubber plant, his head being smacked repeatedly—*thwack, thwack*—against the herringbone fabric of the deposition room wall.

Lassiter put one hand on the sergeant's meaty shoulder and

squeezed hard, just to let him know he was there. "Okay, fun's over. Let's everyone sit down."

The sergeant let go with his right hand, and Hopkins toppled into the rubber plant, a gurgling sound stuck in his throat. Lassiter relaxed and never saw it coming, a lightning *Yoko Hiji-ate*, the sergeant's elbow smashing into his ribs from a foot away. The pain shot through Lassiter's chest, and he gasped.

The sergeant turned to face Lassiter head-on. "You peckerhead lawyers, with all your fancy words and fancy cars and fancy watches . . ."

Lassiter was holding his side, sucking in shallow breaths. "Sergeant, I drive a twenty-six-year-old convertible with leaky canvas, my vocabulary is limited, and my watch is forty bucks, though it's good to a depth of a hundred feet. I'm just an ex-second-string linebacker trying to do my best in an imperfect world."

The sergeant laughed, but there was no pleasure behind it. "Linebackers! Standing up straight, roaming around like they was posing for the cheerleaders. Not like in the pits. Real men gouging, cursing, eating bucketfuls of mud, ending up with your face in some nose guard's crotch."

"Given a choice," Lassiter said, "I'll take the cheerleaders."

The sergeant growled and dropped into a three-point stance, his thick right hand sinking into the plush, burgundy carpet. "Strong side tackle. Blew out a knee my second year at Clemson. Coulda been all-ACC. Maybe it's time for a comeback. C'mon. Let's go."

"Nah, I always hated practice."

"C'mon. You know the one-on-one, nutcracker drill."

"Sure, but it's done with a ballcarrier behind the offensive lineman. The linebacker plays off the block and makes the tackle."

"Shitface there can carry the ball," the sergeant said, moving his head in the direction of the prone Winston Hopkins.

Hopkins whined something unintelligible.

Lassiter said, "Winnie, want to grab your dainty Italian briefcase and pretend it's a ball?"

Hopkins shook his head and mouthed the word "no."

"He's taking a medical redshirt," Lassiter said. "Probably has fumblitis anyway."

The sergeant was still in a three-point stance, head up, waiting for some imaginary quarterback to call the signals. "Then it's just you and me, Mister Linebacker."

Lassiter studied him, planning to keep talking until the sergeant returned to Planet Earth. But the man's eyes were glazed and his breath was coming hard. A little extra baggage around the waist, maybe 250, but a meaty chest and granite shoulders, arms straining against his government-issue shirt, epaulets stretched tight.

Lassiter moved close and stood facing him, legs spread, arms hanging slightly in front of his body, knees flexed. No one cheered.

"Let the record reflect we have taken a short recess," Lassiter said to the court reporter, who looked at her watch, and dutifully recorded the time of the break.

"Jake, I don't think you should . . ." Stuart Zeman was saying, fiddling with a Lady Justice cuff link of gold, black onyx, and diamonds.

"Fifty-two, gap tough rotate," Lassiter heard himself say, signaling a short yardage defense.

"Set, hut-hut-hut . . ." the sergeant intoned.

"Stand 'em up!" a voice thundered in Jake Lassiter's mind, Coach Shula shouting instructions from a distant sideline.

"Hut-hut," the sergeant barked, then fired out straight and low.

Lassiter squared up and delivered a shoulder-high blow with open palms. His wrists howled with pain, but he stood the sergeant straight for a moment. It wouldn't last. Using his weight advantage, the sergeant ducked low, put a shoulder into Lassiter's gut, and slammed him into the cushioned wall with a thud.

Lassiter grunted, shook it off, and said, "Okay, you win."

"Again," the sergeant said.

Zeman groaned. Hopkins whimpered. Lassiter shrugged as if to say why not. This time, the sergeant fired out and hooked an arm around Lassiter's elbow—offensive holding—and was about to drive him in the general direction of Key Largo when Lassiter slid to the right, caught the sergeant off-balance, and slung him sideways against the wall. The crash left two Frederic Remington originals dangling cockeyed.

Sergeant Ferguson picked himself up. "Enough bullshit. Hand-to-hand, commando style." He spread his legs wide, bent his knees, and put his hands on his hips. The *Kiba-dachi*, an attack position.

"Not one of those," Lassiter said, shaking his head. "What ever happened to good old American punchin' and wrasslin'?"

From somewhere on the floor Lassiter heard Hopkins squeaking. It sounded like *son of a bitch* the way Donald Duck might say it.

"Now, Claude," Stuart Zeman was saying. "This will complicate the settlement conference."

The sergeant gestured in the general direction of his lawyer's carotid artery. "Shove off, Zeman. You're one of them. You want forty percent of what I get. I'll give you forty percent of the big one's nose and forty percent of the little shit's tongue."

"C'mon, Sarge," Lassiter said. "Let's talk this over."

"Except talk isn't cheap for you jaybirds, is it?"

"Hey, I'm on your side. Let's just—"

Ferguson feinted with a *Kizami-zuki* jab, then followed up with a *Oi-zuki* lunge punch that caught Lassiter in the solar plexus. He doubled over, gasped, then came up hard, catching Ferguson's chin with the top of his head. The sergeant staggered back a step, then the two men tied up like a couple of professional wrestlers.

The sergeant took a step forward and Lassiter a step back; the sergeant moved his right foot to the side, and Lassiter moved the same direction with his left.

"Personally, I always preferred a waltz," Lassiter said.

"Linebacker, I'll hurt you!"

The sergeant worked a hand free and boxed Lassiter's ear, once, twice, a third time, until the lawyer heard the Bells of St. Mary's. Then Lassiter pulled back and stomped on the sergeant's instep and hooked his right fist into the man's gut, followed by a looping left to the jaw. The sergeant didn't fall all at once. He just rocked back two steps, his legs wobbling, then slumped to the floor. He wasn't hurt, not physically anyway. He had snapped, snapped from watching his wife die of a disease hatched in her mother's womb, snapped from having a piss-ant kid in a custom-made shirt ridicule him, a kid whose idea of a tough day is to lose at squash.

Emboldened, Hopkins finally stood up. Holding his throat, he managed to squeak, "We'll *prothecoot* for *atthalt.*"

"Shut up, jerkoff!" Lassiter ordered.

Zeman was still frozen to his chair. He cleared his throat with a lawyerly harrumph. "I suppose this dashes any prospect of settlement."

"Sethelment?" Hopkins squealed.

The silk-suited plaintiff's lawyer ignored him. "Jake, if you want to cancel tomorrow's mediation, it's all right with me. Let things simmer down. If you seek sanctions, I'll understand." Zeman cleared his throat again. "Noting that the hour is growing late, and with my Ferrari parked vulnerably on Biscayne Boulevard, perhaps we should adjourn."

Lassiter shook his head. "No sanctions, no postponement. Keep the mediation on. Give us your settlement demand. We'll make an offer."

"An offer?" Hopkins stammered. He was moving now, keeping his distance from the sergeant. "No! This guy will crack on the stand. He's a fruitcake."

Lassiter narrowed his eyes and took a step toward his associate. "Hopkins, you don't know people and you don't know the territory. You've got no heart, and you've got no soul. In short, Winnie, you are Grade A, prime-cut partnership material. You really fit in with the gazoonies who run this high-rise whorehouse."

Hopkins stiffened, his eyes fluttering, searching for a rejoinder. "Mr. Tuttle won't like the way you put that."

"Maybe not, but he'll sure love it when you smooch his lily-white ass."

Clever, very clever, Lassiter thought, figuring he just cost himself another ten grand.

CHAPTER

8

Bonds Away

Violet Belfrey walked arm in arm with Samuel Kazdoy, her heart doing little hippity-hops as they approached the front door of the theater. It was shortly after noon, and she'd been his shadow since dinner in his apartment the night before. Violet held her breath as the old man unlocked the front door and wobbled up the stairs to the mezzanine. She'd have to do some damn good acting, but Violet had been pretending for men all her life, and a look of shock can't be any harder than the cowlike moans she'd perfected at age fifteen. Get ready, she told herself, it's Academy Award time.

"What's this?" Samuel Kazdoy asked, looking at a trail of

coupons on the top steps, not yet comprehending. The office door hung open on one hinge, leaning against the inside wall like a drunk at a lamppost. Kazdoy switched on the lights and the scene unfolded. The file drawers were open, metal latches twisted out of shape. A handful of coupons remained, strewn across the floor like confetti. The clock, a memento from a 1948 convention of box manufacturers, lay shattered on the floor, its hands stuck at two-fourteen.

"Oy vay!" the old man wailed. His knees buckled and he caught himself by clutching the desk.

"Tarnation," Violet said, raising the back of one hand to her mouth the way she imagined Bette Davis would do it. "Who woulda done this?"

"Zoll vaksen tsibiliss in zein pupik!"

"Huh?"

"Whoever did it, onions should grow in his navel." A shudder went through Samuel Kazdoy's body and he sagged on his desk, folded over at the middle as if his stomach ached. For a moment Violet felt his pain. Samuel Kazdoy had been nice to her, and now he was hurting. That was bad. But from the look on his face, there must have been a fortune there, and that was good. She couldn't wait to see Harry and help with the counting, but first there was work to do.

"What are we gonna do, Mr. K.?" she asked.

Samuel Kazdoy's eyes were misty and his skin was gray. "Jacob . . . I need Jacob. Hand me the phone."

Bent over the sink in the partners' rest room, Jake Lassiter closed his eyes and tossed cold water onto his face. The sign on the door did not say MEN, just PARTNERS. No women had yet gained entry into what Marshall Tuttle called *The Brotherhood.* The uniformed rest room attendant, a Cuban man in his seventies who pretended not to understand English, stood at a discreet distance with the practiced look of one paid not to observe.

Lassiter was letting the adrenaline ebb, feeling pain for the sergeant who probably wouldn't have hurt him anyway. Claude Ferguson was striking out at the system, not at Jake Lassiter. It was a system that had buried him in endless delay, had tied him up in mind-numbing depositions and repetitive hearings, had pried into his personal life, picking at his wound, treating his loss with impersonal cruelty.

Men had killed his wife, men who went to work each day in suits and ties and met in quiet rooms where they calmly decided to place poisons on pharmacy shelves. These men, Lassiter knew, paid his salary, and the thought made him ill. Even now, in a hundred conference rooms, the bozos in research or marketing or risk management are figuring the cost-benefit analysis of selling death with a jingle and a rhyme, and if a few million-dollar settlements threaten to dent the quarterly report, not to worry, the excess liability coverage will pick up the tab. Earnings up, bonuses all around. The Glory of the Bottom Line.

But are you any better than they are, he asked, another splash of water hitting the face. What are you anyway, besides a moderately skilled practitioner of the fast shuffle and the soft shoe? Liability, now you see it, now you don't. Comparative negligence, assumption of the risk, or that all-time favorite, statute of limitations. Sure, you caught us, but you caught us too late! His job was to excuse, to deny, and to obfuscate. There you are, Jake Lassiter thought. Former second-string linebacker, current All-Pro obfuscator ready to roll up the score with a verdict here, a summary judgment there.

Jake Lassiter leaned on the marble-topped sink with its gold-plated faucets and stared into the mirror. Not a healthy look. Dead eyes. A sour expression. Charlie Riggs was right.

Without looking at him, the old attendant handed Lassiter a terry cloth towel. "*Gracias, Pablo,*" Lassiter said.

"*De nada, Doctor.*"

Once, at a partners' meeting, Lassiter had suggested that partners and associates share the same rest room. "An egalitarian gesture. Lawyers that pee together plead together."

Marshall Tuttle had tabled the motion, then referred it to the Committee on Facilities, but not before saying, "The officers ought not be displaying their wares to the enlisted men. Loss of stature, you know."

"Maybe we need officers with bigger stature," Jake Lassiter had suggested helpfully.

When Lassiter returned to his office, Cindy was missing from her desk, probably riding a chopper with Tubby Tubberville in the Keys. She had taped a pink telephone memo to the top of Lassiter's leather chair, a place reserved for important messages such as emergency hearings and small-craft advisories:

Mr. K.; Mr. K.;
Bonds away,
Gone with the wind.

"What the hell?" he said to himself, trying to decipher Cindy's version of Japanese poetry. Bonds, Lassiter thought. He had advised the old man to keep his negotiable paper in a safe-deposit box and to do his monthly clipping in a bank. Probably didn't listen. Bonds away?

"Oh shit," he said aloud. Then he headed to the parking garage at the pace the coaches use for the twelve-minute run.

A City of Miami Beach police car was double-parked in front of the South Side Theater, its front wheels over the curb and its tail slanted into Lincoln Road, a cop in a hurry. A van for the forensic team, the crime scene investigators, was parked neatly next to a planter on the pedestrian mall. Lassiter pulled his old convertible into the alley and jammed the rusty front bumper against the wall by the fire door.

The crime scene technicians were just leaving, their photos taken and surroundings dusted for prints. Lassiter climbed the stairs two at a time.

In a corner of the office, Sam Kazdoy was slumped in an old sofa. He looked up as Lassiter stepped through the broken door, but the cherubic smile was missing. "Jacob, there you are. I got *tsuris*, real trouble here."

"Hello, Sam. Officer . . ."

The cop's name tag said P. Carraway and he had three stripes on his sleeve. Early fifties, maybe older, big with a potbelly, a red face, and a veined nose that was a road map to every after-hours joint in Sunny Isles. A look that said he burned out so long ago he probably couldn't remember when he liked his job or did it well. The cop didn't say hello or offer his beefy hand. His partner, J. Torano on the name tag, looked bored. Late twenties, short but muscular, a bodybuilder maybe, sloping shoulders and huge biceps straining against a tapered, short-sleeve shirt.

Sergeant Carraway spoke first. "You the lawyer we been waiting for?"

"Guilty."

"Your client here claims somebody stole one to two million in, what'd he say, Georgy boy, bonds?" A nasty, hard-edged voice, the cop watching the lawyer for a reaction. Lassiter kept quiet, still sizing up the players. The younger cop wasn't paying attention to anybody. Carraway asked again, louder, "Georgy boy, what'd he call 'em?"

"Called 'em coupons, and please call me Jorge, like with an *H* where the *J* is," Torano said.

"Coupons. Thank you, Whore-hay," Carraway said, dragging out his partner's name.

Samuel Kazdoy looked up and said in a whisper, "Bond coupons." Then he sank back into the sofa. For the first time that Lassiter could remember, Kazdoy looked every bit his eighty-six years.

"Bond coupons, yesiree!" Sergeant Carraway hooted. The cop wanted to spar with him, Lassiter thought. Shit, might as well lead with your chin.

"What do you mean, *claims* they were stolen?" Lassiter asked.

The red face smirked. "What I mean, Counselor, is we got no signs of forced entry, this mess on the floor is as phony as a fifty-dollar roofing job, and who the hell keeps that kinda dough in a dump like this? What I'm saying in case you're a bit slow on the uptake is that maybe there wasn't a burglary here at all."

Okay, if that's his best shot, no blood on the canvas. Just open with a jab now, get the feel of it before getting into any clinches. "I don't believe you, Carraway. You're sent to investigate a B and E that doesn't solve itself in half an hour, so you accuse the victim. No break-in, huh? Sam, was there a show last night?"

"Eisenstein festival," the old man said softly from the couch. "A twin bill—*Ten Days That Shook the World* and *Alexander Nevsky*—a beautiful show, three hundred people."

"Yeah, yeah," Carraway said. "He told us that, but from what I hear about his customers, most couldn't get up the stairs, much less bust down a door."

Lassiter moved to the middle of the room. "Sergeant, you know what pisses me off? Salesclerks who are rude, TV repairmen who show up three hours late, and policemen too lazy for anything except cadging free drinks and copping cheap feels at topless bars."

"And you know what pisses me off?" Carraway said, his watery eyes squinting. "Lawyers. All of you, the smart-aleck young ones in the PD's office and you downtown types with your bayfront views." He turned to Torano, who was silently doing some slow-motion martial arts exercises by the door. "Yo, Whore-hay, what does a lawyer use for a contraceptive?"

"*No sé*, man."

"His personality."

Carraway laughed at his own joke. His partner kept wheeling around, ready to slash at an invisible opponent, and Kazdoy stayed on the sofa, apparently oblivious to the byplay. "Whore-hay, you hear the one about the lawyer who stepped in a pile of horseshit?"

"No, dígame."

"He looked down and thought he was melting."

Carraway was laughing so hard his face turned purple. With any luck, Lassiter thought, he'd have a coronary, and a real cop could be assigned to the case. "If you're done, Sergeant, maybe we can get down to work. Did you consider the possibility that somebody hides in the rest room, then after everyone's gone and the place locked up, breaks into the office, takes the coupons, and walks out the fire door downstairs and into the alley?"

"Yeah, I considered it."

"And?"

"And I don't have to tell you nothing, smart guy."

"Carraway, my first impression is that you couldn't find your dick with both hands, but maybe I'm wrong. Tell me, am I wrong?"

Carraway studied him impassively, tucked his thumbs in his belt, and said, "All right, the show was over at what, eleven o'clock. The break-in didn't occur until after two o'clock, according to the broken clock. If someone's in the rest room, they don't wait that long. They'd be going bananas by then, anyway. If you'd ever done surveillance, you'd know how slow ten minutes goes by, much less three hours. Plus, like I said before, this crowd ain't exactly a bunch of cat burglars."

Lassiter thought about it a moment, then turned to his client. "Any new faces last night, Sam?"

"More strangers than fleas on a dog." It was Violet, coming through the broken door, filing her fingernails, chewing gum, and walking, all at the same time. "I jes hadda get outta here, it was givin' me the heebie-jeebies, even with such handsome officers to keep me company."

Jorge Torano grinned and flexed his broad shoulders, then resumed his *t'ai chi ch'uan*, or *wing chun do*, or whatever the hell it was. Sergeant Carraway tried to peek down Violet's low-cut blouse. She let him have a quick look, then sashayed to the couch, lowered herself ceremoniously next to the old man, blew on her fingernails, and said, "Last night, had a class here from the university, moviemaking or somethin'. Bunch a guys with earrings and hair down to their ass. Wouldn't of trusted a one of them. Mr. K. and I left here about eleven and I fixed a late supper at his place and so on and so forth as I told these two gentlemen."

And so on and so forth. The phrase rattled around in Lassiter's mind.

"We're looking into the UM class, cinema arts," the sergeant said. "But what the hell were all those bond things doing here?"

Kazdoy was paying attention now. "If I kept them all in a safe-deposit box, I'd have to go there every month to clip coupons. So I clipped enough for the next two years, I don't know, maybe one-point-five million, maybe a little more. The rest are still attached to the bonds in my box at the bank."

Lassiter said, "As for the mess, whoever did it either was looking for other valuables or wanted us to think so."

"Whoever did it should have an onion grow out his belly button," Violet piped up. "That's what Mr. K. said."

"Make him easier to ID," Lassiter said.

"Cute," Sergeant Carraway said without smiling. "But I ain't seen nothing yet to convince me anybody from outside took whatever was in those drawers. Far as I'm concerned, the three of you are as much suspects as some joint-smoking hippies at UM."

The old man whimpered. The sergeant looked right at Lassiter, testing him, seeing if he could get out of a clinch. The cop's hands were on his hips now, his belly hanging over his pants, straining the buttons on his regulation blue shirt. Lassiter was wearing his uniform, a charcoal-gray suit, white shirt, and burgundy tie, and it was time to play lawyer games with the bigmouth cop. A simple strategy, act dumb, sucker the cop into dropping his hands, then unload with a hook to the jaw.

"Interesting theory, Sarge. You got a motive for this allegedly fake burglary?"

"Sure, tax evasion. Ever heard of it, Counselor? Your client here reports an imaginary theft. He still has the bond things plus he gets to take a whatchacallit from the IRS."

Lassiter turned to face the cop straight on. He lowered his voice, a trick used by lawyers and leg breakers alike. The most effective threats are delivered sotto voce. "They call it a casualty or theft loss, and I call your statement slander. You've just published the defamatory statement to a third person, Miss Belfrey here, which creates the cause of action and obviates any privilege you might have had to say it directly to Mr. Kazdoy and his counsel. Now, I'm going to let that one slide, but I'll serve you with process on your favorite barstool the day you open your fat trap to the papers."

Lassiter paused and let the silence fill the room. Then he picked up the volume just a bit. "And, as long as we're talking litigation, let's not forget a civil rights action, depriving Mr. Samuel Kazdoy, one of the city's most respected philanthropists, of his rights under color of law. Plus intentional infliction of mental distress and a few other things my bright law clerks come up with, and even if I don't win the suit, there'll be a helluva fuss, Internal Review investigation, who knows, a lot of trouble for a cop maybe a year or two from pension."

Officer Jorge Torano stopped his Asian isometrics and let out a whistle that sounded like "oh boy." The old man sat up straight, something flickering in his eyes. Violet seemed flushed, expectant and alert at the possible clash of stags in the forest. For a moment Sergeant Phil Carraway didn't move, didn't say a thing. Then he smiled a sloppy grin and put his hands up, palms forward.

"Okay okay," Carraway sang out. "Just doing my job, part of the book, making sure it's not an inside job, don't get your nose outta joint, you never know, sometimes you come on like that and bam! You get a confession. But Jesus, we got no leads here."

Lassiter smiled and walked to a neutral corner. The cop was throwing in the towel. Now that the macho bullshit was over, how to get him to solve the crime and get back the coupons?

"You said no signs of forced entry," Lassiter said. "Who has keys to the front door?"

"Only Mr. K. and little ole me," Violet said, studying a cuticle on her right pinkie.

"And Miss Belfrey has an alibi," Sergeant Carraway said with a wink and a leer. Now the cop was Lassiter's buddy, sharing confidences with him. It took a second but Lassiter figured out the alibi when Violet put an arm around the old man, then gently stroked his neck. It wasn't a sexual gesture, just a comforting one, but the body language was unmistakable. She may not have gotten into the old man's cabinet but she's in his pants, Lassiter thought.

"Mr. Kazdoy said you'd be able to tell us something about these coupons, what a thief would do with them, that sort of thing," Sergeant Carraway continued, his tone finally respectful and professional. Torano groaned and asked if he could leave, had to work out, and the fat sergeant nodded okay.

"Where do you want me to start?" Lassiter asked.

The sergeant pulled out a vinyl-covered notebook. "Well, what the fuck are these things anyhow?" That was as good a place as any, so Jake Lassiter told him to think of Mr. Kazdoy as a lender who gives five thousand dollars to, say, the city of Jacksonville to help build a sewage plant and the city agrees to repay him over twenty years at 8 percent interest, four hundred dollars a year, payable two hundred bucks a pop, every December 1 and June 1, then at the end of twenty years, he gets back the five grand. In the meantime, he pays no taxes on the interest payments.

"I built a box factory in Jacksonville once," Kazdoy said to no one in particular. "Cost me nine million in 1958, would be worth forty million today, but I don't own it."

Lassiter looked toward his client, hoping the old man wasn't losing his marbles along with the bonds. Then he turned back to the sergeant and explained that to get your two hundred bucks, you have to turn in a coupon at a bank. "A bond payable over twenty years will have forty coupons. What the burglars took would have been . . . what, Sam . . . six or seven thousand coupons?"

"Never liked Jacksonville," Kazdoy said. "More anti-Semites than Warsaw." The old man wasn't going to be much help.

Lassiter said, "A securities newsletter will alert all the local banks. But the coupons will more likely turn up out of the country, maybe in the islands at some doper bank good at money laundering. Problem is, these are negotiable securities, anybody can cash them."

Violet Belfrey was trying hard not to show that she was paying attention, but if she kept filing her nails, she'd soon draw blood.

"If real pros masterminded this," Lassiter concluded, "they already have a buyer, maybe in the Bahamas or Switzerland, or someone in organized crime, so they wholesale them for fifty cents on the dollar, let somebody else worry about dropping them at banks all over the country or all over the world."

Now Samuel Kazdoy was coming alive. "Jacob, you get them back for me, *boychik*, one half is yours."

The old man pulled himself off the sofa, struggled for a moment to gain his balance, and then stepped between Lassiter and the sergeant. He turned around, asserting control as he must have done in conference rooms for more than half a century. The events of the day still hung on his shoulders, but a brightness returned to his eyes.

"One half, Jacob. You got a good *kop* on your shoulders, I always said that. You can do it. Just like you got those *momzers* in Hollywood off my back. Just like you saved my driver's license when the sons of bitches in Tallahassee said I was too old. You're my friend, Jacob. You break bread with me and drink borscht with me, now find the bonds for me. If you can keep your mind off the *shiksas* for a while, you'll figure it out."

Carraway snapped his notebook shut. "Should have figured. We do the work, the lawyer gets the money."

Kazdoy turned his attention to the sergeant. "Mis-ter Policeman, who do you think you are, some Cossack, you come in here and threaten me like there's gonna be a pogrom. I been a friend of the mayor since he was a little *pisher*. You don't want to help, he's gonna hear about it."

Sergeant Carraway swallowed hard and swung his bulk toward the broken door. "Fine with me. I gotta open a case number, but nothing says I gotta be a hero. Lassiter, call me when you got something to say."

The sergeant left without promising to call for lunch. Lassiter looked around the office for another few minutes, then said his good-byes and headed down the stairs and out the fire door, opening it slowly, studying the latch. Nothing to see. He ran his hand over the mechanism, the little bolt that locks from the outside but slides open when the bar is pressed from inside.

Hullo! A tiny piece of silver duct tape, like you use to patch a torn sail, and the rest of the latch faintly sticky, like it was covered with the same tape but was torn off in a hurry. Okay, a guy doesn't wait in a rest room all night, somebody tapes a door open for him. Just like Watergate—why not—most of those characters live in Miami anyway.

He stepped into the alley. No one had stolen his car, a canary yellow 1968 Olds 442, or sliced the canvas top in search of a tape player to exchange for a day's ration of crack. Not that a slash and grabber would have found anything to sell. The car had no tape player, no CD, no cellular phone, and the radio was the original equipment: AM only.

The late-afternoon ocean breeze whipped discarded popcorn boxes against the building's foundation and rattled the top of an aluminum garbage can. The temperature was dropping, and it was growing dark. Sliding into the bucket seat of the old beauty, he turned on the headlights. Then he got out, knelt into a catcher's position and looked around. Crushed soda cans, candy wrappers, old newspapers. Street crud, nothing more. A mercury vapor light clicked on two buildings away, bathing the alley in a sickly green light. Then, something glared back from the pavement.

What the hell! He picked it up carefully, touching only the

sides. A photograph, Violet Belfrey's sharp face and round breasts. The photo was clean, everything else in the alley covered with grime. Couldn't have been there long. If Carraway could see over his belly, maybe he would have found it.

Now what does Violet have to do with this? She was in the theater last night and could have taped the door. Lassiter leaned against his old convertible and thought about it. He felt a chill. It didn't make any sense. Violet didn't have to tape the door. She could have given anyone a key. Unless someone didn't want to be seen walking through the front door after midnight. But the picture? Who would be so stupid to leave a picture of one of the culprits at the crime scene, unless it was supposed to be found. Someone could be framing her, but who and why? He would give the picture to Carraway as a peace offering. If they didn't drool over it first, the lab boys could dust it for latents.

Across the alley, an old woman wearing a tattered sweater used a cane to poke around in a dumpster behind a Burger King. Lassiter walked toward her, reached in his wallet for a ten-dollar bill and offered it, but she swatted at him with the cane. He got back into the car, turned the ignition, and listened to 455 cubic inches of rebuilt V-8 growl to life. He was low on gas—at eight miles a gallon, Arab sheikhs should send thank-you cards—and wondered if any stations in South Beach still carried high-test with lead. He flicked on the radio. The talk show host was bellowing at a caller, simultaneously questioning his patriotism, intelligence, and sexual preference. He turned off the radio and ran through all the facts, finishing with one that hit him square in the face. On December 1—less than two weeks—the first coupons would become due. He would have to work fast, and it could all be for nothing. Even now the coupons could be in New York or La Paz or Grand Cayman.

But the coupons were not nearly so far away. They were in a cardboard box that once held Coca-Cola syrup in the storeroom of the Lincoln Road Grill three blocks west of the theater. And there, too, was Harry Marlin, a guy whose prayers would be answered if he could only figure out one thing—how to turn paper into gold.

CHAPTER 9

The Case of the Kosher Kielbasa

The phone message from Great Southern Bank said "Urgent," but that did not necessarily imply a threat to the ozone layer, or even a mildly interesting problem. Thaddeus G. Whitney, the bank's general counsel, might have called because a computer glitch foreclosed the wrong mortgage. Or another customer could have dropped a safe-deposit box on a big toe, or a trusted bookkeeper might have run off to Acapulco with the Christmas Club fund.

Jake Lassiter put the phone message to one side and returned his other calls. He told Bernard/Bernice he would consider suing his/her insurance company for declining payment for a sex change operation on the grounds it was cosmetic surgery. He tried to calm down the mother whose infant was put on the X-ray machine's conveyor belt at the airport by security guards because the baby was considered carry-on luggage. He listened patiently to the Hialeah man who insisted the First Amendment prevented the zoning board from removing *La Virgen de la Caridad* from his front yard, despite the fact the statue was forty feet high, contained blinking lights, and played music that kept the neighbors awake.

Then Jake Lassiter returned Thad Whitney's phone call.

"Shit's hit the fan," Whitney said, each word a little puff, as if the breath were being squeezed out of him. The bank lawyer had a habit of speaking in scatalogical clichés. "You know Humberto Hernandez-Zaldivar, one of your basic Cube developers, gets rich on borrowed money?"

"Take it easy, Thad. I've known Berto since law school. We tried cases together in the PD's office, and I consider him a friend."

"Well, start considering him an asshole. I'll make this brief, so listen up. A few years ago, when all the South Americans were bringing their cash into town, your buddy Berto buys thirty-eight oceanfront condos thanks to an overly generous loan officer I'll tell you about later. When currency controls shut off the pesos and bolivars, the condo market dried up, and he stopped making payments. Bottom line, with acceleration, unpaid interest, penalties and fees, your buddy's about four-point-six million in the hole. Pretty big bucks for a kid floated up from Havana on an inner tube."

"A raft made of tires," Lassiter corrected him. "He was twelve. His mother died in the Straits."

"My condolences," Whitney said coldly, "but frankly, I'm more concerned with our P and L statement for the current fiscal. We may have to call in the regulators, and you know how that frosts my buns."

Lassiter pictured the bank lawyer at the other end of the line. A bland, forgettable face topped by pale wispy hair that threatened to blow away in the first easterly. Slinging the corporate jargon, feet propped on a marble desk, fouling the air with smoke rings and ill humor.

"Just call the loans and sue to foreclose," Lassiter suggested, contemplating the ethics of punching out a client. "The condos give you the security."

"They would, except your old classmate flipped Conrad Ticklin, one of our loan officers. Turned him over for a lousy twenty-five in cash plus an empty condo to play hide-the-weenie with a receptionist from installment loans. Ticklin approves about a hundred and twenty percent financing, and the Cube takes home close to half a mil, over and above the mortgages."

"Bad news, Thad, but the apartments still secure most of the debt."

"You'd think so," Whitney said, "except the bastard slipped in another lien before ours. Closed four million in loans with Vista Bank the day before he closed with us. Theirs are all recorded first. We're the bare-assed second mortgagee on thirty-eight empty, unsold condos. Get it? We're sucking hind tit to the tune of four-point-six-million clams."

Lassiter smiled, taking surreptitious pleasure at the bank's predicament. "That's really a shame, Thad."

"A shame? It's a fucking crime. C'mon, Lassiter. Let's see some of that toughness, pro football star, rah, rah, rah and all that shit."

"Second string, Thad. Story of my life. A step too slow."

"You're telling me. Can you sue the wetback by Thursday?"

Jake Lassiter would have liked to put Thad Whitney in the middle of the nutcracker drill, a pair of linemen tattooing his flabby ass with their cleats.

"You there, Jake? How long will it take to draft a complaint, then set up a meeting with the U.S. Attorney so we can prosecute for fraud?"

"I could sue Berto tomorrow. But I've got a better idea. Let me take him to dinner tonight."

"What the hell for? You hard up for black beans and rice?"

Jake Lassiter paused and held the phone away from his face, putting distance between Thad Whitney and himself. It wasn't far enough. He thought about all the things he'd rather be doing than dealing with the repulsive bank lawyer who was good for forty grand a month in billings. He thought about telling Whitney to take the bad loans and shove them where the sun don't shine. He thought about hanging up and heading for the beach. And he thought, too, how hard it would be to start a *third* career. After a moment, he simply said, "If we sue, we've got to join Vista Bank as a defendant. They'll counterclaim and wipe you out with their first mortgage. This has to be finessed. Let me talk to Berto, and I might be able to help you both out." Lassiter looked at his watch. "Yikes! I gotta get to court."

"So, is this your biggest case, or what?" Sam Kazdoy asked in a whisper that could be heard throughout the courtroom.

Jake Lassiter leaned close to him at the defense table. "I had another false advertising case even bigger, defending Busty Storm when she was appearing at the Organ Grinder. The state claimed there was no way her bosom measured one hundred and twenty-seven. But I won."

"How?" Kazdoy asked.

"Centimeters, Sam. Centimeters."

Their discussion was halted by a stern look from the judge, and Lassiter returned his semi-attention to the witness stand where Mrs. Sadie Pivnick was swearing to tell the truth, the whole truth, and nothing but the truth, just like Abe, may his soul rest in peace, always told her.

The prosecutor, Chareen Bailey, a statuesque African-American woman a year out of law school, went through the preliminaries, eliciting name, address, and background, getting warmed up. Mrs. Pivnick sat there stiffly, eyeing the microphone suspiciously, her dyed hair the color of a copper penny. After establishing that her witness was a regular patron of the Kazdoy All-Nite Deli, Chareen Bailey got down to business.

"Did there come a time, ma'am, when you had a conversation with Mr. Kazdoy about the food in his deli?"

"We talked, sure."

"And when you talked, did Mr. Kazdoy characterize the food he served?"

"Objection!" Lassiter sang out. He stood, more to stretch his legs than to make a legal point. "No predicate laid as to time or place."

Judge Morgan Lewis craned his neck to see over the bench and glanced at his watch. "Overruled. Let's just move it along, Ms. Bailey."

"Thank you, Your Honor," the prosecutor said, bowing slightly. They're still polite when they're green. She turned to the witness. "You may answer the question, Mrs. Pivnick."

"Vad question? Who can remember a question when the three of you keep kibitzing?"

The prosecutor gave her a strained smile. "We'll try it again. Did there come a time when you had a conversation with Mr. Kazdoy in which he characterized the food served in his delicatessen vis à vis the Jewish dietary laws?"

"Vad she say about Visa?" Sadie Pivnick asked, turning to the judge. "My late Abe always insisted I pay cash."

The judge looked down from his perch and smiled tolerantly. "The food, Mrs. Pivnick. Did you ever discuss the food?"

"Oy, the food! The stuffed derma gave me the heartburn. I wouldn't feed it to a dog."

At the defense table, Sam Kazdoy tugged at Lassiter's sleeve. "She's one to talk, that old *kvetcherkeh.* She put so much chicken fat in her chopped liver, Abe keeled over when he was still a *boychik.*"

"That's a shame," Lassiter whispered.

"He wasn't a day over eighty," Kazdoy said, shaking his head sadly.

Chareen Bailey cleared her throat and moved a step closer to the witness stand. "Mrs. Pivnick, what did Mr. Kazdoy say to you as to whether his food was kosher?"

"Ay, *that's* what you want to know."

"Yes, ma'am."

"So why beat around the bush?"

"Mrs. Pivnick, in the courtroom, the lawyer asks the questions, and the witness answers," Chareen Bailey said. "Do you understand?"

"What's not to understand?"

Judge Morgan Lewis sighed and rolled his eyes. "Mrs. Pivnick, just tell us what Mr. Kazdoy said to you."

"All right, already. I asked him about the food, and he said, 'Strictly kosher.' Twice he said it. 'Strictly kosher.' "

Mrs. Pivnick smiled triumphantly at having done her civic duty. Ms. Bailey sat down, and the judge politely asked whether Mr. Lassiter wished to inquire.

Lassiter stood and smiled at the witness, then turned his back. "How is your hearing, Mrs. Pivnick?"

"Vad you say?"

Lassiter wheeled around toward the bench. "No further questions, Your Honor."

As soon as Lassiter was in his chair, Sam Kazdoy poked him in the ribs. "That's it? Perry Mason wouldn't sit down so quick unless it was time for a commercial."

"Trust me, Sam."

"But I never said such a thing. She's *meshugge*."

"She's a sympathetic witness, and I don't want to embarrass her. We'll win or lose on your testimony."

The old man looked at him skeptically.

"Sam, please trust me. You're like family to me, and I'd do anything for you."

"You mean that?" Sam Kazdoy said, his eyes going misty.

"Yeah, I do. And I haven't said anything like that since I told Coach Shula I'd do whatever was best for the team."

"He must have liked that."

"Sure did," Lassiter said. "He told me to retire."

Isidor Pickelner scratched at his beard and waited for the next question.

"What is your official capacity, Mr. Pickelner?" Chareen Bailey asked.

"Officially, I'm the Kosher Food Inspector for the city of Miami Beach. Unofficially, I'm Izzy."

Chareen Bailey leveled her gaze at the witness to tell him this was serious business. "Are you a rabbi?"

"No, ma'am. I'm a *shochet*. I slaughter animals according to the Jewish dietary laws as laid down in Leviticus and Deuteronomy. And I investigate all establishments in Miami Beach that hold themselves out to be kosher."

"What do your duties entail?"

"Ascertaining the ingredients and the method of preparation of foods served in restaurants and delicatessens. Only those four-footed animals that chew their cud and have cloven hooves are kosher. So, a cow is kosher, a pig is not. Creatures that crawl such as lizards or snakes are forbidden. Fish must have both scales and fins, so shellfish is taboo."

"No stone crabs?" Judge Lewis mused.

"Afraid not, Your Honor," Pickelner replied.

"Did you have an occasion to investigate the food served at the Kazdoy All-Nite Deli?" Ms. Bailey asked.

Did he ever. Pickelner claimed he found on about the sausages made of pork!

"*Trayf*, Your Honor. Unclean! Kielbasa sausage posing as kosher knockwurst. An abomination under the religious laws and false advertising under state laws."

Ms. Bailey allowed as how she had no further questions, and the judge suggested it was a good time for lunch.

The courthouse wits could not restrain themselves as they stopped at Lassiter and Kazdoy's table at the Quarterdeck Lounge.

"Hey, Jake, that Reuben's not kosher," announced Marvin the Maven. "No mixing meat and cheese."

"How 'bout the beer?" Lassiter asked.

"No problem."

A few ex-clients wandered over. Luis "Blinky" Baroso, a con man and lobster pot poacher stopped by to say hello. He was being arraigned in federal court for stealing rare ostrich eggs. Stuart Bornstein was eating grilled grouper at the next table. He once tried to cash in on the fast-food craze but went bankrupt when no one would buy into his franchise for Escargot-to-Go. Mike DuBelko was perched on a barstool and saluted Jake with his old-fashioned glass. He owned a service station and was still on probation for pilfering freon from his customers' cars while he changed their oil. At twenty bucks a pound, the freon was more profitable than tune-ups.

Sam Kazdoy frowned when Lassiter ordered a second sixteen-ounce Grolsch. "What now, I got a *shikker* for a lawyer?"

"Don't worry, Sam. I can hold it. Let's talk about the case."

"Why get *fartootst*? What does God care what we eat? What matters is how we treat each other. Which reminds me, have you found the *gonifs* who robbed me blind?"

"Not yet, Sam. With your bonds, the bank, and the windsurfing race, I'm spinning in circles right now. That's why I needed your kosher kielbasa case like I needed a . . ."

"A second hole in your bagel," Kazdoy said.

Judge Lewis was waiting impatiently in the courtroom, but Jake Lassiter was on the pay phone in the corridor.

"Es negocio o es placer?" Berto asked him. "Business or pleasure, Jake?"

"Business. I'm representing Great Southern Bank."

Silence. Then a hearty laugh. "Jake, I'm glad it's you, *mi amigo.* I thought it would be one of those bloodless WASPs downtown, those pasty faces, *sin alma ni corazón.*"

Funny, that's what I said about Winston P. Hopkins III, only in English, Lassiter thought. He felt a kinship with Humberto Hernandez-Zaldivar. "Berto, they've sucked the blood out of me, too. Working for bankers turns you into one of them."

"No, *nunca.* I know you better than you do. We will talk. We will drink wine and eat, and you will tell me what to do, just as you did in law school."

"But, Berto, I'm representing the bank *against* you. I'm supposed to collect money from you."

"Don't worry. We'll work it out."

The phone clicked dead, and Lassiter rushed into the courtroom, where the judge motioned the lawyers to the bench with an imperious wave of his hand. Then he instructed them to move the case along so he could make the daily double at the dog track, and finally he sniffed the air. "Mr. Lassiter, do I detect the scent of alcohol on your breath?"

Lassiter winked a yes. "If Your Honor's sense of justice is as keen as his sense of smell, I have no fear of the outcome of the case."

The judge harrumphed and sent the lawyers back to their

tables. Lassiter called Sam Kazdoy to testify. He ran through Kazdoy's past, his philanthropy, his love of Russian films, and how he brought corned beef and social life to the retirees of South Beach.

"Now, Mr. Kazdoy, you heard Mrs. Pivnick testify this morning?"

"Of course, I heard. You think I'm deaf like her?"

"What do you mean by that?"

"The old *bubbe* bought a hearing aid, twenty-nine dollars mail order."

"Objection!" Chareen Bailey was on her feet. "Outside scope of the witness's knowledge."

"What's not to know?" Kazdoy asked. "You could hear Radio Havana on the *farshtinkener* thing all the way across the street."

"Overruled," the judge said.

"Did there come a time when you discussed your deli's food with Mrs. Pivnick?" Lassiter asked.

"She asked if our chicken was stuffed with matzo meal and prunes, and I said, 'No, with kasha.' "

"Kasha?" the judge asked.

"Buckwheat," Kazdoy explained. "Cook it with some chicken soup and egg, you got yourself a nice stuffing."

Lassiter moved a step closer. "So you simply described your stuffing?"

"Twice, I told her," Kazdoy said. " 'Strictly kasha. Strictly kasha.' She must have thought—"

"I get it," Judge Lewis said, making a notation in the court file. "Mr. Lassiter, do you have anything further from this witness?"

"Well, I was going to ask—"

"Because," the judge continued, "I'm prepared to rule in your favor. But if you want to try and change my mind . . ."

"The defense rests," Lassiter said.

"Your Honor, please!" Chareen Bailey called out, leaping from her seat. "What about final argument?"

"Don't need it. Of course, you're free to appeal to the District Court." The judge smiled, a phenomenon as rare as snow in Miami. "After all, I answer to a higher authority."

CHAPTER

10

Tres Leches

B*erto had said eight o'clock at El Novillo, a Nicaraguan steak* house on South Dixie Highway. Lassiter arrived at eight-fifteen, knowing that his old friend operated on Latin Standard Time and was always late. The menu was covered with cowhide, the bristly hair still attached, and Lassiter wondered whether to pet it or read it. He ordered a pitcher of sangria and waited. Finally, at ten past nine, Berto arrived, greeted the hostess with a smack on the cheek, and after scanning the room, found Lassiter in a distant corner.

"*Hola, chico,*" Berto boomed. "Looks like they put the *gringo* next to the men's room."

"Hello, Berto. Long time." He looked like hell, Lassiter thought. The hair was still black, shiny, and perfectly cut, and the dark tailored business suit was freshly pressed. But the skin had lost its natural ruddiness, the cheeks were puffy, and the smile was forced.

"Jake, you look great, like you could still put the pads on. And you got some suntan for a guy stuck in the courthouse."

"Windsurfing. Keeps me in shape. Haven't made a tackle in a thousand years, but there's a client or two I wouldn't mind using for a blocking sled."

Berto's eyes skimmed the perimeter of the restaurant. One of those cocktail party looks, Lassiter thought at first, Berto checking out the room for more interesting company. But the eyes were jittery, the mouth tight with tension.

Berto caught Jake staring and responded with a prefab smile. "Let's order! I know you Anglos like the Early Bird Specials, so you must be starving by now."

"Why don't you handle it so I don't embarrass you with my Spanish?"

"Excellent idea." Motioning toward the waiter, Berto ordered without consulting the cowhide. "*Traiganos una orden de chorizos de cerdo, otra de cuajada con tortilla con plátanos maduros, dos lomitos a la plancha, término medio, y una orden de hongos a la vinagreta.* We'll order dessert later. Jake, you want more sangria?"

"No, Berto, I want to talk about the loans."

"The loans? The loans are the least of my worries, *amigo.* Stop playing lawyer and listen." Berto looked around again. The restaurant was filled, some families, mostly Hispanic businessmen. Lassiter guessed that he was the only Anglo other than the man who had followed Berto in the door and now sat at a corner table drinking American coffee.

"Jake, let me tell you what's happened to me. I didn't screw around with the bank until I'd already lost the shopping centers. When the economy turned, the bottom fell out of my real estate holdings. The offices, the strip centers, condos . . . all gone. Plus Magda left me when the money ran out. Back to Daddy in Caracas."

"I didn't know . . ."

"I don't broadcast it, Jake. But sometimes, you have to swallow your pride. *A veces es mejor tragarse el orgullo.* It's no disgrace to be broke, eh?"

Lassiter looked into Berto's eyes and shared the pain. He wanted to put his arms around his old friend, not prey on the carcass. Berto smiled. "Hey, Jake, it's not so bad, I've still got this." Berto reached inside his silk shirt and brought out the heavy chain that was his trademark, huge woven links of gold that could have anchored a catamaran in a squall. "Bought it with the profit from my first deal. Told the jeweler I wanted something different. Every Latino in town wears gold chains, *verdad*? Make it *grande*, I told him, links as big around as my *penes*. Jeweler said, 'Ingots don't come that big, how about as big around as your thumb?' "

"It's you," Lassiter agreed.

"I never take it off, Jake, I'll die with my gold on."

Lassiter didn't like the way Berto said it, the casual mention of death, as if it were the next flight out of town.

They were eating now, Berto picking at his food, Lassiter slicing the marinated steak, dipping it first in the sweet sauce of tomatoes and red peppers, then trying the green sauce of garlic, parsley, and oil. The meat was tender, the sauces tangy, the starchy black beans and rice taking some of the sting out of the spicy dishes.

"What about you, Jake? What's new in your life?"

"Nothing. I still don't have a wife, a dog, or a Most Valuable Player award."

Berto pointed at Jake with a fork filled with peppers and onions. "You have this tendency to reject the mainstream, to scoff at conformity."

"Really?"

"It's a contradiction that has always plagued you. A football player with brains and savvy, then a lawyer bursting at the seams of his vest. You frustrate easily and you have a low tolerance for bullshit. You may seem controlled and contained, but you're always on the verge of just chucking it all away. You don't always play the game, Jake, and if you're not careful, you could lose what you've built."

"Look who's talking."

"That's why I can talk. Ever thought about your future?"

"As little as possible."

"You ever gonna get married?"

"What for?"

Berto laughed. "Great question, Jake! I wish I'd asked myself the same question before I'd done about a thousand things."

"Such as."

"*En resumidas cuentas*," Berto said, "to make a long story short, when things went bad, I cut some corners to try and make a comeback."

"You doubled up the loans on the condos, Great Southern and Vista Bank, a neat scam, but fraudulent as hell."

Berto's fork struck his plate like a rifle shot. "Forget the loans. *Jesús Cristo!* The loans are dogshit. I'll tell you what I did. I got a DC-3. I bought a hundred acres just north of the Trail near Naples. I spent a small fortune clearing, filling, building a runway. You get me?"

"Oh no," Lassiter said, shaking his head in disbelief.

"That's right. Only *el idiota* I hired, he built runways in the Bahamas on coral rock, and he doesn't figure on the change in the water level in the Glades. So, first flight we got thirty thousand pounds of grass that I paid cash for, but it's August, and it's raining so hard the animals are leaving in twos, and there's a foot of muck on the runway. Pilot tries to set it down, he skids into a hammock, sheers off a wing, fifteen tons of prime weed goes up in flames. Gators got so stoned, they didn't move for a week."

"You were there?"

"Hell no, but I had trucks there and runway lights and guys with radios and guns. Everyone on the ground hauled ass. By the time the pilot gets out, he's gotta walk. Meanwhile the fireball attracted a state trooper who was cruising the Trail. He nails the pilot, who gives me up."

"I didn't realize. Didn't hear anything. You get indicted?"

"No way, José. I gave them the source in the islands. I have no priors, and it was my first job, I swear. So now, I'm a federally protected witness." Berto gestured to the Anglo man sipping coffee. The man nodded, almost imperceptibly. He wore a plaid polyester sports coat, gray slacks, and brown loafers. Lassiter guessed he was about forty, short blond hair turning gray. The man scanned the restaurant with pale eyes, studying everyone who came in the front door and out of the kitchen.

"DEA?" Lassiter asked.

"Yeah. His name's Franklin, like Ben, only this one doesn't have a first name. All very hush-hush. They deposed me for a week, and now they're setting me up with a new place to go, new name, job, everything."

"Where you going?"

"Not supposed to tell." Berto looked around again, shrugged his shoulders, and said, "Casper, Wyoming."

"You're kidding."

Berto shrugged and signaled the waiter to bring dessert, *tres leches* for Lassiter, espresso for himself. "Can you imagine me with the cowboys, Jake?" Berto looked down at his plate. He still had the charm that had carried him so far, Lassiter thought, but a hearty greeting and a slap on the back could not disguise his anguish. They were silent. Then Berto worked up the old smile and said, "I'm taking Lee Hu with me to Wyoming."

"Who?"

"Not who, Hu. Rhymes with stew, which is what she is for Avianca, based in Bogotá. She adores me. Only nineteen, about five one. You ever have an Asian girl? All they want to do is please you."

"That would be different," Lassiter allowed.

The *tres leches* was delicious, cake soaked in whole milk, evaporated milk, and condensed milk, covered with white frosting. Lassiter could barely move, and it was time to talk business. "Berto, the bank wants to bring charges against you for fraud and bribing a bank officer. Conrad Ticklin spilled his guts, said you gave him twenty-five grand to approve the loan. It's a federal crime."

The espresso cup stopped an inch from Berto's mouth. His eyes narrowed. "Ticklin's a candy-ass! He begged me for the money because he was whipsawed by his wife and his girlfriend."

"Regardless whose idea it was, you bribed him."

Berto scowled. "Yeah, because I tried to help him out. Ticklin's pushing forty-five and has all the charm of a warthog, but he's not as good-looking. He falls ass over elbows for this receptionist at the bank. She's twenty-one, Cuban Catholic, lives at home, and won't see him because he's married. She tells him, '*No puede estar el pollo en el corral y en la cazuela.*' "

"You can't have your chicken in the pen . . ."

"And in the pan," Berto added. "Or put another way, you can't have your *tres leches* and eat it too. So he says he'll leave his wife, and the blessed virgin rolls over. Course he doesn't leave his wife. Now the girl is pissed and threatens to tell the wife *and* the bank, and Ticklin needs money to shut her up.

He gets it from me, she gets a new BMW with a sunroof, Berry gets fired anyway, and I'm stuck with a bribery charge."

"His mistake was saying he'd leave his wife," Lassiter said. "I'll never understand why men do that."

"Jake, your naïveté knows no limits. *El hombre promete y promete y promete hasta que se la mete.* The man promises and promises and promises until he sticks it in."

Two strolling guitarists and a musician shaking maracas were serenading a middle-aged couple, singing "Besame Mucho," the love song that pleads for kisses. Franklin, the DEA agent, watched as if the maracas were hand grenades.

"Berto, I'll try to talk the bank out of going after you, but I'll need to give them something to keep the grand jury away. Do you have any property you can substitute as collateral for the condos?"

Berto grabbed the napkin from his lap and squeezed it, as if wringing out a dishrag and finding it dry. He dropped the napkin and gestured with both hands to the heavens. "My house has three mortgages, and I took all the equity out of the shopping centers to buy the first haul of grass. The property along the Trail took the last cash, and the feds are going to grab that under the forfeiture law."

"Is there anything else, race horses, foreign accounts, other properties?"

Berto looked around again. He seemed to think about it, weighed his thoughts, and finally said, "What the hell. There's one thing. It's not in my name, so the feds haven't found it. If they had, it'd be gone too, to the IRS. When things were good, I put some bucks in an offshore corporation, courtesy of the Cayman Islands. It holds clear title to a three-hundred-acre ranch outside Ocala. Gotta be worth two million plus, and it's not doing me any good. If I touch it the feds will hit me with obstruction or perjury."

Bingo. Another chance to be a hero for the bank, Most Valuable Mouthpiece award. Not much of a thrill, not like breaking into the starting lineup against the Jets because of an injury to the strong side linebacker, but it would have to do. "That's it, Berto. It's clean. Your offshore company can deed the property to Great Southern and you'll get a release on the loans. Will you do it?"

Berto sipped at his espresso and said, "For you, Jake, I'll do it."

"And I'll make sure the bank forgets all about bribery charges. The bank will get close to fifty cents on the dollar which is fine for a bad loan. Vista Bank gets the condos, and you're off to Wyoming."

They sat in silence for a moment. Jake Lassiter wondered what it was like, one day the world tasting of champagne, the next day of ashes. Berto had seemed so strong, so much in control. But inside he was still a twelve-year-old kid floating on a raft across the Florida Straits. He was burned out now, caught in a maelstrom beyond his control—the deals, the drugs, the women, the money.

Always the money. The gods tempt us, Lassiter thought. They offer us riches and sweet smelling women, *tres leches*, each milk sweeter than the one before. But you cannot beat the gods. The grander house, the bigger deal, only mean more borrowed time, more risk. When you build your life on a house of cards, you never know when the joker will turn up. When you wheel and deal and borrow and spend, when your balance sheet is based on forecasts and projections, wishes and dreams, it is only a matter of time. One day, the mortgage comes due, and it all falls down. It only takes a missed step, a tax return that catches the computer's eye, an oil shortage or an oil glut, a weakness for drink or drugs or soft skin.

We are so frail. The gods build us up, then wait. The fall from grace is a spectator sport, and those too meek to take the risks watch from afar and cluck their tongues knowingly.

"I wish I could turn back the clock for you," Lassiter said finally.

"I have no regrets. It was a hell of a ride while it lasted."

"Can you stay out of trouble?"

Berto gestured toward the federal agent. "If Franklin can get me through the week. I have to do a little favor for the DEA, part of my deal. I'm helping set up some doper from out west."

Lassiter frowned. "Sounds dangerous."

"Don't worry, *amigo*. I'll be in and out. The bust won't come down until they bring the stuff into the country from the Bahamas, and I'll be long gone by then."

They looked into each other's eyes, old friends grown apart with the years, drawn together for a moment by a flicker from the past.

"Take care of yourself, old buddy," Lassiter said softly.

"I always do," Berto replied with a laugh devoid of joy.

CHAPTER 11

A Day at the Beach

What would she be like, Jake Lassiter wondered. Until now, Lila Summers had been a two-dimensional vision, a color photograph in a magazine, leaning back from the boom, leg muscles taut, turquoise swimsuit cut high over rounded hip, wild mane of hair frozen in the wind. In a photograph there are neither flaws nor words of rebuke, just timeless youth and beauty and joy.

She was not hard to spot. Every man on Concourse D either stopped dead in his tracks or suffered whiplash from a quick turn as she passed. Lila Summers was breathtaking in a white cotton sweatsuit—deep suntan set off by the snowy fabric—her thick hair butterscotched by the sun, bright hazel eyes flecked with green sparkles. She had a body that could be sensed even through the loose outfit, full breasts and strong legs. California-born and Hawaii-raised, she was tall and walked with a long stride. She carried a pink sail bag weighted down with her gear, but her sturdy arms and shoulders showed no strain. There was no mistaking that she was both an athlete and a woman, a perfect picture come to life.

Keaka Kealia walked a step behind her, his eyes lumps of coal, his skin the ruddy brown of cedar. He bounced on his toes gracefully, without swaying, his head perfectly still. Sinewy muscles stood out on either side of his neck, and his chest bulged through a black-and-red T-shirt with the logo of the World Cup Slalom Event in Japan. He looked like a sprinter, maybe even a wide receiver.

"I'm Jake Lassiter, your host."

"Hello, Mr. Lassiter." Lila Summers's smile was polite, nothing more.

"Please call me Jake. Mr. Lassiter sounds like an undertaker." I'm a fossil to her, he thought.

Keaka stepped between them and extended a hand. Lassiter had to counterattack to keep his knuckles from cracking like walnuts under a mallet. They went through that curious male dance, an arm-wrestling handshake, Keaka at first in control, then Lassiter battling to a draw. He could feel the faint traces of calluses on Keaka's palm, remnants of hundreds of hours' hanging from the booms. Before letting go, Keaka asked, "Do you have the check?"

Lila gave the Hawaiian a pained look. "Keaka, mind your manners, we're in civilization now. Your direct ways might not be appreciated here."

Tarzan and Jane, Lassiter thought.

"I'm only asking because last year I was stiffed in Mexico after an exhibition," Keaka said. "Everything was *mañana*, then *mañana* came, but the pesos never did."

It could have been a witty line, but the Hawaiian did not smile. Not a latter-day Duke Kahanamoku, joking with the tourists after riding waves at Diamond Head. No, this guy had all the charm of a hammerhead shark.

"Quite right to be concerned in this day and age of charlatans," Lassiter said stiffly. "Check's right here." He patted his suit pocket, not liking the sound of his own voice. Uptight and pickle-assed, out of his element with the two great athletes. Wanting to tell them that he didn't always tote a briefcase. But what would they know of a quarterback sack on third and long?

They loaded their gear into Lassiter's old convertible and headed for Key Biscayne where their boards, masts, sails, and booms—shipped ahead from Hawaii—waited in storage sheds on the beach. Keaka and Lila checked into the Sonesta Beach Hotel and twenty minutes later were rigging their equipment in the white sand twenty yards from the Atlantic. Other competitors were fine-tuning their colorful sails, tugging lines taut, and bending masts to the proper angle. It was one of those postcard days, endless blue sky and temperature in the high seventies, wind humming, a steady twenty knots from the east.

The beach was awash with young athletes, deeply tanned and exuberant, so that the pale couple—an old man and a sharp-featured, squinting woman—looked like characters from an Ingmar Bergman film, displaced persons drifting by. How long had it been since Samuel Kazdoy had walked along a beach, decades maybe, but here he was slogging through the deep sand in black oxfords and baggy pants, looking unsteady and ill at ease. Alongside was Violet Belfrey in a short skirt and tight blouse, guiding Kazdoy by the elbow, his chalky arm poking out of a short-sleeve white shirt.

"Keaka, these are friends of mine," Lassiter said. "Violet and Sam, say hello to the greatest board sailor who ever lived." They exchanged greetings and the old man inspected the board, running a hand over a hard rail, the bottom edge that speeds the craft through the water. "Keaka's the first board sailor to have completed a three-sixty, a back sommersault off a wave. Now that it's fairly common, he does them blindfolded."

Violet's gaze locked on the bulge in Keaka's swim trunks. "Ah'd somersault on that thing any ole time he wants," she stage-whispered to Lassiter.

Keaka Kealia silently continued rigging an old board dinged with scars from collisions with coral rocks. The professionals all used custom-made boards with airbrushed designs—rainbows or sunsets or sponsors' logos—but Keaka's board was decorated with the grim face of an ancient Hawaiian warrior, mouth curled open in a bloodthirsty scream. Because he had spent hundreds of hours on it, the board would give him a true reading of the conditions at a new sailing spot. How fast was the current? Were the waves crisp or mushy? Did the wind have holes or was it steady?

Violet was fidgeting, shielding her eyes from the glare. "When the hell they gonna do something?" she asked impatiently. Count Dracula would have been more comfortable in the midday sun.

"They're adjusting the equipment," Jake Lassiter said. "The sail has to be tuned just right for the strength of the wind. Think of the board as a sailboat, except you sail it standing up, and you use your feet and the angle of the mast to steer."

"You should have seen that stinking boat I crossed the Atlantic on, the *Petersburg*," Samuel Kazdoy said. "I was sick the whole time. Swore I'd never go near the water. Never did, not even the Staten Island ferry."

Some of the competitors were carrying their equipment into the surf, boards held overhead, masts pointed downwind. Lassiter tried to bring the old man back into the 1990s: "This is only practice. On Saturday, they'll go for the gold."

"Jacob, did I ever tell you what they said in Kiev about New York?" Kazdoy asked, his mind somewhere between Key Biscayne and czarist Russia. "They said the streets of New York are paved with gold and when I got off that *farshtinkener* boat, I saw a man following a horse with a broom and pail, but . . . but . . ."

". . . But what he was sweeping wasn't gold," Violet said, finishing the story that the old man had told a thousand times. Now Lassiter worried even more about Sam Kazdoy losing his sharpness. Lassiter had seen it happen before, a younger woman of shadowy background drawn to an old man's money. In the beginning it's innocent enough, the woman running errands, tidying up, providing companionship. Before you know it, her name pops up as joint owner on the old coot's brokerage accounts.

Keaka finished tying the clew of his sail to the boom with an outhaul line. When the sail reached the perfect curvature, he jammed the mast into the sand and leaned back from the boom, testing the rigging against the steady easterly. The sail supported all his weight, a precise trim.

Lassiter watched him and said, "Keaka, I brought you a navigational chart, though I doubt you'll need it. I'll be in the lead judges' boat, and if everything's true to form, you'll be right behind us and all the other racers can follow you. But this will give you an idea where we're going. It'll be a Le Mans start from the beach, then forty-eight miles due east across the Gulf Stream, finish just a mile or so off North Bimini at the Great Bahama Bank. There'll be a finish line strung between two barges with checkered flags flying, so just sail under the line and tie up. The awards ceremony and a champagne celebration will take place right on the barge."

"Finish at the Great Bahama Bank," Keaka repeated.

Violet watched him crouch in the sand, her eyes still on groin patrol. "Smart to finish at a bank," she said, nodding sagely. "Easier to pay off the winners."

Keaka ignored her, tugged on his windsurfing gloves, and jogged into the water, carrying his equipment effortlessly. "Practice now," he said without looking at them. Violet watched his muscular body disappear into the surf.

A moment later Lassiter caught sight of Lila Summers, twenty yards down the beach. Her hair was pulled straight back and tied in a ponytail, accentuating her cheekbones, the muscles in her calves undulating as she carried her rig into the water. He guided Kazdoy closer to the shore break.

"Here's who I want you to see," Lassiter said, pointing toward Lila's board as it shredded the small offshore waves. "Watch her bottom turn."

"That's what I'm doing, *boychik*. My eyes still work, even if my *schmeckel*—"

"No, watch how, at the bottom of a wave, she climbs back up the face. Her bottom turn's the best in the business."

"Got some *tuchis* on her," the old man agreed.

Lila rocketed down the face of a wave, her board etching a foamy wake. As the wave ran out of water, her back hand pulled hard on the boom, trimming the sail tight against the wind for an extra burst of speed. At the same time she jammed her back foot onto the downwind side, burying the rail, and the board carved a tight turn and shot up the face of the wave. A rooster tail of spray exploded from the stern.

"Now watch her slashback," Lassiter said. "You won't see her change direction. One second she's going one way, then slash, and she's going the other."

At the top of the wave, Lila shifted her weight to the inside rail and released pressure on the boom to let wind out of the sail. On command, the board pivoted on the shoulder of the wave, just inches from the breaking lip, and cut down across the face, never losing speed. The board was a fiberglass stiletto, flashing in the sun, cutting back and forth, bottom turn at the end of the wave, slicing to the top, then slashing back toward the bottom, Lila laughing into the wind, her honey hair flying.

The old man winked at Lassiter, gave him a sly grin, and said, "You got some eye for the *maidels*."

"Sam, please," Lassiter said. "She's with Keaka."

"So?"

"So, I don't have a chance."

"*Feh*, and if you'll pardon my English, bullshit. You want a piece of property to build a plant, sometimes another fellow wants it too, and maybe he can offer more than you. But maybe he has some unexpected *tsuris*. Maybe the IRS finds out about his second set of books or his unions strike or his wife finds out about his girlfriend. But one thing for sure, you can't do nothing just staring at your *pupik*."

Violet was growing restless and the old man was uncomfortable sinking into the sand. "*Boychik*, we're going to run along and get to the theater. You think about what I told you." He toddled off, Violet hanging on like a platinum blond vulture.

Lassiter watched them go, wondering what he could do to protect his friend. Wondering too if he had any chance of recovering the stolen bonds. And wondering finally if winning Lila Summers might be more complicated than closing on a piece of real estate.

Alone with his thoughts, Jake Lassiter went about his chores as race organizer. Of all the serious board sailors in Miami, Lassiter was the obvious choice to run things. Unlike most of the boardheads who either lived in their beach vans or worked night jobs so they could sail all day, Lassiter was considered semirespectable. Plus he had a secretary and a photocopy machine, essential to organize anything from a car wash to a World Cup athletic event.

First Lassiter checked with Commodore Ralph Whittaker, the old fussbudget who ran the Coral Gables Yacht Club, which was providing the prize money. Next he confirmed starting times with the captains of the lead boat and the chase boat. He spoke to the medical personnel, then verified that hotel rooms would be ready for the network television crews. Finally, he ducked into a cabana, changed into a faded pair of surfing trunks, and rigged his own board. Watching others sail is fine; sailing yourself is better. He chose a six-meter sail, bigger than most competitors would use on a day of strong, steady winds, but when you weigh 220, it takes a lot of canvas—actually Mylar—to get the board up on a plane.

He beach-started in the shore break, hopping onto the board between incoming waves, then guided it into open water. His knees flexed, adjusting to the rollers, and soon he was skipping across the top of the waves, bouncing over moving ledges of water. Offshore, the chop rolled toward land in evenly spaced swells, what the surfer kids called corduroy. Lassiter luxuriated in the strain on the arms, the tendons and muscles of the shoulders stretching as gusts tried to tear the sail away. It was a mixture of pleasure and sweet pain that nearly chased away the gray, cloudy thoughts that hovered over him.

Nearly, but not quite. Thoughts of Sam and Violet, and how the hell he would find the missing bonds. No word from Sergeant Carraway. Thoughts of the reptilian Thad Whitney and the fallen Berto, wondering if he had signed the papers.

Poor Berto.

Lassiter remembered their days in the public defender's office, celebrating with pitchers of sangria and mountains of paella after tap-dancing an N.G. verdict from six citizens, good and true. Thoughts of Lila Summers, too, and whether the beautiful athlete might find some redeeming value in a has-been linebacker who could spin a fair yarn.

Lassiter shifted his weight toward the bow, tilted the mast forward, and pushed the board off the wind. It jibed hard and fast on its rail, and Lassiter flipped the sail around in the extravagant gesture of a matador sweeping his cape. He headed due south on a broad reach, the coastline of Key Biscayne to starboard, the lighthouse at the tip of the island coming into view.

He thought of the partners' meeting he was missing, *a meeting of compelling urgency*, according to Marshall Tuttle's agenda memo. The issue: whether the firm should continue paying for either a tennis club or golf club membership for each partner since the golf memberships cost considerably more. Memos were the lifeblood of the managing partner, whose day began at ten A.M. with a thorough reading of *The Wall Street Journal* and was followed by an hour of making appointments—lunch at noon at the Bay Club, squash at three at the Atlantic Club, and drinks in the Oak Room at five-thirty. In between, he dictated dozens of irrelevant memos, which Jake Lassiter crumpled, then used to practice his free throws.

Finally, Lassiter angled toward shore, surfing over the incoming waves. In shallow water, he hopped off and hoisted the rig onto the beach. What he had in mind was a two-mile jog on the hard-packed sand, and then a pleasant sail back to the hotel. There were only a few people on the beach, Canadian tourists judging from their arctic pallor and French accents, plus a smattering of South American kids from expensive condos near the hotels. He started at an easy pace—*pick it up, fifty-eight*, Coach Paterno yelled from a faraway field. As he neared the old lighthouse that once warned ships of the treacherous reefs, he saw someone familiar. No, not here, what would he be doing . . .

"Berto. Berto, is that you?"

The dark-haired man whirled around, revealing a naked look of surprise, almost fear, Lassiter thought. After an awkward moment of silence, Humberto Hernandez-Zaldivar said, "Jake, *mi amigo*, good to see you."

Lassiter kept running in place. "Berto, what're you doing here?"

Silence.

Lassiter had questioned enough witnesses to read the look on Berto's face. *He's making it up, winging it.*

"I thought I would find out what you saw in this windsurfing," Berto said finally. He was wearing shorts and rubber thongs and a sleeveless top with tiny holes for air vents, a look popular in Little Havana. He nervously twirled a finger around his heavy gold chain.

Next to Berto was an Asian girl who looked about fifteen but must have been the flight attendant he'd mentioned in the restaurant. Then a bare-chested man slowly stood up from where he was crouching in the sand like Johnny Bench behind the plate.

Keaka Kealia.

Jake Lassiter stopped running in place and stood there with his hands on his hips, breathing hard. No one spoke.

Keaka's board was pulled up on the beach, resting on its side in the shadow of the lighthouse, much farther out of the water than necessary to protect it from the shore break. Now what the hell was going on, Berto collecting autographs? Seemed like he should have more pressing things on his mind, like staying out of sight. The DEA agent was nowhere to be seen. A sniper could pick him off from the sand dunes, if there really were assassins.

Berto smiled and regained his composure. "Jake, this is Lee Hu, sweetest tiger lily in the land, and I think you know Keaka Kealia."

"Hello, Lee Hu. Berto, I didn't know you and Keaka were acquainted."

"Just met," Berto said. "Thought I might open a ski shop out west, have windsurfing equipment for summer business. Who better to talk to than the best, right, Keaka?"

Berto's head swiveled to Keaka Kealia, looking for help, but the Hawaiian was silent. Lee Hu looked down at her tiny feet, and Lassiter looked too: nails painted glossy red, her toes positively edible. Her halter top was plastered against her small body by the November easterly. Long black hair fell in bangs in the front and straight to her shoulders in back, where the wind tossed it leeward. The total impression, Lassiter thought, was of childlike sensuality.

"Great, Berto," Lassiter said. "You came to the right place for advice." He didn't believe a word of it and couldn't figure out what Berto was doing with Keaka Kealia. Real estate developer turned doper going into the windsurfing business. What a crock.

Then Berto flashed his old smile and said, "Funny we don't see each other for years, then twice in two days, our paths cross. Must be the stars, *verdad*? By the way, I stopped by your office this morning and signed those papers, the deeds to the bank. Cindy's got them. Glad to get it over with."

"Sorry I missed you," Lassiter said, aware Berto had changed the subject. A diversionary tactic, and any lawyer worth his wing tips would not be thrown off the track. Why had Keaka sailed a mile down the beach to discuss the latest in equipment? Why did he try to keep his rig from view? What was Berto's sudden interest in the sport, and where the hell was the DEA agent?

Lassiter would have loved to grill these two under oath, but he didn't have a subpoena in his surfing trunks. After quick good-byes, he left them there and jogged back over the dunes to retrieve his rig. Nearing a roped-off area, he was careful to avoid the sea grass, which was more than a guy with binoculars was doing. Tourists were always tromping around where they didn't belong. Lassiter wished he was wearing his favorite T-shirt, the one with the slogan "Welcome to Florida, Now Go Home."

"Hey, you're not supposed to be in there, beach erosion," Lassiter called out. The guy lowered the binoculars and scowled. There was something familiar about him. Sports coat. Short blond hair going gray. Sure. "You're the DEA guy. Franklin, right?"

"Get the fuck outta here," the man said, lifting the binoculars again, aiming toward the beach where Keaka, Berto, and Lee Hu still huddled.

"Okay, just glad to see my tax dollars at work. Shame the federal government cut your funds for charm school."

". . . the fuck out 'fore I bust you for obstruction."

"You too?" Lassiter asked. "I know a Beach cop would love to nail me for a B and E. Maybe my picture will be in the post office next week."

The man's sports coat swung open, revealing a shoulder holster filled with a .38. "Maybe so, you don't watch out the company you keep."

"Berto's not a hard guy, just someone who took a wrong turn."

The man laughed. "Who the fuck's talking about him?"

CHAPTER 12

Back to School

O*nly in Miami, Jake Lassiter thought, reading the morning paper* while sipping guava juice in the tiny kitchen of his coral rock house.

Only in Miami was the theft of $1,640,712.50 in negotiable securities considered small potatoes. That was the total Cindy came up with after putting the old man's records into the calculator, and where did that get you? It got you on page 7-B of *The Miami Herald*, only four paragraphs plus a thumbnail photo of Sam Kazdoy, a shot taken sometime after his bar mitzvah but before he lost his hair.

Jake Lassiter had been hoping for more. A lot of publicity

and the burglars, if they were still in town, would have to wonder. Is it safe to leave through the airport or would bags be searched? Are banks on the lookout? Is the FBI involved? But four paragraphs told the world that nobody gave a shit about a B and E, not in a town where there's more than one homicide a day, 365 days a year, and without a good angle, a murder gets five measly paragraphs and a one-column headline BODY FOUND, next to ads for lingerie models and body shampoo massage parlors in North Miami Beach.

The burglary was lost in the day's crime news, heavy even by Miami standards. One hundred grams of cocaine is hardly worth mentioning and it wouldn't have been, except a federal juror stole it while deliberating the fate of an accused drug dealer. The evidence was being passed around the table when it disappeared, probably crammed into a juror's Jockeys for a late-night toot. It was the first time anyone could remember a jury being read its Miranda rights.

Then there was the middle-aged Cuban driver who rammed his Marriott catering truck into the nose gear of a Cubana Airlines jet at MIA. A million dollars' damage to the plane, and a great shot of the driver shouting "Cuba Libre" on the front page. Yes, Lassiter admitted, it was too heavy a news day to pay much attention to a burglary.

The newspaper devoted a portion of its Local page to yet another mystery at the Miami police station, thirty-eight bales of marijuana missing from a padlocked bin in the property room. Two weeks earlier the police lost seven hundred abandoned bicycles that were to be auctioned off for charity when a wise guy took them from an unguarded lot. Then, $150,000 in cash was stolen from the police safe, evidence in a drug case.

Of course the newsboys were going bonkers with the missing marijuana, the papers and the TV stations yukking it up. And why not, more crimes are committed in the Miami police station than on the streets of most cities. Still, the Kazdoy burglary might have gotten some notoriety had a major-league drug dealer not been machine-gunned at high noon in Little Havana by assassins firing MAC-10s. For the third time in a month, a copy editor tried to slip the phrase "MAC Attack" into a headline and for the third time an assistant city editor killed it.

After reading the morning paper, Lassiter still didn't have a lead. Maybe he should confront Violet, one-on-one. Put some pressure on her, more than Sergeant Carraway would do. Except first he had to file three mortgage foreclosures and review title documents to a dozen real estate transactions.

Cindy was missing from the cubicle where she usually perched, cursing at her word processor. Wrong day of the week for riding the chopper in the Keys. Lassiter opened the door to his office and found her doing a pirouette, modeling a bikini for Tubby Tubberville, who overflowed the high-backed chair and whose black motorcycle boots were propped on the oak credenza. Tubby had a round face, a neck that no collar could contain, and powerful arms that ended in thick, stumpy hands. He wore grease-spotted jeans, a T-shirt advertising a Key West oyster bar—"Eat 'em raw"—and a sleeveless leather vest with slots for shotgun shells.

"Make yourself comfortable, Tubby." Lassiter slipped a managing partner memo—scolding secretaries for using the Xerox machine to photocopy their private parts—under Tubby's boots.

"Thanks, don't mind if I do."

"Hey, Cindy," Lassiter said, "how about typing the complaint in the First Savings mortgage foreclosure?"

"Sure, boss, but whadaya think?" Cindy spun three hundred sixty degrees, arching her back to show off her tight bottom in a black-and-yellow cheetah print, the fabric little more than a Band-Aid covering her crotch, a strap as thin as a shoestring between her cheeks, the top a shred of spandex over small breasts.

"I think you're going to catch cold. Now, you two mind if I sit down and bill some time?"

"Ay, bro, don't give me no bull," Tubby said, riffling Lassiter's documents. "All you got here are papers from a bank that don't make no sense, three windsurf magazines with pictures of beach bunnies with some radical deltoids, and a note about a reunion of your old college team."

"Thanks, Tubby. Maybe you could also return my calls and answer the mail while you're here."

"For what you're paid, why not? To you high-rise types, talking on the phone is work. You guys got it good. Private clubs, fancy lunches, pheasant under glass."

"I just eat the glass. Thanks for stopping by and brightening my day."

Tubby lifted his bulk from the swivel chair with unusual grace for a man whose 260 pounds bulged around a five-foot-nine-inch frame. "Don't mention it. But I gotta go work on the Harley and I hate being downtown anyway. Anybody left here who speaks English?"

"Before you go, Tub, let me ask you something. You remember when I was in the PD's office?"

"How could I fergit? You got me off that trumped-up charge. I mean, give me a break, aggravated assault for shoving a guy in a shitkicker bar."

"As I recall, you had a pool cue in one hand and a broken Budweiser bottle in the other."

Tubby shrugged. "House rules. No guns."

"Anyway, you remember my trial partner, Berto Zaldivar?"

"Ay. Handsome devil. Combed that black hair straight back like some gigolo. The two of you were defending poor wretches what couldn't afford real lawyers."

"We were both starry-eyed in those days. It took me a while

to figure out that a three-time armed robber wasn't a saint just because he was indigent. It didn't take Berto as long."

"What about him, bro?"

"You still have friends in the business?"

"What business is that, bro?"

"C'mon, Tubby. Importation."

The big man looked around, as if somebody might be eavesdropping. "I hang loose in a bar in the Keys where half the Bubbas are smugglers and the other half narcs. As long as the fishing boats keep unloading that square grouper, the Keys ain't gonna have no recession."

"Keep your ears open for me about Berto, okay, but be discreet."

"Ain't I always?" Tubby whispered. He slapped Cindy playfully on the bottom and headed out the door.

An hour later, as Lassiter was putting the finishing touches on a motion to foreclose the mortgage of a laid-off airline mechanic, the intercom buzzed. "Don't forget," Cindy said.

"Forget what?"

"Your meeting with Charlie Riggs at the med school."

"Shit, I forgot. Searching for truth and justice really drains the brain cells."

"Another thing, boss."

"Yeah?"

Wind dies at sundown,
Dinner date,
Beach Bunny at eight.

"Thanks, Cindy, but Keaka's going to be there, too."

"No sweat, *su majestad*. Just flash those baby blues and talk some legal mumbo jumbo. He'll be dead meat."

It's not far from downtown to the medical complex near the Orange Bowl. Unless the East-West Expressway—renamed the Dolphin Expressway, no thanks to me—was battened down. Which it was. A dozen Metro police cars were angled across the roadway, lights blazing, cops with drawn guns approaching an overturned trailer truck. Tiptoeing, watching where they stepped as thousands of Florida lobsters spilled out of the rear door of the refrigerated truck and scuttled across the road, sensing the water of a muddy canal nearby.

Not an everyday traffic accident, especially since Alejandro "Monkey" Morales, ex-shrimper and current thief, was pinned inside the cab of the stolen truck. Morales had long ago figured out that grabbing a truck with three hundred thousand dollars' worth of shellfish was more profitable than holding up a bank. And wasn't a federal crime. As the kidnapped crustaceans disappeared into the bushes, Lassiter pulled his old convertible onto the berm and made it to the exit ramp, ignoring the occasional crunching sound under his tires.

The traffic on Flagler Street was at a standstill and Lassiter took a shortcut on Seventh Street, lately rechristened Luis Sabines Way by the city commission, always anxious to pick up a few votes in Little Havana. Municipal debates over street names take almost as much time as haranguing Fidel Castro and soliciting campaign contributions from builders of homes that turn into shrapnel in a stiff wind.

The bridge was up on Twelfth Avenue, newly renamed Ronald Reagan Boulevard, mainly because the former president once ate a *media noche* at La Esquina de Tejas during a campaign swing. The restaurant, at the intersection of the Gipper's boulevard and First Street, had erected a little presidential memorial that looked like a religious display.

Lassiter stayed on Luis Sabines Way, heading too far west, and nearly got lost because the signs on Twenty-second Avenue had been changed to General Máximo Gómez Boulevard. He didn't know Máximo and figured Reagan didn't either, since he couldn't remember half his Cabinet members. Lassiter swung left on the generalissimo's boulevard and again on Eighth Street or, if you prefer, Calle Ocho, to head east again. A tired Chevy with no shocks or maybe three bodies in the trunk was double-parked in front of Tony Perez Bail Bonds, *Fianzas*, according to the neon sign. A parade of homemade floats inched along the other two lanes, celebrating Independence Day on an obscure Caribbean island that, in fact, was ruled by a malevolent despot.

So Lassiter waited, top down, figuring he could miss Charlie Riggs's lecture on the body temperature of stiffs and still have time to talk to him about Sam's missing bonds. Doc Riggs hadn't spent a lifetime sifting scientific evidence of crime without solving a few puzzles.

The sun shone brightly, and the breeze from the bay crackled the American and Cuban flags in front of a Toyota dealership at the corner. Lassiter's mind wandered. He thought of open seas and riding a board through ocean swells. An image of Lila Summers appeared on a beach of cocoa sand. The reverie was interrupted by a steel band clanging by on the left, trying to give Lassiter a headache and succeeding. In front of him, three men, who believed their bare chests made Little Havana even lovelier, sat on the hood of the Chevy, arguing with Tony the Bondsman, who apparently demanded more than a jalopy as collateral. Finally, Lassiter gave the Chevy a love tap with his front bumper, and a wiry fellow on the driver's side stuck an Uzi out the window. Nice move, Lassiter thought. An automatic weapon is better than the traditional bird for getting your attention. Lassiter decided not to lay on the horn. Not the one installed by GM, and not even the one that played "Fight on, State."

Finally, the Chevy moved, and so did he, rolling through a

yellow light at Seventeenth Avenue, now dubbed Teddy Roosevelt Boulevard. Traffic congealed again a block away, alongside turquoise-and-yellow apartment buildings, gussied up with curlicues and bric-a-brac, window air conditioners coughing and dripping. A heavy woman in a rocking chair with a black shawl around her shoulders stared at him through the narrow metal railing of a second-floor balcony. Back on Ronald Reagan Boulevard, Lassiter turned left, crossed the bridge over the Miami River, and headed past Cedars of Lebanon, the various cancer and eye centers, and into the medical school parking garage.

Charlie Riggs was shouting at his class. "Inshoot wounds are always smaller than outshoot wounds, true or false?"

"True," said an Asian woman with enormous round eyeglasses. "The entry wound is always smaller."

"False!" Charlie Riggs bellowed. "One of a number of myths you must forget if you are to learn. Suicides have been called murders by untrained coroners who believed a larger hole in the chest meant the deceased necessarily was shot in the back. Innocent men have gone to prison because of incompetent autopsies."

A hush fell over the room. Riggs paused, then started up again. "Inshoot wounds are always circular. Another myth! It depends on the angle of entry. The bullet always follows a straight path inside the body. False! A bullet can ricochet off the organs. How about this one: The powder burn helps determine the distance of the gun from the body."

"That's true, Doctor Riggs," the woman tried again.

Charlie Riggs peered up into the sloping, theater-sized classroom. "True once, obsolete now. With a smokeless propellant, it's useless. And another one: A good M.E. can tell the caliber of a gun by measuring the inshoot wound."

This time, the class was silent. They learned slowly, but they learned.

"Maybe on TV," he continued, "but I can't do it, and I was studying holes in people when most of you were in knickers. When a bullet enters the body, the skin stretches, then contracts. The hole may be smaller than the bullet by the time you measure the opening."

This went on for a while, Charlie Riggs prancing about the small stage on his bowed legs, unlocking secrets learned in twenty thousand autopsies in a cold, tiled room smelling of rotting flesh and formaldehyde. Then he tugged off his glasses and propped them on top of his unkempt hair. He leaned back against a high laboratory stool, scratched his bushy beard, and told about the Expressway Body, found a few pieces at a time along I-95. Everybody had wondered about the green paint on the femur. Not Charlie. He knew that store-bought hacksaw blades typically are splashed with green paint. When a suspect was picked up, Charlie wandered around the man's garage, pulled a new hacksaw off the wall, and tested the paint. Eureka, a conviction for Murder One.

"But you have to be able to distinguish murder from accidental death," Charlie told them. "A man comes home from work, finds the house locked and his wife stone-dead on the kitchen floor, her throat slashed. The house shows no sign of forced entry. Nothing missing. No sign of a weapon. A hamburger was burned to a crisp in a pan on the stove. A broken plate lay on the floor, an empty gin bottle on the kitchen table, blood everywhere. What happened?"

"Suicide," a young man in a lab coat said from the front row.

"No note, no weapon, no history of despondency. Don't jump to conclusions. What do you do first?"

"Examine the wound," the man said. "Establish cause of death."

Charlie Riggs smiled from beneath the bushy beard. "Good. *Periculum in mora*. There is danger in delay. Her vena cava is empty. She bled out. And suppose you find shards of porcelain in the wound?"

Silence.

Then, from the back of the hall, Lassiter called out, "The plate. You test the plate, Dr. Riggs."

"Correct." Riggs squinted in Lassiter's direction. "Very good for a downtown mouthpiece. And if the porcelain matches?" He looked at his students, waiting for an answer.

"The husband killed his wife with a broken plate?" the Asian woman guessed.

"No, no, no! You still don't have enough facts. *Qui timide rogat docet negare.* Don't be afraid to ask questions. What do you need to know?"

"Her blood alcohol level," Lassiter piped up.

"Right again, Counselor. And suppose it comes up point-three?"

Lassiter answered, "I'd say the lady drank too much gin before lunch and tripped while carrying a plate to the table. The plate broke and slashed her throat. Death by exsanguination. An accident all around."

"Correct," Charlie Riggs proclaimed, happily. "She was a heavy drinker who often passed out in the afternoon. This time it was fatal. Mr. Lassiter, next week, you shall be permitted to do an autopsy if you wish. At least we know you won't kill the patient."

Huddled around a plastic table in the medical school cafeteria, Lassiter sipped black coffee and Charlie Riggs chewed on a sandwich.

"You ought to try the *choripan tejas especial con queso derretido,*" Riggs said, wiping melted cheese from his beard.

"Thanks, Charlie, but in a couple of hours, I'm taking two board sailors out for stone crabs."

"*Menippe mercenaria*, a remarkable animal. Lop off a claw,

it grows another one. Would that we could do the same. Now, Jake, why did you want to see me?"

Lassiter finished his coffee and waited for three young residents in green smocks to leave a nearby table. "Two reasons, actually. You remember Berto Zaldivar?"

"Of course. Your trial partner in the days when you defended people with no morals and no money, before you switched to representing corporations with no morals and lots of money." Charlie gnawed at his sandwich. "Berto was never half the lawyer you were."

"Yeah, thanks. He's had some trouble, and I was wondering if you heard about it."

Charlie Riggs stroked his beard. "Well, for years, I'd see his picture in the social pages, giving money to the Bay of Pigs Brigade, the Mount Sinai Founders Ball, every charity in town. He'd made it, that's for sure. Then he dropped out of sight. Word was he was dirty, FDLE tried to sting him a few times, didn't work. Finally, a year or so ago, one of my friends in the State Attorney's Office, or maybe it was DEA, doesn't matter which, told me they'd nailed him with a fairly sizable load of marijuana. Enough for minimum mandatory fifteen years plus a two-hundred-thousand-dollar fine under Chapter Eight Ninety-three. So he turned and started working for the narcs as part of a plea bargain. That help any?"

"Some. It basically corroborates Berto's story, except he says it was his first dirty deed. You hear anything about him being sent to Wyoming as part of the witness protection program?"

"No, but it makes sense. Problem is, the DEA will use him up first. Make him do just one more job, then one more, then another. Somewhere along the line, he'll either go back into the business or end up in the bay sleeping with whatever fish haven't died of pollution."

Lassiter signaled for a refill on the coffee. "I'd like to help him, Charlie, get him safely out of town, a fresh start, but I don't know how."

"*Amicus usque ad aram*, you're a friend to the end. But forget it, Jake. Once they're into dope, they're gone. Cut him loose."

"I'm not the cutting loose type."

"An admirable quality, albeit an anachronistic one. You're a throwback, Jake. It's one of the reasons I like you so much. Your ideals are as dated as that . . . Le Mans, or whatever it is you drive."

"An Olds 442, Charlie. Four-barrel carburetor, four-speed transmission, dual tail pipes."

"Precisely! You're still a cheeseburger and double malted fellow in a world of quiche and white wine. And you still think all your friends wear white hats. Someday you'll realize that nearly everybody in this town is playing it fast and loose. Bankers who launder drug money, boiler room gold bullion salesmen who cheat widows in Iowa, lawyers who cross the line and become partners with their clients. Everyone's walking a tightrope, and with just a nudge one way or the other, most tumble into the swamp."

Lassiter stared into his coffee cup. "Thirty years hanging around cops and corpses has left you a tad cynical."

"Wake up, Jake. When you read in the paper that a dope kingpin walks because the cops lose the evidence, do you think it's an accident? In case you didn't know it, prosecutors tank cases, judges play favorites, and lawyers crawl in bed with their clients. Berto's descent should not surprise you."

Lassiter looked away and studied a group of residents—haggard men and women—filing through the cafeteria line. So young. Soon they would be experts at picking lead from gunshot wounds, standard fare in a county where gun control means holding it with two hands. "I'm not surprised by anything in this town, Charlie. Now, how about helping me with something else. A crime I can't figure out."

"Murder?"

"No, a burglary. One-point-six million in negotiable bonds from a client."

Charlie Riggs snorted. "Burglary. Ugly Anglo-Saxon word. *Burgh*, 'house' *laron*, 'theft.' A penny-ante crime for small minds. All that stuff about mastermind thieves is mostly fiction, you know. There've been some pretty glitzy B and Es, but mostly just second-rate smash-and-grab artists."

"As I recall, there've been some pretty good jewel heists."

"Hollywood," Riggs scoffed. "Take the Star of India theft from the Museum of Natural History. You know damn well Murph the Surf was just a beach bum from Miami."

Lassiter speared a fried plantain from Charlie's plate. "Nothing as exciting as a giant sapphire here. My client kept the bonds in his office. He's an old man who's got a younger woman working for him, hanging around the office, hanging all over him. She's got a look that says she's been around the track a few times and hasn't cashed any winning tickets yet. My client may be her last race."

"*Auri sacra fames*, the cursed hunger for gold. I assume she has an alibi."

"A most convenient one. She was with my client at the time of the theft."

"She has friends, does she not? A husband, boyfriend, nephew, that sort of thing. Have you done a workup on her, any surveillance?"

"The client won't let me. He's . . . fond of her."

"Fingerprints at the scene?"

"None."

"You've notified the banks, I suppose."

"Immediately."

"So what do you propose?"

"Don't know, Charlie. I could confront her, make the accusation, see her reaction."

"No. *Sapiens nihil affirmat quod non probat.* A wise man states as true nothing he cannot prove. You must have patience and wait. The problem with a burglary is there's no body. Bodies are full of clues. But with a burglary, the thieves take the *corpus delicti* with them. For the time being, you're stuck. Let the police handle it or mishandle it. But examine every clue they turn up. And don't go looking for any geniuses."

"I won't, Charlie. You're the only one I know."

CHAPTER 13

Goddess of Desire

At seven-thirty, Jake Lassiter pulled under the canopy of the Sonesta Beach Hotel and gave his yellow Olds convertible to a goofy teenage valet—"Rad, man, that a GTO?"—who promptly ground the gears. Lassiter gritted his teeth and walked to the veranda overlooking the ocean. In five minutes they appeared, freshly scrubbed and wholesome as a Pepsi ad.

Keaka's short black hair was still wet from the shower. He wore baggy cotton pants and a polo shirt, his arms strung with steel-cable veins. Lila had changed into a simple pink cotton dress, the sleeveless tank top clinging to her breasts and a full skirt falling away from a dropped waist. The long skirt flung easily with each athletic stride. When they walked outside and Lila felt the breeze from the Atlantic, she locked both hands behind her head, cradled her neck, and tossed her hair downwind. The ocean was streaked with creamy light as the moon rose in the east and smoothed a warm glow over her face. The wind was gusty and scented with salt, and as it blew, Lila's skirt gathered between her long, strong legs. She stood there with eyes closed, back arched, and breasts thrust forward, listening to a silent song, laughing into the wind.

Jake Lassiter stood transfixed. Her physical beauty was intoxicating, as natural as a windswept beach. Never had he seen a woman so exquisite, so removed from his world of the mundane and mendacious . . . and never one so beyond his reach. His mind recorded the sight, savored it, and burned it into place.

"God I love the wind," Lila said finally, her hair flying.

"Easterly," Lassiter said. "About eighteen knots, but there's a venturi effect here from the buildings. Feels more like twenty-five."

Idiot! He cursed himself. The occasion called for savoir faire, for poetry, anything but a weather report. Then the moment was gone.

With the top down, they headed across the Rickenbacker Causeway to the mainland, through downtown and across the MacArthur Causeway, the lights from the moored cruise ships twinkling in Government Cut. On South Beach, Keaka Kealia paused before entering Joe's, the famous stone crab restaurant, and said, "Surf here." His head was cocked toward the ocean half a mile away. Lassiter listened and couldn't hear a thing.

"The ocean's just at the end of the street," Lassiter said, "but not much surf, at least not by Hawaiian standards."

"Three feet, maybe a little less," Keaka announced judiciously.

They entered the restaurant, the Hawaiian still listening for the distant shore break, Lassiter wondering if he was being put on. A throng of tourists huddled in the foyer and the adjacent bar, and Lassiter had to elbow his way toward the maître d'.

In Miami, there are three enduring personalities who, like Franklin Roosevelt, have defined an era. There is Shula the coach, Fidel the dictator, and Roy the maitre d'. Without access to Roy, the highlight of your trip to Joe's was standing in line with fifty John Deere tractor salesmen from the Midwest.

Bespectacled and sleek in a black dinner jacket, Roy saw Jake towering over the crowd and waved him to the front. "How do you like the Fins against the Bills Sunday?" he asked.

"Give the points and put your money on Marino." It was the same advice he always gave—give the points, or take the points—but bet on the Dolphins. He was right about half the time.

The captain took them to a corner table under a black-and-white photo of Miami Beach in the 1930s. When they were seated, Lassiter turned to his guests. "Keaka, did you really know there was surf here?"

Lila said, "Keaka has a sixth sense for water. His ancestors paddled canoes from Tonga to Hawaii, and Keaka believes in reincarnation, so he thinks he was a great sailor or King Kalaniopuu from an earlier life."

Lassiter nodded nonchalantly, as if he often dined with reincarnated royalty. "King Kalan . . ."

Keaka smiled for the first time. "He killed Captain Cook."

"And ate him," Lila laughed.

"A lie!" Keaka barked at both of them. "A lie invented by the British. Cook was a fool. He did not know the people or the land but thought he was invincible because he had guns and the natives had only stones and slings."

The outburst silenced the table. Lassiter shifted uneasily in his chair, wanting to change the subject. Anything but cannibalism or the weather. But Keaka wasn't ready to let it go. "Do you know anything of Hawaiian history?"

"Not much," Lassiter answered. "There was one king who united the islands, wasn't there?"

Keaka gave a small smile of approval. "Kamehameha the Great, an invincible warrior. A string of war canoes four miles long. Of course, I am descended from Kamehameha the Great."

"Of course," Lassiter said.

Lila laughed and her hair fell across a shoulder. "It'd be hard to prove. Old Kame-ha-ha had about forty wives."

"Only twenty-one," Keaka corrected her. "Just enough to serve him."

"Give me a break," Lila said, "and pass the pumpernickel while you're at it, Keaka the Great."

Lassiter ordered stone crabs for the table. Boiled and served cold with a tangy mustard sauce, the hard colorful claws contain a meat sweeter than lobster. Keaka Kealia devoured his order and asked for a second portion. He ate quickly, going from one side dish to another, creamed spinach and hash browns and fried eggplant. Together, they put away several cold beers and the room became warmer. Around them was the clatter of plates and the cacaphony of voices. At the table, everything was in softer focus now, the atmosphere changed. Keaka became more talkative, weaving tales of Hawaiian folklore, warriors from the jungle defeating great forces of invaders. Lila's face radiated happiness, her eyes sparkling, and Lassiter thoughtfully concluded that the world's most glorious sight was a dab of mustard sauce clinging impossibly to a cheekbone carved by Michelangelo.

On request, Keaka passed the second portion of stone crabs to Lassiter, but suddenly he winced, and Lassiter caught the platter before it crashed to the table.

"Good reflexes," Keaka said.

"The pass-tip drill," Lassiter replied. "You okay?"

Keaka was silent. Lila looked at him and asked, "Did you soak your elbows today?"

The Hawaiian shook his head. "Later, at the hotel. Don't worry. I don't bother you about your problems."

Jake Lassiter waited, the outsider, figuring they would fill him in if they wanted to.

"Torn ligaments in both my ankles," Lila explained, "from hard landings in wave jumping. But it's really nothing compared to Keaka's elbows. Chronic tendonitis from all that pressure on the arms."

"Can't it be treated?"

"Sure," she said. "Anti-inflammatory pills, cortisone, tendon massage. Nothing works. Keaka soaks both elbows in ice after windsurfing every day."

"Like Sandy Koufax," Lassiter said.

"Who?" Keaka asked without taking his eyes from the claw he was dissecting.

"Pitcher," Lassiter said, making a throwing motion with his left arm. "Struck out fifteen Yankees in the first game of the Series in '63. Had a bad elbow that cut his career short."

"Yankees?" Keaka asked, clearly puzzled. *"Haoles?"*

Lila erupted in laughter. "It's a baseball team, Keaka."

Now Lassiter was puzzled. "What's a howley?" he asked.

"There's a culture gap here," Lila said. "*Haoles* are Caucasians, foreigners as far as the native Hawaiians are concerned. So when you said 'Yankees' . . ."

"I get it," Lassiter said.

Keaka silently ate his stone crabs, ignoring the conversation, seeming not to listen until he looked straight at Lassiter and announced, "You *haoles* are ridiculous. You wear too many clothes, ties that choke the neck and hang down like an old man's limp *ole*. Your women starve themselves and end up with chicken necks and hips sharp as bamboo sticks. You work in offices fifty weeks a year, then come to Maui and lie all day on a tiny piece of sand by your Hyatts and Marriotts where all you see are other *haoles*."

The attack startled Lassiter. Why this resentment directed at him? Lila waited for Lassiter's response, enjoying the verbal combat as if staged for her amusement.

Lassiter joined the battle. "Keaka, if you're saying that modern America has a lot to learn, I agree. But we can't all spend our days on the beach. Somebody's got to grow the grain and make the widgets and even try the lawsuits."

Lila's full mouth parted into a small, enigmatic smile. "Jake, we all must find ourselves, decide what to do with our lives. I know that I would be out of place in a city. And maybe I have no right to say this, but when I look at you, I don't see a lawyer in a three-piece suit and a fancy office. I see an outdoorsman, riding horses in the mountains, windsurfing on unspoiled waters."

Lassiter looked at Keaka. No expression. Back to Lila. Was she teasing him, leading him on?

"I don't know," he said, "you might think I was just another *haole*."

"No, Jake, you'd be different, I can tell."

Keaka laughed without smiling. "Would he know the mountain or the jungle or the sea? There are spirits on Maui that sing, but the *haoles* are deaf. They are forever strangers in my land."

Jake Lassiter cleared his throat and bought some time. Had it been a courtroom, he would have thumbed through some papers, stood up, hitched his thumbs in his belt, and prepared to counterattack. Here he just took a sip of the cold beer and thought it through. First Lila flirts with him, then Keaka insults him. And does it well. I knew the bastard could outwindsurf me, but he's outdebating me, too, Lassiter thought. A surprise witness catching him off guard. He had imagined they would talk about the latest in camber-induced sails and triple skegs, but Keaka was not just a jock and the sparring seemed to be for Lila's approval. How to win? To tell them their lives were meaningless, just waiting for the wind, doing stunts in the waves, empty days of barefoot bliss. But was his life any more meaningful, renting himself out by the hour to balloon-heads like Thad Whitney at the bank?

Finally Lassiter said, "Keaka, you speak very eloquently. Your thoughts are profound and you deliver them poetically. But you overgeneralize. Every culture has its philistines, even old Hawaii, I'm sure. We have no monopoly on evil here."

"It's not poetry, it's history," Keaka shot back. "The English came two hundred years ago to build ports for their ships in the Pacific. Then the American missionaries, who thought nakedness was sinful, so they covered our bodies with heavy clothes and made us stink like them. The *haoles* stole our land and brought disease and killed the whales and swallowed the fish in huge nets. They planted that damn weed, sugarcane, for what, to make Coca-Cola? Then they burned the cane in the fields and blackened the sky."

Any rebuttal, Counselor? a faraway judge whispered in Lassiter's ear. He tried to remember what he knew of Hawaii. The college football team was called the Rainbows, or was it the Pineapples, and a long time ago he had read the Michener book, or did he just see the TV movie and think he read the book?

"Even before the Europeans, weren't there constant wars on the islands?" Lassiter asked. "It wasn't exactly Camelot."

"Right," Lila said, patting Lassiter's arm. Her fingers lingered, and Lassiter's pulse quickened. "Keaka's ancestors used to get all painted up like Indians in a B Western and ride around in war canoes. The Big Island had five or six chiefs ruling different tribes, and they'd cut each other's hearts out."

Keaka narrowed his eyes and gestured toward both of them

with a table knife. "It is an honor to be a great warrior, to die a warrior's death." Then he silently examined a claw that was not cracked, apparently overlooked by the kitchen crew which used mallets to break the hard shells that give the crabs their name.

Lassiter said, "Don't worry, we'll send it back and they'll give it forty whacks."

"No need." Keaka scooped up the claw and it disappeared into a thick brown hand. The fingers closed and Lassiter watched ribbons of muscle pop from Keaka's forearm.

"That's not a walnut," Lassiter warned. "The shell's too thick . . ." A sharp crack interrupted him, the shell splitting into pieces. Blood spurted onto the tablecloth, a piece of jagged shell sticking from Keaka's thumb. Expressionless, he sucked at the wound for a moment, then devoured the meat from the claw.

The show of strength seemed intended for him, Lassiter thought, a primitive warning, a staking out of territory. Had he telegraphed his thoughts about Lila, or did every man?

"I didn't think that was possible," Lassiter said.

Keaka grunted. "It's easy. First you find the weak spot, then you apply pressure." He jutted out his chin and smiled, the look of a barracuda. Then he rubbed his right elbow with his left hand.

"Keaka here is hard as a rock everywhere," Lila said, squeezing Keaka's thigh and simultaneously harpooning Lassiter's morale. "But his elbow tendons are like spaghetti. He doesn't complain, too Hawaiian macho for that, but I know how much it hurts. I wonder how much longer he can go on. We're looking for easier ways to make money."

Keaka shot her a murderous glance. "Listen, I've heard enough about my elbows. It takes more than a sore elbow to stop a Hawaiian. More even than three bullets."

"Three bullets?" Lassiter asked.

Lila sighed. "A Hawaiian fable."

"No. True story," Keaka corrected her. "Haven't you ever heard the saying 'Never shoot a Hawaiian three times or you will make him really mad'?"

"No, must have missed that one," Lassiter conceded.

"Right after Pearl Harbor," Keaka said, "a Japanese pilot tries to get his plane back to its carrier but has engine trouble, so he puts it down on Niihau, one of the small islands. The local constable is a native Hawaiian, big-boned and a barrel for a stomach. He's unarmed, but he puts the little Jap pilot under arrest. The pilot takes out a pistol and shoots the Hawaiian in the gut, but it doesn't stop him. Bang, the Buddhahead shoots him again, but the Hawaiian's big and strong and just getting madder, then bang again, a third shot in the stomach. Then the Hawaiian picks up the Jap and crushes his skull against the plane."

Lila wore the look of a wife who has heard her husband tell the same golf yarn a hundred times. "Moral of the story," she said, "if I ever get mad at Keaka, I won't shoot him, I'll chop his big fat head off."

"You're the only one who would have a chance at it," Keaka said somberly. He turned to Lassiter, his black eyes humorless. "Lila is strong, quick, and fearless as a *pu'ali*, a great warrior."

"But can she type?" Jake Lassiter asked, and the blond warrior rewarded him with a knee-weakening smile.

A cool ocean breeze whipped across the Rickenbacker Causeway as they drove back to Key Biscayne, the lights of downtown Miami bouncing off the bay, the moon high overhead on a cloudless night. Traffic was light and in twenty minutes they were back at the hotel.

"Li'a, I'm going to make a call," Keaka said, heading for the front desk and leaving Lassiter and Lila standing together in the lobby.

Lassiter's look asked the question.

"Li'a was a forest goddess to the native Hawaiians," Lila said.

"Li'a," Lassiter repeated, letting the name linger on his tongue.

"In Hawaiian, it means desire or a powerful yearning. That's why the Hawaiians wrote so many love songs about Li'a."

"Goddess of Desire," Jake Lassiter said. "The name fits. The spirits of the forest are still alive in Li'a, beautiful Goddess of Desire."

"You're a very sweet man, and a very attractive one," she said with a provocative smile.

Now what did that mean? A thousand men must have complimented her name, her face and perfect body, but she was Keaka's alone, Lassiter thought. He looked toward the front desk, where Keaka was using a telephone.

"Probably calling his cousin Mikala on Maui," Lila said. "They've got business deals together. Will you wait with me?"

Only for a million years, he thought, and they sat down in cushioned chairs surrounded by ficus trees in the courtyard.

"Do you really want to get out of windsurfing?" Lassiter asked, his mind spinning.

Lila smiled a soft, wistful smile. "Like I said, I'm not going to give it up to work in an office somewhere, but I've swallowed water from nearly every ocean in the world. I've been stung by jellyfish, cut by fins, and been catapulted onto rocks and coral. If that isn't bad enough, it's gotten boring. Some days, I just don't want to load my equipment, pack six different sails, rig and rerig all day long. It's become routine and dull, sort of . . ."

"Mundane," Lassiter suggested.

"Right, mundane. That's the word."

"Like going to the office, whether you want to or not," Lassiter said.

"Right, or making love to someone just because he's there, whether you want to or not."

He tried to decipher the message on the parted lips that half smiled and half pouted at him. She looked at him for a response. He thought a thousand things and said none. No follow-through. He let the ball slip through his hands with the clock ticking down. Then it was too late, Keaka heading toward them, smiling his barracuda smile, the call apparently a success.

"Mikala agrees we should take care of our business as soon as possible, tonight even," Keaka said to Lila, and his look told Jake Lassiter it was time to say good night, which he did.

"So long, Jake," Lila Summers said. "Thanks for a wonderful evening. When you come to Maui, you'll become a *kamaaina*—a native—or almost one. You'll blend into the surroundings, become part of the mountains and the sea."

She laughed and her eyes danced and Lassiter wondered again if they held a promise or if he was the foil in a private game between these two strangers. He said good night a second time and walked outside, where a different valet looked at his ancient convertible as if it were a two-ton cockroach. Then the wind from the ocean slapped Lassiter's face and he told himself not to be such a goddamn fool.

CHAPTER 14

The Snitch

*Two years earlier, the hurricane had buried the marshy ham*mocks of the coastline under a ten-foot wall of water. The tidal surge, pushed by raging winds, ripped out seawalls and tossed boats onto lawns of waterfront homes. The winds cleaved at the vegetation, shattered roof tiles and rent asphalt felt from its plywood sheathing, splintering trusses from their hurricane straps. Roofs were blown to neighboring zip codes. Road signs were recovered twenty miles away. In an office near the bay, a five-hundred-pound desk flew through a window and was never found. In four hours, the winds and water created three million cubic yards of debris.

Along the southern shore of Biscayne Bay, gusts toppled giant oaks. The eye wall of the storm tore from the ground the shallow-rooted ficus trees and shredded the aerial roots of sprawling banyans. But when the water receded, the red and black mangroves—propped on roots aboveground—were still there, matted with sea grass and debris, gnarled as before. If royal palms were regal in their bearing, the mangroves were the crippled outcasts of a primitive society. Stunted, bent into impossible shapes, rooted in sand and salt, they were the sturdy survivors of eons of evolution and countless storms.

At night, the bowed and hunched trees of the swamp take on ghostly shapes, their silhouettes appearing as the arms of the tortured, reaching out in pain.

Berto splashed through the shallow water, ducking under the branch of a red mangrove, not seeing a curved root. He tripped and fell, banging his knee against the trunk of a submerged, long-dead tree, and dropping the duffel bag into the water. He cursed under his breath, picked up the bag, and kept going. Above him, through the branches of the mangroves, low silvery clouds scudded across the sky, obscuring a slice of moon. He swatted at a mosquito and succeeded in swatting his own ear. Gnats buzzed around his neck and tickled his nose. An unseen animal *splish-splashed* away in the darkness.

What a place to meet, he thought. Like one of those old black-and-white movies. *Creature of the Black Lagoon* or something like that. Man, the sooner you get your citified ass out of here, the better. That's the trouble with the assholes in this business. Too many movies. Passwords on the phone, hand signals, always afraid of wires and bugs. Dress this way, blink your lights three times, meet in the goddamn swamp. What bullshit he had to put up with. If he had it to do all over again . . .

That made him laugh.

If he had it to do all over again! Man, he'd change everything. Maybe he would have stayed in the practice of law, let *clients* sign the personal guarantees to the banks. Didn't he talk to Jake about that in the old days? *Hernandez-Zaldivar and Lassiter, P.A.* Or was it the other way around? But they never did it. What was it Jake always said?

"Berto, the courtroom's too small a stage for you. You've got to have your name in lights."

"With my name, it'll take a lot of lights."

He laughed again, took two more steps and stumbled.

Shit.

The water splashed onto his trousers. Three hundred bucks in Bal Harbour. Not that Franklin would care in his Sears polyester. Where was the guy? Was he so good at his job I won't know he's here?

Berto thought he heard something—a movement, a broken twig. He turned in the darkness but saw nothing, his Gucci loafers sinking into the mud. He strained to hear over the pounding of his heart and the buzz of mosquitoes around his ears. Then a jolt from behind, his feet out from under him, and he landed in the muck, his first thought a wild incongruity—could the dry cleaner get the mud out of his bird's-egg pleated Italian slacks? A moment later a vague feeling that his neck hurt.

"Heavy links," said the voice from behind him. "Gold? You would like gold, wouldn't you?"

The grip tightened on his chain and Berto swallowed and tried to look over his shoulder. A snap on the chain, a knee in the small of the back, and he was staring straight ahead into the blackness. "You'll turn when I tell you," the voice said in a controlled tone barely above a whisper.

Dense clouds covered the moon now, the curtain of mangrove trees closing around them, drawing them nearer in the muck of the swamp.

He strained to talk. "What do you want?"

"The money," the voice ordered.

"In the duffel bag," Berto whimpered. He kicked at the canvas sack at his feet. "*Por favor*, some air."

The gold noose loosened a bit and Berto sucked in a long, greedy breath. At the same time he rubbed his neck, wondering if he could reach the pistol in his ankle holster. It was not going the way it should, not the way it had been planned. Where the hell was Franklin? Another absurd thought—maybe the budget-crunching feds refused overtime for a DEA bodyguard.

"Is it all there?" Another whisper in the darkness.

"Twenty thousand now, the rest when you bring the stuff in. Plus a bonus."

"Liar!" The voice startled him, strange and unfamiliar, and another yank from behind. The chain lifted Berto to his feet, the links digging into his neck, drawing blood. "Turn around," the voice commanded, a firm grip steering him. Berto staggered in a circle, gasping, blinking through tears from the pain, a blaze of lights behind his eyelids, torches of agony igniting the darkness.

Silence, then a whisper again, frightening in its softness. "Are you afraid to die? Maybe you will come back as a warrior, instead of the worthless little snitch you are."

Berto shivered with cold fear. "Please, just take the money," he begged, the words barely audible above the crazed song of a million insects.

"Of course I'll take the money." A hint of amusement now.

The pressure on the chain loosened. Then a hard punch, palm upward, knuckles clenched, aimed precisely at the Adam's apple. In the dark Berto never saw it coming, never flinched. There was a crunch, then a sickening gurgling sound. Berto collapsed into the mud, gasping for breath that would not come.

A second later, powerful, gloved hands circled his wounded

neck. The hands pressed steadily. Deprived of air, Berto's body began to shake, his feet dancing a palsied jig. Pinpoint hemorrhages popped out on his eyelids and scalp, then the cartilage of the larynx *cra-acked* like a chicken's wishbone, and finally, his tongue, elevated by the pressure of the hands on the neck, shot out of the mouth, at first bloody and red, but by sunrise, long after the killer had left, black and grotesque as death itself.

CHAPTER

15

Your Basic Police Work

*Thursday already. The race two days away. Time to take in*ventory, Jake Lassiter thought, knowing he'd come up a few items short. No leads on the missing coupons. No word from the Miami Beach cops, what could you expect? And Lila on his mind, clouding the sky. A vague feeling of uneasiness. Paying too little attention to work. Thaddeus G. Whitney had been calling all day, and Lassiter had ducked him. A bunch of other phone messages piled up, but then Cindy buzzed.

"Your favorite *policía* on line *dos, jefe.*"

"G'day, Lassiter," Sergeant Carraway announced cheerfully.

"Picture was clean, no prints. I'll keep it in my wallet as a souvenir. Hey, the slut's got some pair."

The cop sounded so happy Lassiter wondered if he'd been drinking. No, he was probably a nasty drunk.

"Here's something else might interest you, Counselor. Last night, me and my partner spot a couple greasers prying open a soda machine at Alton Road Texaco after hours. I don't move so good anymore, but Georgy boy, excuse me, Whore-hay, he thinks he's fast, runs on his toes like the girls are watching. Fact is, he's muscle-bound and a meathead, would never have caught up except one of the punks is limping like a horse kicked him—shit, at first I thought he was crippled. Anyway, my partner grabs him halfway down the block, poor kid musta tripped 'cause his collarbone seems to have fractured by the time he's put in the blue-and-white which, by the way, is where I been waiting 'cause I ain't chasin' no more greasers down alleys."

What's he getting at? The fat sergeant didn't move fast and he sure as hell didn't tell a story fast.

"Anyway, while Whore-hay is working up a sweat catching one out of two, I do what you might say is your basic police work."

"Sergeant, spare me the details. What the hell's this got to do with Sam Kazdoy's coupons?"

"I'm getting there, Counselor. I look over at the soda machine, figure I might have me a diet Coke, 'cause I'm watching my girlish figure, and of course, caffeine-free 'cause I'd like to get some shut-eye. Well, what do I see on the ground but a little crowbar they were using to bust open the machine. Wouldn't have thought nothing about it, except we're Mirandizing the kid and Whore-hay, he's a stickler for the rules, tells the little prick he's being charged with malicious mischief, attempted larceny, trespass, resisting arrest with violence, and possession of burglary tools, to wit, one crowbar. So the kid, who's dumber than a lump of yeast, he says it's not *his* crowbar, some guy gave it to him the other night. And where'd this guy give it to you, I ask real innocent. He says, in the alley behind the South Side Theater."

Carraway paused, letting it hang there, basking in the silence. "You like this story, Counselor?"

"It's getting better. He give you a description?"

"Not much a one. Short guy dressed like those assholes in the Everglades, you know, the ones throwing grenades at the snakes, training to overthrow Fidel?"

"Bay of Pigs Brigade," Lassiter said.

"Right, a dark little guy in a camouflage jacket, probably Latino. This mystery man supposedly comes out the back door of the theater, has a . . . discussion with our two soda banditos, ends up giving them his crowbar as a gift."

"What about the crowbar?" Lassiter asked. "Any prints, any scratches?"

"Good questions, Counselor. Very good. You could be a dick. Maybe you are a dick, eh?"

Let him have his fun, Lassiter thought. Making you drag it out of him. Still pissed at the way you rubbed his face in it at the theater.

"Only prints are the kid's. Name's Rodriguez, ain't they all? Lassiter, you know how many pages of Rodriguezes in the Miami phone book. No? Take a guess. Okay, I'll tell you, fifteen fuckin' pages, a septic tank full of Rodriguezes."

"Sergeant, what's this got to do with—"

"You're wondering how Phil Carraway knows this. 'Cause Rodriguez is a juvenile and the old sarge gotta call the dipshit's mother, only the kid's got a bad memory for addresses and phone numbers."

"Sergeant, what's—"

"Now this Rodriguez ain't even Cuban. He's a Puerto Rican, musta got lost on his way to New York. Hey, Lassiter, how come there are so few Puerto Rican doctors?"

Lassiter was silent, knowing the burned-out cop would provide his own punch line.

" 'Cause you can't write prescriptions with spray paint."

Lassiter had to wait for the sergeant to stop laughing at his own moronic joke. "Carraway, the Beach ought to enroll you in an ethnic awareness program."

"Won't do no good, 'cause I hate everybody," he said with obvious pride. "Now, where was I?"

"The prints! What else besides the prints?"

"Oh, I almost forgot. Thanks to the wonders of modern technology, the lab says the brown paint from your client's cabinet matches exactly a speck on the tip of the crowbar, plus some oxidized fragments from the bar turn up in the scratches on the cabinet. You like the story now?"

"Love it. Good work, what's next?" The son of a bitch had been stringing him along.

"Getting the little fucker to tell us where the coupons are."

"What! The kid doesn't have them. He wouldn't be breaking into a Coke machine if he knocked off one-point-six million the night before."

"He might if he didn't know what he had. I'm not buying the shit about getting the crowbar in the alley, little guy in a camouflage outfit, come on."

"Carraway, I don't believe you. Rodriguez is a *lead* to the burglar, not the burglar. The guy who broke in had help from inside, a taped-over latch. The Rodriguez kid would've busted a window."

"Not if he had help from somebody who knew what was there."

"Like who?"

"How should I know? Maybe you and the blonde with the big maracas gave him a new skateboard for bringing out the old man's coupons, so he still has to steal quarters."

"You've lost it, Carraway. They should've put you out to pasture years ago."

"Don't worry. I ain't writing you two up. Too much work. Far as I'm concerned, the kid broke in on his own. By the way, I asked him about the photo, swore on his virgin sister he never saw it. I figure he picked it up in the old man's office, was gonna jerk off later, maybe he did in the alley. You didn't see any pecker tracks out there, didja?"

"Carraway, you're a disgrace. You're shutting down the investigation."

"Not so. Just shifting it. When the kid gets a public defender appointed, we'll offer a deal. Return the coupons, he can plead to trespass, get ten days in Youth Hall, spends more time there than home anyway."

Lassiter gritted his teeth. "There can't be a deal! The kid doesn't have the bonds, anybody can see that. He probably saw the burglar come out of the theater, maybe toss the crowbar into a dumpster. We have to find the guy he saw. And what about Violet Belfrey? You should have put her under surveillance. Who does she hang out with? Does she have a rap sheet. I'll bet you never even checked her record . . ."

"Wrong. Couple liquor code violations when she tended bar in North Carolina. Soliciting for prostitution fifteen years ago in Jax, same thing in Daytona Beach and Fort Pierce—musta worked her way down the coast on her back—all penny-ante stuff. Not a felony charge in the bunch, no break-ins, no grand larceny. Just an over-the-hill piece who's got your client seeing stars. With his money you'd think he could do better."

The sergeant laughed and hung up. It was useless. Carraway just didn't want to work it. I should talk to the kid, Lassiter thought, get a better description of the guy with the crowbar. Maybe hire Tubby Tubberville to tail Violet Belfrey. Wonder if a bearded 260 pounder on a Harley can be inconspicuous. Could go over Carraway's head in the department, but it takes time . . . and Cindy buzzing again.

"Now what?" he asked.

"A very important message, which I have taken the liberty of putting into my own words."

"People have been arrested for using some of your words. Shoot."

" 'If you don't get your two-hundred-fifty-dollar-an-hour ass to the bank, pronto, they'll find a lawyer who will.' "

"Okay, I get it, Thad called."

"Actually, I toned it down. He wasn't as polite."

Lassiter dialed Whitney's direct number. Just as the bank counsel answered with a gruff "Yeah," Cindy popped in the door, looking frazzled. "Another *gendarme*, line *deux*."

"Miami Beach?"

"No, *mon patron*, Metro."

Lassiter frowned and disconnected Whitney, a violation of the managing partner's Ten Commandments concerning the care and stroking of clients.

"Lassiter, this is Officer Joaquin Morales. We'd like you to come down to Matheson Hammock, you know where that is?" A faint Hispanic accent, a very polite tone, one of the new breed of county cops trained in human relations and interpersonal communication.

"Sure, the last bit of nature not paved over or built on. What's up, Officer?"

"A body, sir."

"A dead body?"

"That's the usual kind," the officer said, without a hint of humor. "We need to talk to you."

"Why me? Whose body?"

"The subject is not identified, or rather, I am not to identify the subject to you, sir."

The subject. Damn police lingo.

"Can you come right away?" Morales asked, pleasantly but firmly.

"Sure, but I still don't get it. What am I supposed to know?"

"Sorry, sir, not supposed to say anything else. You could bring a lawyer if you want."

"You know any good ones, Officer?"

"No, sir. They're all sleazebags, sir."

CHAPTER 16

A Crummy Place to Díe

T*here were brown shirts everywhere, the uniform of Metro dep-*uties, county cops standing ankle deep in swampy mangroves that haven't changed since Ponce de León landed on Florida's shores. Officer Joaquin Morales led Lassiter under the orange rope that cordoned off the side road into the hammock. The cop was young, muscular, and handsome, a recruiting poster.

"Watch your step through here," Morales said.

It was as if the trees had been yanked up by a celestial gardener, propped three feet out of the ground. The roots were hundreds of reptiles entwined, grabbing at Lassiter's ankles, trying to spill him into the black, malevolent water. The trees were mostly red and black mangroves, some lignum vitaes, close together, blocking out the sun.

Tiny gnats—no-see-ums, the locals called them—buzzed around Lassiter's ears. There were patches of dry ground, black dirt pocked with holes the size of a man's fist, where land crabs dug their homes. Small black mangrove roots stuck out of the ground, hundreds of them a few inches apart, sharp and deadly.

Maybe all life started in a place like this, Lassiter thought, different organic matters fermenting over millions of years until some protoplasm oozed out of the swamp. Maybe, but what a crummy place to die.

By the time they reached a dry spot where a cluster of cops huddled, sweat was splotching his blue oxford cloth shirt. Somewhere over the canopy of tangled trees, the midday sun shone, but in the bowels of the marshy hammock, it was gray and damp.

Lassiter expected to see a body under a white sheet, neat and clean, ready to be hauled away. But there in a tree, his feet dangling just above the brackish water, Humberto Hernandez-Zaldivar hung from a thick mangrove branch by a gold chain the diameter of a thumb. The chain dug deep into the soft flesh of his neck, and his head flopped to one side. A storm of gnats buzzed in his open mouth. Tiny parasites had already hollowed out one eye, and blowfly eggs were deposited in the corner of the other eye.

Jake Lassiter wasn't ready. He took an involuntary step backward, then braced himself against one of the ugly trees, the skeletons of the swamp. "Berto," he whispered. "Why?"

The cops watched him. Then one came over. Tired eyes, neatly trimmed hair, a face that could have been thirty or forty and had forgotten how to smile. He was dressed in jeans and muddy running shoes. "Farrell, Metro Homicide. Whadaya know?"

Maybe the last Anglo cop for fifty miles if you didn't count Carraway at CMB who wasn't worth counting.

"Berto Hernandez-Zaldivar. He's an old friend of mine."

"No shit. We thought he was the Duke of Windsor."

Lassiter glared at the detective. "He was a friend of mine."

The cop shrugged. "Even dopers got friends."

"Want to tell me what happened?"

"Sure thing. Your buddy was a federally protected witness. Great protection, huh? Best we can figure, he was supposed to meet with a bad guy. DEA agent was tailing the bad guy, maybe gets lost or tails the wrong one. Not rating two babysitters, Señor Zaldivar comes out here after midnight all by his lonesome trying to set up a guy bringing coke in from the Bahamas. Somehow he blew it. That's the problem with amateurs. Their assholes get all puckered up, they forget their lines."

"Why'd you haul me out here?"

"To see what you know about it."

"What would I know?"

"You were seen on the beach with him. And in a restaurant. Plus he's got your business card in the pocket of his chichi slacks."

Chichi. Now there's a word coming from a homicide detective. Guess he's seen a lot of well-dressed corpses—Italian suits, silk shirts, the whole Latino drug shtick. Berto definitely was not dressed for a walk in a swamp. Soft leather loafers, pleated cotton pants, and a loose linen shirt. Lassiter avoided looking at his bloated face, black tongue sticking out to one side, mouth open with the jaw hanging slack, and bloody mucus protruding from each nostril.

"My card?" Lassiter said absentmindedly. "I don't know. He could've had it a while. Could've picked it up in my office earlier this week."

"That so? What was he doing in your office?"

"Sorry, Officer. Attorney-client privilege." One word about the ranch property and the feds could try to void the transfer to Great Southern Bank. Still the lawyer, Lassiter would clam up.

"Didn't know you were his attorney."

"Didn't say I was."

"You wanna get cutesy, I lay a subpoena on you, you come talk to us downtown."

"Fine, you don't ruin your shoes in the grand jury room." It's tiring to argue with cops all day, Lassiter thought. First, the lard-butt from the Beach and now this guy, probably has two hundred unsolved homicides and wishes they'd just go away.

A third man joined them, toddling over on bowed legs, a lab coat stopping just above green wading boots. "I've had my look, Officer, and can give you a preliminary report," he said.

"Charlie!"

"Hello, Jake. Heard they were calling you. I'm sorry about this, sorry I was right about Berto. As the Romans said, *abyssus abyssum invocat*, hell calls hell. I've just seen it so often . . ."

"Charlie, what are you doing here?"

"I was fishing for mullet in the bay off Lugo Point. Had my police scanner on, and when I heard the call, I just waded over. The M.E.'s sending someone out, but what the hell, I've dragged enough bodies out of swamps to help them for a while."

"You establish cause of death, Doc?" the detective asked.

"*Mortui non mordent*, dead men carry no tales. That's blatantly false, of course, and a good thing, or I'd have been out of work these last thirty years. Let's see. There are no bullet or knife wounds. The little hemorrhages on the eyelids, Tardieu's spots, are consistent with asphyxiation, the marks on the neck consistent with strangulation."

Lassiter asked, "Did he suffer much?"

"Afraid so. Sometimes strangulation can be very peaceful. Take a hanging. If the rope just shuts off the carotid artery, no blood gets to the brain, you get drowsy, just fall asleep in two or three minutes. Here, we've got broken laryngeal cartilage, a fractured hyoid bone, and the first collapsed trachea I've seen since a Brazilian carpenter rolled his van over his best friend's throat in what the papers called a love triangle. *Amantes sunt amentes*, lovers are lunatics. Now you crush somebody's trachea, we're talking major-league pain, the body gets air-hungry, involuntary gasps, a lot of struggling."

Lassiter turned away. The fetid darkness of the swamp enveloped him. Tiny insects found his neck, searching for blood. Unseen animals rippled the still, black water.

Detective Farrell listened with a look of casual indifference. Just another corpse, and this one a doper—so much the better—save the feds all those relocation expenses. Finally, he asked, "So what'd the killer use to do all that damage?"

Charlie Riggs scratched his beard. "No ligature marks, except where the gold chain is supporting his weight, so there's no rope or garrote involved. A single bruise on either side of the midline right over the thyroid cartilage. Here, let me demonstrate . . ."

From behind, Charlie Riggs placed his hands around the detective's throat. "See, when I press, the tips of my fingers close over the thyroid. Now, ordinarily in manual strangulation, you have little crescent abrasions or cuts on the throat."

"Fingernails," the detective said.

"Exactly. But no such marks here. I would say to a reasonable medical probability the deceased was strangled by two very strong hands wearing gloves. Football player, weight lifter, guy who swings a pick all day, not a nearsighted pathologist with pencil wrists."

Detective Farrell looked hard at Jake Lassiter. "Awright, Counselor, whadaya know?"

Lassiter thought of seeing Berto on the beach. He wouldn't mention Keaka Kealia, not until he sorted it out. He could remember that later.

"Have you talked to his girlfriend, an Asian stew?"

"Yeah, Lee Hu. Goes by Little Lee. Flies for Avianca. Bogotá, Buenos Aires, Guatemala City."

"Bogotá?"

"Yeah, ain't that interesting? She's dicking a guy who's a known trafficker and every two weeks, just like clockwork, she's in the capital of cokedom. She's bid the route for the past year. Even switched a couple of trips to get it."

"Any priors?"

"Nah, nothing. Looks clean, Japanese parents, grew up on the West Coast. Junior college education, lived with a guy owns a restaurant in the Grove, kind of a hangout for the high-rise cokers. Then she starts shacking up with your late friend here."

Two cops were hauling Berto down, lifting him up by the legs to get the thick gold chain to unhook from the tree limb. The detective continued, "There is one thing, though. On trips she used to room with a Cuban chick. Carmen Ramos. Both of them get off a flight from Bogotá at MIA one day, Carmen Ramos collapses in shock, they carry her off the concourse, dies on the way to the hospital. Had two condoms filled with coke in her vagina . . . one broke."

"Must have figured no one would look there," Lassiter said.

"Well, all the girls know we do body-cavity searches on South American flights if we got probable cause, unless it's the girl's wrong time of month. Well, Carmen Ramos was under surveillance 'cause she had a prior, simple possession here. But get this—she's on the rag—at least she's wearing a Tampax, but the canoe maker downtown says she was clean enough to eat."

Charlie Riggs clucked his tongue in disapproval.

"I don't get it," Lassiter said.

"Must have borrowed the Tampax, maybe from her roomie, Lee Hu," the detective said. His eyes flicked over the corpse. "After all, how many people can you ask for something like that? And if Lee Hu knew what was coming down, she'd have been an accessory. Regardless, the feds have reason to believe that the late Carmen Ramos was working for the late Hernandez-Zaldivar."

"Berto told me the marijuana load in the Glades was his first and last job."

"Counselor, you'd make a shitty shamus if you believe everything a doper tells you. Your pal was a middleman, a wholesaler. Somc Colombian cowboys would get the shit to the Bahamas, he'd buy it there, arrange to get it here by boat, plane . . . who knows . . . pussies."

"You think Lee Hu was a mule?"

"Maybe. Though I doubt if she'd stuff it up her chute after what happened to her roomie."

"I doubt much would fit," Lassiter said.

"Really?"

"From outward appearances."

"Careful, Counselor, you could be a suspect if you're bird-dogging his chippy."

"That's great. One cop accuses me of stealing a million bucks from my favorite client, now you think I killed an old friend. You want to talk about anything else?"

"No. I just wanta know what this slimeball friend of yours was doin' in your office."

"Get a court order."

"You protecting somebody? 'Cause if you are—"

"Don't threaten me. Don't even talk to me."

Lassiter turned and splashed back through the swamp. When he got back to the road, he saw Biscayne Bay on the other side of the clumps of palms. A small wading beach emerged from the dark of the swamp into the bright sunlight that ricocheted off the wide expanse of flat bay. A dozen white egrets flew low overhead, scouting the shallow water, on the lookout for dinner. The breeze that couldn't find its way into the mangroves formed small whitecaps on the clean, open bay.

To the east he could see Key Biscayne and to the north, where the shoreline curved, his high-rise office building dominated the horizon. He walked into the water, leather shoes sinking into the sand, scattering crabs no larger than a toenail. He dropped to his knees, his gray suit pants soaking up the bay. Then he dunked his head and held his breath, held it as long as he could, letting the water cleanse him. When he came up, Jake Lassiter ran his hands through his sandy hair, wringing it out, and he rubbed his eyes, the saltwater from the bay mixing with his tears.

CHAPTER
17

Free as the Wind

H*arry Marlin thought he'd feel like a millionaire by now, but* he didn't. He was just a guy with a problem, a guy trying to cash his chips and he couldn't find the window and here was Violet yammering at him.

"We gotta get them kew-pons to the Bahamas," Violet Belfrey was saying. She had said it so many times Harry Marlin was getting a migraine. Christ, this dame gets something in her head, she don't let go.

"I heard Jake Lassiter talking on the beach the other day," she said. "There's a big bank there, Great Bahama Bank."

"I heard of it," Harry allowed.

"That's where they're paying off the whatchacallits, the water surfers."

"Makes sense," Harry agreed.

"And that first day in the theater with the cops and the old man, I was listening real good, and Lassiter says he's worried about the coupons ending up at banks in the Bahamas. It's what the dopers do with their cash. They wash it."

"Launder it," Harry corrected her.

"Launder, dry-clean, whatever. So I put two 'n two together, we gotta get 'em to the Bahamas, to the Great Bahama Bank."

The Bahamas, the Bahamas, the Bahamas—she was still going. "Okay," he said finally. "I'll take 'em to the friggin' Bahamas."

Violet Belfrey dropped Harry Marlin off at the airport, praying he wouldn't fuck it up. It had to be Harry, what other choice did she have? She couldn't leave town with the cops poking around, so she watched Harry disappear into the crowd, whistling off-key as he carried a heavy canvas tote bag to the Bahamasair gate.

"Stay away from the damn casino," Violet had warned him, remembering how quickly an eagle had flown the coop in Nassau.

"Not to worry, Vi. The slots are for housewives, and roulette's for suckers. Shooting craps, though, I can get hot."

"Har-ry Marlin!"

"Okay, okay." They'd hit a classy casino someday just for the hell of it, Harry thought, maybe Vegas, catch Wayne Newton or, hey, Monte Carlo, wear a tux like James Bond, play one of those fancy card games. Harry couldn't wrap his brain around the names chemin de fer or trente-et-quarante, so he imagined himself rolling the dice, placing thousand-dollar bets, wondering if they played chuck-a-luck in Monte Carlo or Biarritz. He was mentally raking in a pot, when he saw a com-

motion just ahead of him on the international concou[r]
was the Bahamasair gate, and a dozen guys in blue nylon
ets came running by, one so close Harry felt the breeze.
jackets had foot-high yellow letters, POLICE, what they
when knocking down a door in a Liberty City crack house
they don't want a jittery rookie blasting the shit out of
fellow lawmen. Behind the nylon jackets, three or four pla
clothes guys jogged down the concourse, little walkie-talkies
their hands, sports coats flapping over their asses. No gu
drawn, not yet, but something was coming down.

"What's happening?" Harry asked a uniformed securit
guard who apparently had ceded his authority to the real cops.

The guard, a skinny black man with runny eyes, said, "Drug bust, what else? Bahamasair three-fourteen from Freeport. They got a tip, holding it at the gate, gonna search every passenger."

Harry turned around just in time to have a German shepherd stick its nose in his crotch. A woman cop restrained the dog by a leather collar big enough to saddle a thoroughbred. "Whoa, Rex! Sit, boy," she commanded.

The security guard started laughing, a hacking cough of a laugh, and spittle dribbled from the corner of his mouth. "Whatch you got in there, boy? That dog trained to sniff for co-cay-un but he wanta do a short-arm inspection on you. You creamin' in your jeans?"

Harry's eyes darted from the guard to the woman cop to Rin Tin Tin, who was one horny canine. "Jock itch," Harry said. "Had to talcum my privates."

The woman cop regarded him suspiciously, but then two more dogs and their handlers were running down the concourse, and she followed them, dragging off Harry's admirer by a leather leash. Harry decided to get the hell out of there. Who knows, they might seal off the concourse, search everybody.

The airport's not safe for your honest business travelers, Harry Marlin thought as he retreated to the entrance. Welcome to friggin' Miami.

At about the same time that Harry Marlin was bemoaning the lawlessness that closed down Bahamasair, Jake Lassiter sat at his desk, mourning his friend Berto. He'd had twenty-four hours to play it back, Berto at the beach with Keaka and Lee Hu, Franklin behind the dune with the binoculars.

Again, phone messages piling up, only one in verse:

Angry skies,
A foul wind,
The banker calls.

No mistaking that one. Thad Whitney. Half a dozen pink telephone slips. Lassiter buzzed Cindy to tell her he was going over to the bank. Ordinarily she would have hustled him out of there. Not today.

"You're not in the right frame of mind to see that twit," she told him. But Lassiter went anyway, a black tempest of storm clouds brewing in his mind.

*The corner office on the bank tower's forty-first floor was im*maculate—no piles of papers and correspondence, no messy phone messages cluttering the sleek marble desk, no files stacked on the beige carpet. And no smile on the face, much less a pleasant thought behind the bleak visage of Thaddeus G. Whitney, Great Southern Bank's general counsel. Lassiter looked out the floor-to-ceiling window, warmed by the midday sun. On a clear day you could see across the Gulf Stream to

Bimini. Today, it was breezeless and humid, and a haze of auto smog wrapped the high rise in a noxious cocoon.

An unlit cigarette dangled from Whitney's mouth, a pitiful attempt to toughen his doughy face. "Jake, where the hell you been? Jesus H. Christ, you won't believe it."

"What's the problem, Thad?" Lassiter asked listlessly, his mind elsewhere.

"Problem? Your Commie EEOC is the problem. Some shyster just called me and five minutes later a *Miami Herald* reporter because a VP in PB terminated an AAT who also happens to be a DBF."

"Say what? You've got an employment complaint, that's about as much as I picked up."

"Whatsa matter? You play too much football without a helmet? Without my approval, without any oversight by Legal or Personnel, one of our vice presidents in Personal Banking just fired an administrative assistant trainee."

"Yeah?"

"The trainee is a black woman who also happens to sit in a wheelchair."

"A disabled black female," Lassiter said.

"You got it."

Lassiter shook his head. "A potential three-bagger. Race, sex, and handicapped discrimination, all in one case."

Whitney ran a hand through his receding hair, his fingers leaving trails through the colorless strands. He lit the cigarette, which, by now, had gone soggy around the filter. "There's more. She alleges that Phil Bannister, our veep, used to corner her in the hallway by the lunchroom. Small turning radius, she couldn't wheel herself away."

"Keep going," Lassiter said.

For the first time Lassiter could remember, Whitney looked embarrassed. "He grabbed her boobs. Every day for a month, she'd get stuck there, he'd grab her boobs."

"Sexual harassment, too, a home run. I've never had a case with four employment law violations."

"To make matters worse, he was groping her during her coffee break."

"I don't see what difference that makes."

"She's one of your Muslims, was headed to the lunchroom to read her Koran. Bannister told her it was against bank policy to pray during working hours."

"Apparently it's okay to cop a feel."

Whitney shrugged.

"Religious discrimination, too," Lassiter said, "a five-bagger. Legal history in the making. Thad, you'll be in all the legal journals. *Sixty Minutes* will knock on your door. Any idea why your sleazy vice president did it?"

"Bannister's not real popular with the women," Whitney said.

"I don't doubt it."

"They usually take an instant dislike to him."

"Probably figure it'll save time."

"So he's got a thing for paraplegics. Doesn't like women with a moving target. Anyway, when this one wouldn't put out, he fired her without consulting me. Her lawyer's a sole practitioner. I need you to tie up the case, get continuances, take interlocutory appeals, paper them to death, whatever it takes."

Lassiter shook his head. "Not my style."

"What do you suggest?" Whitney asked, his pale eyes narrowing.

"Settle now. Pay her. Rehire her, give a written apology, fire Bannister, and teach the rest of your officers some simple manners."

"Fire Phil? You crazy? He's my golf partner. And spare me the lecture. Bannister could testify the crip came on to him, he felt sorry for her, goes for a charity fuck, she cries wolf."

"You want me to suborn perjury?"

"I want you to *win*. That's what I pay you for."

"You pay me for my advice in your office and my skill in the courtroom," Lassiter said without emotion. "I don't do your dirty work. I don't lie to the court or let a client do it."

Whitney's head snapped back as if he had taken a jab to his chin. "Whose side you on?"

"That's what I'm trying to figure out."

"I'd suggest you do your figuring in a hurry," Whitney said, exhaling foul smoke through his nose.

"Look, Thad, I've had a rough week. I'm just trying to make it till tomorrow. I have a client who gets ripped off for a million and a half in negotiable paper, and I think his lady friend was in on it. Then my old trial partner gets his neck wrung and strung up like a twelve-point buck."

"I heard, actually I read, what'd the paper call him, a 'socialite'? What a hoot. He's a socialite like I piss Pouilly-Fuissé."

Jake Lassiter decided to let that one pass. He couldn't expect much compassion from Thad Whitney, a guy whose Lincoln Town Car wore the personalized license plate 4-CLOSE. Lassiter had seen the newspaper story, ten graphs under a two-column head CUBAN SOCIALITE STRANGLED. Nothing about drugs, but most readers assume it anyway. Funny the way headline writers sum it up for you, a life in a word.

Thad Whitney was saying something. What was it? And who cared?

"It is taken care of, right?" Whitney asked.

"What?"

"Hey, Jake, anybody home? You with me, fella?"

"Must have been thinking of something else."

"So it's signed, right?"

"What's that?"

"The *deed*, for crying out loud! The Cuban's ranch to the bank, the quitclaim deed you promised me. I trust you got the deed signed before this dastardly crime wiped out one of Miami's most eminent citizens. I told the Board last week I'd gotten security for the condo loans, they thought I was hot shit, so I owe you one. With him getting snuffed, you and I look like geniuses to get it squared away like that. We're talking *mucho grande* bonus for yours truly."

The heat rose from inside Lassiter, and he waited a moment, hoping it would pass. He tried to think of something else, something besides moving Whitney's bland little nose in the general direction of one of his bland little ears or maybe opening the door and tossing him into the lobby of the Legal Department, probably getting cheers all around. Lassiter tried to think of clear skies and steady winds and Lila Summers. It almost worked; he almost let it pass. But not quite.

"Yeah, he signed the deed, now I wish he hadn't, wish I hadn't made a jerkoff like you look good."

"Hey, you got some mouth on you." Whitney got out of his chair and began walking around his office, trying to look tough now, ever the asshole. "You forgetting Great Southern's good for half a mil a year to Harman and Fox. Your partners would slice you up like snapper fillet if you blew that."

"Thad, can you get it through your thick head that Berto was my friend and he's dead?"

"My condolences. But he was a turd. You can polish a turd, drive it around in a limo, dress it up in suits and gold chains, but it's still a turd."

Lassiter slowly rose from the chair, his face calm, eyes focused on a distant shore. Whitney saw him coming, got a funny look on his face like he ate something that didn't agree with him, raised his arms, and stepped backward.

With arms that had fought off bull-necked tight ends, with wrists strengthened from tugging a boom through thirty-knot winds, Lassiter raised Whitney off the floor by his lapels, not looking into that bland face, and Whitney flushed with fear.

Then Lassiter shook him, shook him until Whitney's head flopped forward and back, shook him till his own shoulders ached, shook him for Berto and for Sam and for Jake himself, shook him to purge whatever poison ate away inside him, to become free as the wind.

Lassiter didn't hear the door open but there was a gasp and a crash of china as Thad Whitney's secretary dropped the tray she was carrying, two cups of coffee splotching the beige carpeting, a spot to last the ages, to remind Thad Whitney of the day. Jake Lassiter let go then, Whitney crumpling over his desk like a sack of flour.

Jake Lassiter loosened his tie, unbuttoned his shirt collar, and calmly walked to the elevator, trying to figure out what the hell to do with the rest of his life.

CHAPTER 18

Misty Rain

Just before sunset, Jake Lassiter headed to his coral rock pillbox between Kumquat Avenue and Poinciana in Coconut Grove. He parked under a chinaberry tree, kicked one of the rally wheels just for the hell of it and slammed the door, hard. The front bumper didn't fall off, but the grille seemed to frown and from somewhere inside, springs and cylinders and bushings whinnied like an old horse.

The front door of the house wasn't locked, just swollen shut from the humidity. Lassiter opened it with a good drive block—head up, shoulders square—and stripped off his suit and black oxfords. He changed into cutoffs and nothing else and, for no good reason, uncoiled the hose, washed down the Olds 442, and worked up a sweat massaging paste wax into the canary-yellow finish. The exertion demanded a two-pack of sixteen-ounce Grolsch with the porcelain stoppers.

He found three slices of pizza in the refrigerator, the ends curled up like old shoes left in the rain. He dropped the Beach Boys into a tape player almost as old as Brian Wilson and sang along to "Little Surfer Girl," missing the high notes by twenty yards.

Thinking of Lila Summers.

Regressing. A picture from a magazine. A symbol of something, what? Freedom, youth, pleasure.

Overgrown adolescent jerk, he told himself, reaching for another Dutch brew, crawling into the hammock slung between live oak trees. Falling asleep there in the yard, throwing the porcelain stoppers at a redheaded woodpecker with a machine-gun beak. Missing it, too, by twenty yards.

No use going to the office this morning. News of *l'affaire* Whitney had spread—and grown—all over downtown. One version had Lassiter dangling the bank lawyer out the window, a good trick in a sealed-tight skyscraper. No, his partners would swarm over him like mosquitoes on a naked thigh if he went to work.

Besides, Lila Summers was here. Final warm-ups, the race one day away, and Lila was spinning through a balletlike freestyle exhibition just off the Key Biscayne beach. Jake Lassiter dug his bare feet into the sand and, anonymous behind dark glasses, watched Lila perform. She wore a simple, one-piece white suit cut low in the front and high on the hip. Today, her honeyed hair flew free with the wind.

As her board reached a patch of smooth water, Lila dropped into a split, legs spread along the length of the board, then slid to her feet and spun a perfect pirouette, releasing the boom for a moment, relying on lightning reflexes to keep her balance. She grabbed the boom again, headed on a beam reach and put one foot under the windward rail, popped it out of the water so the leeward rail sank, then rode the board on its side until she levered it back into the water. Finally she flipped into a handstand, held it for fifteen impossible seconds, and after lowering her feet to the board, somersaulted over the booms and landed gently on her back in the sail. She was poetry and grace and her movements were all in harmony, fluid motions that looked effortless.

Alongside Lassiter on the beach a television crew was setting up equipment. "Nice trick," said P. J. Jeter, the ABC announcer.

"She's the best that ever was," Jake Lassiter said. "In the history of the sport, no one has ever done freestyle like that."

"Wouldn't mind getting up close and personal with her," Jeter said.

P. J. Jeter, ex-football semigreat, would rather be covering the NFL, but as the junior member of the *Wide World of Sports* team, he hadn't gotten past the Texas Prison Rodeo and the Wrist-Wrestling Championships from Petaluma. In a minute he would interview a dude who looked half black, half Cherokee and parceled out smiles as if they were twenty-dollar gold pieces.

Finally the camera was ready, the microphone checked out. "So how do you like Florida?" P. J. Jeter asked.

"Flat," Keaka Kealia said.

"How's that?" Jeter asked.

"Flat land, flat water."

"How about the women?"

"Not flat."

"I mean, how about the women windsurfers? Anyone here to compare to your longtime companion, the lovely Lila Summers?"

"French girl, good form, one German girl, very strong, others, don't know their names."

Oh shit, this is enlightening. "Bet you miss Maui, eh?"

"Yes."

A yes-and-no guy. Might as well interview Marcel Marceau.

"Your love for your island home is well known. What is it that makes Maui so special?"

"History. There is much to be learned if you listen to the land and the sea."

Bet they talk more than this guy. "I'm sure there is. What lessons would you like to pass on to your fans?"

"In the Iao Valley there was a great battle two hundred years ago. Chief Kalanikupule ruled Maui but was attacked by much greater forces. Kalanikupule would have been killed, but he created a diversion by sending a warrior in his chieftain's garb into the valley while he escaped into the mountains."

Now what the fuck does that have to do with windsurfing, P. J. Jeter would like to have asked. Guy's probably stoked out of his mind on Maui Wowie. "Okay, let's talk about your world speed record . . ."

Lassiter listened for a moment, then caught sight of Lila Summers foot-steering toward shore. She called to him, "Take one of Keaka's boards. He's busy being a big shot."

Jake Lassiter's brain cells did not have to appoint a committee. If she'd told him to hang by his heels from the hotel balcony, he'd have asked which floor. Keaka Kealia already had rigged four different slalom boards and Lassiter settled for a middle-of-the road nine footer with a five-point-eight-meter sail. He peeled off a faded Penn State T-shirt, hitched up his trunks, and beach-started by hopping onto the board in the calm water just beyond the shore break. In a minute he was next to Lila Summers, who was appraising his form. The wind was kicking at about eighteen knots and an angry cord of steel-gray clouds hung over the horizon.

"It'll take me a little while to get used to the equipment," Lassiter said.

"Don't worry, you're doing great," she said. The board was custom-made for Keaka's specifications and Lassiter, taller and heavier, expected it to be sluggish. Instead, the board turned so quickly on his first jibe, he barely had time to flip the sail to get going on the other tack.

After a few minutes in the swells, Lila yelled above the wind, "I'm tired of shredding back and forth."

"Follow me," Lassiter shouted back. More comfortable now, he raked the boom in tight and trimmed the sail, catching a gust that shot him in front of Lila. She laughed and pursued him down the coastline. The wind was humming now, twenty knots with stronger gusts as the sky darkened and they neared the lighthouse at the tip of the island, the condos and hotels out of sight. Lassiter remembered the strange trio there—Berto, Keaka, and Lee Hu—wondered again what he had barged into. He felt a sharp twinge realizing Berto was gone, then the sting of guilt, because he was enjoying this moment, enjoying the breeze and the water and the company of a young woman, pleasures Berto would never know again. While he was thinking about it, a gust caught him standing up too straight, and a second later, the mast whipped forward, slinging him off the bow. He landed on his back and skipped like a stone another twenty feet.

"You okay?" Lila yelled as she luffed the sail to slow down and pull alongside.

Lassiter came up spitting water, his neck hurting, his ego bruised. "Sure, no problem. Just was thinking about something else. Zigged when I should have zagged."

"Concentration, it's the most important thing. Stay there a second." In a moment, Lila Summers was beside him in the water, their boards floating alongside. She faced him while they both treaded water, the hooks from their harnesses clanging against each other.

She was close enough to kiss, so he did, her lips salty and yielding. She kissed him back and wrapped her legs around him and his neck stopped hurting, and then the skies opened and a hard rain pelted them, and still they kissed but now the swells tumbled over them, growing with the squall that roared from the northeast.

"Getting a little radical out here," Lassiter said, coming up for air. "I have an idea."

"I was hoping you did."

With the wind howling like a betrayed lover, they water-started in unison, two sails whisked out of the water on cue, each sailor slipping into the foot straps and hooking harnesses to the booms, the storm a raucous symphony around them. Tricky now with the swells building and the wind rising to gusty crescendos then falling off to diminuendo lulls.

Lassiter luffed the sail and took a cautious approach. Once past the tip of the island, they headed west into the protected waters of the bay, Key Biscayne taking some of the sting out of the wind. In a few minutes they were at Stiltsville, a collection of twenty wooden houses on stilts smack in the middle of the bay. After Hurricane Andrew, half the structures had splintered into driftwood. The ones that remained were sagging onto their pilings and needed a fresh coat of paint, if not a complete rebuild by structural engineers.

Reachable only by boat, the houses sat empty most of the time. Fifty years ago, you could shoot craps there. Now doctors, lawyers, and bankers owned the houses and used them mainly for weekend family outings with an occasional extra-curricular session on a weekday afternoon for the married guys.

Lila Summers followed him to a white house with faded

green shutters and a wooden deck. They tied their boards to one of the stilts and climbed weather-beaten steps to the front door. The house belonged to his law firm, and like many a grown man's toys, was little used. Lassiter opened the combination lock, and with the squall raging and the cold rain chilling them, they hurried inside. The house was dark and stuffy, so they opened the shuttered windows on the leeward side to let in some air without the rain.

They found towels and a bottle of red wine. He dried her, and she dried him. They talked about the storm and about the race and about everything except the subject at hand: each other and the possibilities that awaited. After a moment, Lila explored the house, her bare feet leaving wet imprints on the floor. She padded through the large, open Florida room, a mounted sailfish dominating one wall, a nautical map another. She walked through the two bedrooms in the back, then rejoined Lassiter at the counter in the kitchen.

She drained her glass of wine and said, "I was still in high school when I met Keaka. I looked up to him. I still do. He's the only man I've been with, and he's been completely faithful to me."

It was the beginning of intimacy, Lassiter knew, plus a medical background, so important these days.

"What about you?" she asked.

"I've never been with Keaka," he said.

She ran her hand through his hair. "Are you one of those men who doesn't talk?"

He talked. He talked about the women who had sailed through his life, Susan Corrigan, the sportswriter, Dr. Pamela Metcalf, the English psychiatrist, Lourdes Soto, the private investigator, and Gina Florio, the ex-Dolphin Doll who kept dancing in and out of his life. Then, in the spirit of the times, he told her he had a blood test every six months at the county health department, and the only thing wrong came from eating too much red meat.

She gestured with her glass for more wine. Then the hand that held the glass circled his head and she pulled him toward her. They kissed softly. He cradled her face in his hands, and the kiss lasted, and with eyes closed he heard the small waves breaking against the pilings. Rain pinged off the metal roof. In the distance, thunder echoed. Wordlessly, Lila stepped out of her white suit and pulled the drawstring on Lassiter's old surfer trunks. The squall had worked its way around the tip of Key Biscayne and the wind roared, and even with the shutters open, it was dim inside. In the Florida room, they lay on the floor on their towels and explored each other's bodies, and Jake Lassiter imagined they were floating on a raft, for the wooden floor seemed to pitch with the waves, his equilibrium still at sea. They made love tentatively at first but then Lila arched her back and her breasts pressed against his chest and she tightened her strong legs around his buttocks and locked him tight into her.

Lila purred in his ear. He moved slowly, and she tugged at his shaggy sun-bleached hair, gripping hard until it hurt. Pulling back his head, she nibbled at his lower lip, then bit down hard enough to draw blood. He never winced, but bit her back, though gently. She sucked at his wounded lip, and their tongues danced, and they kissed harder and deeper until their teeth struck.

A flash of lightning reflected off the water and illuminated the room. Thunder rumbled, and the house seemed to vibrate.

With his eyes closed, Lassiter felt the tide surge toward a distant beach, heard water breaking against a rocky shore. He imagined a beach of red sand and a jungle of green vines. He thought of valleys carved in volcanic rock, pictured a thousand war canoes lit by torches on a black sea, and saw orange flames rising from molten lava. He felt the wet heat rising from both of them as their gears meshed, and they moved to the same silent music.

Later, they lay there together, bodies slicked with sweat and salt water. He looked at her but didn't say a word.

"Jake, don't blink those blue eyes at me," Lila Summers said. "I know what you want to ask but won't, so here it is. It was pleasurable, enjoyable. You're a wonderful lover. The fact that it wasn't a hydrogen bomb—that it's never been—shouldn't bother you. It doesn't bother me."

Lassiter was silent. "And don't pout," she said. "You're a very special man, everything I thought you would be, strong but sensitive, and it was very nice, really."

Very nice. Very nice is okay for Granny Lassiter's pot roast, not this ethereal experience. At least it had been that for him. They were silent. The rain still pelted the roof, but lighter now. Lassiter walked to the window in a daze, his joy tinged with disappointment. A brown pelican sat on one of the wooden pilings, its pouch empty, scanning the shallow water. Small waves sloshed against the pilings, a sleepy sound.

Jake Lassiter looked at Lila, naked on the towel, and saw the last train leaving the station. There would be no more women like this—young and beautiful and unspoiled. She has never tasted defeat, he thought, and cannot imagine it. How long had it been since he figured he would never sit on the Supreme Court or stake his life on principle like an Atticus Finch? How long since he realized he would never be All-Pro, or All-Anything? It was creeping up on him and the train started moving now, and he would run for it and leap aboard and wherever it went, it didn't matter.

"Li'a, Goddess of Desire, I want to say things to you that no one ever has. My head is full of music and poetry but it's all jumbled up, and all I can think of is, Grow old along with me . . ."

". . . The best is yet to be," she said, and he raised his eyebrows and Lila laughed. "Don't look so surprised. We studied poetry at Seabury Hall on Maui, but to tell the truth, I always found Robert Browning a bit sappy. I preferred Housman":

Now you will not swell the rout
Of lads that wore their honors out,
Runners whom renown outran
And the name died before the man.

"But that's a little melancholy, isn't it?" Lassiter asked. "An athlete dying young."

"Not melancholy at all, an athlete or warrior going out in a blaze of glory."

Jake Lassiter shook his head, in the mood to talk of romance, not blazing death. "You didn't happen to learn any poems about Li'a at your highfalutin school, did you?"

Me 'oe ka 'ano 'i pau 'ole . . . With you an unending desire.

"Perfect," he said. "The rest?"

Here in the beating heart.
Do not thrust away the glimpse
Of our drenching in the misty rain.

"It's beautiful," Lassiter said. "Our drenching in the misty rain. What a sensual thought."

"Maui is a very sensual place. It could be our place."

She stood there, naked in front of the window, and Lassiter looked into the star bursts of her eyes and wondered if a second mission could drop the hydrogen bomb. But soon, it would be dark, and windsurfers don't have running lights. As he slipped into the cold, wet swim trunks, his desire waned. They locked up the house, untied the boards, and headed back to Key Biscayne.

The weather had calmed, and the wind was nearly too light now, the typical pattern after a series of squalls. Three gray gulls, shrieking stridently, kept them company as they sailed up the coast. A single osprey, the Florida fish hawk, soared above them and dived suddenly, snatching a fish with its talons. The fish struggled for a moment, but the piercing claws would not release, and bird and prey disappeared toward land.

The beach was deserted in front of the hotel and they carried their equipment up the beach. As they neared the raised pool deck, Lassiter stopped suddenly and said, "How can Maui be our place?"

She looked puzzled.

"Keaka," he said. "What about Keaka?"

"What do you mean?" she asked, innocent as a child bride.

"Where's Keaka while you and I are riding horses in the mountains, windsurfing on unspoiled waters?"

"Does it matter?"

"Do you love him?"

"Love," she said, pursing her lips and cocking her head as if trying out a new word. "Oh, Jake, you are a romantic, aren't you? Look, I love what Keaka is. I love his strength and his pride and his independence. He's free, and not many of us are."

I'm not, Jake Lassiter thought. I'm tied to a clock and time sheets and to bloodsucking clients. "How could I be free?" he asked, not liking the sound of his own voice.

"By doing what you enjoy most."

He laughed. "I'm too slow to cover the flanker over the middle. All I can do is put facts together, examine witnesses, argue the law, write briefs—all useless skills except to sell your life by the hour, lease each heartbeat to corporations and robber barons."

"Jake, there's something for you in the islands. There's . . ."

"*Lila*, there you are!"

Keaka carried a board under each arm, biceps pumped from hard sailing, looking powerful and dangerous. "You left your rig on the beach, you know what the blowing sand does to the sail."

"Lots more sails where that came from," Lila said.

Without acknowledging Lassiter's presence, Keaka looked hard at Lila. "I know you're tired," he said, "but it's our last race. After this, I've got other plans."

"I know, I know."

"Let's get cleaned up now," Keaka said. "I have to meet somebody on business."

"Not the same business as the other night, I hope," Lila said.

"No, even easier, and more profitable."

Jake Lassiter wondered if he'd suddenly become invisible. Finally Lila turned to him and said apologetically, " 'Night, Jake. See you tomorrow. Thanks for filling me in about the location of the reef. Jake was very helpful, Keaka."

"I'm sure he was," Keaka Kealia said, shooting Lassiter the sideways look of a Doberman pinscher. "Say, lawyer . . ."

"Yeah."

"You got a bruise on your lip. You bump into something?"

"Grabbed the boom with my face."

"That's what I thought. Got to be careful when you're out of your element. Got to be real cautious or you can get hurt."

Keaka smiled a malevolent grin, then hauled his rig back toward the hotel garage, Lila following behind. Alone now, a pair of images drifted through Lassiter's mind—that first night outside the hotel, Lila's hair flying, back arched against the wind, and now, her kisses still lingering on his lips.

It was after six o'clock when Lassiter found a pay phone to check with Cindy at the office. "Where you been?" Cindy shouted at him. "I waited so long for you, I'm missing happy hour at the Crazy Horse. Jeez, what a day, all hell's broken loose since you beat the crap out of Thad Whitney."

"Cindy, I didn't beat the crap out of him. We just bumped into each other."

"The way I hear it, you sucker-punched him, then trashed his china cabinet. Your partners are really pissed. The MP's been reading the office manual all day. They're gonna court-martial you or something, conduct unbecoming a partner. Maybe they'll forgive you if you apologize to Thad."

"I will . . . the same day the pope marries Madonna. What else?"

Cindy paused, and Lassiter imagined her running a finger through a permed curl, deep in thought. "Jake, don't get in over your head. I don't mean to be lecturing you since you're my boss and you're God knows how much older than I am. And you're a real together guy, except . . . except what you don't know about women could fill Biscayne Bay and flood Miami Beach. So don't go off the deep end, okay?"

"Hey, Cindy."

"Yeah?"

"Throw me a life preserver."

CHAPTER

19

The Partners

H*arry Marlin hoped she knew what she was doing. Christ, who* was this guy anyway? You don't just call somebody you don't even know and say, how 'bout taking some hot goods to the Bahamas for me. But that's what Violet did, called a stranger at a hotel.

The Bahamas. Still got Bahamas on the brain. Now we got another partner, if he goes along with it. She sees the guy once and all she remembers, he's the color of cordovan loafers, he's sailing to the Bahamas, and his wang's like a loaf of bread stuck in his shorts. Meets a guy on the beach, guy that knows the old man's lawyer, for Christ's sake, and brings him in on the deal. Said she had a feeling about the guy. Bet she did, too.

How the hell would Harry recognize the son of a bitch, he wasn't gonna stare at the crotch of a guy walking into the bar, particularly the Organ Grinder, a topless joint on Collins Avenue just a block off the ocean.

Harry used to hang out there, knew the turf and felt at home. He could have gone to see the guy, but let the son of a bitch take a cab from his fancy-pants hotel. Probably wouldn't even come. Told Violet he'd be there at eight, had to be back early because of the race tomorrow. Needed his sleep, friggin' Boy Scout.

The Organ Grinder was nearly empty. Two guys, truck drivers maybe, sat around the three-sided bar that framed a small stage. They watched a hopelessly bored stripper, down to a red G-string, titless babe with short black hair, skinny with a soft ass, wrinkled and white like two scoops of cottage cheese. This place couldn't attract your prime-grade talent, Harry thought, not for dollar tips in the garter belt.

"*. . . I'm not perfect, but I'm perfect for you-ou . . .*"

Music so loud your ears hurt, whatshername singing, Grace Jones, built like a licorice stick, hair cut like a Marine, a wild look like she'd bite it off she had half a chance.

The skinny stripper unhooked the G-string, wrapped it around a metal pole on the stage, rehooked it on the other side, and strung her legs around the pole, humping it to the music. Not bad, mushy ass and all, not bad and Harry felt a stirring.

Where was the guy anyway? Goddamn noise giving him a headache. Ever since Buddy Holly died, music'd been shit. Tried to hum it, "*All my love, all my kissin', you don't know what you been missin'.*" But the tune in his head couldn't compete with the blasting tape:

"*. . . You're gonna have to face it, you're addicted to love. Might as well face it, you're addicted to love . . .*"

When the music stopped, so did the stripper, boom, as if the factory whistle blew and the assembly line crashed, you weren't gonna get one extra bump outta that bitch. Then she stretched out a leg and with her high-heel sequined shoe, she flicked off the light switch that illuminated the stage a whorey red.

Another girl would be out in a minute, but Harry wasn't in the mood. It was eight-thirty and he would wait another five minutes, then fuck it. Harry went to the rest room in the back hauling a tote bag. He took a leak, studied the graffiti, felt for a forgotten quarter in the condom machine change slot, then came back out. In the rear of the joint, near the tables for private dances—ten-dollar minimum—was an aquarium. Funny, a bunch of fish in a place like this, but there it was. Harry walked over, aimlessly, looking at the fish, killing time.

Harry could tell from the way light reflected off the tank that someone had opened the front door, but he didn't turn around. He was watching the tank, and as he did, a cream-colored lionfish sneaked up behind a blue-and-yellow angelfish, tailing it like a cop on surveillance. The angelfish would wiggle right, the lionfish would wiggle right, flaring its large gills, the mane of a lion. They swam inside a little cavern, out again, up and down, and finally, the lionfish grew tired of the game. It came from behind the angelfish and swallowed it whole, just swallowed it, no bites, no struggle. One second there were two fish, then there was one.

At about the same time that the Miami Beach fish population decreased by one, Harry saw a reflection in the glass tank, a man behind him, strong guy, the silhouette of sinewy muscles bulging from each side of his neck. Harry felt a shiver, then turned around to see the unsmiling face of Keaka Kealia.

They shook hands, Harry's knuckles ricocheting off each other like billiard balls on a clean break.

Harry massaged his right hand with his left and said, "A

guy walks into a bar with an alligator and asks the bartender if they serve lawyers . . ."

Keaka was studying the smaller man as if he were a moderately interesting chimpanzee at the zoo.

" 'Sure,' the bartender says. 'Good,' the guys says. 'Give me a beer and my gator a lawyer!' "

Keaka didn't smile.

"It's a joke," Harry said. "But I'm worried about the lawyer."

"Lassiter?"

"Yeah. He'll be there, won't he?"

"In the lead boat, nothing to worry about."

They talked about the coupons, Harry lifting the canvas tote bag with two hands. Keaka said, sure he could get them to Bimini if they fit into a backpack. The added weight, no problem, he was the best in the world. Customs? No problem. Customs doesn't check guys coming over on a sanctioned, nationally televised windsurfing race.

"Okay, partner, you know where the Great Bahama Bank is?" Harry Marlin asked.

"Yeah," Keaka Kealia said, showing the first trace of a smile. "It's not hard to find."

"I'll meet you there."

"What?"

"At the bank. I'll meet you at the Great Bahama Bank. At a teller's window. You bring the coupons and we'll settle up, a nice safe place for both of us, no monkey business there."

Keaka spoke slowly then, as if he hadn't understood what Harry said. "You want me to meet you at the Great Bahama Bank?"

Shit, Harry thought, this guy is two pickles short of a Whopper. Gotta explain it all twice. "That's right, partner, any problem?"

"The Great Bahama Bank," Keaka Kealia repeated. "That's where I'll be."

Good, Harry Marlin said, relieved to have worked it out. Then Harry said that he'd be watching during the race, he'd be right behind, and not to be threatening or anything, but he'd be packing heat.

"No problem," Keaka Kealia said, baring his teeth in what Harry Marlin mistook for a smile.

"Easy as pie," Harry told Violet that night. "The sucker's gonna do it for a ten percent commission—that's what I called it, a commission. He's taking the risk for a lousy ten percent and we'll deposit more than a million in the Great Bahama Bank, just like some cocaine kingpins."

"You gave him the coupons?" Violet asked.

"Not to worry, I got his pecker in my pocket."

"Harry Marlin, you ain't got but lint in your pocket."

"Vi honey, I wish you wouldn't be always putting me down that way. I got feelings, you know."

"You? C'mon, Harry, you're as sensitive as an aluminum foil condom. Now, tell me everything."

"I told him I'd be on his tail, put the fear of a steel-jacketed .357 Magnum right into him."

But Harry hadn't seen any fear. He had watched the dark guy leave the bar, walking on the balls of his feet, head perfectly still, shoulders back, a cocky walk, an alert walk, like he could see all around him.

If the guy wasn't so dumb, Harry Marlin thought, I'd be worried about him.

"Not much time to make plans," Keaka Kealia told Lila Summers in their suite at the hotel. The sliding door on the balcony was open and the wind from the ocean rustled the drapes.

"Better call Mikala. Has a friend here from 'Nam can get us a plane."

"What about the *haole*?" Lila asked.

"Stupid and weak," Keaka said. "Thinks the Great Bahama Bank is a place to cash checks, has hands like a baby's ass."

"*Haoles*," Lila said, shaking her head.

"Thinks he can shoot me from a boat crossing the Gulf Stream."

"Not unless he's Buffalo Bill," Lila said, laughing. They emptied the multicolored coupons into a yellow waterproof backpack, filling it. Lila hefted it and whistled. "It's a load."

"It's our big chance."

Lila walked to the balcony door, letting the ocean breeze cool her. "There's a risk. The DEA knows we're here, especially after the other night."

"The DEA's looking for drugs coming into the country, not bonds going out," Keaka said. "That's the beauty of it."

CHAPTER

20

The Name's Marlín

If you look at a map of southeast Florida, you see a string of islands. Just offshore from Miami are Miami Beach, Virginia Key, and Key Biscayne, all sedimentary barrier islands that began as sandbars, the ocean currents depositing tiny particles of limestone and quartz over the millennia. The islands farther south along the Florida Keys began as coral reefs, the skeletal remains of ancient marine animals. The early sailors—Spanish, English, and Dutch—faced a perilous journey through the Straits, avoiding the Florida Reef to the west and the Great Bahama Bank to the east.

A ridge of limestone sand only six feet below the surface,

the Great Bahama Bank runs close to the Biminis, which appear on maps as an artist's mistake, tiny splashes of ink from a fountain pen. No casinos or fancy nightclubs on these islands. Just waters rich with fish and saloons with shutters open to the southeast breeze. Ernest Hemingway fished and wrote and drank in the Biminis and did all three better than anyone else. More than four hundred years earlier, a Spanish explorer set out for Bimini, lured by tales that the island's waters could turn old men into youths. Juan Ponce de León never found the fountain of youth but on Easter Sunday in 1513 he saw the sedimentary barrier islands of Miami Beach and Key Biscayne. Rather than step ashore, Ponce de León sailed northward along the coastline of what he believed to be an island he named Florida. He landed near what is now St. Augustine, far from Bimini and without finding magic waters to soothe the aches of a fifty-three-year-old explorer.

Two years later he again sailed, this time exploring the southwest coast of Florida. It was there, probably near Sanibel Island, that the Spaniards came upon the Caloosa Indians. Like the native Hawaiians encountered by Captain Cook two hundred years later, the Caloosas were warriors. They were deadly with bow and arrow and hurled spears from crotched sticks. When the soldiers commanded the Caloosas to convert to Catholicism, the proud warriors responded with battle cries and a hail of arrows, killing many of the Spaniards, including Ponce de León.

Europeans had discovered the New World.

"Better secure your gear below, Charlie," Jake Lassiter said. "We'll be going too fast to troll, and bouncing through the chop, you may break something."

Charlie Riggs frowned and held on to the rail of the *Big Daddy*, an excessively well-equipped fifty-eight-foot Hatteras that was swaying at anchor three hundred yards off the Key

Biscayne shore. "Don't know why I agreed to this. I could be in Bimini in thirty minutes by seaplane, have my first *Acanthocybium solandri* by noon."

"Sounds serious. Can you take penicillin for it?"

"Wahoo, Jake. Ever see one burn up a reel? Just a flash of steel blue . . . *whoosh* . . . like a rocket, it's gone."

"Well, the fish will wait, and I need your help," Lassiter said.

"You want to chat or you expecting a body to pop up?"

"I don't know what's going on. The other day, at Matheson Hammock, I didn't exactly tell Detective Farrell the truth, the whole truth, and nothing but the truth."

"Ah, and you want to atone for your sin, *expiatum peccatum.*"

"Not really. I want to tie some loose ends together, then go to Farrell. For starters, I'm trying to figure out what Berto was doing on the beach a day before he was killed."

"Getting a suntan was out of the question, I suppose."

"He was with the best board sailor in the world, a guy who also thinks he's a reincarnated Hawaiian king and seems to yearn for the good old days of war canoes and flaming arrows."

Charlie reached into a pocket of his bush jacket and withdrew his pipe. He tamped tobacco into the bowl and struck three matches in the ocean breeze before giving up. "Am I supposed to find anything suspicious in that? I'm sure Berto saw many people his last few days, some of them far more unsavory than an athlete with a sense of ethnic heritage."

"It's hard to explain, Charlie, but the two of them didn't fit together. No common ground. Certainly not windsurfing . . ."

"Then perhaps drug smuggling . . ."

They both let it hang there.

"Sorry, Jake, but I've never adhered to Chilon's admonition, '*De mortuis nihil nisi bonum.*' If I only spoke kindly of the dead, I'd have very little to say. Little indeed."

A white-coated waiter offered them piña coladas from a tray. A prerace buffet was in full swing, the yacht club brass, some ABC dignitaries, and assorted hangers-on spearing cold shrimp and slathering duck pâté on crackers. Lassiter and Riggs moved farther down the rail, but the partygoers crowded their way. A man in a faded madras sports coat loudly was engaged in animated conversation with Paul Flanigan, the boat's owner, and a yacht club honcho.

"What the hell we gonna do tonight?" the man asked.

"Nothing to do on Bimini but fish, drink, and screw, and you can't fish at night," Flanigan said. He was an old Bimini hand, two-time winner of the Adam Clayton Powell Memorial Fishing Contest.

Jake Lassiter led Doc Riggs toward the stern. Lassiter pointed toward the beach. "There he is, rigging for the crossing. Here, use these." Lassiter handed over his binoculars.

Doc Riggs peered through the high-powered lenses. "Strong, athletic, not much else I could say from here."

"Keaka Kealia is the fastest sailor who ever lived," Lassiter said. "He shattered the *Crossbow*'s record by more than four knots."

Riggs thought about it a moment. "Which means he broke the forty-knot barrier."

"Right. A space-age trimaran goes thirty-six knots, and nobody comes close for ten years. Then a descendant of Polynesian warriors obliterates the record standing on a sliver of fiberglass with a tiny patch of sail."

"Which tells us what, Jake?"

"That he's tough, single-minded, fearless. Probably egocentric. Loves a one-man sport, not a team player."

"But a killer?"

Lassiter shook his head. "Who knows? When we get to Bimini, we'll talk to him. I'll tell him about Berto's death. You watch for his reaction, judge his respiration for me, watch for an increase in body temperature."

"You really think I can do that?"

"You're the human polygraph machine. You've done it before."

"Jake, I hate to shatter your illusions, but I was faking it. When I got a confession out of the woman who brained her husband with the frozen rack of lamb, I was making it up as I went along. She went for it and gave me the murder weapon before it defrosted."

"Maybe you can fake out the reincarnated Polynesian king."

Charlie Riggs laughed. "*Rex non potest peccare.* The king can do no wrong."

The racers would put their boards into the water in the shadow of the old lighthouse. They would head due east where the bottom falls away quickly to two hundred feet just north of Fowey Rocks, and soon they would reach the Gulf Stream, a warm, choppy river flowing north, the water two thousand feet deep. Then on to the Great Bahama Bank, the bottom coming up suddenly again near the Biminis.

Two Zodiacs, inflatable boats with egg-beater motors, were ferrying race officials and medical personnel to a Magnum 63 that would follow the sailors while the *Big Daddy* would lead them. Though the Magnum was glitzy and had twin staterooms furnished like luxury hotel suites, it was long and sleek and could hit sixty miles an hour.

Even had he seen the last passenger to scramble into the Zodiac, Jake Lassiter wouldn't have known him. No one else on the Magnum knew him either, and by the time the strangely dressed man climbed unsteadily from the ladder and onto the deck, he could have been the answer to the question: What's wrong with this picture?

"You can't come aboard in those shoes," said Commodore Ralph Whittaker, an aging mariner whose white slacks and white shirt with epaulets matched his white mustache and beard.

The man stood on one foot, took off his worn leather loafers, and climbed aboard. The big toe of his right foot peeked through a hole in his thin black sock. The commodore eyed the man suspiciously.

"Marlin," the stranger announced with authority, as if the name demanded recognition and respect.

"You have the wrong boat," the commodore said. "No fishing here. We're bringing up the rear of a race."

The man tried again. "Harry Marlin."

"No blue marlin, no white marlin, no hairy marlin, whatever that is. This is no fishing trip, just a bunch of Hawaiians and hippies and Krauts and Frogs and what have you."

"The *name's* Marlin! Harry Marlin. Jake Lassiter said I could go along." It was a bluff, but it couldn't fail, Harry figured. He'd hung around the sponsors' tent long enough that morning to find out which boat Lassiter was on, and then headed for one of the others.

"All right then," the commodore said, warming up. "There's plenty of room on this baby, eh. Help yourself to a Bloody Mary." Which is just what Harry Marlin did, to steady his nerves, then below he went, wondering if the boat was going to rock back and forth like this once they got going. He still wore his jacket, the green-and-black camouflage number from the army surplus store, while everyone else was in short-sleeve knits and shorts. Harry was wearing shorts, too—khaki safari shorts like an English gentleman in India—but with the camouflage jacket, they made him seem even more out of place. He didn't care. The jacket hid a shoulder holster, and it held a loaded Police Bulldog .38 Special.

Jake Lassiter trained the binoculars on the beach again, this time searching for a sailor in a one-piece suit, cut low in front and high over the hip. He found her, tugging on a skin-tight wet suit. Nearby, Keaka Kealia adjusted the weight of a yellow waterproof backpack that was slung across his shoulders. Lila wore an identical pack. Up and down the beach, the young competitors stood on the bleached sand, loosening up, stretching hamstrings, their minds visualizing the rough crossing, preparing for a test of body and mind in the same, silent ritual athletes have employed since the days of ancient Greece.

The starter blew the air horn, one minute until the start. The athletes, sun-darkened bodies in stark contrast to the white beach, moved to their positions. The horn sounded again, and the twenty-eight competitors grabbed their rigs and lugged them into the water, a Le Mans start. Lila struggled a bit as she beach-started, the backpack swinging free under one arm. Keaka hopped onto the board and was the first sailor through the shore break, Gary Koenigsberg three board lengths behind. Mickey Kerbel, a former Israeli paratrooper, cut upwind of Koenigsberg, stealing his air, and briefly taking second place. Leslie Weeks, an Australian woman, was next. A Canadian whose sail was emblazoned with a maple leaf was close behind. Françoise Duvalier seemed to be leading the women.

Within minutes, all the boards were in open water, and the pack thinned out. The water was calm except for the wind chop. Unlike the smaller boards that become airborne on the lip of the slightest wave, the big cruising boards stayed in the water as sailors leaned back, trimmed their sails tight, and headed toward the horizon. As they neared the Gulf Stream, they routinely adjusted to the ocean swells with reflexes that had been honed on waters from the Tasman Sea to the Mediterranean. Some cursed themselves for rigging too big as the wind pounded at a steady twenty knots from the north, guaranteeing five hours of unremitting pain on shoulders, elbows, and wrists. Others yearned for more Mylar as they had rigged too small. In the front, his sail trimmed perfectly, Keaka Kealia led the pack.

Jake Lassiter watched from the stern of the *Big Daddy* as Keaka broke for an early lead. From the bow of the Magnum trailing the last racer, Harry Marlin watched, too, but soon lost sight of him. Harry had figured that the added weight of the coupons would drag on the Hawaiian, holding him back. Nearly every competitor carried a small pack containing water bottles and granola bars, but those, he thought, weighed far less than the coupons. The Magnum was getting reports from the ABC helicopter, and Harry learned he had been wrong—Keaka Kealia was leading the race, far out of sight of the trailing boat. Shouldn't worry, though, where was the bastard going on that board, the Bermuda Triangle?

From the *Big Daddy*, Lassiter looked for Lila but couldn't see her. Lost in the pack somewhere. He thought she would lead the women, but there was local talent Carolyn Kvajic leading with Françoise Duvalier from France second, and Luisa Vázquez from Cuba third. Where was Lila?

Three Bloody Marys and two dozen raw oysters on an empty stomach. That is not the prescribed breakfast for someone about to cross the Gulf Stream, but Harry Marlin did not know that. Among the many other things that Harry Marlin did not know was that he was prone to seasickness. He learned this fact after slurping down oyster number six, a juicy Apalachicola.

Harry had spent some time in small motorboats lazing on the flat water of Lake Okeechobee, waiting for bass to jump aboard. It was different here, the Magnum pitching over the chop, kicking spray onto the deck. Harry decided to stay dry below, nursing a fourth Bloody Mary, sweat beading on his forehead, bile churning in his stomach.

The windsurfers were battling the chop, too, bouncing over small waves, feeling it in knees and ankles, fighting off muscle cramps, fatigue, and stiff backs from being locked into one tack for hours, straining against the wind.

"ABC says the Hawaiian's still leading, about half a mile in front of Kerbel and Koenigsberg," the commodore said, poking his head below to grab a cup of tea. "Hey, you feeling all right, Mr. Marlin?"

Harry nodded and mouthed the word "fine," but his eyes were glassy and he looked like he'd be over the rail any minute.

"Hang in there," the commodore said. "You'll feel better when we're out of the Stream."

Harry lay down on a cushioned built-in sofa and tried to sleep, but he couldn't. Sweat poured from him. He burped and tasted half-digested oyster. Whose idea was this, anyway? Violet's, of course. Everything was her idea.

The Magnum was bouncing over the waves now, and Harry gritted his teeth and concentrated on keeping his stomach from somersaulting.

Time passed.

Slowly.

Queasily.

Excruciatingly.

He felt weak, disoriented, but finally the water calmed. They were out of the Gulf Stream. Harry climbed to the deck on shaky legs. The radio crackled from the helicopter. Keaka Kealia was a mile in front, Françoise Duvalier leading the women.

"Almost there," the commodore told anyone who would listen. "That Hawaiian has it locked up. He's got us for the appearance fee plus first prize, he'll be laughing all the way to the bank."

Despite his discomfort, Harry Marlin smiled to himself. The Hawaiian'll be laughing all the way to the Great Bahama Bank, but I got the last laugh 'cause that dumb-ass is doing it for 10 percent. Shit, I'd a given him a third, easy.

A mile off the coast of North Bimini, the Big Daddy *pulled under* a finish line strung between two barges, the checkered flag popping in the wind. Paul Flanigan killed the engines and prepared to tie up at the barge. From the stern Jake Lassiter could see Keaka Kealia a hundred yards behind them, heading for an easy victory. The ABC helicopter circled overhead, capturing the winning moment on videotape. A round of applause went up from the yacht club members on the *Big Daddy*—those still sober enough to bring their hands together—and Keaka nodded as he sailed by. Which is what he did, sailed right by, didn't stop, didn't tie up at the barge for the awards, the champagne, and the calypso band.

Jake Lassiter saw it happen: Keaka Kealia tipping the mast slightly forward, shifting weight to his front foot, falling off the wind. Heading southeast toward Turtle Rock. The trip across the Florida Straits was a beam reach, 90 degrees off the wind. Now Keaka was on a broad reach, 135 degrees off the wind, the fastest angle for the board, and with the trade winds humming at close to twenty-five knots in the open waters, he was zipping along, bouncing off small chop, the board planing now with only the stern in the water.

"Charlie, wake up and look at this!" Lassiter shouted.

Charlie Riggs opened his eyes but didn't move from the deck chair. A plaid blanket was tucked up under his chin. "*Quid nunc?* I always get sleepy on boats."

"The reincarnated warrior just called an audible."

"Hmmm?"

"Called his own number, but damned if I know the play."

On the Magnum, still two miles from the finish line, the radio crackled again with static and someone's voice from the helicopter. Harry Marlin couldn't make out the words. The commodore strained to listen, then fiddled with his mustache. His face had a look of consternation. "Didn't stop? Hell's bells."

"What's wrong?" Harry Marlin asked, sensing trouble even through a haze of Stolichnaya and seasickness.

"Copter says the Hawaiian finished, just kept on going, bearing off to starboard."

Harry's stomach lurched, and not from the oysters. The son of a bitch was way out of sight. What was happening? Then that old feeling—fear and shame, letting Violet down—the same feeling when he came back empty-handed the first time from the theater.

Time to take control. "Let's go get him! He double-crossed me, the bastard."

The commodore had his thumbs in his belt and looked sideways at Harry. "Take it easy, Mr. Marlin. It's his problem if he doesn't stick around for the ceremony. I'll take it up with the board of directors. He could be disqualified for conduct unbecoming a yachtsman, might have to forfeit the first prize. This is quite unprecedented, you know."

"Screw the prize and screw you!" Harry shouted, and the commodore blanched. This friend of Lassiter would never be admitted to the yacht club, the commodore quickly decided.

Harry Marlin stood there in his camouflage jacket, safari

shorts, and stockinged feet, the hole in his sock, larger now. He felt helpless.

But only for a moment.

He had never pulled a gun on anyone, ever. Until now.

Harry reached inside the jacket, and drew out his Police Bulldog .38 Special, and summoning his deepest voice, ordered the commodore, "Follow that friggin' board."

CHAPTER

21

Race to the Bank

Jake Lassiter heard a roar, two roars really, and he tried to separate them. First was a grinding yowl from overhead, where a twin-engine Grumman, a small seaplane, flew at two hundred feet, heading in the same direction as Keaka Kealia. Second was the throaty roar of two Italian MTU motors, four thousand horsepower in all, powering the Magnum across the water, cutting a path through the windsurfers who were trying to finish the race.

The big boat scattered the racers, red and blue and turquoise sails flattened against the water. Startled by the cacophony, some of the sailors jumped out of their foot straps. Others were swamped in the wake. Bedlam on the high seas.

"Pisshead powerboaters!" yelled Gary Koenigsberg after he coughed up several jiggers of the Atlantic Ocean. "Slow the fuck down. This ain't the Santa Monica Freeway."

Lila Summers never fell. From her position deep in the pack, she seemed ready for the madness. When the boat sped by, she spread her legs wide on the board and luffed the sail. Her big Mistral pitched in the Magnum's wake but she kept her balance and slowly made her way toward the finish. The other racers cautiously water-started, cursing the huge Magnum. Then they took off in pursuit of the second prize.

The Magnum won the second prize, theoretically at least, as it was the next craft under the finish line. Its crossing did not go unnoticed on the barges. Couldn't have. It flew by at sixty miles an hour, kicking up a spray that doused the victory cake, nearly electrocuted the electric bass player, and sent the calypso band's steel drums rolling overboard. The Magnum carved a tight turn just past the *Big Daddy* and headed southeast after Keaka Kealia.

Jake Lassiter and Charlie Riggs watched it all, unable to do anything, stuck on a boat of drunken yacht clubbers swapping fish stories, oblivious to the commotion, while Keaka Kealia, a low-flying seaplane, and the pursuing Magnum headed for points unknown.

Harry Marlin aimed his .38 Special at the right ear of Commodore Ralph Whittaker, who stood a foot behind the hired captain of the Magnum. The captain, a twenty-three-year-old Marine mechanic with tattoos on each forearm, was thrilled. It was his first chance to open it up and the baby was purring, bouncing over the water, kidneys jarred on every smash. Harry held on to a rail with one hand and tried to steady the gun with the other. His arm was growing weary.

He had barely thought about it a minute ago. Just decided to hell with it, a man's gotta do what a man's gotta do. He had pulled the gun when the commodore refused to give chase, pulled it out like it was the most natural thing in the world. Felt good grabbing it from under the camouflage jacket, just like in the movies.

Now he was thinking about it. Thinking hard. Shit. What had he done? Gave his real name back there when he climbed aboard. Got his prints all over the boat. No more flipping hamburgers in South Beach, not even if he wanted to, because he'd just bought a one-way ticket out of town. But isn't that what he wanted? It better be, because those coupons were everything now, and some two-bit punk was trying to heist them. Christ, can't even think, the old salt babbling away.

"You've committed a felony on the high seas," the commodore bellowed over the roar of the two engines. "I'll see you in Admiralty Court. And this race is FUBAR—fouled up beyond all recognition. I must warn you, if you're taking us to Cuba, I seriously doubt we have sufficient fuel, at least at this speed."

Harry drew back the hammer on the revolver. "Shut up, fish bait! We're not going to Cuba, we're going to the bank."

The seaplane landed in the shallows near an exposed cluster of rocks. Less than a mile away, Keaka Kealia headed toward the same rocks, his sail vibrating with a high-pitched hum in the strong wind. From the bridge of the Magnum, Harry Marlin saw it all, had it figured out now.

Harry ordered the captain to pull between Keaka and the seaplane, and at near top speed, the Magnum swung in a wide arc in the shallow water, tumbling liquor bottles from the shelves, knocking club members into each other below deck. The Hawaiian was fast, but the Magnum had closed the gap and in a matter of seconds would cut him off. Killing the engines, the captain eased the boat directly in the path between Keaka and the waiting plane. The engines died, and in the silence, Harry Marlin could hear the gentle slap of waves against the hull. He could see Keaka Kealia heading straight for them.

Keaka had two choices. He could keep going straight at the boat and be splattered against its sleek hull, or he could bear off and head downwind to avoid the collision, but if he did that, he would lose his speed and would pass by the stern of the Magnum at a crawl. Even the dumb *haole* might pick him off with a clear shot like that. So he did neither one. He leaned back hard against the boom and raked the sail over the board, using every last breath from the wind. Unhooking the harness line from the boom, Keaka Kealia pumped the sail furiously to build speed, wincing with each movement as the tendons of his elbows, already swollen from the crossing, flared with pain. He watched the rollers hit the sandbar near Turtle Rock, and with the timing practiced on a thousand waves on Maui's north shore, he took aim.

*Harry Marlin stood motionless on the deck watching the Ha*waiian approach, catching a glimpse of the yellow backpack. When he could see the grimace on the dark man's face, Harry fired. The noise and jolt of the gun startled him and he hopped backward, tromping on the commodore's deck shoes. "Jumping Jesus!" the commodore shouted. "You don't shoot a sailor for leaving the course, you just penalize him."

Wildly, again and again, Harry shot into the sky and into the water as the boat bobbed and dipped in the waves. Harry was trying to shoot a moving target while his own foundation was slipping out from under him. Sergeant York couldn't have hit the broadside of a barn in these conditions, and Harry Marlin was no sharpshooter, just a guy who kept a gun under the lunch counter in case some freaked out *Marielito* with a Saturday night special showed up at closing time. Finally, Harry stopped shooting and simply watched. The crazy son of a bitch was coming right at him, right at the side of the Magnum, and there'd be a helluva mess of blood and splintered bone to clean up.

Then Keaka had what he wanted, the perfect wave. He got all of it, a huge roller, and just as the Magnum dropped into the trough, Keaka's feet lifted against the foot straps and hurled the board off the lip. Airborne, he pumped the sail again, getting more lift, and he looked down to see Harry Marlin's balding head, and Harry ducked, just in time, because the sharp fiberglass fin would have parted what was left of his hair. A spray of salt water spattered his back. Keaka's board was flying now, bow up, sail taut with wind. It landed on the far side of the Magnum, Keaka luffing the sail a moment. Then he hauled it back in, hooked into the harness line, and headed straight for the waiting seaplane.

The young boat captain tried to start the Magnum, but it wouldn't turn over, just sat there coughing and sputtering, a million-dollar piece of junk, while the Hawaiian sailed away on a slab of fiberglass with a pole stuck into it. The captain tried again, muttering something about flooding out. Harry spat every curse he ever knew and invented a few more. He got off one more meaningless shot as the Magnum heaved in the waves and Keaka approached the seaplane. Harry screamed at the captain, who was hitting switches and twisting dials. He cursed the Hawaiian and every member of his family. He stomped his stockinged feet. Finally, his eyes filled with tears of frustration as he watched Keaka Kealia ditch his board and swim to the plane, where two hands hauled him aboard.

Keaka Kealia leaned out the door waving, holding up the yellow pouch, yelling something at him. With the boat's engine dead, Keaka's voice carried across the open sea. "Here we are, partner," Keaka called out, spreading his arms over the clear, shallow water, holding the pouch effortlessly at one side. "Here we are, the Great Bahama Bank."

Suddenly a sharp pain, the same shoulder that had taken a direct hit from an aluminum baseball bat. Shit, I've been shot, Harry Marlin thought. But he was wrong. He'd been gaffed, hit square on the shoulder blade with a four-foot gaff. The commodore had a death grip on the other end and was barking orders. "Now hear this! Under the law of the sea, Mr. Marlin, you're under arrest. You will report below at once. We will arrange a suitable brig in conformance with the Geneva convention."

What could have been the commodore's finest moment crumbled. By some miracle Harry Marlin still held the gun. The thick army jacket had absorbed most of the blow. Breathing heavily, Harry pointed the .38 directly at the commodore's crotch and said, "Now hear this, Admiral. Get this tub back to Miami or I'll blow your nuts from here to Hawaii."

Hawaii being what was on Harry's mind at the time, Hawaii where he figured the bastard was heading, not on the little seaplane, of course, probably from here to one of the other islands, then to Mexico City maybe, and then Honolulu, and then, what the fuck was the name of that other island?

"Where's that thieving motherfucker from?" Harry demanded.

"Keaka Kealia?" the commodore asked.

"No, Michael Milken. Of course, Keaka Kealia, you asshole."

"He's from Maui."

Maui. Wait'll I tell Violet where her beach boy friend with the load in his drawers is off to, Harry thought. Violet and her big ideas, hire the jock. Well, fuck him, if he thinks he can screw Harry Marlin like that, 'cause old Harry will be right behind, right on his tail. Thinks he's tough. Let's go at it on dry land, and the sooner the better.

Then Harry did something he'd wanted to do most of the day. He leaned over the rail and let go of four Bloody Marys and two dozen oysters that had been corroding his gut like battery acid.

He wiped off his mouth on the sleeve of the camouflage jacket. "Maui, get ready, 'cause here I come," Harry Marlin said to the sea.

CHAPTER 22

Bímíní Blues

The racers straggled in, tied up and sprawled out on the barge, exhausted. Most said to hell with the champagne, just leave a six-pack and lemme alone. Lila Summers had finished midway back, helped some by not falling when the Magnum roared by, but she was exhausted too. Jake Lassiter helped her climb aboard the barge, where she peeled off her wet suit and sprawled out on a deck chair, eyes closed, chest heaving. He covered her with a towel and asked what Keaka was up to, but she just shrugged and rolled her eyes.

Maybe Keaka snapped, Lassiter thought. The reincarnated warrior heading for his own Valhalla. But what the hell was going on with the commodore in the Magnum? He wouldn't answer radio calls.

It was nearly dusk and the ABC producer kept asking when the awards would be given. P. J. Jeter stood nearby, microphone in hand, but with no one to interview. Presiding on the barge, Paul Flanigan convened an emergency meeting of the yacht club board which, after several rounds of Tequila Sunrises, concluded that there was no requirement to show up for the awards ceremony and declared Keaka Kealia the winner. "*Victor in absentia,*" Charlie Riggs agreed.

Lila Summers accepted the check for Keaka and brush-kissed Jake Lassiter, who handed it over, filling in for the missing commodore. François Duvalier, the surprise women's winner, gave Lassiter a better kiss than he deserved while Lila watched. He loved the look in Lila's eyes, like she might have bashed Françoise with her daggerboard if she wasn't so tired.

For a race with a bizarre finish—a windsurfer and a chase boat that disappeared—the atmosphere on Bimini was strangely calm. Bimini can do that, mellow you out. The judges' boats ferried the racers to the Big Game Club, where some serious drinking was under way in the Rum Keg Bar. Lila Summers squeaked across the lobby on bare feet, carrying the yellow backpack. Lassiter brought her sail bag with a change of clothes that he had stowed on the *Big Daddy*.

"Give me twenty minutes," she said, "then come to the room." The mystery of the missing Hawaiian wasn't so important now. Lila was supposed to be sharing a cottage with Keaka, but Lassiter was willing to pinch-hit. He stopped at the restaurant, got two bowls of conch chowder, an order of service, four broiled Bahamian lobster tails, a loaf of Bimini bread, still warm, and a six-pack of Grolsch, ice-cold.

Twenty minutes later—okay, so maybe it was fifteen—he knocked on her door. Room service, he said. Lila was just stepping out of the shower, white towel wrapped around her, its folds revealing full hips and flat stomach. She smiled at him, a tired but happy smile, kissed him gently on the forehead and grabbed one of the beers.

They devoured the food and drank the Grolsch, and Lassiter stepped out of his shorts while Lila undraped the towel, and on a cool bed with a breeze rattling the latticed windows he held her, his face buried in her wet hair, her skin still faintly salty from the sea. He nibbled at her pouty lower lip and she responded, and he slipped down under the sheet, caressing her breasts, brushing her stomach with light kisses. She purred a sweet song and her breathing quickened and her body moved to a faster beat, but in a moment she stopped moving and her breathing became slow and regular, and in another moment he figured it out . . . Lila was fast asleep.

O for 2. No hits in two at-bats. At least the first time I got some wood on the ball, he thought. This time I whiffed. Couldn't even keep her awake. Damn, maybe the beer was a bad idea.

Jake Lassiter pulled the sheet over Lila, who lay on her side now, her silhouette of slopes and curves visible in the darkness. He crawled in beside her and fell asleep. He dreamed of a jungle covered with swampy mangrove roots that grabbed at his legs and snaked up to his neck, where they tied intricate knots and strangled him, and he yelled and kicked and woke up in a sweat with Lila Summers holding him and whispering that everything was all right. And soon it was, because she kissed him and aroused him and with Jake Lassiter on his back she straddled him and guided him into her. With strong legs she slowly eased up and down, telling him to lie still and he obeyed, and she tightened herself onto him and rocked forward and back and when he finally gasped, she smiled, and he knew so he didn't ask. He knew it had been for him, Lila's way of saying not to worry about her, it didn't matter. He thought about it and was happy and sad at the same time and then he slept again, this time without dreams.

When Jake Lassiter awoke, there was something wrong. The telephone jarring him awake was wrong. The space next to him was empty, the sheets cool, and that was all wrong. He could feel the emptiness in the room. The phone still clanged, an ugly sound.

"I hope you're with the girl," the husky voice on the phone said.

"What?" Lassiter asked, propping himself up on an elbow, clearing the cobwebs. "Who's this?"

"Tubby Tubberville here, at your service. I'm at the front desk."

"Tub, what the hell, didn't know you could ride a chopper across the Straits. What're you doing here?"

"Cindy sent me over on the first Chalk's puddle jumper this morning. She was worried about you, what with the commodore hijacked and you not answering your phone all night. Plus all hell's broken loose at the firm. According to Cindy, your partners had some kind of emergency meeting to consider your future, or lack thereof. Some dude at the bank claims you nearly broke his neck. Gonna charge you with assault."

"Forget the firm and the bank. What do you mean about being with the girl?"

"The cottage you're in is registered to a Mr. Kealia and Ms. Summers. Your room's been empty all night so I hope you're in there with the girl, not the guy. Don't want any of my notions about you going down the drain."

Lassiter struggled upright and swung his feet onto the cold tile floor. "What's this about a hijacking?"

"If you're both decent I'll drop in and tell you."

"Only seems to be one of us here. C'mon in, number four."

Lassiter looked around. The wet suit was still hanging in the bathroom but Lila's sail bag with a change of clothes was gone. So was the yellow backpack. He had last seen it sticking out from under the bed last night. And there was a note on the dresser.

A note the morning after.

Oh shit. How did he know it wouldn't say to bring home a jug of wine, a loaf of bread, and thou?

Dearest Jake,

You don't know how close I came to staying. Grow old along with me, the best is yet to be. *You're very special to me and you deserve the best. But I am not for you. Too much has happened. There are things you don't know. When you learn them I pray you will not hate me. I know how you feel about me and hope I have not caused you pain. But please do not follow me. It is dangerous.*

Love,
Lila

Tubby came in, swung his bulk around, and looked at the empty beer bottles and the remains of the lobster tails. "Whoo-ee! Big-time lawyer buck nekkid, looks like you had yourself an orgy here."

Lassiter ignored the crack and handed Tubby the note. "Here, play Dear Abby for me."

Tubby scratched his beard, wrinkled his broad forehead, and moved his lips as he read. "Sorry, bro, a Dear Juan letter, as they say in our hometown. What's this 'dangerous' shit? Got anything to do with yesterday?"

"What happened yesterday?"

"Boy, are you out of it, she must be some piece . . . sorry,

Jake . . . but don't you know about the Hawaiian dude cutting out, then some friend of yours makes like *Miami Vice*, shootin' at him from this speedboat, goes back across the Stream, disappears at the Miami Beach marina? Meanwhile, nobody's seen hide nor hair of the Hawaiian, who hops on a seaplane and takes off."

"What friend of mine?" Lassiter asked, straining to focus on one fact at a time.

"Guy named Marlin, used your formerly good name to board the chase boat, then hijacks it. By the way, the Coast Guard wants to chat with you about it."

"Great. Tell them to stand in line behind Miami Beach burglary and Metro homicide. Also, tell them I don't know any Marlin."

Tubby began eating the crust from last night's dark Bimini bread. "Now what, bro?"

"How long ago your flight get in?"

"About an hour, and fifteen minutes later the plane headed for Nassau." Tubby finished the bread and wiped a paw across his mouth. "I know what you're thinking. Yeah, maybe she was on the plane outta here. Or maybe she took a boat going anywhere. You thinking of chasing her, proclaiming your devotion?"

Jake Lassiter had been thinking just that. But could he catch her if he didn't know where to start? He needed time to figure it out. His head was spinning. Marlin, who the hell was Marlin? And Keaka, where'd he go? And Lila, what did she mean, *it is dangerous*?

Lassiter stood up and pulled on his undershorts. "What about this Marlin, the hijacker, what'd he look like?"

"Short guy, balding, probably Latino, wearing an army jacket."

"A what?"

"You know, one of those camouflage jackets."

"Holy shit," Jake Lassiter said. He turned it over, the description the Rodriguez kid gave of the guy coming out of the theater, a short dark guy in a camouflage jacket. He did the B and E. Could be a coincidence, lots of those jackets around, or could be the same guy, now dropping my name, taking the commodore's boat, then hauling ass after Keaka Kealia, who leaves by seaplane. What's Keaka got to do with it? It didn't fit together, not yet. "Anything else? What'd the commodore say?"

"Said you're never to set foot in the hallowed halls of the yacht club again."

"Did Marlin say anything to him? Like what he was doing there?"

"Said the Hawaiian kid double-crossed him, that's all."

Keaka in on the theft, Lassiter thought, doesn't make sense. The bonds were stolen before he even got here. Could be just transporting the coupons, but they'd be too heavy. You couldn't sail like that and carry all that weight. Even Keaka Kealia couldn't do that. Lassiter wished Charlie Riggs was there to think it through, but the sun was already high in the east, and he would have been off at dawn in pursuit of the wily wahoo.

Tubby reached for another piece of the bread, dipped it into the remains of the conch chowder, then let it slip from his fingers. He bent down to grab the soggy bread from the floor and came up with a scrap of paper, which he crumpled and tossed into the wicker wastebasket. Jake Lassiter saw it out of the corner of his eye, a delayed reaction, the fine print in orange ink finally registering.

"Tubby, what the hell was that?"

"Hmmm. What?"

Lassiter was in the basket now, unfolding the scrap of paper, barely an inch wide by three inches long. His heart raced. "City of Gary, Indiana Environmental Improvement Revenue Bond 6.85 percent," a coupon worth $171.25.

Oh no, it couldn't be.

His mind sought an explanation other than the only one that made any sense.

There it was and had been all the time.

Right under his nose, or rather, his bed.

How stupid he had been.

Keaka Kealia hadn't transported the coupons. He had created a diversion, like some ancient warrior whose forces were outnumbered, King Cantaloupe, or whoever. He had lured the enemy into chasing shadows.

Lila Summers carried the coupons.

Lila Summers was weighted down by the contraband. That's why she lost the race. Lila Summers was the mule. And Jake Lassiter, what were you? The horse's ass, he told himself. Should have figured it out, instead of being swept away by her beauty. Don't get *farchadat* by the women, Samuel Kazdoy always told him.

Jake Lassiter sat back on the bed, paralyzed. His insides were empty, hollow, his guts scooped out. The pillow still carried her sweet scent. He thought about the note. He ached for her just as much as before, only it was a different kind of pain now.

Tubby found a half-empty beer bottle and drained it. "Hey, bro, you look like somebody just stole your girl."

"No, Tub. My girl just stole my bonds."

"Huh?"

"My client's bonds, though I was starting to think of them as half mine. I was thinking of Lila as half mine, too. Isn't that stupid?"

"Don't think I follow you," Tubby said.

"I'm going to need your help, Tub. What do you have planned the next few days?"

"Workin' on the Harley, some fishin', the usual. I'm yours."

"What's today, Tubby?"

"You do need help. Sunday, bro."

"Call Cindy at home, have her get us connections tomorrow to Maui, first-class."

"Sure thing. You're paying, I'm flying, but can I ask a question?"

"Shoot."

"Are we goin' after the bonds or the blonde?"

Jake Lassiter knew the answer. Lila had the bonds. And had him. Stole his heart and his client's bonds. He wanted to bring them both back, but could he? And what about Keaka? Funny, that was what he asked Lila on the beach. What had she said—she loved Keaka because he was free. Would she still love him if he were doing five to seven at Raiford for BRC—buying, receiving, and concealing stolen property? Let him windsurf in the urinal trough. But she was guilty too. Sweet Lila, how could she?

He could change her. He would talk her into turning over the bonds and leaving Keaka. Tubby would provide extra muscle in case things got ugly. Jake would use his connections to get her immunity. They'd come back to Miami. And live happily ever after.

He thought about it.

Dumb.

Very dumb.

It was the dumbest idea that ever worked its way into his consciousness. But he didn't have any other ideas.

"The bonds *and* the blonde, Tubby. We're going to get them both."

CHAPTER 23

Bottoms to the Moon

When Captain James Cook, commander of the British ship Resolution, landed on the Big Island of Hawaii in January 1779, he was accorded the honors of a chieftain. Priests in feather capes sang chants in his honor, and local chiefs brought him pigs and fruits and native wines.

The chiefs' generosity caused a food shortage among the commoners, who soon grew weary of the visitors. Within weeks, the Hawaiians began stealing the British seamen's supplies. Cook responded with a vengeance, burning houses in retaliation for a stolen goat, flogging those suspected of petty crimes. Still, the thievery continued—blacksmith's tongs, nails, finally a small boat.

Captain Cook himself led a small expedition of Marines that last day, hoping to take King Kalaniopuu hostage, to be held as ransom for the boat. As with later military disasters—Ponce de León and the Caloosas, General Custer and the Sioux—the white strangers woefully failed to comprehend the determination of the natives on whose land they had intruded. The Hawaiians attacked the British with rocks, fence posts, and wooden clubs. The British Marines fired one round from their muskets but were overwhelmed before they could reload. Though the entire battle took place on the lava rocks at the shore and Cook's dinghy waited beyond the surf line, he did not attempt to make it to that haven. James Cook, the world's greatest ship captain—conqueror of the Pacific, explorer of Tahiti, Hawaii, and Alaska—could not swim.

One of Kalaniopuu's chiefs stabbed Cook. Other warriors crushed his skull against the lava rocks. Then, with knives descended from the Stone Age, the Hawaiians stripped Cook's flesh and returned it to the British ship, believing Cook's men would want it. Instead, the British were horrified and returned to England having concluded that the Hawaiians had eaten portions of their captain and expected them to do the same.

The *haoles* had discovered Hawaii.

Harry Marlin didn't know Maui from Coney Island, but he booked the first flight. Five and a half hours Miami to L.A. on American, a three-hour layover and then five hours and twenty minutes to Honolulu, another layover, and finally a commuter flight ninety miles to the small city of Kahului on Maui, the Valley Isle of the Hawaiian chain. And so Harry Marlin emerged from the small plane . . . bleary-eyed, groggy, dehydrated, and constipated.

Pausing on the top step of the stairway, Harry blinked

against the harsh sunlight. Across the runway, through the trees, he could see colorful sails zipping by, windsurfers at Kanaha Beach Park, less than a mile from the tarmac. Sons of bitches. He hated them as he hated Keaka Kealia, imagined them young and tanned and getting all the pussy they could handle. A strong trade wind from the northeast nearly toppled him from the stairs. A real tank town, Harry thought, not even a jetway for the big planes rolling up nearby. And that wind. Good thing he didn't wear a toupee, it'd be in Samoa by now.

"Aloha," said the Asian woman at the foot of the stairs, placing a lei of fragrant white plumeria over his head. "Maui *no ka oi.* Maui is the best." The day was warm and the sky cloudless and the woman stood smiling at him, her straight black hair blowing in the wind. Harry Marlin despised the place.

He rented a four-door Chevrolet Celebrity and drove to the hotel in Kaanapali. He wasn't thinking of the coupons, not yet, because at the moment he had only two things on his mind—taking a crap and getting some sleep. Tomorrow he could set out after the bastard who ripped him off.

Harry passed through the central valley of the island, the towering peak of Haleakala to his left, lost in the clouds, the lower green mountains of west Maui to his right. On both sides of the road, fields of sugarcane swayed in the wind. He passed the smokestacks of the processing plant at Puunene, the aroma like sweet summer corn hot off the grill. But the air turned bittersweet, the sky blackened nearby, hundreds of acres being burned to strip away the cane's useless leaves.

The hotel was a jungle and a menagerie filled with plants and animals. Harry Marlin stood in the open-air lobby beneath a seven-story Japanese banyan tree. Flowers everywhere. Pink lokelanis, the Maui rose, were mixed with crimson bougainvilleas, the heart-shaped anthurium, and the exotic bird of paradise. Plumeria added fragrance as strong as burning incense.

Then the animals. The fish, Japanese koi, orange and black, swimming in a stream, getting fat on pretzels as they swam by the bar in the lobby. There were parrots and macaws and cranes, and nearby, miniature penguins hopped into their little pool. The birds all tweeting and the flowers reeking and the walls all teak and glass. Makes the Fontainebleau look like a flophouse, Harry Marlin thought.

In fact, the hotel was ersatz Hawaii, a jungle the way Walt Disney might have imagined it, where the palm trees were stripped of their coconuts so that mice were not attracted, and the birds, like the concierge, worked an eight-hour shift, nine to five, then back to the cages. An upscale tourist's ideal, a touch of exotica but no mosquitoes for three hundred bucks a night.

Harry shrugged off the bellman and carried his own bag, riding the elevator to the eighth floor. He took one look at the view—the Pacific Ocean, the island of Lanai—closed the curtains, and fell into bed. He slept soundly, the sleep of a man who does not know enough to be afraid of the dark.

The waitress chirped *g'morning* and said, "How 'bout starting with some papaya juice and all-bran cereal, great for the digestive tract?" She was young with a ponytail and eyes that had never seen trouble and was probably a health food nut, Harry figured. California written all over her. The type that wouldn't dream of a cheeseburger sizzling in grease at the Lincoln Road Grill.

Harry had the papaya juice and the bran but his digestive tract was still as congested as I-95 in rush hour. Then he set out in his rented Chevy in search of Keaka Kealia. It had taken only a couple of questions in the hotel to learn that the windsurfers all hung out in Paia, a town on the north shore.

Yeah, I know Keaka, everybody knows Keaka. That's what all the suntanned, long-haired, glassy-eyed kids said in every shop, but nobody had seen him since the trip to Miami. Paia had turned out to be little more than a few dusty blocks crammed with windsurfing shops and hippie restaurants serving mahi-mahi burgers.

The day wasted, Harry returned to the hotel and tried to figure out what he would tell Violet. He dialed her number and got the machine—"y'all leave a message"—and figured she'd call him back. *Where on God's green earth you been?* So Harry wasn't surprised when the phone rang in his room. It was a woman's voice, all right, but young and sweet. No, definitely not Violet.

"Mr. Marlin, you don't know me. I am with Keaka Kealia. He asked me to contact you. He very much regrets that the two of you had a misunderstanding."

"Misunderstanding! Look, honey, that bastard stole my hard-earned grubstake."

"As I say, Mr. Marlin, Keaka regrets your misunderstanding and wants you to know he has a great deal of respect for you, the way you traveled all the way here, your courage in coming to a strange land."

Okay, Harry Marlin thought. That's more like it. Found out I was nosing around, got nervous, wants to deal. Even better than me making the first move. Dumb bastard shows his weakness right off the bat.

"Tell him to save the grease job, just gimme back my property, he can keep ten percent just like we agreed and I'll forget how he double-crossed me."

The sugary voice continued in the same tone, "Keaka asked me to arrange a meeting with the two of you."

"You think I'm gonna meet your pal in some dark alley, forget it."

"Mr. Marlin, I'm in the lobby. Would you care to join me at the Banyan Bar in, say, ten minutes? We can discuss the meeting there over drinks." The voice still even, smooth, but a nice lilt on the word "drinks," a bit of interest there.

Why not? Safe place, young babe in a hotel bar, maybe hot to trot. What was it Violet was talking about, the old man saying something about his lawyer falling for the Hawaiian's girlfriend, she was a real number. Okay, gonna meet her, maybe one of those nymphos. But how 'bout this chicken-shit bastard sending his squeeze to do the dirty work. I'd never do that to Violet.

Only a few customers at the bar, some watching the fish swim under the bridge, a few couples talking at tables, one guy at the end of the bar staring into a drink.

"Mr. Marlin." A woman's voice, sweet and soft.

Harry turned around. Okay. All right. The Hawaiian had good taste in cooze. Harry gave her a grin that countless women had found resistible. "Yeah, that's me."

In a dainty sweeping motion, the young woman extended her right arm and shook Harry's hand with a grip that couldn't break an egg. "So pleased to meet you," she said.

"You got a name, honey?"

"Lee Hu," said the petite woman with a shy smile. "My friends call me Little Lee."

Harry Marlin didn't notice the man at the end of the bar watching them, didn't notice anything but Little Lee's big dark eyes and compact body. He ordered drinks, Perrier for Lee Hu, a Blue Hawaii—pineapple juice, vodka, and blue curaçao—for himself.

"*Okolemaluna*," she said, hoisting her Perrier.

"Huh?"

"*Okole*, that's butt or bottom. *Luna*, that's moon. So, bottoms to the moon, or bottoms up."

"Gotcha," he said, sipping at the straw, it being hard to toss down a drink served in a hollowed-out pineapple. Wouldn't mind seeing her old-koley, Harry thought, a tight little bottom on this one.

They talked. Yes, Keaka had the coupons, had stashed them on the slopes of Haleakala, the extinct volcano. She would meet Harry in the morning, take him there. Keaka had a new proposition, she said, a fifty-fifty split.

Harry used the miniature umbrella to stir a second Blue Hawaii—not much vodka there—and said he would sleep on it. Shit, he would grab it, grab half the coupons and get the hell out of there. Then he asked her if she'd like to have a nightcap in his room. A polite no-thank-you. Okay, can't blame a guy for trying, can't get a hit if you don't swing the bat. She'd pick him up at seven A.M. Better get some sleep. Maybe the digestive tract would be working in the morning, Harry hoped as he headed to his room.

A Hawaiian man, early forties, in khaki slacks and an aloha shirt, moved from the end of the bar where he had been nursing a drink and slid next to Lee Hu. "What do you think?" he asked.

"It should be easy. He's a fool, he makes eyes at me like I'm a pushover, spends six-fifty for a drink that looks like toilet bowl cleaner. He has no sense of who he is, his limitations, or where he is, the dangers."

The man smiled and squeezed her arm affectionately. "Good work, Little Lee. It's no wonder Keaka likes you so much. You catch on quick."

"Compared to bringing a load in from Colombia through Coast Guard and Navy reconnaissance, this is child's play."

"We'll see you in the morning then."

He started to get up, but she touched his arm lightly and said, "Tell Keaka not to get careless. There was a bulge in the sports coat, a gun I suppose."

"I saw it halfway across the lobby. Don't worry."

"Mikala, you'll take care of Keaka for me?"

The man nodded. "He takes care of himself pretty well. And he's my flesh and blood. Anybody touches a hair of his head, I blow the guy away."

CHAPTER 24

Island Cop

First-class on United, L.A. to Maui nonstop. To Tubby Tubberville, it was like dying and going to heaven. "You mean I can have all the little bottles I want?" he asked the flight attendant. "Just line up the Jack Daniel's like so many tenpins and see them fall down."

Jake Lassiter watched the bulk in seat 3A with concern. "Easy, Tub, we've got work to do when we get there."

"Sure, bro, you're looking for the dame what left you and I'm making sure nobody sticks a shiv in your back. A little angel tit to warm the throat ain't gonna hurt none."

"You're not forgetting the coupons, are you?"

"The bonds and the blonde, I remember." He yelled at the flight attendant. "Hey, sweetie, there a movie on this wagon?"

They were halfway across the Pacific and Jake Lassiter was trying to figure out where to start. He could have gone to the police in Miami, of course, and with his testimony could have gotten an arrest warrant, but for whom? For Lila. The only evidence of criminal conduct was the bond coupon on the floor of the cottage. He could have Lila arrested but not Keaka, and what he wanted was the opposite. He needed to trap Keaka, to find him with the goods, to get Lila's help and win her freedom in return for her testimony.

It had better work, because there wouldn't be a lot waiting for him at home. The executive committee at Harman & Fox had suspended him pending an inquiry of the charges brought by Thad Whitney, who was claiming a severe case of whiplash, not to mention mental anguish.

"This flight ain't half bad, eh, bro?" Tubby said happily somewhere over the Pacific.

"Glad you're enjoying it. It's lasting longer than most of my relationships." Lassiter put his head back and tried to sleep but could not, visions of Lila streaking across his mind. Lila laughing at him, waving handfuls of colorful coupons, tossing them like confetti, the dark warrior Keaka watching with evil amusement.

At the airport in Kahului, they rented a Pontiac Grand Am and drove to Makawao, a rural town upcountry on the lower slopes of Haleakala. It was only a few miles from where Lila grew up, and from the mountain, you could see the windsurfing beaches on the north shore. Because Lila loved the upcountry, Lassiter believed she might be there. If not, it was a good place to start looking. What was it Keaka had said? The mountains and valleys talk, or something like that. Lassiter was ready to listen.

"Somehow, Tubby, I pictured you as a faster driver," Lassiter said as they crept up the mountain in the rental car.

"Yeah, well ain't in no hurry. Cindy complains too, says I drive too slow and screw too fast. Used to do 'em both at the same time with biker chicks, but that was before Cindy. Settled down now. Cindy's talking about marriage when she's not telling me what to do—lose weight, get a real job, sell the Harley, buy a condo."

Lassiter laughed and did his best to carry a tune, " '*She'll redecorate your home, from the cellar to the dome, then go on to the enthralling fun of overhauling you.*' "

"Huh?"

"Henry Higgins, *My Fair Lady*."

"Ain't none of 'em fair," Tubby Tubberville said.

They were upcountry now, the temperature a few degrees cooler. The sugarcane and pineapple fields yielded to pastures with horses standing vigil, cattle grazing, and hibiscus growing wild. They registered at the Makawao Inn and headed down to Paia. He knew from the windsurfing magazines that Keaka and Lila lived in the little town near the Sprecklesville Beach. He doubted they would be there. On the main street and in the shops, they asked their questions. The answers were always the same. Nobody had seen Keaka or Lila since they'd left for Miami.

Tubby eased the Pontiac by their house, an old stucco number on a dusty street with overgrown lawns. No signs of life, neighbors said nobody there for weeks. A short ride to Hookipaa, the most famous windsurfing beach in the world. Lassiter asked several of the beachers but came up empty until he found a dark-skinned Hawaiian teenager with spiked, bleached hair. He was using sandpaper to smooth the rough spots out of a fiberglass fin. "That Keaka a radical dude, he may be on Molokai," the kid said.

"Molokai?" Lassiter asked.

"The dude loves the jungle there. Gets high on it. Weird dude."

Lassiter asked, "Where on Molokai would the dude be?"

"Don't know. Big jungle."

Molokai was only a few miles across the Pailolo Channel, but there was virtually no development, just cattle ranches on the high plains and a jungle on the east end facing Maui. If Keaka was in there, no one could find him. And if Lila was with him? Lassiter's spirits plunged. He decided to do what he hadn't done in Miami.

The County of Maui police station in Wailuku sits at the foot of the West Maui Mountains, green and jagged, a beautiful backdrop to the small downtown. An old banyan tree shades the building, a sturdy structure with a red barrel tile roof, a holding cell downstairs, and a small office crammed with typewriters, communications gear and computers upstairs.

A pleasant young woman in uniform ushered him into the captain's office, a cramped room with maps on the walls, pictures of soldiers in a jungle, an honorable discharge from the U.S. Army, and a framed medal tarnished at the edges. The captain was swarthy and stocky, mid-forties, his uniform neatly pressed, short sleeves rolled up over solid biceps. His name tag read M. Kalehauwehe, and he watched Lassiter scan the mementos.

"Nam," the captain said. "Flew a chopper, Cobra gunship, had three shot out from under me, two more burned up flying flat out. Loved those Cobras, like little bees buzzing, blasting the shit out of anything that moves. Got thirty-caliber machine gun, twenty-millimeter cannon, grenade launcher, aerial rockets, and TOW missiles. Shit, I could destroy a town with one Cobra."

"You must have some memories," Lassiter said, letting him play them back. He was going to anyway.

The captain nodded and settled back into his wooden chair. "Brass said I was hell on engines, the way I flew. After I was grounded, learned something new, ordnance specialist, C-4 plastique. Looks like clay the kids play with. Hit it with a hammer, nothing happens, but send an electric charge through it, ka-boom! Wired a toilet once, blew porcelain up a VC's ass and out his Adam's apple."

"Guess he was really on your shit list," Lassiter said, but the captain didn't get it, just kept talking.

"Had a problem with VC stealing our jeeps. So we'd bait 'em. Leave a jeep out but wire it with plastique. Bastard turns on the ignition, his balls end up on the far side the Ho Chi Minh Trail. But they catch on, get little kids—orphans, ragamuffins—to start the jeeps for 'em while they hide in a ditch. Then we catch on. I rig up a gizmo, the ignition doesn't blow the plastique, just starts a timer that sets a spark in three minutes. By then the kid's gone, the VC slimeball gets in, ka-boom!"

Captain Kalehauwehe smiled with contentment. Time to bring him back to his job. Lassiter said, "Guess police work is a breeze after those experiences."

"Yeah, just a bunch of Filipinos cutting each other up and tourists losing their wallets. What can I help you with?"

Lassiter told part of the story, held back part, told him a client was burglarized, lost a bunch of valuable securities—didn't say how much—and circumstantial evidence implicated Keaka Kealia, did he know him?

Sure, everybody knew him, great athlete. No, he'd never been in any trouble, at least nothing more than the rest of the kids here, maybe a few fights when he was younger, never lost one. No, hadn't seen Keaka in some time, usually with his girlfriend, what's her name, Lila, right.

The captain asked if Lassiter had an arrest warrant or an extradition order. No, well, not much we can do for you, just coming in here accusing a well-known citizen of being an accessory to a felony. Where you staying? Makawao Inn. We'll let you know if anything turns up, have a pleasant stay, Mr. Lassiter.

Okay, Jake Lassiter thought, the cop was a little defensive. Understandable, I come in here with a story like that. He'll probably call Miami Beach and check it out. Shit, Carraway will tell him a skinny kid named Rodriguez took the coupons.

Captain Kalehauwehe escorted Jake Lassiter to the door and watched him walk to his car. Then the captain returned to his office, closed the door, picked up the telephone, and dialed a familiar number. A woman answered the phone.

"Hello, Little Lee," the captain said. "Tell Keaka we've got some work to do."

"More, Mikala, more besides the stupid little man?"

"First him. Then a smarter, larger one," Captain Mikala Kalehauwehe said.

CHAPTER

25

House of the Sun

At the time when the earth became hot,
At the time when the heavens turned about,
At the time when the sun was darkened,
To cause the moon to shine,
The time of the rise of the Pleiades,
The slime, this was the source of the earth . . .

FROM "KUMULIPO," A HAWAIIAN SON OF CREATION

T*he islands that are Hawaii sit atop the largest structures on* earth, volcanoes that extend five miles from the ocean floor to peaks ten thousand feet above the sea. The oldest of the islands, Kure, was formed more than twenty million years ago. Today, it is a tiny reef fifteen hundred miles northwest of Maui, eroded into a semicircle that will eventually disappear beneath the sea.

All these islands—from the largest and youngest, Hawaii, the Big Island, to the smallest and oldest, Kure—were born from the same womb, a hot spot boiling with magma beneath the surface of the earth. When the pressure builds in this underground reservoir, steam surges upward, searching for the path of least resistance. Then molten rock erupts from the innards of the earth, and if the volume is great enough, a new land mass is formed.

The mantle of the earth moves slowly over the hot spot, a few inches each year to the northwest, and with the millennia each island moves with it. While Kure slowly disappears under the ravages of erosion, the Big Island of Hawaii grows even now as Kilauea continues to erupt and add silvery rock to the land.

The ancient Hawaiians, the Polynesians who crossed the ocean in giant sailing canoes, had their own explanation for the explosions and the crimson flow of molten earth. The fire goddess Pele lived in the heart of the volcano, shifting from Kauai to Oahu to Maui before settling in Kilauea on the Big Island in search of the perfect home and perfect lover. She thought the chief Lohiau would be that lover but he fell in love with her younger sister, Hiiaka, and when the couple tried to escape, Pele drowned them in the caldron of fiery Kilauea.

Pele, it seems, is a jealous lover.

Haleakala. Haleakala here, there, and everywhere, Harry Marlin thought. Postcards in the gift shop, a tourist film on the hotel's TV channel, busloads of hicks leaving at four A.M. to see sunrise at the Haleakala crater like a bunch of friggin' pilgrims. Four A.M., for Christ's sake, time to call it a night, not start the day. Haleakala, that's all there was here except for the beaches and Harry Marlin didn't travel six thousand miles for a suntan or for a ride up a mountain to take snapshots of a burned-out volcano. A one-horse town, that's Maui for you.

Harry studied the literature, as he called it, at the concierge's desk. Haleakala, House of the Sun. *Hale*, "house"; *La*, "sun." That's where the girl, Little Lee, said the coupons were, and that was the only good reason to go up the mountain, as far as Harry could see.

He showed up fifteen minutes early. That was smart, he thought, take a look-see, scout the perimeter for wise guys. At seven o'clock sharp, Lee Hu pulled into the driveway. Hard to miss her, the engine of the Chevy Blazer 4x4 rumbling in the still morning air, awakening the snoozing cabbies. Now if this wasn't a sight, Harry thought, the little dumpling driving a souped-up truck, actually a jacked-up truck, thirty-nine-inch wheels and a heavy suspension system lifting the cab high off the ground. The front bumper was a foot-high beam of thick steel with a heavy winch attached. Seven high-powered spotlights were attached to a rail across the roof, nearly enough wattage to play a night game.

"You got yourself *some* wheels there, Little Lee," Harry Marlin said, hoisting himself onto the bottom rung of the built-in ladder and poking at a tarpaulin that covered the truck bed. You never know, Harry thought, could be some jungle boy with a machete back there.

The bed was empty. Empty but not clean, a residue of twigs and tiny leaves stuck to the crevices of the metal bed. Harry knew from the smell that the truck wasn't used by a Japanese gardener. No, this baby's been hauling the kind of grass that mellows you out.

Harry stood there for a moment, not getting in, just hanging onto the side of the customized truck, the engine vibrating with quiet thunder as Lee Hu kept it in neutral. There was a moment of hesitation, and Lee Hu saw it.

"It's Keaka's truck but he usually keeps it on the farm he owns with his cousin," she said. "Rough terrain, you need power and big wheels, rugged suspension. They've dropped a four-hundred-and-twenty-seven-cubic-inch engine into it, has five-fifty horsepower, a six-hundred-lift hydraulic cam, TRW pistons, high-volume oil pump, the works. You ought to see it on mountain roads."

Christ, this one talks like Mario Andretti, Harry thought. "We're going on a mountain road, aren't we, to get to the volcano? I read about the winding road."

"Oh no," Lee Hu said with a smile. "We'll go a much quicker way. C'mon."

Okay, sometimes you just got to take a risk, Harry thought, hauling himself into the cab. Lee Hu eased the truck into first gear, let out the clutch, and stomped on the gas, burning rubber and scattering birds as they tore out of the lushly landscaped hotel grounds and headed down the coast on Highway 30.

Harry kept his eyes on the outside mirror to see if they were being tailed, but the road was deserted except for hotel employees coming to work. Lee Hu drove south five miles to Lahaina, a nineteenth-century whaling village now overrun with tourists and T-shirt shops, an ice-cream stand on every corner. They were on Front Street along the harbor, the shops still shuttered, a few breakfast places opening, the island of Lanai visible across the channel.

Lee Hu turned into a side street and drove a few blocks to an empty softball field. She pointed to the middle of the field. "Here's how you'll travel. Much faster, much more comfortable than Crater Road."

A helicopter sat in the infield. Two men stood near first base, one lean and strong—so he's here—the other a massive hulk of dark Hawaiian manhood. Lee Hu pulled the truck alongside the first base line, Harry admiring the way she downshifted. Then he got out and stood face-to-face with Keaka.

"Hello, partner," Keaka Kealia said, smiling at him, like they were really buddies.

"Hullo yourself. Been looking forward to this." Have to show some toughness, let' em know Harry marlin don't roll over for nobody. Like the girl said, came six thousand miles.

Fucking A, kid, Harry Marlin got balls the size of coconuts.

Keaka still smiled. "Say hello to Lomio."

Lumbering toward Harry, Lomio was a load. He was smaller than a Patton tank but looked just as lethal, and he sure hadn't missed any meals. He wasn't built like Schwarzenegger, no rippling lats or carved washboards here. More like a sumo wrestler, big all over, the neck of a Brahma bull with huge, sloping shoulders, arms without definition, just thick slabs of meat. He wore a turquoise aloha shirt, his stomach ballooning underneath, but with no trace of softness, more like he'd just swallowed a watermelon. His face was the color of overdone toast, and if he knew how to smile, he was keeping it a secret.

"How you doin'," Harry said, eyeing the big man warily. Lomio grunted in return.

Keaka laughed and patted his friend's beefy shoulder. "Lomio isn't used to strangers. He lives on the other side of the island, even beyond Hana, no paved roads, go in and out by copter. Few *haoles* there, few anybody there. He helps out on a farm I own with my cousin."

"Looks like you could hitch a plow to him, wouldn't need a John Deere," Harry said.

Keaka smiled in a relaxed, natural way, like it was every day he made a deal to split up more than a million bucks. He was wearing shorts and a T-shirt. Barefoot, he looked harmless enough, just another kid from the beach, though this one had taut veins popping out on each arm and muscles that rippled with each movement. Even his wide, dark feet looked muscular.

"Lomio's more of a caretaker than a farmer," Keaka said. "He keeps trespassers from disturbing our crops, but he's really very gentle, a lover, not a fighter. Lomio translates to Romeo, you know."

"Didn't know," Harry Marlin said, thinking this Romeo's Juliet was probably a holstein. Harry also figured they weren't growing pineapples on the other side of the island, but that was none of his business. *His* business was . . . where, buried in an extinct volcano? He pointed at the helicopter. "So where we going in this thing?"

"To the crater. We're waiting for the pilot. But first, do we have a deal? An even split, fifty-fifty."

"I don't like it, but I'm an easy guy to get along with. Just to avoid any . . . uh . . . unpleasantness between you and me, okay, fifty-fifty, even Stephen."

Keaka Kealia extended a powerful brown hand and said, "Shake, partner. I knew you were reasonable."

Harry Marlin tried not to wince as the handshake cracked his knuckles. He turned around in time to see Lee Hu pull away in the truck, the huge tires biting into the red dirt and stirring up a dust storm. "Good-bye, Mr. Marlin," she called out the window. Harry stared after her uneasily, somehow feeling more exposed now, thinking nobody would put a bullet in his head with a lady on the premises.

"Little Lee's afraid of heights," Keaka said, as if reading Harry's mind. "Refuses to fly unless she's mellowed out on *pakalolo*."

Harry stared at him blankly.

"Marijuana. Maui Wowie," Keaka explained. "If you want, we'll get you some."

"Maybe later."

Lomio had already hauled himself into the passenger compartment of the helicopter, a sleek beige craft with brown stripes. There were two doors on each side, one up front for the pilot and a larger door to a separate compartment for the passengers. Harry looked into the window of the passenger compartment. Five seats, two facing the rear separated by a small bar with a cut-glass brandy decanter, and three deeply cushioned seats facing forward. The interior was beige trimmed in brown leather. You could have a pretty good poker game back there.

Lomio sat in one of the seats facing the rear, opening and closing the compartment door by twisting the spring-loaded metal handgrip. The door opened with a whoosh, pushed by a pneumatic plunger. He did it again and again, like a child with a favorite toy. Christ, this elephant's got the IQ of a sponge, Harry thought.

"He loves the copter," Keaka said, "loves to play with the cyclic, the stick. We have to keep him out of the cockpit or he'll foul up all the instruments."

"Glad you told me. I was afraid he was our pilot."

Keaka laughed again. Harry wondered why everything seemed funny to the Hawaiian this morning. Suddenly, a police car whipped onto the ball field, a trail of dust kicking up in its wake. Harry turned, took one look at the car and nearly started running. "What the hell!"

"Don't worry," Keaka said. "He's my cousin and he's the best copter pilot on Maui." The police car slid to a stop, and a man looked out at them through the open window. Keaka said, "Mr. Marlin, say hello to Mikala Kalehauwehe, captain in the County of Maui Police Department."

"Hello, Officer," Harry Marlin said.

The captain nodded, got out of the car, took off his regulation shirt and replaced it with an L.A. Raiders jersey of silver and black. "You like the copter?" he asked Harry, who shifted from foot to foot, trying to assess the situation.

"Yeah, it's a fine-looking machine." Harry knew cops on the take. Hell, in Miami, you were lucky if they didn't steal nickels and dimes from the parking meters, to say nothing of the ones in bed with the drug dealers. But here, halfway around the world, not my turf, and I'm using a cop to pick up stolen property.

"Let me show this baby to you while I check it out." Mikala put on his aviator sunglasses and smiled easily. "Usually, it's on the farm, but I flew it in last night, humming like a Stradivarius. Ever fly in one of these? Hey, Lomio, hope we have enough horses to get this off the ground with you in there."

The cop was chattering away, being friendly, too friendly maybe, Harry thought. The kid, too. They're gonna give me half of a fortune and they're happy about it, maybe stoked on what'd he call it, a pack of lolo.

"A beauty, huh?" The cop ran his hand over the smooth curve of the nose. "Made in Italy, those Italians know design. An Agusta A-109, two engines—good to have two, in case one peters out on you, right? Didn't have that in Nam, the Cobra's engine goes, you better have some flat land in sight. Now, this baby cruises at a hundred seventy-five, can take a thousand pounds of cargo or people. You want to take some *pakalolo* home with you, we'll stop at the farm. Now, this is what they call the executive configuration of the passenger compartment, five people, three facing two, can have a meeting, fix drinks, whatever. So make yourself at home, we'll be there in no time."

The guy seemed all right. Just a fly-boy who loves his planes, Harry hoped.

"Just one thing before we take off." Mikala pointed at the bulge in Harry's sports coat. "Standard procedure, I gotta take that gun in your shoulder holster. No firearms near the fuel tank, state law."

State law! Friggin' cop is fencing stolen property, growing weed, but he's worried about aviation regulations. "I 'spose you'll make me fasten my seat belt, too," Harry said.

"Absolutely."

Harry handed over the gun. Now, if you don't mind, the cop was saying, still smiling, his voice apologetic, assume the position, and with a gentle but firm grip, he spun Harry around until he faced the fuselage, kicked his feet apart and expertly frisked him, patting the polyester sports coat, under the arms, back of the pants, then up and down each leg, right into the crotch where one pat smacked Harry's testicles into each other, hard enough for his eyes to water. Sorry, old habit, the cop said, then with Harry's gun, he climbed into the cockpit, put on green earphones, and began fiddling with the dials.

Keaka stepped gracefully through the rear door and sat down. He offered Harry a hand and pulled him in, Harry settling into a seat directly across from the big man. Sitting that way, his knees wedged against Lomio's shins, it was impossible not to look at the huge Hawaiian. The big man was unshaven, a three- or four-day growth erupting scraggily from the dark face, a forest here, a desert there. His dirty neck was creased with rolls of tissue, muscle or fat or a mixture of the two. An ugly yellow boil the size of a kumquat festered maliciously above his shirt collar. His black eyes were lost under heavy lids and he had yet to offer a smile or a decipherable word.

Harry was still concentrating on the dull ache in his groin when the four rotor blades started churning. The engines whined and the copter lifted a few feet off the ground, hovered a moment, then shot upward toward a rendezvous with the House of the Sun.

Harry Marlin had read the brochures but still didn't know his geography. He didn't know that Haleakala was east and that the trip should be entirely across land, first around the West Maui Mountains, then through the central valley, then up the gentle slopes of the extinct volcano, past the ring of clouds to the ten-thousand-foot level. Because he was unaware of these things, Harry Marlin was not alarmed that the helicopter was flying south across the Auau Channel, then the Kealaikahiki Channel—literally, the Path to Tahiti—then east over the small island of Kahoolawe. All this took a matter of minutes in the fast Italian helicopter, and then they were flying east over the open ocean toward the Big Island of Hawaii.

Harry Marlin did not know the difference between Maui and the Big Island. He thought only of a mountaintop with riches buried inside. And, sure enough, in the distance two volcanoes were visible. The twin peaks of Mauna Loa and Mauna Kea on the Big Island stood more than thirteen thousand feet above the sea, even higher than Haleakala on Maui. Below the two giants was Kilauea, a third volcano.

There is a difference, however, between the volcanoes of the Big Island and Haleakala of Maui. Haleakala last erupted in 1790. Kilauea's last eruption began only three months ago, and lava continued to pour through its vents and spill down its side to this very day.

The helicopter flew five hundred feet above the water, rapidly closing the distance to land. Harry Marlin leaned against the window and watched the waves peaking beneath them.

Keaka broke the silence. "Now we renegotiate."

Oh shit. "Whadaya mean?"

Keaka's smile was gone. He looked at Harry through eyes black and hard as coal. "Fifty-fifty is not fair."

"C'mon, a deal's a deal."

"New deal," Keaka said. "A fair deal."

"What's fair?" Harry Marlin asked, afraid his voice betrayed a shudder deep in his bowels.

Keaka shrugged as if there could be no dispute. "All for me and none for you."

Harry exhaled loudly. He tried his best fuck-you look, vaguely aware that it wouldn't have frightened a kitten. Then Harry sized up the situation. The Hawaiian kid on one side of him, the door over the ocean on the other side, and a monster stepping on his toes facing him. And the crooked cop had his piece.

"Not exactly fair," Harry said, his throat tightening against the fear.

Keaka stretched his arms in front of him, lazily, but the triceps sprang into shape, cords of well-defined muscles a few inches from Harry's nose. Keaka spoke again, softly. "It's my copter and they're my coupons and these are my friends, and I'm going to have to ask you to leave."

"Leave?" Harry was sweating now. He could feel his face heat up, imagined it a searing red, hated himself for it.

Keaka was expressionless, his voice still calm. "Lomio, I wonder if the *haole* can swim. Many of them can't. Hey, *haole*, would you believe that Lomio can hold his breath three minutes and free-dive to forty feet for Kona lobster. Lomio, should we see if the *haole* can swim?

The big man grunted and seemed to smile. At least the corners of his mouth turned horizontal from their previously slack, downward arc.

"Wait," Harry pleaded, "if you want the coupons, keep 'em, they've been more trouble than they're worth. They're yours, let's get back to the hotel." The posturing was over. Harry knew what he was doing, knew it more clearly than anything he had ever known. He was begging for his life.

"That's very generous of you, but they're already mine. What else can you offer me? Nothing. You have nothing to bargain with. Maybe you could tell me where the other *haole* is, the lawyer, but I know that from Mikala, so you can give me nothing but your life. And after you die, the lawyer will die."

Lomio nodded his massive head in approval, and he really did smile, revealing teeth large and gray like granite tombstones.

"Lomio, did you know this *haole* tried to shoot me? If he did that to you, what would you do?"

The big man shrugged, his massive head tilting toward the

window, an unmistakable gesture, pointing to the open sea. The copter seemed to list in that direction.

"Hey, there's land coming up," Harry Marlin whined, bargaining for time. "Just put me down there, anywhere, and let's forget all about it."

Keaka moved closer to him. Their shoulders touched and Harry inched away until he was squeezed tight against the door.

"Lomio, I think the *haole* is afraid of the sharks. Hammerheads down there, tiger sharks, too. But the grays are the worst. Of course, they don't usually eat everything. So if your head floats up somewhere, my poor cousin Mikala has another death to investigate, keeps him from helping me on the farm. Maybe it's better if we don't drop you here."

Harry Marlin prayed then, prayed that they were just trying to scare him, to get him on the first flight home, but then he forced himself to look into Keaka's eyes, the lumps of coal now ablaze with withering hate. The fear hit him then, waves of heat and then cold from the pit of his stomach. But Harry didn't panic. He kept his eyes open, watching for a chance to cheat death.

Harry looked out the window and saw the breakers that tumbled close to shore, and with one hand he unbuckled his seat belt and with the other reached for the handle with the spring grip and twisted it. The door opened a crack. The big man made no move to stop him. Harry pressed against the door with all his weight but the pressure from the wind pushed back, closing it. Harry twisted the handle and pushed again but the door wouldn't budge beyond an inch or two and then they were over a rocky coastline and the fall would kill him. He slumped back into his seat.

Keaka laughed and this time his teeth showed and his black eyes danced. "If you want to leave, just say so. Mikala can hover and the door will open easily, no wind resistance to keep it closed."

In a moment they were over the lower slopes, on a detour around the massive peak of Mauna Loa flying toward the eastern shore. They rode in silence until they were above Kilauea and the helicopter bucked and pitched in turbulent air currents.

Harry pressed his face against the window, the glass hot against his cheek. He looked down and what he saw was a vision of hell, a lake on the summit of the volcano churning with red lava, a pot boiling with molten rock at two thousand degrees, torrents of heat rank with sulfur rising around them. The helicopter hovered now, Mikala trying to hold it steady in the updrafts.

"Say hello to Pele," Keaka said. "Would you like to visit her? She is always looking for new lovers."

Harry was silent, sick to his stomach from the turbulence and the fear.

Keaka grabbed Harry by the back of his neck, and pressed his face to the scorching window. "The fools built houses on the coast road below, all *haoles* like you. They thought they were safe there, ten miles from a sleeping volcano. But Pele sleeps restlessly, and when she awakes she lets out a roar. Each day the flow comes from the bowels of the earth. Sometimes the lava is fluid like a river out of control, the *pahoehoe*. No man can outrun it. Then there is the *'a'a*, full of rocks and cinders, and though it is slow, no man can stop it, not the *haoles* with all their machines and technology. Pele adds to the island, gives us a new coastline. Probably somewhere in California, even before the lava has cooled, *haoles* are planning stupid condominiums for the new land of Hawaii. But Pele has issued her warning. Already, she has breathed her fire on the *haole* houses along the sea, big stupid houses like the big stupid *haoles.* And little stupid *haoles* like you, Harry Marlin from Miami Beach. You were born stupid and you will die stupid."

"No, please," Harry whimpered.

"Do not fear, little man. I will make you immortal. In a few weeks the lava will cool and harden. In months it will become rock. In years wind and rain and dust will carry spores and seeds into the crevices, and from the smudge of grease that had been your worthless body, a flower might grow. And in ten thousand centuries, the same wind and rain will eat away at the rock and the rock beneath it, and the Big Island of Hawaii will disappear into the sea from which it came. Ashes to ashes and dust to dust."

There was a rapping on the wall separating the passengers from the cockpit. Keaka looked up and rapped back, twice. "Mikala's in a hurry. The fumes will corrode our engines. *Haole*, are you ready to meet Pele, to love her forever?"

Lomio reached over and grabbed Harry marlin under each arm. Harry neither resisted nor uttered a sound. He just wanted to get it over with, what he knew was coming, to replace the agony with the pain that would be short and the nothingness that would be forever.

Propping him half out of the seat, Lomio used one hand to turn the spring-loaded door handle, and the pneumatic plunger pushed the door wide open while they hovered. A blast of sulfur, harsh and hot, filled the compartment. With two hands, Lomio swung Harry out the door holding onto his wrists, and Harry did something he had not done in three days on Maui. He unlocked his rectal sphincter and let it go, soiling his pants. A second later, he was hanging there, swinging back and forth by his wrists, his sports coat blowing in the wind from the props. Harry felt the heat through the soles of his shoes, the rising steam from the blast furnace burning his face. He looked up at the big man, who was smiling broadly, his face lathered in sweat.

Lomio let go, the copter hung there a moment, then lifted skyward. At the same time, Harry Marlin fell, arms flailing, trying to fly, Icarus on his way to the sun. Then, spread-eagled, he dropped straight and landed facedown, his descent into hell barely causing a ripple in the flow of boiling red and black lava. In an instant Harry Marlin's clothing was incinerated, and in another second his flesh melted and then the flames of centuries consumed every bone and organ, and having swallowed him, the molten river moved slowly down the mountain and what had been Harry Marlin became a piece of the island itself.

CHAPTER 26

Crater Road

Another day down the drain. No sign of Keaka, no sign of Lila, and damn sure no sign of Sam's coupons. Jake Lassiter returned to the Makawao Inn to find two messages. The first one had to be from Cindy:

Long days without lawyer,
Long nights without biker,
Call home at last light.

The other . . . holy smokes . . . *Meet me on top of Haleakala by the observation building, five o'clock today. Lila.*

Lassiter found the desk clerk who took the call. A retiree from Arizona with leathery skin, a gravelly voice, and a good memory, he said a woman called just before noon. "Left no number, what she said is right there on the slip, word for word."

"Five o'clock," Lassiter said aloud, but mostly to himself.

"Kinda funny time to meet up there," the desk clerk said. "Nearly dark, colder than my ex-wife's bosom."

Someone from the board shops in Paia told Lila he was there, Lassiter thought. And she wants to see him but doesn't want to be seen. Things are looking up. But something about the message bothered him. What? So impersonal. On Bimini, the note had said "Love, Lila." No love here, maybe it'll take some misty rain for that.

It was almost three o'clock, and Lassiter knew they would have to get going. In his room, he tossed a sweater into a gym bag. Then the phone rang. Maybe Lila.

"Hey, *jefe*. You takin' care of my big guy?"

"It's supposed to be the other way around, Cindy. You calling him or me?"

"You mostly. Tell the Tubber I been cleaning his trailer, throwing out all the junk he doesn't need."

"Better wait till he gets home, then you tell him. What else?"

"Well, get a load of this. Seems they identified the boatnapper, the guy who says you're his pal, one Harry Marlin."

"Never heard of him," Lassiter said.

"Keep listening. According to Sergeant Carraway, the Rodriguez kid identified Marlin's mug shot as the guy coming out of the theater that night with the crowbar. Marlin has a record, just *un poco* of this, *un poco* of that, bolita and gambling stuff mostly, but he's the number one suspect in the burglary."

"Great, they arrest him?"

"Can't find him, but Carraway says to tell you that a guy named H. Marlin booked a flight, Miami to Maui, about twenty-four hours before you two adventurers left town."

Lassiter thought about it. The boatnapper Marlin yelling that Keaka double-crossed him. Now Keaka, Lila, Marlin, and Jake all on Maui. Okay, we've got enough to play bridge. "I'll be looking for him. Talk to you tomorrow. Have to—"

"There's more, Jake. Carraway interviewed Violet Belfrey, and guess what, she's got a boyfriend named Harry Marlin. She says she casually mentioned to her beau that Mr. K. gave her a bunch of bonds in his office, never dreamed old Honest Harry would do anything like this, he being a hard-working guy and all. She's just sick to death about the whole thing."

"As Doc Riggs would say, that's *deridiculus*!"

"I take it you doubt the lady's story."

"It's all too convenient. She had the alibi of being with the old man all night. Her boyfriend pulls the B and E. I mean, who's she kidding? Sam must want to string her up."

"No dice. Feels sorry for her. Told her the burglary wasn't her fault and says you'll straighten everything out."

"What the hell's that mean?"

"Don't ask me. You're the lawyer. I'm just a lowly typist cum philosopher."

Straighten everything out, Lassiter thought. How? Now there were two bad guys, Keaka Kealia and Harry Marlin, and two bad gals, don't forget about them. Violet Belfrey and Lila Summers. But Lila wanted to come over to the other side. Isn't that why she was calling? She wanted to join Jake's team, which meant joining Jake. At least that's what he hoped.

"Anything else?" he asked.

"Well, if you're interested in your formerly brilliant career, you're still suspended here pending a Senior Council meeting tomorrow. The partners have been kissing *mucho tuchis* at the bank. I think they're going to put a new regulation in the office manual. You can't beat up a client without prior written approval from three members of the Executive Committee."

"Cindy, I didn't beat anybody up."

"Whatever you say, *su majestad*. Anyway, that's the news from Lake Okeechobee, where all the women are strong, the men shitty, and the children on dope."

"Thanks, Cindy. Tubby and I will be back harassing you and loving you in no time."

"Sure thing, but who's gonna do which?" Cindy laughed and hung up.

It was cool and misty at the lower elevations. Low gray clouds hung over the Silversword Inn and a fine rain fell at the three-thousand-foot level. They passed farmers' fields planted with sweet onions. Cattle and horses grazed in open pastures. Then the road became steeper, twisting higher past clusters of boulders on the lower slopes of the extinct volcano.

The Pontiac crept around the curves, nearly coming to a stop on some of the hairpin turns, and Jake Lassiter grew fidgety. "Want me to drive, Tubby? This is taking forever."

"Nothin' doing. I gotta earn my keep. Whatsa matter, afraid she won't wait? Hey, weather here ain't like on the postcards."

By the time Tubby pulled into the parking lot near the observation building, they could see their breaths in the dim light. Clouds filled the giant crater, obscuring the thousand-foot cinder cones and blurring the bright red sand. A cold wind whipped across the unprotected peak. The few cars still at the summit began to leave. Soon they were alone and darkness came, the clouds obscuring the stars, the blackness enveloping them.

They waited.

No one came and no one went.

Not D. B. Cooper, not Jimmy Hoffa, and not Lila Summers.

Tubby kept the engine running with the heater on. "Hey, bro, we sit here all night, we're gonna run out of gas."

The only sounds were the off-key chugging of the Pontiac's engine and the occasional rumbling of Tubby's stomach. Nearly six-thirty.

"A little while longer," Lassiter said.

"If you don't mind my saying so, I think we're on a wild-goose chase. She's putting you on, a cockteaser if you ask me."

"Another few minutes," Lassiter said, wondering if he'd been twice the fool, once on Bimini—thoughts of the empty bed knifing him even now—and here in the vastness of the dark volcano. They sat in silence, finally making small talk like a couple of bored cops on surveillance.

"Hey, bro, you like lawyering for a living?" Tubby asked.

"It has its moments."

"Whadaya do all day, I mean when you're not in court pulling the wool over some judge's eyes?"

"You think a lot. You plan strategy. You consider the strengths and weaknesses of your case, your witnesses, your evidence. Sometimes you bluff, sometimes you fold, sometimes you call. You play poker with ideas."

"What cards you holding now?"

"Nothing but jokers, Tub. Tried to draw to an inside straight, a sucker bet. I thought I had a chance to break out of the mold, but maybe I belong back in Miami with all the grubby lawyers, playing their games, posturing for judges and juries and corporate boards."

"Hey, at least you grabbed for the gusto."

"Tub, you've reduced my life to a beer commercial."

"What the hell else is there, bro?"

By seven o'clock, they'd run out of talk and called it quits. Tubby eased the Pontiac back onto two-lane Crater Road, both of them silent. They were alone in the night—not another car or light—as they took the winding turns at a crawl.

Lassiter heard it first but thought it was a plane. The noise grew louder in the darkness. "Tub, is there a car behind us?"

"Don't see nothin', but somethin's stirring up a ruckus."

There was a crash from behind, a scream of metal on metal, and Lassiter's neck flipped back, then forward. He might sue this asshole for whiplash. Tubby's foot slipped off the gas pedal as a second jolt hit them.

"Some jerkoff without lights, must be drunk." Tubby's eyes darted from the winding road to the rearview mirror. "Maybe a Jeep or pickup truck, got a big-ass bumper on that baby. I'll let him get around us."

Tubby pulled partially off the road onto the narrow shoulder and came to a complete stop, but it was behind them again, banging away. The taillights burst, the clatter of broken glass mixing with the shriek of metal and squeal of tires, a nightmare of noise shattering the night.

Tubby hit the brakes hard, but the roaring engine rammed them again, shoving the Pontiac a hundred yards along the gravel berm.

Lassiter yelled at him. "Tubby, he doesn't want to pass us! He wants to push us off the mountain. Step on it!"

Tubby jammed a giant foot on the gas, but he had to brake to make one of the hairpin turns, and it was there again on their tail. Then a burst of light, a painful blast, headlights on high beam plus a row of spots, bleaching them against the black backdrop. Momentarily blinded, Tubby sat on the brakes, and again it smashed into them, caving their rear bumper into the trunk.

"Them folks at Avis gonna be pissed." Tubby yanked the wheel toward the center of the road as they were pushed again toward the berm. Then he stomped the accelerator, and while their pursuer was getting back onto the road, Tubby made it around the next bend, where he cut the headlights and slid off the pavement onto a gravel area by a lookout site. During the day, you could see a huge valley below, all the way to the north shore beaches. At night, it was a black hole.

Tubby smacked Lassiter in the shoulder. "Out, bro, hit the deck!"

"What're you talking about?"

"Go, get out, one of us gonna make it, you're not doing any good sitting next to me. Now git while the gittin's good."

Tubby leaned across and opened the passenger door.

Lassiter hesitated, stuck one foot out of the car, then stopped. "No, Tub. I'll—"

"Out!" Tubby yelled again, and bashed Lassiter with a beefy forearm.

Lassiter hit the gravel just as Tubby was putting the Pontiac back onto the road, but there it was again, screaming around the turn, a blaze of lights leading the way. Facedown on the cold earth at the edge of the universe, Lassiter saw a souped-up Chevy Blazer with huge tires.

The Blazer growled viciously, circled the Pontiac, blocking its path, then swung around, and faced it head-on. The truck revved its engine and shot forward, splintering the front bumper, crushing the top of the hood, and exploding the radiator. The Pontiac stalled and Lassiter heard a sickly hacking sound as the engine gasped and sputtered. The Blazer backed up and charged again, giant wheels churning away in four-wheel drive. Another crash, the Blazer pushing the Pontiac backward, then a scraping sound as the car broke through the guardrail. It tumbled end over end, eerily silent, and then there was a flash of flame and an explosion deep from the dark valley below.

The Blazer backed up, its rooftop lights a cold, malevolent glare. Lassiter could see two shapes in the front, a huge man behind the wheel, a smaller figure next to him, but he could not make out their faces. Had they seen him? They were looking in his direction.

Lassiter buried his head in the cold gravel, shame sweeping over him. Total helplessness, total humiliation. He had been unprepared. Like Captain Cook who did not know the people or the land. So now, Lassiter lay there, his grief mixed with rage, his guilt overwhelming him. He tried to block it out with a heroic fantasy—Jake Lassiter, the avenger, springs at them, pulls them from the truck, throttles them to death with his bare hands. He pushed the fantasy away. Temporary insanity, a brief moment of wanting to die with Tubby. Then reality. There was nothing he could do, but that only added to the shame. His head stayed buried. The truck pulled slowly away and headed down the mountain, its powerful engine throbbing in the night.

CHAPTER

27

Ready to Die

"*Jake, is that you? Thank God you're alive.*"

It was Lila's voice, no mistaking it, the call to the Makawao Inn coming fifteen minutes after he hung up with Maui police.

"I'm alive," he said.

"I heard on the radio, an accident on Crater Road, a car over a *pali*. They only said the car was rented to a tourist from Miami, wouldn't give the name until next of kin are notified. I was afraid it was you."

"That so?" His voice was cold.

"Jake."

"It wasn't an accident."

"I . . . I was afraid of that. The road isn't dangerous if you stay close to the *mauka* side, toward the mountain. The *makai* side, toward the sea, has guardrails. So when I heard—"

"Thanks, Lila, but I'll call Triple A if I need some driving tips."

She was silent and Lassiter thought he could hear the pounding of surf in the background, but maybe it was just the connection. "Jake, I'm sorry. I know you're upset. What more can I say?"

"You can explain why you set us up."

"What are you talking about?"

"The message you left here, to meet you at the crater."

"I left no message, Jake. A couple of boardheads in Paia said you were looking for me. Then I heard the radio, an accident involving someone from Miami, and I knew you'd be in danger here, so I naturally thought it was you. You have to believe me."

"Have to? Why? Because you're Li'a, Goddess of Desire—or is it Goddess of Death?"

She took a breath, then asked, "What happened last night?"

"What happened was a Chevy Blazer rigged like a battle cruiser played chicken with us on a cliff."

Lila spoke in a whisper. "That's Keaka's truck."

"I figured, and that's what I told the cops."

"The cops?"

"Yeah. Meanwhile, my friend tossed me out of the car, so I'm here with a scraped knee and he's burned to a crisp. I walked most of the way down the mountain. Finally a farmer picked me up before dawn. I called the Maui police, talked to a captain who told me he'd put homicide on it and to stay put till he gets here to take a statement."

"A captain? Who?"

"Hawaiian name. Kale-ha-ha or something."

"Kalehauwehe."

"Yeah, that's it."

Lila was quiet and Lassiter tried to decipher the silence. Then, betraying no emotion, Lila asked, "And he knows where you are."

"Of course he does." Lassiter was growing impatient. "Like I said, he's coming up here. Besides, I told him where I was staying the first day I got here."

She let out a little laugh, but there was no amusement in her voice. "That's how they knew to leave the message. Mikala must have been surprised to hear from you this morning. Get out of Makawao. Now!"

"Forget it. I'm through taking travel advice from you. Besides, I seem to have lost my car."

"Jake, listen to me. Mikala Kalehauwehe is Keaka's cousin. They're the largest growers of marijuana on Maui. They're ruthless, and Keaka's flipping out on his kill-the-*haoles* crap. When I left him, he was planning to kill the robber who took the bonds."

"Burglar," Jake corrected her listlessly. "That'd be Marlin."

"Jake, wake up. You're in shock or something from last night. You're in danger."

He remembered her note. *Do not follow me. It is dangerous.*

"Jake, what can I tell you to make you understand? In Miami, before the race, Keaka killed someone, a coke smuggler we were going to do business with, strangled him with his bare hands, do you understand?"

"Yeah, he killed a doper, it happens all the time." As Lassiter was saying it, a thought crept into his head, a druggie in Miami . . . strangled. "What smuggler?" he asked.

"I don't know his name. He wanted to get a few keys into Miami, a small deal really. Brought it from Bogotá to Bimini, was going to fill one of Keaka's old boards with it. They'd reseal the board, glass it over, and Keaka would bring it into the states by seaplane after the race."

"Why'd Keaka kill him?"

"Because the Cuban double-crossed him."

Oh no. "What Cuban?" Lassiter asked.

"The smuggler. Keaka got a call from Mikala, who had set it up. Some guy in the DEA in Miami who used to fly with Mikala in Vietnam warned him the Cuban was a snitch. Keaka was being set up—customs, DEA, everybody would be waiting to rip open the board. So Keaka strangled the snitch and hung him in a swamp by his gold chain."

Jake Lassiter was coming awake, the fog clearing. "Where are you, Lila? Can you lead me to Keaka?"

"Jake, what are you talking about? Just get out of there. Get a cab if there's one in that town. Anything . . . borrow a car, steal one, just get off the mountain. Mikala is probably on his way to Makawao right now. Do you understand? Meet me in Kihei at Paradise Fruit. Ask anybody for directions to the fruit stand. I'll be there in an hour."

Maybe it was the wild West character of the town that made him do it, Jake Lassiter thought. Tumbleweed blowing down the street, dust covering the sidewalks, ranchers and farmers tending to business in their quiet way, cowboy hats pulled down, sheepskin collars turned up. In the upcountry town of Makawao, Jacob Lassiter, Esq., attorney-at-law—admitted to practice by the Florida Supreme Court, three federal district courts, plus the United States Supreme Court—became a car thief. Or, more accurately, a pickup truck thief.

There were no taxis in town, but a pickup truck with its engine running—a sooty gray Mitsubishi packed with sweet Kula onions—was parked in front of the Upcountry General Store. While the truck's owner was buying a fifty-pound bag of fertilizer, Lassiter hightailed it down the mountain past herds of Angus, across the Central Valley, through towering stalks of sugarcane, and into the south shore town of Kihei.

Paradise Fruit sits across the street from the Pacific Ocean on Kihei Road, an unsightly stretch of condos and strip shopping centers built by Californians who strive to make Maui look like Burbank. Lila Summers wasn't there. Lassiter ordered a banana smoothie, a rich drink made with sweet stubby bananas, fresh pineapple, and orange juice.

The smoothie finished and still no Lila.

Maybe being set up again, he thought. Maybe Keaka would come crashing through the plywood walls of the fruit stand in his tanklike truck, squashing pineapples and papayas and Jake Lassiter with a reinforced-steel bumper.

He bought a coconut macaroon and ate it in two bites. What was making him hungry—thoughts of Lila or death, or were they one and the same? Boy, the mind plays tricks after you've seen a friend killed. Jake Lassiter was fondling the passion fruit and munching a second macaroon when he turned around and there she was. Sun-streaked hair pulled straight back, her face tanned, full lips slightly parted, gold-and-emerald eyes still innocent and inviting.

"Lo-li-laa," he mumbled, mouth full of macaroon.

"Jake, you have a milk shake mustache and crumbs on your chin. You really know how to knock a girl off her feet, don't you?"

"Bad timing," Lassiter said, wiping his mouth with a bare arm.

"Good choice, very filling and healthy, good to have in your stomach before a flight."

"We going somewhere?"

"You, Jake. You've got to leave. Go home, get out of here before Mikala and Keaka find you. Mikala will kill you to get you out of the way. Keaka will do it for fun."

"Nice crowd you hang around with, or isn't hang around the right description? Nice crowd you conspire with, carry their garbage, take a cut."

Lila took a step backward and turned toward the ocean. She

stared at the horizon, keeping her thoughts and her expression hidden. "I'm not with them, not anymore. There isn't time to explain everything to you. I know I've hurt you and now you're striking out at me. Try to put yourself in my position. I met Keaka when I was a kid. He was different from the other boys."

"So was Ted Bundy."

"Listen, Jake. In the beginning, he wasn't violent. He just wanted to return to an earlier time, to live off the land and the sea. Somewhere it went wrong. His disgust with the *haoles* led to disrespect for their laws. The drugs, the violence . . . it started slowly and got worse. Sure, I went along, I admit it. But I got out after Miami."

"What do you mean, *got out*? You were the mule, you carried Sam Kazdoy's bond coupons to Bimini."

"I didn't know whose they were, that you were involved in it."

Lassiter laughed a hollow, sad laugh. "It doesn't matter *whose* bonds they were. It's still a crime. But it so happens the bonds belong to my client."

"So you came for the bonds, not for me."

He could have told her the truth but the truth hurt too much. "That's right. Does that disappoint you, Lila, that I'm not the romantic fool you took me for?"

"I was sort of hoping that you were," she said wistfully, her eyes moist. "Romantic, I mean. I thought you were, and it made me realize how little I was getting from Keaka." She put both arms around his neck and drew herself up to him, the fullness of her breasts against his chest. He kissed her, wanting her more than ever, knowing the bonds had never been as important as this. But at the same time his mind was working overtime, the brain rattling off the charges against her—conspiracy to transport stolen property, grand larceny, buying, receiving, and concealing stolen property, and the biggie, maybe accessory to first-degree murder. Her rap sheet could be a mini-series. And Keaka—two first-degree murders, Berto and Tubby, three if he killed Marlin. The two of them were Bonnie and Clyde at the beach.

"Jake, it's wonderful to be in your arms again," she whispered in his ear. "I've missed you so. That morning, leaving you on Bimini, it was awful. I cried all the way to Nassau."

"It's a twenty-minute flight," he said.

"I mean it, Jake. It was the worst day of my life. I kept thinking about what I did, and I don't mean carrying the bonds. That was no big deal, but leaving you that way . . ."

"What'd you do with the coupons?" he asked, Sam Kazdoy's lawyer again.

"Keaka met me on Nassau. No hassles with the Bahamian government, no searches or anything. We flew Air Canada to Toronto. Same thing, they don't bother Americans. I had them in a carryon, could have been my toiletries. Only things we declared were two bottles of duty-free rum. Then we went to Vancouver on the same plane. We spent the night and took a Continental flight to Kahului. No problem there, just a couple tourists coming home from Canada. But, Jake, the whole trip, I kept thinking of you."

He wanted to believe her, wanted to hear more about how she missed him, but part of him was on assignment. "Where are the coupons now?"

"Keaka has them. I don't know where, probably stowed away until Mikala figures out what to do with them."

"Where's Keaka?"

"Forget about Keaka," she said, kissing him again. Why did he get the impression she used her kisses as tools of distraction, the same way he fouled up witnesses with irrelevancies? Was that it, were her kisses irrelevant?

A voice inside forced him back, took him somewhere other than where his body wanted to be. The voice told him there was unfinished business and a score to settle, told him to use his wits and maybe a weapon, too, told him things would never be the same. Finally it told him he could kill.

"Where's Keaka?" he repeated.

"Jake, can't you understand? You're out of your element here. If Keaka pulls a gun, you can't object like it's a courtroom. Even if you found him, even if you had a gun, what would you do? I don't see you shooting anyone. And Keaka won't surrender. His greatest wish is to die a warrior, to join his ancestors and be reincarnated as a king."

"Maybe I can grant his wish. Look, he killed Berto, a friend of mine for a long time. Berto made some mistakes, screwed up his life, but he didn't deserve to die. And Tubby Tubberville. Tubby was a big teddy bear. I blame myself for bringing him along. I was riding shotgun without a shotgun, and I was useless. Now, where is Keaka?"

She looked at him through misty eyes. "Not on Maui."

"Where?"

Lila shook her head sadly, as if already regretting what she would say. "In the jungle on Molokai. He has a campsite in a clearing."

"How do I get there?"

"You don't. He's on high ground above the beach. He can see a boat approaching during the day or hear it at night. Besides, there's nowhere to land a boat."

Keep asking questions, fast and simple, no time for a witness to take a breath or fabricate an answer. "How'd he get there?"

"Windsurfs across the Pailolo Channel. He fishes and hunts and picks fruits. But he also has weapons—not native spears either—guns, and he's good with them."

"How do you know all this?"

"Because I used to go there with him. That's always what we did after a job, sort of a native celebration at beating the *haoles*. He would have sailed there early this morning, after killing your friend."

"His job isn't finished if I'm still breathing, is it?"

"No, but now that Mikala knows you're alive, he'll probably handle that himself. They'd consider it fairly easy—you're just not in their league when it comes to this—and they'd want Keaka to lay low."

"Does Keaka have a telephone or a shortwave radio on Molokai?"

"No, that would be too modern, too much *haole* influence."

"So he would have gone there believing I'm dead. Mikala couldn't tell him I'm alive. I'd have the element of surprise."

"It would be your only advantage," she said quietly. "Everything else favors him, including the fact that he's a killer and you're not."

Jake Lassiter was already planning. "Last night there were two men in the truck, a bigger man driving."

"That would be Lomio, part Samoan, part Hawaiian. He works for them. Lomio loves the truck and doesn't mind hurting people. He'd still be on Maui, on the farm."

So three enemies out to kill him—Keaka, Mikala, and Lomio. And Jake Lassiter didn't know whether he could trust Lila Summers. He went fishing. "Why aren't you with Keaka?"

She looked away. There was something about the pause Lassiter didn't like, another evasive witness framing a reply, testing how it sounds in the mind instead of just letting the lips speak the quick truth. Finally she said, "After he killed the Cuban doper, I told him I was tired of the violence. I wanted it to stop. He promised it would. Then we got home, and he said he would kill the robber, sorry, the burglar who hired us to take the coupons to Bimini. I knew then it would never end. Keaka didn't want it to end."

"So you left him?"

"Keaka pretty much guessed what happened on Bimini,

called me a *haole* slut, asked me to choose sides. We said some nasty things to each other, then I left. I've been staying with a girl friend in Kihei. Keaka didn't tell me about the setup on Crater Road last night. He would have been afraid I'd warn you."

"Would you have?"

"Of course."

"Why? Why betray your first lover, the man who taught you so much?"

"I wouldn't look at it that way. I just want you to live a good life and be happy and grow old and die in bed and not on a rocky mountainside."

It wasn't quite what he wanted to hear. An all-American *because I love you* would have done nicely.

"Lila, I'm going after Keaka, with or without your help. It would just be easier if you're on my team."

She looked away again, turning toward the ocean. She was silent for a long moment, and Lassiter stood there, smelling the sweet fragrances of the tropical fruits, waiting. Finally, she told him where to put a board in the water, at Makaluapuna Point on the northwest coast of Maui by the lava rocks called Dragon's Teeth. It was nearly deserted there, she said, only the nearby plantation village of Honokahua framed by a double line of Norfolk pine trees.

At the house in Kihei where Lila had been staying, she opened the garage and hauled out an old eleven-foot board, her harness, and a rig.

"Don't drift too far downwind," she told him, "and sail port of the lighted weather buoy to get through the rocks on the Molokai side."

In the fading light, she handed him a stainless-steel Colt Python to carry in the pouch of a harness. He wanted to ask what she was doing with the gun, and what jobs with Keaka ended in their jungle celebrations. But he didn't ask. He just put the gun in a sandwich bag and pressed it closed by its plastic zipper, sealing it like an office worker packing his lunch.

"You don't have to do this to prove anything to me," Lila said. Then she kissed him, long and slow, as if it were the last time, and as she turned away, Lassiter thought he saw a tear in the corner of her eye. But then again, maybe it was the light.

He could have said that he wasn't trying to prove anything to her, but he didn't say that. He could have told her what it felt like to lie facedown in the cold gravel as your friend is dying in a burst of flames—dying instead of you—but he didn't say that either. He didn't say anything. He just threw the board, the boom, the mast, and the sail into the bed of her old Mazda pickup. Then, as the sun set over Lanai and the coast of Maui was bathed in a peaceful orange glow, he drove to Makaluapuna Point, looking for the rocks called Dragon's Teeth, wondering if anyone is ever ready to die.

CHAPTER 28

Hello and Goodbye

It was from early Polynesians—Tahitians, Samoans, and Tongans—that the seeds of Keaka Kealia grew. Lean and strong, Keaka surfed Maui's north shore, another island boy dark as a kukui nut. Surfing taught him balance and agility, and a thousand years of history imbued him with courage and a love of the wind and sea. When windsurfing came to the island from California, he learned that too, first on an old twelve-foot floater without foot straps, a Model A relic of the sport. With his natural strength, Keaka sailed for hours in thirty-knot winds over rough seas.

In the beginning he did not own a harness, the vest that

hooks into a boom line and relieves pressure on the arms, so he developed stamina beyond that of the others, though the tendons of his elbows swelled from the constant strain. He luxuriated in the drag of stretching muscles, a blend of pleasure and pain, a natural euphoria from the sheer physical act of conquering the sea. While still an amateur, he completed a 360, a complete flip, lifting the bow off a wave, mast upside down kissing the water, then bringing the board all the way around, landing smoothly, and trimming the sail to pick up speed in search of the next wave.

By eighteen Keaka Kealia had grown into a rugged, handsome man, dark eyes set on a wide face, lithe and graceful in every movement. He worked part-time in a rental shop, giving lessons to the tourists, occasionally bedding down teenage girls from L.A. who were lured, yet frightened, by his hard brown body and brooding demeanor. Unlike the other beach boys, his mind was not socked in by a fog of Maui Wowie. He read books, studying the ways of his ancestors. The old Hawaiian folk songs spoke to Keaka, told him of the gods and of the spirits of the sea. He longed for that age, to gather fish from the ocean and ride above it on a board descended from the voyaging canoes of his ancestors.

He watched with disgust as developers built condos hard by the beach. To find sanctuary from the tourists and the time-share hucksters, he sailed nine miles across the Pailolo Channel to the island of Molokai and made a campsite in the jungle there. A century earlier, the island was deserted except for a leper colony, and Keaka, always aware of links to the past, appreciated the irony.

He cleared an area on the slopes of the Kamakou Reserve and slowly built a *hale*, a thatched hut. He removed the bark from the timbers with a stone chisel and dried *pili* grass in the sun for the roof. He made water bottles and *poi* bowls from gourds, and he slept on a *lauhala* mat of woven leaves. He hunted pheasants and goats and cooked his prey over open fires. At night Keaka Kealia dreamed he was a warrior of King Kalaniopuu, and with weapons of stone, he attacked Captain Cook's pale sailors, crushing their skulls and gutting them with sharpened sticks. Those he did not kill he drove into the sea, then watched with joy as they floundered in the surf, disappearing forever from view.

Jake Lassiter wished he had a wet suit. There was a chill in the night air, and the black water even *sounded* cold slapping the rocky shore. His feet felt it first, then his chest, as spray from the shore break hit him.

He beach-started in the shallow water that broke across the volcanic shelf and, looking down, thought he saw a human skull wedged between two rocks, reflecting the moonlight. A wave pounded the rocks, and the skull, if that's what it was, disappeared.

The crossing shouldn't be that difficult, he told himself. He had made longer trips, though not at night and not in unfamiliar waters. And not with murder on his mind.

Is that what it would be if he crept into Keaka's camp and pounced on him under a sky lit with stars? Sure it would, he decided. First-degree, too. Premeditated and cold-blooded. No, that's wrong. His feet were cold; his blood was hot. Hot with thoughts of Berto strung up in a swamp and Tubby pushed over a cliff. And Lila—what had Keaka done to Lila Summers, what had he made her? A thief? Yes, surely that. They were in it together in Miami, and who knows what before then. A murderer? No, he couldn't bring himself to acknowledge that Lila had anything to do with the killings. That was all Keaka's doing, he told himself. Then told himself again, just to make sure.

The wind let up at sundown, just a puff by Maui standards, twelve to fifteen knots from the northeast. He could sail on a starboard tack all the way across the Pailolo Channel. From the beach at Honokahua he could see Molokai, silhouetted in the darkness, rising like a black monolith, its southern coastline a jungle devoid of lights. The night was clear and a three-quarter moon cast a milky glow on the peaking waves. Lassiter fell once getting beyond the surf line, but once was enough. Freezing now, a shivering, bone-deep cold.

The water was choppy and the board pitched beneath him, but in a few minutes his legs were making the adjustments, knees bending, weight shifting without any message from his brain, just doing it on autopilot. At the same time, his arms were letting out the sail and raking it in, allowing the rhythm of the wind and water dictate the movements. It was peaceful here on the black sea and he wanted to enjoy it before the quiet was shattered on a desolate island.

The dark monolith grew larger and Lassiter was aware of how small he was, bucking the waves on a fiberglass board, an infinitesimal speck on a vast sea. It made him think of the insignificance of what he would do, at least in the universal scheme of things. If Keaka would die, or if he would die, the moon would still pass through its phases, and the tide would still rise and fall. We are born, puny and weak, and set afloat on the waters of a small planet in a runty solar system, and if we capsize, as we surely will, there will be others, just as puny, to take our place. Everything we have created, good and bad, will fade and crumple and be lost to the winds of time. Those who mourn our departure will pass, too, so that all memories of us will die in the flicker of a cosmic eyelash. Rather than depress him, these thoughts calmed Lassiter with the knowledge that life was so fleeting, it was useless to waste precious moments in a state of fear.

He was thinking these thoughts, wondering if he would be alive to share them with Doc Riggs, when he felt something. Felt it before he heard it.

The water beneath him moving.

Suddenly, an explosion.

A deafening concussion and a wall of water that engulfed him.

The sea rose from beneath Lassiter and hurled him into the blackness. He belly-flopped into the channel, graceful as a rhinoceros. He kicked twice and surfaced, eyes stinging, a gash on the forehead where the boom had sideswiped him. His first thought was that his board had hit some unexploded Japanese mine from World War II. But treading water, Jake Lassiter saw it, or at least part of it: the mammoth tail of a humpback whale visible forty feet above the water, the rest of the animal hidden below. Then a prehistoric shove, the tail whipped once, and the beast slipped under the sea. Another wave swamped Lassiter, and he tasted salt water, raw in his throat.

Save the whales! My ass.

It was the migrating season for humpback whales, and one had breached alongside of him. Lassiter was still treading water when he realized that his board wasn't next to him. He had lost precious seconds watching the whale, and the board had drifted away. If Lassiter were ten feet above the water, he could have seen the moon glowing off the fiberglass or illuminating the sail. But he was mostly under the water, kicking his legs to keep his nose high enough to breathe. Lila's harness was too small for his chest and pressed hard against his rib cage. It had no flotation material and the weight of the metal simply made him heavier. He was growing tired. He could swim in the direction he thought the board had drifted, but make a mistake, chase the wrong receiver, the coach would scream, and the board would be halfway to Tahiti.

He looked through the darkness toward Molokai. He looked

back toward Maui, getting his bearings, then swam twenty yards downwind and there it was, the boom lying across the stern of the board, waiting for him to pick it up. The wind was barely strong enough to water-start, but he got it going, then checked his gear. The Colt Python was still snug in the harness pouch, but the three pounds of stainless steel now bashed his shoulder blade with every wave. He carried something else, too: a ton of fatigue. His arms were dead, and his legs no longer responded to the sea, the adrenaline having been sapped. He thought of a November homecoming game played in a sleet storm in old Beaver Stadium, his uniform and pads weighted down by icy water, black high-tops caked with frozen mud.

Wasted. Out of shape. Winded, breathing through the mouth now. His mind wandered. Too much happening too fast, he thought. You don't run into many whales if you spend your days trying lawsuits in an old courthouse on Flagler Street. And you seldom lose a night's sleep walking down the mountain after seeing a friend killed.

He could hear the water breaking now over shallow reefs. In the distance he saw the tiny lights from the town of Kaluaaha where the road ended on Molokai and the jungle swallowed the night. He looked for the lighted weather buoy and it was there, just as Lila said it would be, and he had a clear passage through the rocks to the shore.

Then there was a sound. At first Jake Lassiter thought it must have been a phenomenon of the wind whistling through the rocks. It was a voice without direction. It came from nowhere and everywhere.

"Aloha, haole."

Lassiter heard it again, closer this time. "*Aloha, haole.* Are you looking for me?"

Beside him now, emerging from the darkness, riding easily over the small waves, was Keaka Kealia. He was sailing ten yards away, hands lightly grasping his boom, wearing a loincloth made of animal skin. The Hawaiian out for a nighttime joyride, Lassiter thought, crazily, the danger not yet sinking in. Then he saw it dangling from Keaka's shoulder—an Uzi, the Israeli submachine gun. The water was growing more shallow, but the waves were increasing as they passed over the reef and Lassiter was unsteady. Keaka sailed slightly behind him and Lassiter kept shooting glances over his left shoulder.

"I'm still here, *haole*. I want to see what you do when you get to shore, if you get to shore." Then Keaka raked in the boom, pulling the sail over the board, leaned back, and shot by Lassiter, cutting inches in front of him, heading toward the beach, the Uzi swinging ominously from his shoulder.

There were not many choices, Jake Lassiter thought. He could head for shore, ditch the rig in the surf and swim in, hiding in the massive boulders along the rocky beach. Or he could try to reach the gun in his pack, and then . . .

A flash of light interrupted him, the moon reflecting off the bottom of Keaka's board. The Hawaiian must have jibed, for now he was headed straight at Lassiter, jumping over the lips of the breaking waves while Lassiter surfed down their front heading in. Another wave, another jump, and Keaka was bearing down on him. They were on a collision course, drawing closer with each second.

Keaka hit a wave, timed it just right, and lifted off. Then with his ankles, he pulled the board onto its side, perpendicular to the water, a mule-kick. The board's sharp fin whizzed by Lassiter's ear and slashed a three-foot-long tear in his sail.

Lassiter toppled into the water, his harness still hooked into the boom lines, the torn sail wrapped around him, his head under water, his lungs out of breath. Keaka Kealia brought his board out of the jump and landed gracefully as a cat, never losing his balance. He jibed and swung back around to find his prey floundering under the sail, trying to kick himself free.

Keaka shouted at him, "*Aloha, haole!* Hello and good-bye."

Struggling under the water, Lassiter never heard the Hawaiian.

Keaka held the boom with one hand and sailed by slowly, luffing the sail. He aimed the Uzi at the back of Lassiter's harness, still wrapped in the sail, and squeezed off a quick burst of nine-millimeter shells. Then Keaka raised the gun above his head and sailed to shore singing ancient war songs in the language of his ancestors.

CHAPTER

29

The King of Siam

Jake Lassiter was afraid of drowning. Taking a bullet was a secondary concern. Tangled up under the sail, still hooked into the boom, he flipped the quick-release bar on the harness and swam under the board and out the other side. He was just surfacing when he heard the popping of the Uzi, and after a quick breath, he went under again. He held his breath until his lungs gave out, and then he held it some more, exhaling air until there was nothing left. When he came up a second time, Keaka was gone, though his voice could be heard, a maniacal wailing in the night.

The waves pounded Lassiter and spun him around. He lost

his sense of direction, tried to figure out where he was, finally deciding somewhere between the devil and the deep blue sea. Treading water, he bobbed in the waves, knowing it would take a superhuman effort to swim to shore and avoid being sliced to ribbons on the coral. He took a breath, stretched out, and body-surfed fifty yards on the next good-sized roller. He stopped, treaded water again, and tried to locate the boulders in the moonlight.

Then another voice, only this one familiar and sweet, and for a moment Jake Lassiter wondered if the bullets hadn't really hit him, and maybe he was drifting off to wherever you go if you haven't been a saint but you never strangled kittens either.

"Jake, are you all right?" Lila's voice, a whisper among the waves. He turned to find her and caught a breaker in his open mouth and swallowed salt water again, but there she was on a board, talking to him. "Climb up. Just grab the last foot strap, pull yourself up to your knees, and hang on."

It was a bumpy ride, the board bouncing in the surf, his extra weight fouling up Lila's balance like a little brother on the back of a kid's bike. Then the shore break caught them and slammed the board hard against a rock at water's edge. There was a *cr-ack*, and they tumbled into the water, the board nosing up on a boulder. Her fin had snapped in two. She retrieved the broken piece, nearly a foot long, curved and sharp as a saber, and hauled the rig onto the beach. The beach was narrow and rocky and ended in a black jungle of bushes, trees, and towering ferns. Without pausing to rest, Lila dragged the board into the heavy undergrowth. She came back and knelt beside Lassiter, who was lying on his back at the water's edge.

"Are you all right?" she asked.

Lassiter coughed and gave back some of the Pacific Ocean. "I'm alive and five minutes ago I didn't think I would be, so I'm fine. What are you . . . how did you . . . why?"

"Jake, I knew you wouldn't let me come along, but I wasn't going to let you get killed. Do you understand now you have no chance here?"

He sat up but didn't answer.

Lila said, "I was about a quarter mile behind you when I heard the gunfire. Keaka must think you're dead. Somewhere in this vegetation, he has two or three boards and complete rigs. We can get some rest, then sail back before sunrise."

"Sail back? No. I came to do a job, and . . ."

But he stopped himself, because he knew it was just talk, he was just jabbering away on autopilot. *You start something, you finish it.* Yeah, sure. Hit that line. Sis, boom, bah. Talk's cheap, until you've been shot at and left for dead.

He surveyed the damage. His board and rig were gone. The harness and gun, too. All he had left were his boxer trunks and a million goose bumps. If he didn't get shot, he might die of hypothermia. "All right. We'll sail back. If I ever get back to the mainland, the closest I'll get to the ocean will be Kansas."

Lila crouched in the sand, her face luminous in the moonlight. "We should split up and look for those boards. Try not to make any noise. Keaka's camp is only a mile up the slope and he's often out at night, walking in the jungle."

She used the sharp point of the broken fin to draw a map in the sand, showing Lassiter the location of Keaka's path into the jungle and advising him to stay clear. Lila headed west along the beach, Lassiter east, poking into the bushes, looking for the boards. His feet were cut from the rocks and he was freezing. The black boulders lining the shore took on shapes of strange animals and seemed to follow him. The wind picked up and died and sounds came from the rocks, howls and shrieks and taunting laughter. He thought of all the places he would rather be, the list filling a dozen yellow legal pads in his mind. Who would go on a mission like this? A *putz*, Sam Kazdoy would say.

He couldn't tell how much time had passed. A few minutes, a half hour. He didn't see Lila, and he didn't find any bonds. Then, a hallucination. What else could it be, a nude woman on the deserted coast of Molokai? There in front of him, not twenty feet away, backlit by the moon over the channel, a petite young woman emerged from the sea, water dripping over small breasts and onto her firm stomach. She looked directly at Lassiter but was silent. Even in the dark, she looked familiar. She looked to her left and Lassiter followed her gaze and as he turned, the moon burst into a thousand suns, his brain jolted as if hit by a sledgehammer. He was on his knees, fighting off the nausea, straining to focus his eyes.

Through the fog he heard Coach Shula yelling at him, or was it Paterno? "Keep your feet, Lassiter! Body square to the line, don't get blindsided by the tight end. Damnit, eighty-two just cleaned your clock. Now get up and hit somebody!"

Lassiter stood up but didn't see the tight end. They might have scored by now, who knows, you drift into the middle, the lights go out.

A voice again, rattling around in his brain, but not the coach. "What's this neighborhood coming to? A man can't take his *wahine* out for a midnight swim without some trash drifting ashore."

Somewhere through the haze, Lassiter saw two Keaka Kealias and two nude women, and they were dancing around him as if he were the Maypole. "You surprised me, *haole*," Keaka said, the Uzi still slung on his shoulder. "I thought you would stay in your air-conditioned office, but I learned that you were here, at first I thought for Lila, then I learn, for the bonds. You are a foolish man, because you can't have either one. You should have stayed home with your big, cushy job and your flat water. You could have lived to be an old man, playing gin rummy at your country club. You are even more of a fool than the little man, Marlin. The goddess of the volcano spared you last night on Crater Road. It was a signal for you to leave, to go home. But you ignored it, violated the *kapu* of the gods, and now you must pay the price."

Keaka seemed to be waiting for him to say something, but the cobwebs were still hanging on. "Why are you on Molokai, *haole*? The bonds are not here. They are in my favorite place, a place known only to me and that *haole* slut you like so much."

"I came to kill you," Lassiter said.

That made the Hawaiian laugh. "Good. You will die on the rocks like Captain Cook, a stupid *haole* like yourself."

The world was coming into focus now, and Jake Lassiter saw that Keaka's loincloth was gone. *In naturalibus*, Charlie Riggs would have said. The Hawaiian stood there with his feet spread apart, hands on his hips, a warrior king surveying his kingdom, now sullied by an intruder. Lassiter summoned a calm voice. "I should advise you that I left explicit instructions as to where I was going. If I'm not back in the morning, there'll be a search party."

Keaka laughed again. "Who did you tell, Captain Kalehauwehe? You seemed to tell him everything else." He gestured with the Uzi to start walking toward the jungle.

Then another voice. "Keaka, don't do it. Let him go, he can't hurt you." Lila Summers was there, coming out of the darkness, trying to rescue him again.

Keaka was startled, but only for a moment. "What a pleasant surprise. My two *wahines* together. Lila, unlike you, Little Lee knows which side to choose in a fight. Even after what happened in Miami, she is with me, though she doesn't care much for you." He turned toward Little Lee. "Lila used to be my friend and lover, but lately the bitch has been hanging around with *haole* scum."

"Let him go," Lila said again, firmly. But whatever power she once had over him was gone. Keaka just smirked at her, enjoying the situation, his two women there to witness his power, his unsheathed masculinity on center stage. Lee Hu had wrapped a towel around her small body and glared at Lila.

Keaka held out his arms as if to embrace both women. "We will all go to the camp, to my *hale*. It will be like old times. It is a fine place for a man and his *wahines* to make love."

"Has it come to this?" Lila asked. "Are you conquering me, too?"

"If you had been loyal to me, it would not have been necessary."

He gestured with the gun to begin moving. Keaka stayed at the rear, holding the Uzi lightly by the vertical clip. The path was rugged and uphill, strewn with rocks and overgrown with barbed limbs. Every step brought a branch in the face, sharp twigs cutting across neck and shoulders. Lassiter's feet were bleeding from tiny cuts and his head throbbed with pain. His legs barely moved. His mind kept playing tricks on him, black-and-white footage from World War II, the Bataan Death March.

They came to a clearing where a small fire glowed orange. Lee Hu threw two logs into the coals and sparks flew into the night. Keaka stood by the fire and Lee Hu knelt before him as if she were his subject, and he the king. The image brought something back to Lassiter. What was it Lila had said that first night in the restaurant? Keaka thought he was the reincarnation of Kame-ha-ha the Great or something. Another crazy thought, Lassiter said to himself, wondering if he was delirious from the salt water and one smack to the head. And then suddenly, it became clear to him, so clear that he laughed.

"What's so funny, *haole*? Do you find your own death humorous?"

Keaka stood there with legs spread, hands on his hips, his

Hawaiian manhood thick and proud, tumescent from the excitement of a kill, maybe more exciting than the other kills because two women were here to watch.

"Lila said you think you're a king," Lassiter said. "And what you look like is the king of Siam, Yul Brynner in *The King and I.* Strutting around with your hands on your hips, only difference is he wore silk knickers, you're letting your pecker hang out, but either way, I keep waiting for you to sing 'Shall We Dance?' "

Lassiter laughed again, a wild laugh, and Keaka studied him silently. Lassiter looked him square in the eyes. "What's the matter, King Cantaloupe, do you find this a puzzlement?"

And then Jake Lassiter began singing. And dancing. Hands on hips, feet splayed east and west, he pranced around the clearing and belted it out, an old show tune filling the jungle.

"Is a puzzlement. There are times I almost think nobody's sure of what he absolutely know-ows. Everybody finds confusion in conclusions he concluded long aaa-go-oh. And it puzzles me to learn that though a man may be in doubt of what he know-ows, very quickly will he fight, he'll fight, to prove what he does not know is so-oh . . . et cetera, et cetera, and so forth."

Keaka self-consciously took his hands off his hips. It was working, Lassiter thought, a distraction from what Keaka wanted, which was for him to grovel and beg for his life. Forget it, Lassiter thought, he would die first. Then a rueful smile. Yes, that's exactly what he would do. But for now he was onstage in the clearing, a space about the size of the area between the bench and the bar. He had performed there before for judges and juries. Now Keaka was the court of last resort, and Lassiter was acting for his life.

Lila knew what was happening, was laughing and applauding. Lee Hu looked confused, and Keaka was sullen.

Lassiter kept up the patter. "What's the matter, Keaka, don't you like Rodgers and Hammerstein? Too bad, they're my favorites. When I was in college, I played Jud Fry in *Oklahoma.* Hey, you'd be good in that role, it's the villain, but I guess you're not into Americana. Wish I could remember the last verse of the king of Siam's song, maybe you could join in, something like this, *Every day I try to live another day-ay. Every day I do my best for one more day-ay . . . But, is a puzzlement.*"

"Shut up, *haole!*" Keaka barked. For the first time his eyes betrayed doubt, fear that he was the butt of some joke.

"No, I'm going to keep talking. And you can shoot me if you like. If that is what great warriors do—strike down shivering, unarmed men. Will that impress your *wahines*?"

Keaka crossed his arms in front of his chest to make the biceps stand out and said, "You deserve to die. You miserable *haoles* stole our land and diseased our women and—"

"Don't look at me," Lassiter said with a shrug, interrupting the diatribe. "I don't even own a condo and my urologist will testify I've never had crotch rot."

Keaka raised his voice. "You made *kala*, money, your god. You are descended from pigs and goats—"

"There you go again," Lassiter said, "insulting my ancestry. Reminds me of a trash-talking tackle from the Jets. *Yo momma this, yo momma that.*"

Lila Summers was laughing again, signaling Lassiter that this was the right approach: show no fear, mock the king. Lassiter wondered how long he could keep this up, when would Keaka end it with a short burst from the Uzi?

"Whadaya going to do, Keaka, kill me? I can see the headline, JUNGLE MUSICAL CLOSES; ENRAGED CRITIC KILLS STAR."

"*Haole*, you think you are so funny." Keaka's eyes were black slits. "Do you want to die laughing?"

"Sure, laughing or screwing," Lassiter said, and Lila roared. "A dying man gets one last wish and Lila knows what mine would be. You don't have any red satin sheets in your tepee there, do you, chief?" It was going so well Lassiter planned to come back in another life as a stand-up comic.

Keaka scowled. "Lila, you like the *haole*'s jokes, maybe you'd like to die with him."

"If that's what you want, it's your gun," Lila Summers said without a trace of fear.

Turning to Lee Hu, Keaka said, "The *haole* slut is only half a woman. She has no soul, so she cannot reach climax. Li'a, Goddess of Desire, hah. She is without desire. She is dead inside."

"Hey, pal," Lassiter heard himself saying, "if you can't cut it in the sack, don't blame her. When we played hide the sausage in Bimini, I had her lit up like a slot machine hitting jackpot. The birds fell from the trees and the fishes leapt from the sea. I'll tell you, Keaka old buddy, when that woman comes, she registers a ten on the Richter scale, shock waves all the way to Pasadena."

Lassiter was running out of tales, but he didn't want to stop. Somehow, he thought that Keaka wouldn't shoot a babbling man. "I'm not one to kiss and tell, but that's the way it is. And from what I hear, you're just a little quick on the trigger. Slow down. You'll enjoy the scenery more. I'm here to tell you, when this women gets hot, the sheets start smoking."

Lila picked up the cue. "Keaka always thought it was my fault that he couldn't satisfy me. Jake, you're the most exquisite lover a woman could ever want. In Bimini, I thought I would die from the pleasure. What do the French call it . . . *petit mal*, the little death."

"Liars!" Keaka fumed, but his voice exposed doubt, and his manhood dropped a bit. Lassiter decided against making a crack about that. It was a fine line he was walking—one insult too many or too deep and the Hawaiian's confusion could turn to rage. But it was working, Keaka's mind occupied, thinking of the shame of the *haole* unlocking the mystery of his *wahine*, while his warrior's body betrayed him.

Jake Lassiter used the time to size up the situation. As long as Keaka had the gun, there would be no chance. Even unarmed, Keaka would be the odds-on favorite to retain his title as king of the jungle. When's the last time he had even hit anybody, Lassiter tried to remember, figuring the grief-stricken sergeant in a carpeted conference room didn't count. Then there was the bearded guy in the bar, big guy with a big mouth. Should have figured he was a cop, needed a friendly judge to quash the assault charge. And how many years since he had hit a blocking sled? Latest physical contact was shoving around a paunchy bank lawyer, not worth any points here. Still, hand-to-hand was his only chance.

"C'mon, Keaka. Drop the gun. You're a tough guy. Show the ladies how tough, just you and me, *mano a mano*, like in the swamp in Miami."

Keaka looked puzzled. "The swamp?"

"He was my friend. Berto."

A look of confusion gave way to recognition. Keaka smiled a cruel grin. "The Cuban in the swamp."

"That's right, tough guy. Why don't you try to strangle me like you did him?"

Keaka lowered the gun barrel to think about it. Finally he laughed and said, "You *haoles* haven't gotten any smarter in two centuries."

Lassiter didn't know what that meant, but no matter because he was busy measuring distances. Keaka stood fifteen feet in front of him. Lila had moved, a step at a time, closer to Keaka, almost in the line of fire. What was she doing? Did she think he wouldn't shoot her? Was she trying to give Jake a chance to make a break into the jungle? Keaka still held the Uzi lightly by the clip, the shoulder strap carrying most of the weight. Lassiter wondered how long it would take—what millisecond of time—for the great athlete to turn the barrel toward him and squeeze off a rapid burst. And how long would Lassiter need to take two steps forward and dive at Keaka, knocking him into the fire? Too long. Keaka would catch him in midleap with a fusillade through the chest.

Lassiter saw it then. How could he have missed it? Six feet away from Keaka was a machete jammed into the exposed stump of a banana tree, handle angled up, blade glowing orange in the light from the fire. He could dive for it, the stump would give some protection. If only Lila would take one more step toward Keaka, he could leap behind her, two pass receivers on a crossing pattern. Okay, then what? *Hit the ground and roll, yank it free from the stump—young Arthur about to be king—then come up swinging.*

Keaka glared at him. "Are you ready to die, *haole*?"

"Not till I answer the pressing questions of our time. In the song *Moon River*, who the hell is 'my huckleberry friend?' "

Can I do it? Is he too quick for me?

"And if a train leaves Chicago heading west at eighty miles an hour, and another leaves Los Angeles heading east at ninety miles an hour, which one gets to Omaha first, and why not stop in Kansas City, instead?"

"Are you through?" Keaka asked.

"No, I'd like to consider the question of how the iguana evolved over several million years on the Galápagos Islands when the islands themselves are only two million years old."

No choice in the matter. Die either way, at least there's a chance if . . .

"I am going to kill you now," Keaka said, placidly.

"Some geologists think there are older islands that disappeared into the sea, and the animals drifted to the Galápagos on rafts of driftwood and seaweed . . ."

Waiting for the moment, a diversion.

"Isn't that something?" Lassiter continued. "Just like your ancestors paddling canoes from Club Med or wherever to Hawaii."

"You will suffer pain such as you have never known."

Lassiter tried to dry his palm on his trunks but they were still wet. His feet ached from the cuts and his legs were concrete pillars. And Keaka was talking again. "Lila, you have offended me and you should be punished. I could let you stay with Lee Hu and me, and both of you could service me. Or you can die. The choice is yours."

Lassiter worked up a laugh. "Isn't there a third choice. Like a week in Philadelphia?"

Out of the corner of his eye, Lassiter saw the machete blade. Visualized it now. *Two huge steps, the dive, the roll, the grab.*

Keaka glared at him. "I am talking to the *wahine*. In a moment, I will deal with you, *haole*."

"Take your time," Lassiter said. "I charge by the hour, and my next lunatic doesn't come in till noon tomorrow."

Wrap your hand around the wooden handle, then a tight, compact swing to the gut.

"I choose to live," Lila said, taking a long step toward Keaka, as if enlisting in the Army. It was a signal, Lassiter thought, and he bolted to the right, took two steps, then leapt toward the tree stump and the machete. He'd never had any speed—4.85 for the forty on a good day, and that before knee surgery—but he didn't have far to go. He would have made it, too, if his legs hadn't buckled as he tried to launch, just plain gave out, and he sprawled in the brush, his mouth full of dark brown sand, briars scratching his forehead. The machete was five feet—a million miles—away.

Keaka watched without excitement. He swung the Uzi to his left, hefted it to just below shoulder height, and waited until he had a clear shot at Lassiter's back. He never saw Lila's hand come up hard, an uppercut, her fist full of a blue fiberglass fin, sharp as a saber, slashing upward. It caught him right below the navel, and with one fluid motion she slid the blade through his belly, a clean incision, luxuriating in the feel of the smooth tear, placid as a housewife trimming a pie crust. As the point dug in, Lila twisted upward, tearing muscle and tissue and organs, and the fin came to rest stuck in the bottom of his sternum. Keaka dropped to his knees and the Uzi fell to the ground. Keaka stared in disbelief at his wound, blood pouring from his abdomen, staining the sand. Lee Hu gasped, then turned and ran into the jungle.

Lila picked up the gun and tossed it to Lassiter, who was still on all fours. "Take care of this," she said, turning her back to Keaka who lay on his side, nearly in the fire.

Slowly Keaka came to his knees, keeping his innards from coming through the tear by pressing his hand hard over the wound. From deep within himself, from a thousand years of warriors and chiefs and steel-backed men who paddled canoes across raging seas, he blinked through the pain.

Lila took two steps toward the jungle in the direction Lee Hu had run. Lassiter turned and saw Keaka, a grotesque figure, hunched over, approaching Lila from behind, one hand pressed to his abdomen, the other high over his head holding a heavy log. In the light of the fire, Lassiter could see flames spurting from the log and could hear Keaka's flesh crackling. Lassiter raised the Uzi but Lila stood between him and Keaka and he could only yell, "Lila, behind you!"

The warning was a second too late, and the flaming club began its descent, but then Keaka cried out and the torch fell harmlessly to the ground. Now the hand that had clutched his stomach was holding the elbow, the swollen tendons that had lasted so many hours in so many oceans, thickened and brittle, snapping like old guitar strings.

Catlike, Lila sprang to the tree stump and dislodged the machete with one hand. She brought her arms back, and with a left-handed swing, a slight uppercut—Ted Williams in his prime—she brought it around, right foot stepping forward, and Lassiter heard the air rushing by the thirty-inch steel blade.

The machete neatly sliced Keaka's ear in two, the top half falling to the ground like a banana slice. Then the jungle exploded with the sound of a coconut axed in two, the blade fracturing Keaka's skull. The machete broke, the blade lodged in his temple, the wooden handle still in Lila's hands, a broken Louisville Slugger. The two of them stood there for a moment, Keaka's eyes glassy. Then he crumpled to the ground.

The king's greatest wish had been granted. He had died a warrior's death and would join his ancestors for eternity.

CHAPTER

30

Pu'uo Mauí

Ho'oheno Li'a	To Cherish Li'a
"Auhea 'oe e ka ipo pe'e poli,	Listen, lover with a hidden heart,
'O ke anoano waili'ula.	Overpowering mirage.
A he lei mamo 'oe no ke ahiahi	You are evening's lei of saffron flowers
E 'uhene ai me Li'a i ka uka.	Exulting with Li'a, Goddess of desire, in the forest.
"Me 'oe ka 'ano 'i pau 'ole,	"With you an unending desire,
A nei pu 'uwai e 'oni nei.	Here in the beating heart.
Mai ho 'ohala i ka 'ike lihi mai	Do not thrust away the glimpse
Pulupe ai maua i ka ua noe."	Of our drenching in the misty rain."

Jake Lassiter and Lila Summers spent the night—what was left of it—at Keaka's campsite. Lila slipped out of her wet swimsuit, a one-piece yellow number, and dried off on a *lauhala* mat of woven leaves in the *hale.* Lassiter removed his trunks and put on one of Keaka's loincloths.

Lila stifled a laugh. "You look good in that, Jake. It was Keaka's favorite. He shot a wild goat for the skin."

"If my partners could see me now, a deep-carpet lawyer in a goatskin jockstrap."

They found some *poi* that Keaka had stored in gourds and mixed it with smoked fish. Lassiter started eating with his fingers. "Think you could make this stuff in Miami?" He knew what he was saying, sort of asking what she had planned for the rest of her life.

"Get me some taro, the Hawaiian staff of life," she said, "and I'll make *poi* till it's coming out your ears."

Jake Lassiter squatted on his haunches in the little hut and sliced several passion fruit, sucking at the tart jelly inside the skin. Lila studied him in the light of a kukui nut candle and said, "You're starting to look like you belong here, Jake, like you fit in with the land and the sea."

Now what did that mean, he wanted to ask but didn't, that she was going to stay on Maui but that he could share her *hale* anytime? She had to know that now—after killing Keaka and with Mikala still around—she'd have to leave the island too. Lila slid back on the mat, making room for him, and then she patted a spot that must have had his name on it. She was sitting there in the flickering light, inviting him to partake of her after the *poi* but Jake Lassiter was strangely empty, devoid of desire. Lila cocked her head, studying him, her full mouth in its perpetual pout. She leaned back, bracing her arms on the ground, her breasts thrust forward. Her eyes glowed, and her cheeks were flushed.

"Maybe one of us should stay outside and keep watch," he said, gesturing toward the door with the Uzi.

"Jake, we're alone here, trust me."

"What about Lee Hu?" he asked.

"It'll take her till sunrise to get to Pukoo, if she can get out of the jungle at all. She'll call Mikala, but he can't get his helicopter in here so he'll go after the boat he keeps at Maalaea Bay. By the time he gets there from his home upcountry, we'll be long gone. When the sun comes up, we'll take two of Keaka's boards and get back to Maui. Until then . . ." Lila gestured again toward the mat, but Jake Lassiter shook his head. Still no fire in his loins, not on this night.

He crawled under the low door of the *hale* and walked to the fire, now just a cluster of hot coals. Strange that he wanted to be alone just then, strange that he was down. He had won, had survived. Sometimes after winning a trial, the battle over, depression would set in, too. Maybe that's what life was all about, the conflicts full of fury yet joyful, the lulls a peaceful despair.

It shouldn't be that way, he decided, trying to will himself into better spirits. He had the girl. Why wasn't he happy? What was wrong? Tubby's dead, that's one thing, he knew. He hadn't thought about Tubby since he'd put the board in the water at Honokahua, had been too worried about his own hide. But it came back now.

Keaka was dead, too, hard to forget that, his twisted body pitched headfirst in the clearing only inches from the fire, the machete blade still jammed halfway through his skull, blood from his gut blackening the sand. Lila Summers had done the job, expertly and efficiently, with no wasted motion.

Or emotion.

Had done what he couldn't do. Now she wanted to thrust and parry on the very mat where she and Keaka had made love to celebrate their triumphs over the *haoles*.

Lassiter's mind was playing Ping-Pong with a moral dilemma. The body's still warm and she's got her replacement lined up. Not even a momentary pause for mourning her dead lover. The sight of the butchered carcass draining the old libido from me, maybe stirring hers up, Lassiter thought. He summoned a rationalization: She's just different from me, nothing wrong with that. He ducked his head back into the *hale*. "I think I'll sit outside for a while. Doubt I'll be able to sleep after all this."

"It's okay, Jake. I understand. Tomorrow, though, I'll demand your attention. And I want to tell you how wonderful you were out there, the way you threw Keaka off-balance, the way we worked together to defeat him."

"Thanks, Lila, but you did it. You saved my life—twice today, by my calculations."

"Someday you'll return the favor."

"I was hoping it wouldn't be necessary, that we could get away from the violence, get away from here."

"What about the bonds, Jake?"

The bonds.

The bonds and the blonde.

He had forgotten half the reason for being there. What was it Keaka had said about the bonds? He tried to remember. "Where's Keaka's favorite place?" Lassiter asked.

"What?"

"On the beach, before you showed up, Keaka said the coupons were in his favorite place. What'd he mean?"

She looked puzzled. "Is that all he said?"

"I was a little groggy, but he said the bonds weren't on Molokai. They were in his favorite place and you'd know the spot, something like that."

"Keaka's favorite place," she repeated. "I don't know. On Maui there are so many beautiful places."

"But some place had to be special."

She wrinkled her forehead and closed her eyes. "Maybe . . . the crater, Haleakala." She thought about it for a moment. "Keaka never wanted to stay in the park cabins, that was the *haole* way. We used to spend the night outside, camping near the Pu'uo Maui cone. We'd dig a hole in the ash at the base of the cone and store our food and sleeping bags there. Then we could sneak in past the rangers anytime we wanted and camp under the stars. The coupons could be there, buried at the foot of Pu'uo Maui."

"Are you sure?"

"No. But it's a good guess, the best I can come up with."

"We can go tomorrow."

"Sure, Jake, but you can't just carry a pick and shovel into the crater, the rangers would have a fit. We'll hike in at the end of the day and camp out. We'll dig after dark, take all night if we have to, and get out by sunrise."

"Tomorrow night, then," Lassiter said. "Now, shouldn't we bury him?"

Her shrug was almost imperceptible. "If you want to," she said evenly.

Together they dug a pit using an adz, a stone lashed to a timber they found inside the *hale*. Lila struggled to remove the machete from Keaka's skull, placing one foot on the back of his neck for leverage. If she felt any sentiment, her face did not reveal it. If she had suffered a loss, it did not show. Not a moment's grief, not a second of reflection.

They tumbled the body into the pit, covering it with leaves and branches. No one offered a eulogy, but Lila looked down at the fresh grave, and said, "Keaka, wherever you are, I hope you're as happy as I am."

Back inside the *hale*, Lila stretched out on the mat and covered herself with a *kapa* blanket stitched from tree bark. Outside, animals screeched and cawed, and twigs snapped in the darkness. Lassiter watched Lila until she curled up and closed her eyes, and her breathing came in heavy, even breaths. It only took a minute or two, and there she was, purring away, her face peaceful and angelic. Lassiter crawled out the low door and sat, cross-legged by the shallow grave, listening to the music of the jungle, waiting for the dawn.

In the daylight, they easily found Keaka's boards, the sails neatly folded, the booms tied to the masts. The crossing was easy. No whales and no Mikala, only problem a rising sun staring them hard in the face. When they came ashore on Maui, they left the rigs on the rocky beach and drove in Lila's pickup to her girl friend's place in Kihei. Lassiter finally slept, napping at midday. Lila gathered what they would need: warm clothing, sleeping bags, shovels, flashlights, a thermos with coffee, a bag of papayas, and some sandwiches.

They drove upcountry in her pickup truck, through Pukalani and then higher in the Kula District, finally up Crater Road to the summit. They entered the Sliding Sands Trail, walking down from the observation area. The crater was filled with clouds, blowing in from Hanakauhi, the Maker of Mists, and they could barely see the bright red floor. Closer up, the rocks revealed other colors—yellow, lavender, silver, and black streaks, the remnants of ancient lava flows.

Coming down the trail, Lila had pointed through the clouds to the small rise she said was their destination. Later, on the floor of the crater, she gestured and said, "There's our cone, Pu'uo Maui."

Lassiter's broad shoulders sagged. "But that's a mountain. It didn't look that big from above."

"You get no sense of perspective from on top," Lila said. "There's nothing down here recognizable to compare to the cones, so they all look small. I'll try to remember where Keaka and I camped. It was away from the trail so we couldn't be seen."

The cone was a miniature volcano itself, rising nine hundred feet from the floor of Haleakala, with an indented crater of its own on top. Lila was puzzled. "I remember there were bushes and *pili* grass nearby."

They found an area on the far side of the cone with patches of *'ohelo* berries. "It could be around here," she said.

Could be, Lassiter thought, knowing it was futile. There was no way they could just jam a shovel into the red sand and come up with a million bucks. It was getting dark, and the temperature was dropping.

Lila kept looking for familiar landmarks. "Problem is, it's constantly changing in here. Look at the ripples in the sand. New plants grow and die. Others are covered by the blowing sand. We used to camp anywhere we wanted and now looking around, the size of this place, I just don't know. I'm sorry, Jake."

"Don't worry. It doesn't matter."

And it really didn't. He wasn't sad about the money. He thought about it and figured he didn't care about the bonds after all. He'd really come for Lila, it had just been hard to admit on the way out here. After Tubby was killed, there had been another purpose, revenge, and with Keaka dead, it seemed like it should be over.

Darkness came quickly, and with it the mountain air grew cold. Then the sky lit up. The clouds disappeared and the stars blazed, thousands of them, more than he'd ever seen, sparkling against the black velvet sky, a king's ransom in gemstones. They set up camp in the twinkling light, zipping their sleeping bags together, making a comfortable nest for two. The heavy sweaters came off and so did everything else.

They made love, the crisp night air outside, their bodies warm in the sleeping bag. And this time it was different. Maybe it was the place—the stars and the rocks that were born so long ago, a universal silence except for their own murmurs—maybe it was him, maybe it was a million things, but what did it matter, because Lila responded as she had not before, her breathing quickened, and then her breasts heaved and her body shuddered, then rested and shuddered again, and she gave out a short cry, and then another. They both lay there, bathed in each other's sweat, and this time Jake Lassiter didn't ask because he knew, and Lila opened her eyes and dewy tears ran down her sculpted cheeks and Lassiter kissed each salty drop.

Jake Lassiter looked toward the heavens, and in the clear, thin air, it seemed he could touch the stars. The entire world sparkled, the thousand-foot cinder cones etched in relief against the night, the flickering suns burning with fires of antiquity, the woman whose legs entwined his. If only this moment could be frozen for eternity like the bed of an ancient lava stream. Lila was his and he had only one goal: to get her out of Maui and home with him. To hell with the bonds, he thought, and he slept like a man with no enemies and a future as bright as the sky.

CHAPTER 31

Silversword

They could see their breath in the morning air. They could also feel the mist, cold droplets from the clouds. The outside of the double sleeping bag was soaked.

Lila was up, puttering around the campsite, while Jake lay there in the warmth she had created. "Jake, look at this!" Her voice rose with excitement, and at first he thought she might have found an old landmark, a key to the treasure he had all but forgotten. But Lila stood motionless in front of a four-foot tall plant, sleek gray leaves at its base, a burst of purple flowers pointing upward. Propped there in the black sand, the leaves shimmered, nearly white.

"Silversword," Lila said. "In full bloom. Take a good look. They only bloom on Haleakala, nowhere else on Maui, nowhere else in the world."

He pulled himself out of the sleeping bag, and hopped into his undershorts. "It's breathtaking."

"But sad, too."

"Why? It's glorious. A plant flaming out of the rocks and sand, it's almost unearthly."

"Sad because it won't last," Lila Summers said. "The silversword grows for twenty years without blooming, just a bush in the desert. Then it blooms, but only once, a brief flash of colors, then dries up like an old kitchen mop and dies."

They stood there, absorbing the beauty of the plant, struck by its splendor against the stark landscape. Tears came to Lila's eyes. What was she thinking, Lassiter wondered in the silence. She was moved by the sight of the plant, so beautiful, so near death.

Such a strange reaction. When she butchered her former lover, not a trace of emotion. Now, on the lunar landscape, tears for a flowering bush. What did it mean to her, he wondered. Was the realization sinking in? That she had to leave the island, now and forever, this was her last time in the crater, the last glimpse of a silversword in bloom?

Still looking at the shimmering plant, she said, "Will you always remember last night?"

"For the rest of my life."

"Remember the silversword, Jake. Remember it and think of me."

"I'll think of you all the time, especially if we're sharing the same sleeping bag."

But she just shook her head sadly and began gathering up their belongings.

By the time they ate their papayas and gathered their gear, the sun was sizzling over the rim of the crater. Lila paced around the base of the huge cone, but even in the morning light, she had no idea where to look, no way to guess where Keaka had buried the treasure. She scuffed at a few rocks, then gave up. You could dig more holes than Con Ed and have nothing to show for it but a ton of sand and rocks.

It was time to get off the mountain, to get away before Mikala set out to avenge his cousin's death. Which is what Lila predicted he would do. He's a killer, she said, not up close with his own hands like Keaka, but more of an assassin, a methodical professional. Lassiter remembered the talk in the police station, the pride Mikala took in the slaughter in Vietnam.

After the long climb up the trail to the observation building, they loaded their gear in Lila's old pickup and started slowly down Crater Road. Six miles below the summit, behind a sharp bend in the road at the eight-thousand-foot level, a few cars were pulling into the entrance to the Halemau'u Trail, which led to the rim of the crater. As they passed the parking lot, it pulled out behind them, a 1979 Chevy Blazer with a reinforced steel bumper, a row of spotlights, and a rumbling engine. Two tons of terror, a nightmare on wheels.

CHAPTER 32

Déjà Vu

Lila Summers hit the gas, but the engine backed off—the Mazda could have used a tune-up—then revved and tore around the next curve. The Blazer closed the distance, its fortified front bumper drawing a bead on them. Then it just hung there, a foot or two feet behind, taking every curve with them. Lila slowed, the Blazer slowed; she sped up, the Blazer sped up.

"They're toying with us," Lassiter said. "Do you have any weapons in here?"

"Nothing here but the windsurfing gear in back," she replied, never taking her eyes off the road.

He remembered Tubby, déjà vu, and he figured he wasn't

doing any good this time either. "I'm going back there," he said, opening the door and watching the pavement streak beneath him. Lila didn't say a word. No meek feminine protests—*don't do it, Jake*—not from Lila Summers. She was calm, her athlete's reflexes taking care of the driving. If he could help out, fine. If not, just stay the hell out of the way.

Jake Lassiter took a deep breath, and then, holding onto the shoulder harness, swung a leg over the side of the bed and pushed off. A strange thought in midair: the image of Jackie Kennedy climbing over the trunk of the black Lincoln convertible. What was she doing, hauling ass to get out or helping the Secret Service guy in? And what was Jake Lassiter doing, jumping to safety again or picking up arms to fight? His hand caught the roll bar in midleap; it steadied him and he dropped into the bed.

The Blazer hadn't changed position, still hanging back a foot from their rear bumper, growling like an angry beast. Wasting no time, Lassiter took inventory. The harnesses, booms, and mast extensions were rolling around at his feet. So was an eight-foot wave board. Lassiter grabbed the board and tossed it at the Blazer. The driver braked quickly, and the board crashed to the pavement, the fiberglass shattering, the Blazer crunching over it. Then, as if angered, the beast hit the Mazda pickup a jolt from the rear, sending Lassiter toppling forward. Not much time now. He picked up a boom, a five-foot-long aluminum wishbone covered by a rubber handgrip. He bounced it off the hood of the Blazer, a flea brushed from an elephant's hide. Next, one of the heavy aluminum mast extensions: It fit in the palm of his hand like a nightstick. But it pinged on the Blazer's windshield and fell harmlessly to the road.

Then Lassiter saw an old sail rolled up in the corner. He crouched down and opened it. The five plastic battens were not in the sleeves. Good, the sail would be more flexible. It had four vertical panels of different colors from the leech to the mast sleeve. From the head to the tack, it was fourteen feet long, about four feet across from sleeve to clew. It was the right size and it might work, but he would need the element of surprise and more luck than he'd had so far.

The sun glared off the Blazer's heavily tinted windshield. It was ten feet behind them now, and Lassiter stood, spread-eagled, holding the sail, which filled with wind, threatening to take him over the side. He waited until the Blazer charged them, then let go. Five square meters of brightly colored Mylar crackled in the wind, then flew to the windshield. Brakes squealed but the sail stayed put, draping the cab of the Blazer like a shroud. They were on a curve now and the Blazer went straight across the uphill lane into the *mauka* side of the road, where the huge front wheels vaulted over a clump of boulders and slammed into a grassy slope.

Lila Summers hit the brakes, squealing the tires and sending Jake Lassiter sprawling again. He landed hard on a shoulder that had been separated three times and dislocated twice. She expertly slid the Mazda into a 180-degree turn.

Now what? Lassiter thought they'd beat it down the mountain, but Lila was streaking back up the road, nearing the Blazer where the passenger door was opening—the driver's door was pinned against the slope—and as a man stepped from the high cab, Lila swung the Mazda off the road toward him. Lassiter felt the jolt and heard a *th-ump* but from the bed of the truck could not see what happened.

Lila brought the Mazda to a stop and Lassiter jumped out. Sprawled across their hood and front windshield was one of the largest men he had ever seen, aloha shirt pulled up over his huge belly. Lila Summers sat motionless, her hands on the steering wheel, calmly contemplating the sight of the big man's navel staring through the windshield like a Cyclops.

Blood flowed from the man's nose and trickled from one of

his ears. One eye was closed and a nasty welt was forming on his forehead. But he wasn't dead, not even unconscious. He was at that very moment pulling himself up with one hand and tearing off the Mazda's radio aerial with the other. From in front of the pickup, Lassiter grabbed the man's foot to pull him off the hood, a task no more difficult than dragging a tractor trailer up a hill. The foot, wrapped in a size 15EEE Reebok running shoe, jerked Lassiter toward the hood, then with the kick of a plow horse sent him tumbling into the sand at the side of the road. A sumo wrestler, or maybe defensive line material.

The big man slid off the Mazda and got to his feet, shaky but massive, whipping the aerial back and forth, heading for Lassiter, who crouched on his haunches, his hands trailing along the ground. No one said a word.

The big man got closer, the aerial whining in the air, and Lassiter stayed put. When the man was close enough that Lassiter felt the breeze from the metal whip, he sprang forward, tossing two handfuls of red sand in the man's face. There was a yelp, the aerial fell, and the man's hands came up to his eyes.

Lassiter hit him, a good left jab to the right eye, then a short right to his huge belly. The big man simply grunted and blinked, still clawing at his eyes. Lassiter planted his feet and got a lot of hip behind a left hook. The timing was good, but the aim a little high, and it caught the big man square in the middle of his sloping forehead. Slugging Dave Casper's helmet with a roundhouse right in the AFC Championship game had probably hurt more, but maybe not, Lassiter thought, his knuckles flaring with pain.

The giant grunted again and hit Lassiter in the chest with an open palm. The impact knocked him back three feet. A great pass blocker. The man wiped the blood from his nose, and twisted his face into a vicious smile. "Hit me again, *haole*."

Lassiter didn't, but Lila did, clobbering him from behind with a mast extension, then a second time, and the man crumpled like a buffalo shot through the heart.

"Let's get him off the road," she said, looking each way for traffic. It would have been easier with a crane. They pushed and rolled him into a gulley and Lila quickly brought some sturdy quarter-inch boom line from the Mazda.

"Help me get his hands behind his back," she told Lassiter. Working quickly, she bound the big man's wrists with a sheepshank knot. He was facedown in the gulley, moaning softly. It took both of them to turn him over.

"Hello, Lomio," Lila said softly. "You're not as quick as you used to be, but you're just as ugly. And you look like you've been hit by a truck." Lila laughed, and a chill went through Jake Lassiter. He tried to think. What was it about this moment, about that laugh, but it wouldn't compute and he stored it away.

Lila was bent over the bleeding man. "Now, Lomio, tell me where they are. You would have been with Keaka when he hid them."

The man was silent.

"Oh, Lomio, Lomio! Wherefore art thou . . . bonds?" Lila said to him theatrically. Enjoying the moment.

Lomio spoke through swollen, bleeding lips. "Up my ass, *wahine laikini*."

"Lomio, that's very crude, calling me a whore." Then she smashed the mast extension into his ankle. Metal shattered bone. Lomio's face contorted in pain but he made no sound.

Lila scowled and turned to Lassiter. "C'mon, Jake. Let's put him in the back of the truck. We'll have to baby-sit him until he tells us where the bonds are."

"What if he doesn't know?"

Lila laughed, the same mocking, chilling laugh. "We'll find

that out, too, if we handle it right. By the time he dies, he'll tell all his family secrets."

By the time he dies. What the hell does that mean? The big man was hurt, sure, but the injuries weren't fatal. And here's Lila talking about him dying like it was inevitable, like they were going to . . . well . . . finish him off.

Lila was very businesslike, no trace of emotion. No anger, no fear. Okay, she's not like me, Jake Lassiter thought. So what? She's not like anybody I've ever known.

Except that laugh, the taunting of Lomio, that was familiar.

It reminded him of someone, and the memory gnawed at Lassiter, calling back a night of terror and doom.

She sounded just like Keaka Kealia.

CHAPTER

33

Dead Is Dead

Lomio refused to move, so they propped him against the pickup, and when Lila threatened to break both his kneecaps, the giant used his one good leg to hop into the bed. Lila gagged him and pulled an old sail over his head, the smell of sweat and blood fouling the morning air.

They drove down the mountain and across the Central Valley into Lahaina. On a deserted street near the waterfront, Lila parked the pickup under an angel's-trumpet tree, huge white flowers hanging downward in the shape of a horn, the exotic scent of musk heavy in the air.

"What're we going to do with him?" Lassiter asked. It was clear who was in charge.

"Get him to talk, then find a hole to stuff him into."

"It'd have to be big enough for a moose."

Lila's eyes lit up. "Or a pig. Jake, have you ever been to a luau?"

"No, and I'm not too hungry just now."

"That's okay, we don't have time to eat. We'll just let Lomio soak up the cultural experience of his ancestors, a long line of Samoan goat-fuckers."

Her voice was hard. Lila continued to surprise him—so much toughness, so little compassion. Lassiter wondered if part of the attraction was her strength and the danger it courted. Was his button-down life so boring that he needed battles in the jungle and attacks on mountain roads to keep the blood flowing?

They drove another block before turning into an alley where the sign said DELIVERIES ONLY, LAHAINA BEACH HOTEL. Close to the beach a pavilion was set up for the evening luau. Lila pulled to a stop behind a row of pink Tecoma trees and killed the engine.

She pointed to a pile of leaves and banana stalks in the shade of the trees. "That's an *imu*, an earthen oven. The boys would have put the pig in there a couple of hours ago. It will take six or seven hours to cook this way, so they shouldn't be back for a while."

Lila found a pair of windsurfing gloves in the pickup and they walked to the *imu*, where she started peeling away the leaves on top. Underneath was a mound of black dirt. "Jake, bring the shovels from the truck."

He did, checking on Lomio in the back. The man was conscious, but he wouldn't be doing calculus today. Lila began digging and uncovered sweet potatoes, bananas, taro, and fish wrapped in ti leaves. She removed the food gingerly, feeling the heat through the gloves.

"The leaves make steam," Lila explained. "They gut the pig and put hot stones in the body cavity to cook from the inside out."

"The first microwave," Lassiter said. "Didn't know you were so domestic, a real Hawaiian homemaker."

She laughed. "A luau was not done every day, more of a celebration during *makahiki*, a period of peace."

"Not very appropriate today."

"No, this is war and Lomio is the enemy. Jake, I'll need your help to get the information—smoke it out of him, you might say."

Lassiter's look stopped her, but she recovered quickly. "Just to scare him, Jake, that's all."

"He doesn't look like he scares too easily."

She studied Lassiter a moment. "Lomio has to think we'll kill him or it won't work."

Lassiter paused, listening to the distant traffic. In the heavy foliage alongside the *imu*, they were hidden from the street and the hotel.

"Okay, what do we do?" he asked.

It took both of them to haul out the pig, the pungent smell of the steaming pork rising from the ground. Then they went after Lomio. He seemed even heavier now, trussed with the line, not helping out, just sagging his three hundred pounds onto the ground after they dragged him out of the truck bed. They tried to pick him up but he struggled, so they rolled him like a beer keg to the edge of the *imu*. Then Lila removed the gag and pushed him in, Lomio landing on his back on top of the leaves.

A cloud of steam rose from beneath Lomio and his face turned a scorching red, but still he was silent. Again Lila read the look on Lassiter's face. "Don't worry, Jake. It's no worse than a sauna. Unless we keep him there all day, he'll be okay, just lose a few pounds, which he ought to thank us for."

They waited several minutes. Lomio seemed to have mastered the pain.

Lila squatted at the edge of the pit and leaned close to the big man. "Where are the bonds?" she demanded.

Lomio spat in her face. She calmly picked up a large banana leaf and placed it on his chest. Then she dropped a hot lava stone on top the leaf and stepped into the pit, her sneaker pushing stone and leaf against him, his massive chest caving inward to avoid the pain. The leaf was sizzling, leaving its shape as a tattoo on Lomio's skin.

Jake Lassiter had seen enough. "Lila, no . . . forget it!"

"Only a second, Jake. This should do it. Lomio, where are the bonds? Or would you like me to remove the leaf and leave the stone there?"

They both heard it at the same time, a rustling of bushes in the direction of the pavilion, someone walking toward them. Jake Lassiter reacted quickly, standing up, putting a finger to his lips, letting Lila know he would take care of it. She nodded and whispered to Lomio. "One sound, and you're dead, fat man."

Lassiter walked in the direction of the noise, his mind flashing like a neon sign with the crimes he had committed—assault and battery, false imprisonment, kidnapping, extortion, and now maybe desecrating a luau in violation of some old Polynesian law.

Coming through the oleander trees, walking straight toward him, was a man in his thirties wearing neatly pressed white slacks, moccasins, and a bright green aloha shirt. The man didn't see him. He was preoccupied with the task of walking and unzipping his fly at the same time. A second later, the man had his precious cargo in hand. He was no more than twenty feet from the *imu*, hidden behind the trees.

"Howdy," Jake Lassiter called out in his good-neighbor voice.

"Whoa, whoops." The man took two steps backward and tucked himself in. "Didn't expect to see anybody out here now. Just about to take my pre-luau piss. For good luck. Name's Guy Ryder, master of ceremonies."

Lassiter decided not to shake hands. Guy Ryder had a booming voice and a smile filled with porcelain crowns. Lassiter smiled back. "Don't let me stop you. When a man's gotta go . . ."

"Right you are. Now where's that damn *imu*? I always piss on it for good luck."

"What? No! That would be a health code violation. You know, I'm a wholesale butcher back in Des Moines. Those damn regulations can drive you crazy, temperature controls in the freezer, rodent hair counts. But pissing on the pork, I mean, that's gotta be verboten everywhere."

"Just a little hosing on top of the leaves, that's all."

Jake Lassiter scowled, an angry tourist now. "Well, I'm supposed to take the little woman to that looey-ow tonight and she'll be damn sure unhappy if I tell her what you use for barbecue sauce."

Guy Ryder threw up his hands, revealing his still unzipped fly. "Okay, okay," he said, looking for a nearby bush to finish the task.

Lila Summers could hear every word of the baritone voice of Guy Ryder. She had replaced Lomio's gag and at the same time removed the banana leaf from under the stone. Then she put two more stones on his chest and one on his stomach, and ripping open his pants, jammed one against his testicles. The heat singed Lila's fingers through the gloves. Lomio writhed in silent agony. His skin sizzled and the acrid smell of burning flesh rose from the pit. Lomio's face was crimson; then the color drained to a ghastly pallor. Sweat poured from his body and his jaws were clenched in pain.

Lila listened as Guy Ryder's voice grew faint, saying something now about how lazy the Hawaiians were, sometimes he had to help clear the tables, think of it, Guy Ryder, a former Top 40 deejay in a semimajor market, a busboy for Christ's sake. Lassiter kept him company all the way back to the pavilion.

Lila removed the gag. "The bonds, Lomio. Where's Keaka's favorite place?"

Through parched lips caked with dried blood and spittle, Lomio said something. Lila Summers leaned close, her ear near the big man's mouth.

"Ooo-lay," Lomio seemed to say, then fell into unconsciousness.

Guy Ryder was counting place settings as Jake Lassiter walked back, just moseying along, another tourist with time on his hands. By the time he got to the trees, Lila was shoveling dirt into a mound on top of the *imu.*

"Where is he?" Jake Lassiter asked, knowing the answer even as he said it.

"Having high tea with Queen Kapiolani. Come on, Jake, I've put all the stones back in. Help me with the dirt and leaves, then let's go. If you're hungry, take a couple sweet potatoes."

Jake Lassiter didn't want sweet potatoes. "He's dead, isn't he?"

"Jake, lighten up. He killed your friend, burned him to a crisp. As they say, what goes around comes around, a little symmetry in life . . . and death. I've given your friend some justice, something you wouldn't do. If I had more time, I'd have cooked him medium-well, poached the bastard real slow."

"You buried him alive?"

Lila shrugged. "What difference does it make if he was dead earlier or later? Dead is dead."

Lassiter stared at her blankly, his mind trying to work up a rationalization. Sure Lomio deserved to die. He tried to kill us, helped kill Tubby, Lassiter thought. But there are laws. We're not in the jungle, he thought. Or is that exactly where we are, and not just here in the islands, but everywhere?

He thought about Lila. She was right about one thing—dead is dead. No use dwelling on the huge Samoan; he was on his way across the river and Lassiter hoped there'd be a burning sulfur pit waiting. But later, Jake Lassiter knew, he would face his own trial, the moral questions of Lomio's death, the determination of his own culpability.

"Jake, snap out of it. He talked."

"He told you where the coupons are?"

"I think so."

"What'd he say?"

Lila laughed. "I'm glad you haven't forgotten about the money. For a while, you seemed more interested in playing nursemaid to somebody who wanted you dead."

"I'm still Sam Kazdoy's lawyer. I'm supposed to bring the coupons back."

"We can talk about that later. He told me Keaka's favorite place was his *ule*. It means penis."

Lassiter shook his head. "Your boyfriend could've been a chapter in Freud's *Pleasure Principle*."

"What he must have meant is the Iao Needle. It's a pinnacle of volcanic rock in the West Maui Mountains. Keaka used to say it reminded him of his *ule*. What he said to you about his favorite place was a play on words, a joke, or as close to a joke as Keaka ever came."

"So where are the coupons?"

"Putting two and two together, probably buried on top the

Iao Needle about twelve hundred feet above the floor of the valley."

"How'd he get up there?"

"The top of the Needle isn't really sharp. It's sort of a nob, just like . . ."

"Yeah, I get it."

"Keaka would have climbed to the top."

Lila's cheeks were flushed and strands of her hair were slick with sweat. She seemed animated, alive with excitement. Maybe the killing breathed life into her, Lassiter thought. The thought hung heavily on him. Two deaths by their hands. Okay, with Keaka, it was us or him. But Lomio? Lassiter told himself Lila did it to avenge Tubby. But she didn't even know Tubby, so maybe she did it for good old Jake Lassiter. But she did it, he now believed, for the thrill. Maybe the money, too. And that was eating at him. The bonds belonged to Sam Kazdoy. Bring them back and half belong to Jake Lassiter. Lila Summers hadn't said anything about bringing them back. They hadn't talked about it. They hadn't talked about much; they just did things, and everytime they did something there seemed to be a body on the ground.

Holding the microphone loosely as he'd seen Neil Diamond do in Vegas, Guy Ryder led fifty tourists from the pavilion to the *imu* under the pink Tecoma trees. This was a shitty job, worse than being a disc jockey in Quad City, Illinois, but after you skip town eight months behind on the alimony, you have to feel lucky to be the assistant entertainment director at a second-rate hotel on Maui.

"This is Hawaii's most authentic luau, an experience you won't forget," Guy Ryder was saying in his booming voice. "Get those cameras ready. But first let me say *mahalo*, a big

Hawaiian 'thank-you' to these great guys who did the cooking. In ancient Hawaii, the men cooked and the women did the serving, and it's the same here. Not like the mainland. Know what my ex-wife made for dinner? Reservations."

The tourists tittered and gathered around as three local teenagers wearing made-in-Taiwan loincloths pulled off the leaves.

"When Captain Cook discovered Hawaii," Guy Ryder intoned, "he didn't call room service. No siree, the chiefs—and all the Indians—invited him to a feast. Of course, after feeding Captain Cook, the Hawaiians had him for dinner, but we won't be *too* authentic, eh? Now have your luau coupons ready when Leilani comes to your table."

Guy Ryder didn't get too close to the *imu*. The black dirt would have stained his white cotton slacks, and the smell of scorched pig always made him nauseous. He stepped away as the teenagers hauled the blackened carcass out of the ground. There was a rush of air, fifty tourists sucking in their breaths. Then a management consultant from Newport Beach who would have rather been playing golf said to his wife, "First time I ever saw a pig wearing Reeboks."

CHAPTER

34

The Crooked Rainbow

B*efore Haleakala existed, there rose from the sea the shield vol*cano that was to form the West Maui Mountains. For the next million years, molten rock erupted beneath the Pacific and exploded two thousand feet into the air, its boiling rain cascading down the mountain. Time and again the hot magma withdrew into the earth and a caldera, a depression, formed. Carrying the magma to the surface were dikes, channels in the rocks, and with time, they grew hard and the eruptions ceased. Then clouds pushed by trade winds were snared on the craggy peaks and the rains came, torrents streaming down the rocky landscape, and after twenty thousand lifetimes, the rains had carved an amphitheater into the ancient volcano.

To the early Hawaiians, it became *Iao*, Cloud Supreme, a holy place considered the valley of kings, for it was there they buried the *alii*, their chiefs. Less than a dozen years after Captain Cook landed, the peacefulness of the valley was shattered when Kamehameha the Great launched his forces from the Big Island and pushed the army of Maui's King Kalanikupule into the sacred valley. The pure waters of the stream ran red with warriors' blood and skeletons remained visible for decades. A mile from the battlefield stands the Iao Needle, a spire of volcanic rock twelve hundred feet high.

Two busloads of Japanese tourists were clicking away, their Nikons and Canons recording the lush valley scenes for folks back home. Jake Lassiter and Lila Summers crossed the walking bridge over the Iao Stream and headed toward the Needle. The steep slope looked impossible to scale, at least without ropes and pitons and Sir Edmund Hillary leading the way. But Lila said she had done it before, with Keaka, naturally, when they were younger, sneaking around to the far side, away from the tourists.

Lassiter stretched, spit in his hands, and dropped into a deep-knee bend. He started gingerly up the overgrown trail, hand over hand. Lila scampered past him with feline grace, balancing on a rock, grabbing the roots of a small tree, steadily making progress until the angle of the Needle shielded her from view.

"Don't worry about me," Lassiter called after her. "I'll catch you at the top."

But now he was thinking.

Strange thoughts.

So many questions about Lila. How could she dispose of Keaka and never blink an eye? And how did she get the big

Samoan to talk? What goes on in that brain of hers, and what code of conduct does she live by? And what would I have with her? What have we had so far? Just kissing and killing. And *shtupping*, Sam Kazdoy would say.

How is the old man doing? Is Violet Belfrey still hanging on? Have to get back to Miami, the coupons under one arm, Lila Summers on the other. Then what? Talk, plan our lives. She'd learn to be—to be what?—more civilized, less homicidal?

He was tired and his mind was running away again, a dinner party in Miami, Lila talking to him. *Jake, the new attorney general doesn't like the onion soup. Should I jam his hand down the garbage disposal?*

Lila, we don't do that here, we just wait for him to leave and then suggest to the other guests that he's gay.

Welcome to polite society, Lila Summers.

A rock clattered down the slope, startling him. He let go of a tree branch and it snapped back and smacked him across the nose. The trail was no more than a drainage gulley now, thick trees blocking out the sun. Lila was far out of sight, clambering up the slope like a mountain goat. Lassiter tried to pick up the pace, but he was distracted, plagued by bizarre thoughts.

What if she found the buried treasure but said it wasn't there? She could send him on his way, then get it later. Crazy. *Estás loco*, Berto would've said.

Poor Berto. Dead in a swamp, his woman runs off with the guy who snuffed him. Maybe women, like the rich, are different from you and me, Berto, old buddy. Tougher, I guess. The evidence was mounting in support of that case. Maybe not evidence beyond a reasonable doubt, but look at the facts. Lee Hu, there's some fidelity for you. And Violet the Vulture, cozying up to the old man, then wham, her boyfriend swipes the bonds. And Lila Summers. There's more to her than kisses and a suntan.

The slope was even steeper near the knob of the Needle. Lassiter's right knee—ligaments patched, cartilage removed—ached with every step. He was climbing through a fine mist that turned to a light rain. Finally, the trees gave way, and on all fours, he scurried into a clearing at the summit. He rested for a moment, hands on his knees, sucking in air. *Time out.*

Lila sat cross-legged near a sheer cliff on the far side. Sweat and dirt streaked her face, and her hair was matted with brambles. Beside her was a small hole, the dirt the color of cocoa. In her lap was a yellow waterproof backpack caked with mud.

Ignoring Lassiter, she peeled open the Velcro latches and dug in with both hands. She closed her eyes and let her hands drift unseen inside the pack.

"Feels so good," she purred. "Come try it."

"Nah, don't think I could get off on it." But he joined her anyway, four hands rummaging through small slips of paper, the prize of eagles. And she was right. It felt damn good, a fortune trickling through their fingers . . .

East Chicago, Indiana Environmental Improvement Revenue Bond, Youngstown Sheet and Tube Project; Jackson County, Mississippi Pollution Control Bond, International Paper Company Project.

. . . hundreds spilling out in glorious colors. They played with their treasure, reading aloud the tuneless names of municipal sewage projects.

A bright sun had broken through the clouds and mist. A dewy line of sweat beaded on Lila's upper lip. She said, "We've got to get off the island as soon as possible, and we can't use the airport. Mikala will have cops everywhere."

"Just don't ask me to ride a sailboard to San Francisco."

"I'm thinking of a larger boat. My girl friend's father has an old Hatteras docked at Maalaea, the *Crooked Rainbow*." As she said it, they both looked up, because above them was a rainbow, its colors brightly etched against the sky. They laughed and kissed, and rolled on top of each other on the wet ground, and for a moment, he forget about the questions without answers.

When they untangled and stood up, Lila said, "I'll call my girl friend and make sure the boat's gassed up and the keys on board. We'll leave at sunrise for Oahu, and we can fly out of Honolulu for wherever you want."

"Miami, of course," Jake Lassiter said, and Lila sat there looking at him as if she wanted to say something but it could wait.

Lila stuffed the coupons into the pack, and Lassiter walked toward the cliff. Haze filled the valley, but still the view was spectacular. He finally felt at peace with his surroundings. It was starting to sink in.

The bonds and the blonde.

He had them both. Then he felt Lila behind him and started to turn toward her. Something stopped him.

There is a sixth sense, some prehistoric synapse so little used as to be virtually extinct in man. It lets us feel a shadow, a movement unheard and unseen at our back. When man was a hunter, when his knuckles still scraped the forest floor, his senses were honed by constant danger. Today, we are oblivious to the bleat of taxicab horns, much less the cry of a bird in the wilderness.

Not knowing why, Lassiter stopped and turned the other way. He felt Lila brush by him, gasp, and stumble against his planted leg. He whirled back and watched her fall into the vast open space; then his right arm shot toward her. He didn't know how his right hand closed over her wrist. He didn't tell it what to do, it just reacted. Once, in his rookie year against the Bills, he'd let the tight end breeze by him over the middle. Never seeing the ball, Lassiter had stuck out his hand. The pass was underthrown and smacked flat into his palm and stuck. Brilliant interception, the papers said.

He held her wrist tight, her body dangling into space. Their eyes locked, and Lila looked up at him, her mouth twisted into a spasm of fear. Far below her the stream trickled over volcanic rocks, and mist rose from the ancient burial ground. Chilled, Lassiter hauled her back onto firm ground with one solid tug.

Lila sprawled onto the grass, rubbing the shoulder that had held all her weight. "I don't know how I could have been so clumsy." She smiled weakly. "This time you saved *my* life, Jake. I was so frightened that . . ."

"No way I could have dropped you. I had you solid."

She picked up the pack and tossed it over an arm. "For a second I thought . . . you know . . . if I were gone, all the bonds would be yours. If it had been Keaka instead of you, he might have just let go, then laughed about it."

Jake's eyes narrowed. "I'm not Keaka."

Lila used a pay phone at a tourist information booth to call her girl friend. Then they drove out of the Iao Valley and through Wailuku, passing only a few blocks from the County Police Department. Inside the building at that moment, Captain Mikala Kalehauwehe was reviewing transcripts of wiretaps on half a dozen telephones. He had no warrant for the taps, but he had a friend at the telephone company who owed him a favor for looking the other way when the evidence had disappeared in his son's cocaine case. Nothing had turned up on any of the lines from the windsurfing crash pads around Paia on the north shore. Nothing from the girl friend Lila used to hang around with in Kihei. Nothing anywhere until the phone rang. It was his friend from the phone company. They'd just picked up a call.

CHAPTER 35

Slashback

Signing the register as "Mr. and Mrs. R. Bonds," Jake Lassiter and Lila Summers checked into a small motel in Maalaea, a tiny town wrapped around the shoreline of a flat bay. They looked over the *Crooked Rainbow* at the marina. Twin diesel engines ready to power them out of Maui at first light. With Lila on the flying bridge checking the console, Lassiter crawled into the engine compartment.

"Clean, tanks full, fuel lines in good shape," he called out. "Let's see if the battery is topped up."

He popped the battery cover and inspected the chambers. "Everything fine down here."

He hoisted himself out of the engine compartment onto the deck. Lila was above him on the bridge, staring at the horizon. "Great boat," he said. "Maybe we'll get one like it. Catch some grouper and snapper in the Keys. Find an uninhabited island, watch the sun set in the Gulf—"

"Jake," she interrupted him, "I was thinking it might not be such a good idea to go to Miami."

"What?"

"If we go to Miami, you'll have to give back the bonds."

He crawled the ladder to the bridge. Lila settled demurely in the captain's chair, knees tucked under her chin, the picture of innocence. She swiveled the chair toward him and cocked her head, waiting.

"I give back half, we keep half," he said. "That's my deal."

Her smile was backed by iron. "No, Jake, *you* keep half. That's your deal. The half is yours, not ours."

"What do you mean? If it weren't for you, there'd be no coupons at all, none. What's mine is yours."

"What if you get tired of me? What if you do what Keaka did, find someone else, and all of a sudden the money's yours, not ours?"

Jake Lassiter took a moment. So that was it. "That's what happened? I thought *you* left Keaka because of the violence, the murders. That's what you told me."

She was silent. The jury shall not infer guilt from the fact that the defendant remains silent. That's what a judge would say. But in the real world, it's just the opposite. *Cum tacent clamant*, Charlie Riggs used to tell him. When they remain silent, they cry out with guilt.

"You lied to me," Lassiter said.

She put her hand on the throttle and looked past him, toward the open sea. "A white lie. I wanted to stop you from going after Keaka, to keep you from being killed. I thought if you knew how dangerous he was . . ."

"So what did happen with you and Keaka?"

"He was flipping out on his Hawaiian king crap. He wanted to have twenty-one *wahines* to serve him like Kamehameha the Great. Lee Hu and I were the start of the harem. I told him thanks but no thanks, I didn't think he was that hot one-on-one."

First the killings, then a lie, now the bonds, he thought. What other surprises would there be? Time for cross-examine, starting with a leading question. "So what do you want to do with the bonds, keep them?"

"Of course. We earned them."

"Like Hitler earned Poland."

"Jake, don't be foolish. We've got them. Why would we give them back?"

"Because they're not *ours*!" he thundered in his courtroom voice.

She looked at him as if he were a slow learner. "Jake, we killed two men to get them."

The *we* hung there, taunting him, but he ignored it and went back to basics. "Lila, we'll get half, maybe eight hundred thousand. Isn't that enough?"

"How much would that be after taxes? And how much income would we earn on what's left if we just invested it?"

Now she's angling for an M.B.A. from Wharton. "I don't know, Lila, I'll ask my accountant. What difference does it make?"

"It wouldn't be much, would it, I mean for two people to live on."

"Maybe enough for a boat, some papayas and wine. Just drift to wherever the trade winds take us."

"Oh, Jake." She moved next to him and touched her fingers to his lips. Her warm breath brushed his cheek. "I want more than that. Sometimes you just see me in a bikini on the beach."

Her breasts pressed against his rib cage. He fought off the

distraction. "What's wrong with that? It's a glorious lifestyle and you fit there, outdoors, *au naturel.*"

Lila Summers smiled, an indulgent smile. "All of us have to grow up. Keaka understood. What he did wasn't legal, but there are worse things than growing *pakalolo.* Then he started looking for a big score, and frankly, so did I."

"Why? For the money? For material things?"

"Jake, it's such a big world. There's Paris and London and wonderful hotels and restaurants and shops."

So that's what the money means to her, he thought. Not just the time to read great books and drop a line in the water to catch your supper. No, she wants supper served by white-gloved waiters.

"Look, Lila, if you're worried about us, about me, let's make a deal. When we get the money, the half, let's split it down the middle, four hundred thousand for you, four hundred thousand for me. Fair enough?"

She wrinkled her forehead and walked to the rail, turning her back and staring again at the horizon. Lassiter's mind raced. What if she says no? *They're ours, Jake. We earned them. All of them.*

He didn't want to face the question. Would he give it up for her, turn his back on Tubby, who died helping him, and on Sam, who trusted him? Overhead a half dozen black-crowned herons circled the shoreline, their bleats mocking him.

But then Lila turned back to him and said, "Okay, Jake. We'll do it your way. We'll take the boat to Honolulu, then fly to Miami. The eight hundred thousand is all yours. And so am I, for as long as you want me."

A quick turn, Lassiter thought. *Slashback.* One second she's going one way, up a wave, then slash, she jibes and rockets down again. First she's the Goddess of Desire, sun-drenched hair flying in an ocean breeze, then with a blade or hot rock in her hand, she's a one-way ticket to the morgue. Another turn, the air calm after a squall, all sweetness and springtime.

He reached for her, and she kissed him, and he closed his eyes and lost himself in the kiss. When their lips parted, she smiled and laughed. "Hey, what's a girl got to do to get some dinner around here?"

They showered and ate at a small restaurant, feasting on seafood Provençale—shrimp, scallops, and calamari cooked in a casserole with tomatoes, onions, mushrooms, and wine—and Lassiter had the waiter dust off a bottle of Cristal champagne.

When they returned to the room, Lila's cheeks were glowing and she kissed him with an exploring tongue. They were both exhausted, but they made love as they had in the crater. She locked her heels behind his buttocks and demanded all of him, her grip loosening only when her moans built to a crescendo and she exhaled a series of short cries that caught in her throat.

When she lay next to him, her head on his shoulder, nuzzling his neck, his mind took over from his loins. So much she had kept from him. Why? Lassiter held her in his arms and pushed back the questions. He told himself he should be happy. He had the bonds and Lila Summers, too. But his mind wouldn't let it go, kept asking questions. "Committing crimes," he whispered in the dark, "doesn't it bother you?"

"Taking the bonds from the little man after he had stolen them didn't seem like a crime."

"And the killing?"

She sighed. "Keaka was going to kill you, maybe me too. He had to die. Lomio killed your friend. He deserved to die. The Cuban would have sent Keaka and me to prison if he could. He deserved . . ." Lila stopped in midsentence, a cloud crossing her face. Her eyes darted quickly to Lassiter lying next to her. He saw the look and let it pass. Then it sunk in.

He rolled over to look her squarely in the eyes. "Why the mention of Berto? You had nothing to do with that."

"Of course. But . . . I don't know. He's dead, too."

And dead is dead.

Lassiter was still trying to focus, to see something tucked in the shadows of his mind. That night on Molokai. Everything had happened so fast then. What was it Keaka had said? Then he remembered.

"Lila, on the beach that night, I asked Keaka to fight me, *mano a mano*, like he did with Berto in the swamp."

"Yeah?"

"Why was Keaka so confused? He looked like he didn't know what I was talking about, finally said something about *haoles* still being stupid after two hundred years."

"Did he say that?" she asked, yawning and stretching like a tawny cat.

"Yeah, he did. And one other thing. He said Lee Hu doesn't care for you. Why not? What'd you ever do to her?"

Lila didn't raise her head from the pillow. "I don't know, Jake, maybe she's jealous because I was Keaka's old girlfriend."

"Yeah, maybe. It's just funny. Keaka kills Berto and walks off with his girlfriend, but she ends up hating you."

"What are you getting at?"

"Berto was my friend, a guy soft as a dish of flan. Who killed him?"

She sat up. "What difference does it make now?"

Lassiter rolled onto his back, his lawyer's mind racing, the evasive witness all but admitting the crime. Maybe she was right. What difference does it make now?

Dead is dead.

The words kept pounding at him. She already was a killer, sending Keaka and Lomio off to the happy hunting ground. But he still had to know.

"Lila, did you kill Berto?"

Lila ran a hand through the thick mane of her hair and looked away. "All right. Most of what I told you already is true. Keaka and I *were* going to bring coke in from Bimini in a hollowed-out board. Mikala tipped us. The Cuban, your friend, was a DEA snitch. Keaka was going to take care of it himself, get the money, and you know, kill him. But Keaka was being followed. On the beach he saw a man watching him through binoculars. Keaka doesn't, or didn't, miss those things."

"But that was Franklin, the DEA agent. He was guarding Berto."

"Maybe sometimes. But once we hit town, he stuck to Keaka like a sunburn. On the beach, in the hotel lobby, everywhere. So a small change in plans. Keaka spent the better part of the night in the hotel bar, with the DEA agent two tables away watching him. I went to the swamp and took care of the Cuban. There wasn't much to it, one karate punch to the throat, then I crushed his windpipe."

Jake Lassiter closed his eyes and saw Lila squeezing the life out of Berto, showing no more emotion than if she were cracking a coconut on the beach. He stood up, but all the stuffing was out of him, his bones filled with mush. He sat down again and studied the top of his bare feet.

"Jake, now I've told you everything, why I left Keaka, the killing in the swamp. Don't worry, that's all there is, nothing more, really."

That's *all*, Lassiter thought. A homicide in Miami, conspiracy to transport drugs, receiving stolen property, two homicides here. At least she hadn't tried to overthrow the government. He looked at her. She'd just confessed to first-degree murder but didn't beg for forgiveness, didn't shed a tear. You could grow old waiting for Lila Summers to cry over spilled blood.

"Jake, besides the fact that Keaka was getting to be a pain

with his Hawaiian macho crap, there was another reason I left him."

"Yeah?"

She rolled onto her knees and hugged him from behind, her breasts warming his back. "I wanted you."

Jake Lassiter was silent.

"And I still do," she said. "I care for you. You're like an overgrown puppy that needs protection."

Sure I need protection, Jake Lassiter thought. Who wouldn't after hanging out with a woman who strangles, slices, and buries them, one after another? He thought about it some more. The violence hadn't bothered her at all. Should have figured that, the way she'd dispatched Keaka and Lomio the past two days. A man dies and her missing orgasm roars into town like a runaway train. Another man dead, her engine heats to the red line. Keeping her satisfied could decimate the male gender. And what did she see in him, Lassiter wondered, a dreamer in wing tips and button-down shirts who thinks he can take this strong, beautiful, violent woman and wrap her up in a pink ribbon.

"Do you still care for me, Jake?"

He wasn't proud of the answer, but there it was just the same. "Does the sun still rise in the east?" he asked quietly.

Lila Summers arose before dawn and silently gathered her belongings. She looked down at Jake Lassiter, lying on his side, clutching the pillow where she had been. She reached into her duffel bag and pulled out a dive knife, felt the jagged edge, cool to the touch. Kneeling by the bed, she placed the sharp point within an inch of Lassiter's jugular and held it there. Seconds passed. She held the knife steady, studying him, listening to his breathing. She moved the knife to his temple, then brushed back his shaggy hair over an ear. She leaned close, grazed his ear with a soft kiss, and whispered, "I love you, Jake, as much as I can love."

Lila carefully placed the knife on the nightstand, making no sound, pulled on a pair of shorts and a halter top and quietly left the room. Over one shoulder she carried a duffel bag with her clothing. Over the other shoulder, just as it had been in the race to Bimini, was a waterproof yellow pack crammed with treasure.

Jake Lassiter thought he was dreaming. He heard Lila's voice saying she loved him. Must be wishful thinking or wishful dreaming, his mind was saying, shaking off the sleep. He stretched out a leg to find her.

Nothing. He reached with a hand.

The bed too cool.

His eyes opened.

Nothing.

He got up. No Lila in the bathroom. A quick look around, no yellow pack.

It was happening again, Lila gone, the emptiness spreading. He jumped into his pants. Barefoot, he ran outside. The dock was only two hundred yards away. It was not quite dark and not quite light, a slice of the sun behind him rising over the peak of Haleakala in the distance. Puffy clouds dappled the calm bay with pale silver shadows.

Barely twelve hours since he'd saved her life, and she chooses the money instead of him. His mind racing, the image from the top of the Iao Needle flashed back. How strange that the great athlete would stumble. How unlike her to show such fear.

Then he saw it all for the first time. Her eyes were pleading with him not to let go.

He'd had a good grip on her and the leverage to haul her

up. And he was strong. No way he would drop her. Unless he meant to. Which is what she feared. Keaka Kealia would have dropped her, she said. And she would have pushed Keaka off the cliff, too. Or anyone who happened to be in the way at the time. Including Jake Lassiter. Because there wasn't much difference between Keaka and Lila, and Jake Lassiter had known that for longer than he cared to admit.

And now he knew it all. She had killed Berto and tried to kill him. She had tried to push him off the cliff and, dangling there, thought he knew. But he hadn't known until now. He never figured she would kill him for slips of paper that could be exchanged for more paper that could be exchanged for cars and furs and jewels. Now he stood paralyzed in the ashen morning light.

Seconds passed.

Then he ran after her. Or after the bonds. He didn't know which.

He ran toward the end of the dock, his feet picking up splinters from the wooden planks. He heard the engines turn over before he saw the *Crooked Rainbow*. It began to pull away, Lila on the flying bridge, guiding the big boat into open water, leaning a little on the throttle. He neared the end of the dock and had to slow down to keep from falling in.

He yelled her name.

She didn't turn around.

Jake Lassiter would remember many things about the next few moments of his life. One was that Lila Summers didn't turn around. She must have been able to hear him, even over the rumble of the twin engines. She wasn't that far away and he had good pipes. But she didn't turn, she just watched the water in front of her and kept heading toward the open bay. Later, remembering the scene, he decided she had heard him but wouldn't turn, because tears were running down those granite cheekbones. He wanted to believe it, but he would never know.

The rest was frozen. Slowly, so slowly, like a dream. Jake Lassiter stood there yelling, but no words came out.

First Jake Lassiter saw the flash.

Next he heard the roar.

Then he felt the concussion.

The flash was orange, the smoke black, a fireball from within the Hatteras, reaching to the sky, scattering a dozen gulls, drowning out their cries. A splintering of wood, fiberglass, canvas, plastic, and metal.

The huge gas tanks exploded, one after another, launching a thousand missiles of shrapnel, the boat tearing itself apart, leaving nothing above the water, and what was left floating was disintegrated or burning, tiny pieces of indistinguishable matter disappearing into the tomb of a black sea.

CHAPTER

36

Aloha

Jake Lassiter was standing at the end of the dock, staring at the burning wreckage when the first police car pulled up. Captain Mikala Kalehauwehe got out and walked slowly toward him. The cop could have been checking parking meters the way he took his time. Behind him was Lee Hu. Found herself another beau, Lassiter figured later, her mourning taking its usual twenty-four hours.

The captain stopped when he was four feet away. His eyes were hidden behind aviator sunglasses, and when he spoke, his voice was detached and calm. "Looks like you missed your boat, lucky for you."

Lassiter was silent and the captain continued, "Damn shame how some people forget to hit the blowers and clean out the exhaust fumes before turning the ignition. Those fumes ignite, they blow the fuel tank to kingdom come. A real shame, to die like that, but at least it's quick, lot better than having your guts ripped open or being cooked to death."

Jake Lassiter moved a step toward him. He could take the cop right there, could crush his skull against the wooden piling. The cop spread his legs and rested his right hand on the butt of his revolver. He returned Lassiter's stare.

"Still investigating those two homicides. Seems the hotel's entertainment guy spotted someone suspicious hanging around the *imu* that day. A *malihini*, a tourist, tall guy with an acre of shoulders, dirty blond hair. Hey, somebody puts out a BOLO, you could get picked up."

Lassiter kept an eye on the cop's right hand and said, "Or maybe somebody talks to the FBI and DEA, they drag the bay, come up with evidence of plastiques and a timer. Wonder how many people on this island know how to rig something like that?"

The cop's voice hardened. "I could bust you right now if I wanted. Accessory to two first-degree murders, no bail, a guy could have an accident in the county jail waiting for trial."

Lassiter looked at the bay where orange flames still licked at black fuel spread across the water. A dozen bleary-eyed tourists gathered on the dock, gawking at the scene. Lassiter turned back, staring into the reflection of the fire in the cop's sunglasses. "If that's supposed to scare me, forget it, I'm done being scared. Nothing you can say, nothing you can do, means anything. Do you understand?"

The captain studied him.

"Go ahead, arrest me. I'll sing a tune about a corrupt police captain that'll get headlines all the way to Tokyo."

Lassiter watched Mikala Kalehauwehe sizing him up.

Maybe figuring he underestimated the *haole* first go-round. I'm still alive and that beat the odds, Lassiter knew. A guy who could cause trouble. They both heard radios crackling, a woman dispatcher's voice, two more police cars pulling up at the end of the dock.

"You want to talk, go ahead," the captain said. "Or if you want, it's over, no more blood. There's a flight to the mainland this afternoon. Be on it." Which is what Jake Lassiter did, there being nothing to do on Maui but get framed for two murders, maybe get shot in the back by a cop in a holding cell.

Jake Lassiter returned to Miami the day somebody stole the mayor's gun. And somebody else stole the fast-food bandit's gun. The newspapers were brimming with stolen gun stories.

Most readers hadn't even known that Mayor Rafael Benitez kept a city-issued 380 Beretta automatic in the glove compartment of his city-issued Buick. Apparently, the mayor needed protection in case citizens objected to an increase in cable television rates. Mayor Benitez lost the pistol when his car was stolen from his reserved parking place in front of *Les Violins*, a downtown nightclub where he solicited advice and cash from the Hispanic Builders' Association.

The fast-food bandit lost his gun and then some. Trying to hold up a *supermercado* on LeJeune Road, the bandit ran into two female vice detectives taking a break from a "John detail." The bandit loped into the parking lot carrying $104.75 from the cash register and when he laughed at two women in leather hot pants who ordered him to freeze, they peppered him with five shots in the chest. In the confusion that followed, a bystander with a fine eye for firearms picked up the bandit's Desert Eagle .357 Magnum and coolly walked away.

Neither event would have mattered much to Jake Lassiter if Metro hadn't cordoned off two lanes of LeJeune Road, backing him up into a vicious gridlock on the way home from the airport. Not that he was in a hurry. Jake Lassiter was in a fog. The flights from Maui to the West Coast, then to Miami, were a blur. He hadn't talked to anyone, hadn't touched the cardboard airline food.

After working his way out of the traffic jam south of the airport, Jake Lassiter drove to Cindy's place where they talked about Tubby. He held her while she wept and then he left.

The next day, Lassiter lay in the hammock behind his coral rock house between Poinciana and Kumquat. He unplugged the phone and didn't bother to read the mail. At sundown, he coaxed the old yellow convertible to turn over and drove toward Key Biscayne, where he parked on the sandy berm of the Rickenbacker Causeway and walked under the bridge. Leaning against the third piling from the end, a short man with bowed legs in canvas shorts expertly flicked a wrist, and his casting reel whined in the evening air.

"If I were you, I'd use an oil-colored George-N-Shad rubber fish, maybe three-quarter ounce," Jake Lassiter said.

The man turned and waggled his bushy eyebrows. "If you were me," Charlie Riggs said, "you would have called an old friend when you had some trouble out there in the islands. And I'm using a Bang-O-Lure shallow running plug, blue on the back, white underneath."

"How'd you know?"

"Cindy called last night. Figured you'd get around to me when you felt like talking."

Lassiter watched the water ripple over the plug. "I miscalculated, Charlie. I tried to help Sam and Berto and let them both down. Tubby, too. He was a good man, and he's dead because of me. And a couple guys who weren't so good. Plus a woman, a woman who was beautiful and fearless and lived by no rules except her own. Maybe I could have changed her, saved her . . ."

"Did you learn from your experience?"

"Yes, but too late."

"No. We give ourselves the name *Homo sapiens*, which means 'wise man,' but of course, we are not born that way, and we don't gain wisdom from books. We learn how to live by living. *Vive ut vivas*—"

A splash interrupted him, then a flash of silver erupted from the water, and Charlie's rod bent violently toward the bay.

"Tarpon, Charlie!"

"*Megalops atlanticus*, a great game fish, eh?" Charlie Riggs jerked the rod tip straight up, and six feet of fighting fish exploded into the air, then began its run. "*Deo volente*, my twelve-pound line will hold."

After giving a hundred yards of line, Charlie turned the tarpon with thumb pressure on the reel, and the fish jumped, end over end, and hit the water again. Then it threw the hook and was gone.

"Sorry," Jake Lassiter said.

"Doesn't matter. Can't eat 'em. Too many bones. And I never mounted a fish in my life. Would have liked to land it, but sometimes, the big ones put up such a fight, they don't survive it. With some animals it's better to just enjoy their beauty, leave them alone."

"You trying to teach me about life, Charlie?"

"Just about fishing, Jake. Just fishing."

The next morning, Jake Lassiter drove to the Kazdoy's All-Nite Deli where he knew Sam would have his hot tea and prune danish at seven-thirty sharp. Lassiter spotted his friend's bald head over the back of the red vinyl-covered booth. There alongside him was the platinum mop of Violet Belfrey. Just like a couple of kids sharing a soda.

Jake Lassiter told Sam Kazdoy that the bonds were gone, torn to shreds in an explosion. It was okay, Kazdoy said, could use the write-off, lots more where those came from, and his stock portfolio was doing fine. And good thing too, because a married man's got obligations. "A what?" Jake Lassiter asked him.

"A married man," Sam Kazdoy said again, and Violet Belfrey flashed a seven-carat rock and they each twirled gold wedding bands, shiny in the fluorescent lighting.

Lassiter was about to mumble congratulations but the waitress called him to the phone.

"Thought you'd be there," Cindy said, trying to put the old bounce into her voice. "Got some good news for you. The partners' executive committee says you're to come back to work, *pronto*. They want you and need you."

"I suppose that's good," Lassiter said without enthusiasm.

"It didn't hurt your case that Thad Whitney called. Seems the wife of the bank president has a problem. Her poodle bit a neighbor down in Gables Estates. Well, the families haven't spoken for years before this happened, some dumb dispute over whose yacht smacked the seawall. Now the neighbor hits them with a big suit over the dog, he wants punitive damages, the works. Thad the Cad says you've got to handle it or he'll take the bank's work elsewhere."

Only thing worse than a slip-and-fall, Lassiter knew, was a dog-bite case, the bargain basement of the legal profession. "It's my penance," he said. "Thad's way of getting even."

"Jake."

"Yeah?"

"Please come back. I miss you."

Lassiter hung up and returned to the table where Sam Kazdoy held each of Violet Belfrey's bony hands. "You're too late to be best man, but you can still wish us *mazel tov*," Kazdoy said.

"Sure, Sam."

"Jake, *boychik*, you look all *farchadat*, like you're in a daze.

Nu? We're off on our honeymoon. Flying to Los Angeles to-night, then tomorrow, a cruise to Hawaii."

"Hawaii?" Jake Lassiter said as if he'd never heard of the place.

"Hawaii," Sam Kazdoy repeated. "Travel agent booked us into whadatheycallit?"

"Maui," Violet pitched in.

"Right. Good to get away from all the crime around here, go someplace peaceful. Maybe you can tell us what to see, the sights, I mean. I know what I'll be seeing at night, and I don't need a tour guide for that."

"Careful, Sam," Lassiter said. "At your age, sex can be risky, even fatal."

The old man's eyes twinkled and he patted Violet's hand. "If she dies, she dies." He laughed and Violet Belfrey flashed a grin that would frighten a watchdog.

Kazdoy reached out and gave Lassiter's arm a grandfatherly squeeze. "*Shalom*, Jake."

"*Aloha*, Sam."

Jake Lassiter rigged his board on a chilly December day, a northeaster sweeping across the coastline, the sky ashen gray. He bucked over the chop near shore then sliced into the open ocean, a hard rain piercing his skin like a million needles, the wind singing a mournful song through the sail.

He sailed due east, far from shore until he saw no land. An Atlantic ray, six feet across, shot under his bow. A dolphin followed him, leaping gracefully alongside. The sun would set early now but still he went on, his back to land. Tiring, he dropped the boom and let the sail fall into the water. He sat down, straddling the board, his feet dangling in the warm waters of the Gulf Stream, drifting farther from shore. He wanted to keep going, to float into the abyss and let it swallow him.

Suddenly a splash, the dolphin leaping again, its silver skin gleaming in the late-afternoon sun. Once more, closer now, a silly dolphin smile grinning at him, inviting him to play. Then the dolphin turned and headed west, toward land. Follow me, the dolphin seemed to insist. Lassiter watched until it leapt one last time. Then he uphauled his sail, jibed once, and headed back to shore.

Jake Lassiter returned to work. He avoided partners' meetings and stayed away from bar association luncheons. He tried his cases without fanfare, deriving no pleasure from the victories, no pain from the defeats. And when he was alone he would think it through, step by step. What had he done wrong? Would Tubby still be alive if he had acted differently?

Would Lila?

Always Lila in his mind. He remembered the warmth of her body next to him in the crater, the sweetness of her breath visible as puffs of white steam in the mountain air. He could feel her pressed against him and could hear the short gasps catch in her throat. He could see the silversword bloom, but once, in the morning sun, Lila watching it in awe.

Could he have changed her? Or would that have stripped away whatever it was that made her singular? The questions kept coming. And coming back to the same one. What *had* he done wrong? He figured out part of it. He had mistaken youth for innocence and beauty for purity. He had been swept away by the myth of a woman of beauty, grace, and talent, a woman without flaws.

We are all flawed, Jake Lassiter thought, but Lila's were fatal. In her the bad had swamped the good. He knew now that he had adored a totally amoral creature devoid of compassion. Where he saw the sun and a warm breeze, there were only shadows and a graveyard chill. But still he wanted her.

After a while he tried to banish her but could not. So he gave in to it. Each night, just before sleep, he summoned up again and again, the image of a woman so young and beautiful, so beyond his reach as to be an image in a dream. He saw Lila then as he did that first night when a stiff breeze carried the salt air and gathered her skirt between her legs. He captured the image, focused it sharply, and erased everything else. So he had it always, a memory for eternity, Lila Summers standing there with eyes closed, back arched and long hair flying, listening to a silent song, laughing into the wind.